# John Ruffini

Lavinia

Volume 2

John Ruffini

Lavinia
Volume 2

ISBN/EAN: 9783742852472

Manufactured in Europe, USA, Canada, Australia, Japa

Cover: Foto ©Andreas Hilbeck / pixelio.de

Manufactured and distributed by brebook publishing software
(www.brebook.com)

John Ruffini

Lavinia

COLLECTION

OF

BRITISH AUTHORS

TAUCHNITZ EDITION.

VOL. 538.

LAVINIA

BY THE AUTHOR OF "DOCTOR ANTONIO."

IN TWO VOLUMES.

VOL. 2.

LEIPZIG: BERNHARD TAUCHNITZ.

PARIS: C. REINWALD & Cᴵᵉ, 15, RUE DES SAINTS PÈRES.

COLLECTION

OF

BRITISH AUTHORS.

VOL. 538.

LAVINIA
BY
THE AUTHOR OF "DOCTOR ANTONIO."

IN TWO VOLUMES.

VOL. II.

LAVINIA.

BY

THE AUTHOR OF "DOCTOR ANTONIO."

IN TWO VOLUMES.

VOL. II.

LEIPZIG

BERNHARD TAUCHNITZ

1861.

LAVINIA.

CHAPTER I.

Search.

We must now go back to the night of Paolo's second visit to the Joneses. When at half-past eleven he had not returned, Thornton began to feel uneasy lest his young friend should have lost his way in the huge city. Nothing more natural than that Paolo, in the state of pre-occupation in which he was, should have forgotten the name of the street where he lodged, and, supposing that he had not lost it, forgotten that he was carrying his address written down on a card in his waistcoat pocket. After all, he may be still with those people, soliloquized Thornton; they keep late hours, and, in all probability, they had other visitors besides Paolo. No doubt he is there: however, the shortest way to certainty is to go and see.

First informing Madame Françoise of his intention, and begging her not to sit up for him herself, Thornton departed. One o'clock was striking as he stepped out of a citadine at 25, Boulevard des Capucines; he rang the bell and made straight for the porter's lodge. Monsieur the concierge was snoring in his bed, madame his spouse taking a nap in a large arm-chair.

"Monsieur et Madame Jones, if you please?"

Madame la concierge was out of sorts, of course, as all Parisian concierges are always, but more especially after midnight, and knew of no such name as Jones.

"Pardon," said Mortimer, fumbling in his pocket, "I mean an English family."

"We have but one," grumbled the female cerberus; "a pretty time to pay visits."

"Monsieur is too gracious,". coo'd the worthy matron, on receipt of a five-franc piece. "I am at monsieur's service. If all the world were like monsieur! but they are not reasonable, indeed they aren't."

"An English family consisting of three persons," resumed Mortimer; "a tall gentleman upwards of forty —"

"And a short elderly lady, as round as a ball," interrupted the portress; — "Madame Jonasse — I know them, I know them; second floor above the entresol. Always late, just come in."

"Have they been out?" inquired Mortimer, breath-less with surprise.

"It is their rule, monsieur; and a pretty fuss they made both in going out and coming in, with this into the bargain, that they brought the fat one home in a swoon."

A young gentleman must have called on them about nine o'clock. Pray," continued Thornton, almost beseechingly — "pray try and recollect whether it was before or after they went out."

"Nobody came for the Jonasses this evening, except a lady — Madame la Générale — what's her name? She came to fetch them apparently, for they all set off together. I am positive I drew the cordon for no gentleman, young or old; perhaps Antoine did. I say, Antoine, *mon ami* —"

Mortimer begged the porter's lady not to trouble her snoring husband, she had told him pretty nearly all that he cared to know. His heart foreboded some disaster, as he ran up the stairs to the second floor. He forgot all the awkwardness of calling up a family of strangers at that hour. He had scarcely touched the bell before the door opened.

"Is that the doctor?" cried a voice from within; and before Mortimer had taken two steps forward into the anteroom, out rushed Miss Jones from a door opposite. "Oh, Mr. Thornton," she exclaimed, "what of Signor Paolo?"

"I came here to put the same question to you," said Thornton. "He has not returned to the hotel."

"Not returned to the hotel? You don't know where he is?" and Lavinia wrung her hands.

"I don't know where he is," said Thornton. "Have you not seen him? Surely, you waited for him at home."

"I didn't, I could not," replied the poor girl; "I left a note·to explain everything to him. My maid says he read it, did not speak a word, but went away in a sort of hurry, and looking angry."

Thornton, with a gesture of terror, exclaimed, —

"What folly, what cruelty! you don't know what you have done."

"Oh! Mr. Thornton, don't speak to me in that way just now; don't, for God's sake, upbraid me. It is all come upon me at once. Aunt is so ill."

A violent pull at the bell interrupted the speakers.

This time it was the doctor in company with the man who had gone in search of him.

"Don't go away till I come back," said Lavinia to Thornton, as she showed the physician into Mrs. Jones's room.

Thornton sat down to wait, trying hard to think of some clue as to where Paolo could have gone. It might be, that under the smart of bitter disappointment, Paolo had walked straight before him, without thinking of where he was going, seeking relief in movement; and in that moment he most likely lay somewhere exhausted; it might be that, in an access of despair — Thornton shrunk from clearly articulating, even in thought, the last hypothesis, which suggested itself to him. Paolo's fate would depend on the degree of excitement under which he might have been labouring, and Thornton lacked the data on which to ground any adequate estimate of his poor friend's previous state of mind. Bitterly did he reproach himself for having allowed the Italian, a stranger to Paris, and in such peculiar circumstances, to go out alone at night.

Miss Jones returned to the anteroom more discomposed than when she had left it. The doctor had tried in vain to restore Mrs. Jones's consciousness; he was now about to have recourse to bleeding her in the foot. Lavinia had but a minute to spare. Mortimer made the most of it, to put questions and elicit answers. Thus he learned much that we already know, but to him quite new; for instance, the *contretemps* which had attended Paolo's first visit, and the shock he had then received. Lavinia also told him, more at length, the description her maid had given her of Paolo's manner when the note was handed to him; first, as if he did

not comprehend what he was to do with it, his mute
rage when he did read it, and the wild look in his
eyes, when he turned away into the street. All this
formed a chain of evidence so decisive in Thornton's
opinion, that he could not restrain the exclamation of,
"Then it's all over with him."

"Don't say so; don't say so, for pity's sake," implored the distracted girl; "how can you be sure he is
not waiting at your hotel?"

Thornton took compassion on her, and feigned a
hope that he did not entertain, or, to speak more
to the point, believed he did not entertain. There
was no time for further discussion. Upon the understanding that any fresh information which might reach
either of them should be immediately communicated to
the other, they separated.

Thornton had the moral certainty that he should
not find Paolo waiting for him; he would not have
hesitated to have wagered his fortune, his life, that he
should not find him; and yet, when his anticipation
was realized, his heart sank within him, just the same
as if it had been full to the brim with the most sanguine
expectations. Having read in his troubled looks, that
he was uneasy at his young friend's protracted absence,
his landlady had sat up for him, in spite of his request
to the contrary. Thornton was too thankful now to
have some one to advise with, not to confess that he
had been on a fruitless errand, together with such circumstances of the case, as might justify his fears, without, as he supposed, compromising any third person.
Madame Françoise was not a woman for nothing; she
divined all that Thornton withheld, but with more than
usual discretion kept her discovery to herself, while she

gave solid, good advice. Two o'clock in the morning is not the hour best calculated to institute inquiries about missing friends; however, madame recollected having heard, that at the prefecture of police, there was a *bureau de permanence*, that is, an office kept open all night for the convenience of such persons as might happen to require instantaneous help from the municipal powers. Mortimer grasped eagerly at this information, and, accompanied by Madame Françoise, he set out at once for the prefecture of police.

It was not without difficulty that they were admitted within its gloomy precincts, and even after that was accomplished, it was only by dint of perseverance in questioning every policeman on watch, that they at last obtained the necessary directions how to reach the office they were in search of. The prefecture of police, be it observed, independently of the associations it evokes, has, or rather had, a particular frown of its own, which is anything but attractive, even in the glare of day. By the lurid light of flickering gas-lamps, on a stormy night in March, it was forcibly suggestive of Limbos, and Dantesque bolgias, — an illustration of darkness visible. Mortimer felt his blood grow chill in his veins, as he bethought him that Paolo might have been taken up as a vagabond, and might possibly be in one of yonder cells with iron gratings. A low archway was pointed out to Thornton and his companion, and they were told that, passing through it, they would find themselves opposite to a door, which door gave access to the *bureau de permanence*. Following these directions, they were speedily in a spacious room, so faintly illuminated, that the eye required some time to get accustomed to the semi-obscurity, in order to discern that

the three or four heaps strewed over the floor were so
many human beings. Lying at full length on wooden
inclined planes, or *lits de camp*, these human beings
were, in fact, *sergents de ville*, one of whom asked the
intruders their business there, and on being told that
they desired to speak to the police inspector for the
night, once more asked if the case was one that pressed.
Mortimer having replied in the affirmative, the *sergent*
who had been spokesman, got up, knocked at a door,
went in, and returning almost instantly, bid the two
visitors enter.

A military-looking gentleman, whose rather disordered attire, and half awakened appearance, testified
to interrupted slumbers, was seated at a table, on which
stood conspicuous a capacious ledger. His features
would have been commonplace, but for the eyes, which
were intensely quick and searching. He motioned his
visitors to seats, and listened to Thornton's short statement in unbroken silence, then said, —

"Have you any positive reason for believing that
the young man in question meditated self-destruction?"

Mortimer hesitated an instant, then replied, that
positive reason he had not, but that he knew the young
man to be capable at a given moment of taking any,
and extreme resolutions into the bargain.

"I don't ask of what he may be capable or not at
a given moment," observed the sharp-eyed officer; "my
question is, has he been, to your knowledge, actually
contemplating suicide?"

Mortimer recoiled from entering on the multiplicity
of details, and the sort of dissection of Paolo's heart,
which alone could have given the police superintendent
a clue to the probable frame of the missing young

man's mind on leaving the Boulevard des Capucines,
and replied, —

"I cannot take upon me to say that I believe he
had any such intention when he parted from me."

"Then," subjoined the night inspector, "I cannot
consider this a case of emergency, or one in which
delay might be fatal. We are here only for such. A
few hours' absence could never justify my putting the
public force in motion. Paris swarms with places, in
which a young man may spend a night with no other
danger than to his purse and health. If we were to
humour the alarms of parents or other relatives, natural
enough, to be sure, though nine times in ten ground-
less, there would be no end of useless trouble provided
for us. The line must be drawn somewhere. Should
this young man not return home to-morrow, renew your
application before evening, and you will receive, in the
ordinary course of business, such assistance as we can
afford." So saying, the night inspector rose, and civilly
bowed his visitors away. The Parisian is essentially
polite, and, let it be said to his honour, whenever he
is forced to meet a request with a refusal, or communi-
cate anything little agreeable to hear, rarely aggravates
the annoyance by any omission in point of form.

Thornton never closed his eyes that night, and
went much earlier than necessary to renew his application at a particular office, which had been pointed
out to him as the one most eligible for his business.
He wrote down, as desired, the name and description
of the missing Paolo, the last place he knew he had
been at, gave his own name and actual place of abode,
and received the assurance that all possible diligence
should be used in tracing out Mr. Mancini, and in con-

veying to the applicant Mr. Thornton whatever information might be gathered.

Thornton offered money as a stimulant for the search, but his offer was declined for the present; perhaps, at a later stage of the proceedings, he was told, he might be called on to defray some extraordinary expenses. He was advised also to advertise his missing friend in the newspapers, a step of which he had already bethought himself.

From the prefecture of police, he repaired, at Madame Françoise's suggestion, to an agency of publicity in the Place de la Bourse, where an article was concocted and immediately sent for publication to the leading newspapers, embodying the name, country and personal description of the missing individual, concluding with the promise of a large reward to any one who should convey to Rue de Rohan, No. 1, any information that should lead to a discovery.

Thornton went next, God knows with what heart, to the Morgue, and, by means of a handsome gratuity to the president of that lugubrious establishment, secured the certainty of an immediate summons, should anybody be brought there whose appearance in the least corresponded with the description he left. Madame Françoise accompanied the English gentleman on all these expeditions, being most especially useful in smoothing away, with her womanly tact, that host of minor difficulties, and microscopic jarrings, which a man of Thornton's misanthropic turn, little relying, and not caring to dissemble how little, on the benevolence of his fellow-creatures, could not fail to create for him.

Having thus done all that his judgment suggested, Mortimer drove back, wearied and worn out, body and mind alike, to the hotel, where he found a note from Miss Lavinia awaiting him. It said, —

"Aunt has recovered her consciousness, but lost her speech: judge of my state. I know not what to answer to her anxious looks — mute inquiries I am sure they are about Signor Mancini; your silence tells me clearly that you have got no clue yet. I entreat you, in common charity, to come to me. I long to know what you have done, what you hope, what you fear. I am so miserable that I feel entitled even to your indulgence.

"L. J."

Thornton went to her, and, heart-broken as he was, tried to comfort her. He had all but detested her in her days of flightiness and successful beauty; repentant and bowed down, he felt for her. Thornton had less in him of the misanthropist than he believed.

Thus days and weeks passed on with little or no change. Mortimer called every day at the Boulevard des Capucines; was shortly admitted to the sick chamber, and arranged a tolerably probable story about Paolo, a sudden call to Rome, connected with the sale of his great picture of Brennus — which the invalid's enfeebled state of mind thankfully accepted for truth. Mrs. Jones, in fact, had had a stroke of palsy, her left side was paralyzed, and her mental powers were also slightly affected. For the rest, she was going on as favourably as could be hoped, and had partially recovered her speech. Paolo's fate continued an impenetrable mystery. Thornton caused copies of the avertisement inserted in the newspapers, to be separately printed in huge letters, and placarded far and wide over the walls of Paris; he set detectives to work, paying them liberally, and further stimulating their zeal by the promise of a fabulous *pourboire* in the event of success. All was to no purpose. He received indeed an avalanche of written communications, most of them circulars from different trades-people or associations, who, putting to profit the knowledge of his address, urged on him, the one their merchandise, the other their shares. However, of the correspondence that was anonymous, some nine out of ten of the notes bore reference at least to the subject of the advertisement. One was to the effect, that if Thornton would go on such a day, at such an hour, to such a place, he would hear all about the frightful tragedy; another was to the purport, that if a bank-note of twenty pounds were sent by post to such an address, the writer of the letter would call on the advertiser, and conduct him to the house where the missing youth was forcibly detained; a third gave the information that the young Roman had been seen last near the Forest de Bondy riding on a broomstick, and so on. There are wits so witty that every circumstance affords a field for their talents. After a few fruitless essays made in person, Thornton, as advised, handed to the police all such communications, out of which, of course, nothing came.

Thornton's spirits sank under the futility of his every effort; indeed, the intensity of his depression, after the departure of the Joneses for England, fairly frightened Madame Françoise. Mrs. Jones, ever since her last attack of illness, had never ceased sighing for England, as if England were to be her panacea. No sooner did the physicians withdraw their veto to her travelling, than the family set off for London. Great as the deprivation was for Mortimer, it bore still harder on Lavinia, who, as the prospect before her darkened apace, grew every day more alive to the value of a real friend, the more precious too that Thornton was also *his* friend. Thornton, on his side, lost in Lavinia the only creature that suited him in his forlorn condition, the only heart that could sympathize in full with him, the only safety-valve from his lapsing into despair. Lavinia gone, he felt alone in the world.

Madame Françoise watched with daily increasing disquietude his haggard looks, his long fits of absence of mind, his starts of feverish, useless activity, and by-and-by a terror seized upon her lest he should lose his reason. So greatly had his misery impressed her, that when the long-expected notice to quit her premises within a week, was served on her, the good woman had not the courage to abandon him to himself, and at once resolved to put off to a better time the realization of her cherished plan of going to live with her married daughter at Evreux. Instead of that, she secured comfortable apartments for Mr. Thornton and herself at a lady friend's, who kept a *maison garni* in the Rue Neuve des Augustins. As soon as they were installed there, new advertisements and new placards were printed and issued, in order to give the advertiser's new address. The police also, the man in charge of the Morgue, and Miss Jones, now in London, were duly informed of the change. Mortimer did all this scrupulously but without any spirit, like one who discharges a duty for conscience-sake, but hopes no result from it.

CHAPTER II.

Paolo's Progress.

It is mortifying and appalling to think how little may suffice to defeat the best-laid scheme. Here is a case in point. The combined resources of a well organized police, and of a system of publicity, spreading the knowledge of a fact far and wide through every grade of the population, the two great engines and contrivances of modern civilization, kept at bay, or rather put to nought by one or two insignificant circumstances, which an adept in the calculation of probabilities would have disdained to cast up in his reckoning. Thus it now and then happens that a machine, most ingeniously devised on the most irrefragable principles, does not answer in practice: owing to what? — to a slight friction which has been overlooked.

Prosper and his wife saw no daily paper. Benoît, scarcely able to spell, never resorted to reading. Mr. Perrin, the only person about Paolo likely to interest himself in the news of the day, had systematically given up all periodicals, save those of his craft, which had no advertisements but medical ones. Thus far newspapers had no hold on our hero's surroundings. Nor had placards any better chance with people who, like the omnibus check-taker and his wife, never left their domicile either by night or day, and in whose immediate neighbourhood, supposing them occasionally to have strayed into the street, no bills were or could be put up; for the suite of shops on either side of Mr. Prosper's establishment, and the low parapet opposite, that is, on the side overlooking the river, afforded no space for the labours of the bill-sticker. Prosper's establishment, if the reader recollects, was situated on the Quai Montebello, opposite Notre Dame. Mr. Perrin, when out of doors, was constantly preoccupied with the cases of his patients, and, above all, too short-sighted to have noticed the huge sheets of printed paper, even had they been half as large again; and as to Benoît, his five minutes' walk from what he called his "den" to Prosper's "shop," lay through narrow unfrequented lanes, where nothing but the internal interests of those lanes ever excited attention. Remained that quickest and surest conductor of all news, the un-rivalled trumpeter, gossip; but indulgence in gossip, whether actively or passively, presupposes leisure, and life was such a continual race to each and all of Paolo's attendants, more especially since he had fallen among them, that they had no time to spare for gossip, even without taking into account a circumstance which had closed their lips against the but too natural itching to impart confidentially, each to a few bosom friends, the portentous intelligence of the handsome stranger picked up in the street, and ever since the tenant of Mr. Prosper's back parlour. —

During his first and second night under that Sama-ritan's roof, Paolo had raved a good deal in an un-familiar jargon, which Benoît had oracularly pronounced to be Polish, but which the better informed Mr. Perrin declared to be Italian. Now Benoît had been quartered at Pont du Var in 1833, and with his own eyes had beheld many an Italian come from the opposite shore to seek a refuge on French soil. Benoît had served in Africa, and there known more than one Italian refugee in the foreign legion. Benoît had also got acquainted in Paris with Italian exiles; and whether in Paris, Algeria, or the Pont du Var, had invariably seen them roughly handled, narrowly watched by the police, now and then sent to prison, or unceremoniously despatched to the nearest frontier under an escort of gendarmes. Benoît's experience on this particular matter had crystallized itself into two distinct axioms: first, that Italian and refugee were one and the same thing; second, that the police had permanent orders to track out Italians, with a view to their expulsion or imprisonment. Applying his profound wisdom to Paolo's case, Benoît, after various thrusts at his imaginary adversary, addressed the following short and striking oration to Prosper and his wife, —

"*Motus!* the lad is an Italian; you know what that means; shut up your lips, or, '*cré nom*, we shall have the police and all the *bataclan* down on us here."

The matter had been referred on the morrow to Mr. Perrin, who had shrugged his shoulders without saying yes or no. As the proverb, "Silence is acquiescence," was known to the applicants, they all accordingly held their tongues. Thus it came to pass, that, chance aiding and abetting, police, newspapers, placards, and even the clangor of gossip's big trump, were set at defiance. Paolo's whereabouts continued hid as if it were a crime.

The hand-to-hand struggle between fever and the lancet was long and fierce, and more than once did the doctor's leaden-coloured face, on the reappearance of symptoms supposed to be conquered, turn of a cadaverous green. When the enemy was at length put to flight, it left behind a ruin, a wreck, a corpse you would say, but for that thin vapour issuing from his lips on the mirror, the only proof of yet unsuspended vitality. For fully three weeks life oscillated and flickered like a torch in the wind; after that it began to burn slowly but regularly again. Paolo was declared out of danger, another fortnight, and he had entered the phase of convalescence.

One of the inevitable consequences of any acute disease which has its seat in the brain, is that of a period, more or less long and intense, according to the duration and intensity of the disorder — a period, we say, of torpidity and sluggishness in the cerebral sensorium, and the functions dependent on it, which sometimes amounts to temporary imbecility. Such was the case with Paolo. Life was certainly fast regaining its hold of him, but animal life alone; the sentient being, the Psyche, lay still asleep. He would sit up on his bed, and for hours stare vacantly at the wall, chequered by some stray sunbeam, or play with the children, as thoughtless and unconcerned as a child himself. Whenever Prudence, Prosper, Benoît, or Mr. Perrin came into his room, he always smiled good-naturedly, but never spoke unless first spoken to, and then only in monosyllables, never asked questions, never evinced the least sign of surprise or curiosity at the strangeness of the place he was in. The only occurrences which appeared to arouse his interest, were his meals, which he ate with great relish. When able to leave his bed, he would sit for half the day in an arm-chair at the window of the back room, and watch with the same mute delight the manœuvres of a sparrow, or the movements of Benoît, lording it over baths and douches at the bottom of the court-yard opposite, and looking, as he moved amid thick volumes of smoke, much like a droll representation of a half-marine, half-infernal deity.

See him next by the side of Prosper's official desk, promoted to the stirring joys of the waiting room, and ready to applaud the bustle of the scene.

"It's like a sea-port, is it not?" chuckles the little omnibus official, nudging the invalid; "no wonder there's such a competition; find me another conveyance, combining cheerfulness, comfort and speed, ready to take you to *any* part of the town at any moment of the day or night. You'll see it yourself as soon as you are strong enough for a drive; and remember the company is always respectable — lawyers, physicians, merchants, employés, rentiers, not to speak of people of rank like that grey-haired gentleman opposite, with a red rosette in his button-hole — an officer of the Legion of Honour, very likely a general in plain clothes; an officer, not a chevalier of the order — chevaliers wear a red ribbon. Look at those horses now;" and Prosper, whistle in hand, would slap the powerful animals on the neck, accompanying the caress with a side glance at Paolo, which meant to say, "Did you ever see horseflesh equal to that?" The *esprit de corps* which prompts us to make much of the banner under which we serve, must be strong indeed, that even this poor, ill-paid, ill-lodged, ill-warmed drudge should put his pride in a concern which made him such a scanty return.

Then followed the days of those beautiful drives in Mr. Prosper's omnibus, and those long sittings in the mild spring sun in the Jardin des Plantes, or in the Tuileries, with Madame Prudence by his side, to give him treats of galette *ad libitum;* then came strolls, gradually lengthening, in the one garden or the other,

where gentle-looking old men and women would stop,
gaze at him wistfully, and observe to each other, in
passing, "Poor lad, how weak he looks; ah! youth
after all, is no buckler against illness." Perhaps memory brought him back now and then a momentary
whiff of the past; the image of a tall, black-haired girl,
of a tall, grey-haired gentleman — images faded as the
personages of a. tale read long ago, and more than half
forgotten. But it was so much trouble to think and try
to recollect, so as to put in colour into those vague outlines, that he was fain at once to let them slip away.
How far easier and more agreeable to watch those
beautiful lions crouching down, majestic even in the
captivity of their cages; those restless monkeys, for ever
playing mischievous tricks to each other, startled into a
second's immobility by the bells they had unconsciously
set ringing in their gambols; or to gaze on the reflection
of the sun playing in the rippling waters of the great
basin in the Tuileries, and making them into an endless
cascade of sapphires and rubies.

One evening he was on the Terrasse aux Bords de
l'Eau, when the setting sun had dyed the noble river
below a Tyrian purple. Paolo was looking at this
never-tiring spectacle, when his attention was attracted
by a small steamer issuing from below the bridge De
la Concorde, and in its onward course leaving behind
a long white panache of smoke. Paolo watched with
unusual eagerness the progress of the little craft, until
he saw it stopped and moored in front of the Pont
Royal. This sight stirred up a confused recollection of
a similar scene, a scene he had witnessed somewhere;
was it lately, or long ago? A scene in which the setting sun, a large expanse of water, and a big steamer,

with Thornton on its deck, figured. He hesitated, then said in an excited manner, pointing to the steamer, —

"Thornton is there."

It was the first time, since his illness, that the name and figure of Thornton had risen up clearly in his recollection. That evening Paolo, with the air of one imparting a solemn secret, gave the name of Thornton to Prosper, Benoît, and Mr. Perrin, one after the other. Mr. Perrin asked, —

"Who is Thornton? An Italian?"

"No."

"An Englishman?"

"Yes."

"Is he your father, your brother; in short, any relation to you?"

"Thornton," said Paolo, "is my friend."

"And where is he to be found?" questioned Mr. Perrin.

Paolo tried very hard to recall where, but in vain.

However, the sleeping Psyche was at last awakened, and began to throw light on the past. Thread after thread of memory's involved skein was disentangling itself in Paolo's mind. Within a few days, he recollected every incident up to his arrival in Paris, but from that period down to the present moment, all was indistinct, like objects seen through a mist, pierced, however, by salient points, such as the shouting in the streets of persons in masquerade attire, Miss Jones in a ball dress, a huge building brilliantly lighted, and a violent cold that had made his teeth chatter. It was only by the recital given by those good Samaritans, his hosts, of the circumstances attending his entry under their hospitable roof, that he was able to fill up, by

2*

induction, the gaps in his memory. There was one among these, however, which defied his every effort, and that was the name of the street in which Thornton and he lodged, on their arrival in Paris. He had heard it so seldom, and that too at a time when his mind was beginning to be so strangely confused, that his having altogether forgotten it was nothing extraordinary; and, as for identifying street or house from its appearance, no chance of that, considering that he had never seen either by daylight. Prosper and his wife might have gone on to eternity repeating to him the titles of all the streets they could recollect, without ever hitting on the right one, but that the inventive genius of Benoît devised a method which won the day at last. He bought one of those cheap and popular Paris guides, in which not alone streets, squares, and places, are marked, but wherein you will find the narrowest passage, leading nowhere, accurately noted down. Once in the possession of this, Benoît read over every appellation from beginning to end. This scheme may appear obvious enough, but so was the way to make the egg stand upright, once hit upon by Columbus. As soon as the old bath-man pronounced the word Rohan, Paolo exclaimed that that was the street. Madame Prudence immediately set out with him, but alas! when they reached the spot, the Rue de Rohan no longer existed; all its buildings had been demolished a month previous. Then Paolo became, for the first time, aware that two full months had elapsed since the evening he had left Madame Françoise's house, never again to re-enter it. Yes, he could remember now that it must have been in the last week of March, and now it was the last week of May.

Paolo bore the disappointment with much more equanimity than his companion, who protested that it seemed done on purpose to vex a saint — that it was frightful. Indeed, to be perfectly truthful, we ought to say that Paolo did not look at all disappointed. The revival of his mental faculties had not extended to this sensibility: his affections continued to slumber. He was abundantly indifferent to everything; and the very impressions, which he received from such parts of his recollections, as would have quickened his blood, and set him in a blaze two months ago, were now languid in the extreme — indeed, any thoughts he had about Lavinia or Thornton left his heart undisturbed.

Paolo's recovery of relative health of body and mind coincided, or thereabouts with the 24th of May, a date sacred in the annals of Prosper's family, and to commemorate which the little omnibus superintendent granted himself a holiday — the only one in the year — a holiday of six hours, from mid-day to six in the evening. On the 24th of May, 1845, Prosper and Prudence had lost their only girl, a child of four years old, and on all successive 24ths of May ever since, they had never failed to go and hang garlands of flowers, and wreaths of immortelles on the small iron cross, which marked the resting-place of little Annette in the cemetery of Mont Parnasse. They resolved on the present anniversary to take Paolo with them, and make a great day of it. Accordingly, husband and wife, dressed in mourning, the children in brown blouses with leather belts, Paolo in his only suit of clothes, marvellously brushed for the occasion, with one of Prosper's caps to replace his lost hat; and last, not least, Benoît, dressed for once like any common mortal, started at noon in

one of the Company's omnibuses, and were duly set
down at the Barrière d'Enfer, from whence they proceeded on foot to the cemetery.

At one of the many shops furnishing funereal wares,
which swarm in the neighbourhood of all the burying
grounds of Paris, Mr. Prosper provided himself with as
many wreaths as there were persons in his party, and
distributed one to each, the children included; they then
proceeded to little Annette's tomb, where each one laid
their fragile emblems of a never-dying regret. Prudence
threw herself on her knees, an example immediately
followed by Prosper, Benoît and Paolo, and calling her
boys to her side, bid them kneel also, and joining their
hands, made them repeat a short prayer, in which they
begged their little sister, now a bright angel in heaven,
to intercede for them with the blessed Virgin, so that
they might grow up good, and a consolation to their
parents, as she herself, the dear lost one, had been.
Madame Prudence made no extravagant display of sensibility, but her brown face was rather whiter than
usual, and her usual cheerful voice was low and broken.
Prosper was very red when he got up, and he was a
long time brushing the dust from the knees of his
trousers, while Benoît was violently chewing a quid —
quite an imaginary one — and looked pugnaciously
ready for a thrust at some one, but he checked himself
in time.

After this, they walked about the grounds for a
couple of hours, comparing notes about this and that
gorgeous monument, forming conjectures as to whether
the little coffin just brought in was that of a girl or
boy, expressing warm sympathy for the tall woman in
black, who looked so careworn, and for the elderly

gentleman in the shabby coat, praying so earnestly over a tomb; all this interspersed with remarks innumerable on the pleasantness of the spot. And certainly, if anything can make the abode of death pleasant, these neat, quiet verdant cemeteries of Paris must do so, .with their trim alleys and walks, their rows of trees, and fresh groves, their profusion of flowers round the well preserved tombs, their concourse of visitors of all classes, at all times, with all the tokens, in short, of the great care of the living for the dead.

"Three o'clock — *en marche!*" commanded Benoît, after consulting his watch. A last farewell and a last prayer at the foot of little Annette's cross, and they took the road to the barrier, and into the wine shop opposite the omnibus stand, where they had a quiet dinner, composed of *purée aux croutons*, *fricandeau à l'oseille*, omelette, salad — accompanied by a bottle of wine with the yellow seal; which being disposed of, Benoît ordered a fresh bottle, while Prosper carefully undid a paper parcel and placed on the table what at first sight might have been mistaken for a huge nugget of silver. But the children knew what that shining coat meant, and saluted the "*cussy*" with screams of joy, that a lump of real silver would never have excited. The cake being cut in slices, and distributed, and the glasses filled, Benoît rose and gave the health of his young and esteemed friend, Mr. Paulot Mangchinié, which was drunk with hearthy good wishes, attested by a merry clinking of the glasses one against the other. Paolo looked more pleased and excited than he had ever done since his recovery, especially when the two minor Prospers went up to him, and putting their arms round his neck, kissed him.

And now, both Benoît's bottle and pipe being empty, and time short, they stepped into a departing omnibus — Benoît on the *impériale* for the enjoyment of a fresh pipe — and twenty minutes later, they alighted at the bureau ruled over by Mr. Prosper, as satisfied, if not more so, with their six hours' holiday, as many bigger and more consequential people with their six weeks' tour on the Continent, or stay at some fashionable town by the sea-side. Fortunately for the poor and busy, who have to work hard for their daily bread, the fewer their occasions for self-indulgence, the greater and keener the enjoyment they derive from them.

CHAPTER III.
The stern Soberer.

Mrs. Jones bore better than could have been expected the fatigue of her journey to London, where, however, her stay was but short; for the medical celebrities of the capital, immediately consulted, if differing *toto cælo* in the treatment they recommended, were unanimous in advising country air and tranquillity. Accordingly, aunt and niece, with part of the household, went to Mr. Jones's country seat, near Guildford, within an hour by rail from London.

The change was at first fraught with favourable results. Old sounds, old sights, old associations — all that combination of mysterious agencies and influences, which constitute home, attested their power, and revived the invalid; but the improvement lasted only as long as the novelty of the impressions, and the decline that followed seemed by contrast more continuous and speedy. Poor Mrs. Jones saw, and felt herself die inch by inch. Stroke followed stroke in quick succession, and the palsy, hitherto confined to the left side, made its way slowly but surely to the right, like an enemy who carries subterranean approaches round a besieged citadel, previous to storming it. The little walk taken morning and evening was reduced to once a day, and had gradually to be curtailed, till it dwindled to nothing. The only way she could now enjoy the air, warmed by the April sun, and the sight and smell of spring flowers, was in a Bath chair; but even this had to be given up in course of time, and an hour or two spent on a sofa, drawn close to a window, became the only solace accessible to the dying woman — a solace which, alas! had to be renounced in its turn, for Mrs. Jones could no longer rise from her bed.

It was at this pass, that all the fond devotedness, which graced Lavinia's heart, revealed itself thoroughly. She lavished treasures of filial tenderness upon her aunt. Ah! if Paolo could have seen her now, looking more like an angel than a woman, as she kept watch over her sinking friend! From the beginning she had unwillingly allowed any one to share with her in the duties of a fond nurse and attendant, yielding only when Nature despotically asserted a claim to repose. But as the dear one's time on earth visibly shortened, love conquered the body's weakness, and day and night there she was by the bedside, day and night devising new schemes to procure more ease for the patient — that relative ease which is but a diminution of pain — there she was insensible to fatigue, inexhaustible in words of encouragement, of hope, of endearment. Was

Lavinia not richly repaid by the calm she imparted, by the smiles she elicited, by the blessings bestowed on her? More than a hundredfold did she receive back in return for her every loving-kindness. She did not, perhaps, recognize at the time the great blessing that fell on herself, while ministering to Mrs. Jones's spiritual comfort; but surely portions of holy writ, the eternal truths of Scripture, recited and thought over by the lamp of a sick room, under the very shadow of death, seldom fail to assume a new and living significance in the mind of the reader, and to mould themselves into practical precepts of life.

At intervals Mrs. Jones referred anxiously to Signor Mancini, wondering why he had not joined them in England. Lavinia, poor girl, needed no reminder about Paolo; a thought of him mingled with her most painful pre-occupations. Gentle and loving as he was, how he would have sympathized with her, had he known of her affliction. Not one of his words, which had ever borne the least reference to her present sad trial, but she recollected as vividly as though spoken only the day before. How truly had he said, that neither youth, nor fortune, nor health, had ever proved an impenetrable shield against the shafts of sorrow, which, through the breast of some dear object, found a sure passage to the most fortunate of mankind. How many times, under how many shapes, had he not tried to impress on her, that affections were the salt of life, the only reality worth pursuing here below.

The truth of his words struck home to her now. But for the love she felt, but for the love she inspired, what would have been in this hour of extremity her poor aunt's fate? The answer was ready: rich in money, surrounded by luxury, as she was, Mrs. Jones would have been left, in these her last days, to the mercenary care of hirelings. For, as to Mr. Jones, he had never once omitted going daily to town, had never returned an hour earlier to his dinner, had never shortened by five minutes the time dedicated to his wine, nor once refrained from finishing the day by a comfortable evening's nap in the easy-chair by his wife's bedside. When he spoke, if he spoke at all, it was on topics strangely at variance with the atmosphere of the room; in general, however, he confined himself to a good-night, accompanied by one or other of those would-be consolatory banalities, which, in Mrs. Jones's all but hopeless state, meant less than nothing. The servants on their side made up for the official look of condolence, which they thought becoming to wear in their master's presence, by making twice as merry when out of sight.

As the sufferer's strength decreased, so did the lucidity of her mind increase. One evening, after she had lain in a lethargic state throughout the whole day, Mrs. Jones seemingly awoke, and, calling to Lavinia, bade her come close to her, that she might not lose a word of what she was about to impart. A burden had long pressed heavily on her conscience, said Mrs. Jones — a burden she must throw off, otherwise she could not die easily. Then, with a clearness never once at fault, she went on to make to the astonished girl the following disclosure.

When, now more than thirteen years ago, Mr. Jones had been prevailed on by his wife to adopt and take charge of the only daughter of his eldest brother, Mr. Jones had done so on the express condition, that the existence of the little Lavinia's parents, and the early circumstances of the family into which she was about to enter, should both be kept a secret from her. Mr. Jones, rich and a man of growing importance, was already ashamed of his former calling, and, wishing to have what he styled a real gentlewoman in his niece, believed he was taking the best means to secure her becoming one, by trampling under foot one of God's commandments. Mrs. Jones, out of fondness for the child on whom she doted, accepted the bargain, and Lavinia accordingly grew up in the belief, confirmed by the silence of her uncle and aunt, that she was an orphan. Her father, on his side, who had renounced all intercourse with his daughter (Mrs. Jones believed for a certain sum of money), kept faithfully out of the way. For the tacit deception she had practised, partly out of fear of her husband's wrath, though still more so out of apprehension as to the consequences, which any divulging of the truth might bring to a niece she adored, repentant Mrs. Jones now humbly asked and easily obtained forgiveness.

It is easy to imagine that Lavinia, not only startled, but deeply affected by this revelation, was anxious to hear something more of her unknown parents. Mrs. Jones had never known Lavinia's mother, who had died shortly after giving over the child to her relations; and of her father she had seen very little. The first time was shortly after her marriage to Mr. Mark Jones; he was then a man perhaps of six or seven and thirty, but looking much older, and very careworn. She knew he had been a bankrupt more than once; but the brothers not being on good terms, she met him but rarely: and from the moment she and her husband had taken charge of Lavinia, all sort of communication had utterly ceased between her and her brother-in-law; even his abode had been carefully concealed from her. She had, however, discovered, through the loquacity of the servants, that he came by stealth now and then to see her husband. After these visits Mr. Jones had always been out of sorts, complaining of his brother, and calling him a drunkard. As to the poor man's being dead or alive, Mrs. Jones had not the slightest clue to guide her; the last time she had seen him was in the street, just before they went abroad, and he appeared sadly broken down. She would have spoken to him, but for being with her husband. This was all the information Lavinia could gain about her parents.

The aunt completed her confession by making known to her niece her own and her husband's humble origin and beginning in life. She reproached herself the more with having concealed these circumstances, as she now saw that Lavinia might have found, in the knowledge of them, a counterpoise and a corrective to the ideas and aspirations, imbibed from a training far above her station, and fostered by the self-conceit, the preposterous notions, and example of Mr. Jones. His chase after gentility had been the bane of their life. Regarded with feelings of resentment, or ridicule, by the class he had deserted; despised by his superiors, whose notice he courted; haunted by a perpetual fear of meeting some one acquainted with a past he would fain have forgotten himself, Mr. Jones, ever since he had been bitten by the gad-fly of pride, had made himself one of the most disturbed of mortals. Lavinia had surely not forgotten their precipitate and mysterious flight from Florence in the heat of August. Well, that was entirely induced by Mr. Jones having come across an old patron; in fact, one of his first customers, my Lord Berriton.

As to herself, sighed Mrs. Jones, her health and spirits had declined from the very commencement of this mad straining after an unattainable fashion, from the moment when she had had to resign a wholesome sphere of activity and usefulness for one of inert luxury, in which she felt not only displaced, but every taste, duty, and habit of which jarred with all her former tastes, duties, and habits. Thence it was that she had, somewhat hastily she allowed, encouraged her niece's growing partiality for Signor Paolo; being satisfied by what she had seen of the world, that a union entered upon, even with scanty means, but based on mutual affection and esteem, and some moderation of desires, had more chances of happiness than one of those dashing matches between two spoilt children of fortune, which leaves nothing to wish for but the condiment of love; the couple concerned being too much in love with themselves, to have any left to bestow on each other.

These were the last confidences that Miss Jones received from her aunt. Before another day reached its close, the lips that had made them were sealed for ever here below, and she who had listened to them lay on a sick couch, shattered in body and mind. But the wholesome seed of more than one kind, which had fallen on heart and soul during this painful probation, was not likely to be lost; and we may confidently expect that once the first shock be over, Lavinia will rise from the trial quite a renovated being, strengthened for all good purposes. Sorrow is the *toga virilis* of the soul. He or she, who has never seen face to face that stern soberer, Death, knows but little of life and its aims.

CHAPTER IV.

Counter-search.

A MIGHTY consultation was being held in the back parlour of Mr. Prosper's establishment, under circumstances promising little for the quick settlement of the point in question, inasmuch as, out of the four plenipotentiaries assembled in conference, two, Benoît and Prosper, were constantly bounding in and out of the room, and thus causing perpetual delay to the proceedings.

If there were ever two galley-slaves by trade, the two were Benoît and Prosper, and if one of the two was a greater galley-slave than the other, that one was Prosper. For people do not douche nor steam themselves for ever: and therefore Benoît might have moments of respite, could even remember having sat down to his dinner, and finished it without interruption; whereas such a luxury was unknown to Prosper. His labours knew of no solution of continuity. People do loco-move for ever. There was an uncouth machine stopping before Prosper's dwelling every five minutes, and there was Prosper every five minutes seeing passengers out of it, and passengers into it, comparing notes, settling with the conductor, and whistling to the huge conveyance to move off; more to do yet — back to his bureau to serve out new correspondence tickets, and numbers of precedence, besides affording information to all who ask for it. Five minutes were soon used up at this rate, and again a warning whistle carried him to the street to begin the foregoing performance anew; and so on and on from seven in the morning to twelve at night. And thus Prosper being whistled away every five minutes, and Benoît telegraphed to from his den in the courtyard, let us say on an average every seven minutes, one or both were always missing, and the deliberation flagged.

The question just now under consideration had been mooted by Paolo, and seconded by Madame Prudence, and was this: Should Paolo go to the police to make inquiries after Thornton? The initiative taken by the young Roman betokened a new phase in his psychological condition. Paolo's feelings were at last roused, and friendship at once asserted its rights. To find his benefactor, to reassure and be reassured, were the paramount desires of his heart. Even had he been without those strong cords of an almost filial affection which bound him to the Englishman, other considerations would have impelled him to the search. With Thornton he should find the means of discharging that part of his debt to his kind hosts which money could repay, and of getting back to Rome. Paolo had left money enough in his lodgings in the Rue de Rohan, to meet both exigencies, and naturally Mortimer would have seen to the safety of his property. Paolo was eager to leave Paris — a sort of nostalgy had seized upon him.

Having decided with himself that the most probable clue to Thornton's whereabouts was to be obtained from the Joneses, he had made up his mind to the effort of calling there. The recollection of Lavinia was linked with many painful, though still confused associations, so that he knew not whether he should like to see her again or not. He had gone to the Boulevard des Ca-pucines, but only to be thrust into deeper darkness. The Joneses had been gone more than two months, and the tall English gentleman who had been latterly in the habit of calling on them had never shown his face there since their departure. Paolo had then be-thought himself of the police, and some questions hav-ing revealed his intention of going to that office, the present consultation had been the result.

Madame Prudence was of opinion that he ought to go, and might do so with safety, provided she were with him. Prosper was for referring the matter to Mr. Perrin, and abiding by the doctor's advice, but was prevented from developing his thesis by the whistle, which summoned him out of doors. Benoît combated any notion of the kind with might and main.

"Go to the police!" remonstrated the ex-sergeant, getting down from the window-sill, in which he had been seated, with a jerk that sent both his slippers across the room in opposite directions. "Throw him-self into the wolf's jaws, you mean; and once in, who is to get him out, *quoi?*"

"I have committed no offence," said Paolo, quietly; "why should I be in danger with the police?"

"Let them alone; they'll find plenty of reasons for putting you out of sight. Take it as a rule, a refugee is always giving offence to somebody."

"But I am not a refugee," said Paolo.

"Not a refugee!" repeated Benoît, standing aghast.

"Not a refugee!" repeated Madame Prudence and Prosper, who was making one of his hundreds of en-trances.

"No more than you are," persisted Paolo.

"An Italian and not a refugee!" said Benoît, scraping his bald pate; "it's out of nature;" and by way of reconciling himself to the absurdity, he made a thrust or two at the wall. "Are you sure that you are not a ref— D— the boy with his signals. *On y va.* I think all Paris wants to be vapoured to-day — *quoi!*" and away the old fellow shuffled.

"If you are not a refug—" Prosper began, but he had just time to add — "d— the whistle," and he bolted away.

Paolo and Madame Prudence, thus left alone, did what, under the circumstances, was the only reasonable thing to do — namely, put on, he his somewhat greasy casquette, she, her faded bonnet, and went out at once. Prosper, whom they met on the threshold of the office, patiently listening to a complaint lodged by a very fat lady against the conductor, who had not stopped immediately on her signing to him so to do — Prosper, we say, faintly attempted to dissuade his wife from taking a step he was morally sure would be displeasing to his godfather.

Madame Prudence, who harboured some seeds of jealousy as to the great ascendency exercised by Benoît over her husband, retorted that his godfather was at full liberty to be pleased or displeased, but that she and Signor Paolo were neither of them children, nor yet, thank God, in any need of leading-strings, upon hearing which Prosper wisely let things take their course. Truth to say, the omnibus official's belief in Benoît's infallibility had received a severe check ever since the latter had peremptorily pronounced Paolo's case to be one of cholera, and had been proved to be grossly in error. And now the morning's discovery that Paolo was not a refugee, when Benoît had declared the impossibility of his being aught else, could not be overlooked by even so dutiful a godson as Prosper. Benoît's prestige was fading away fast, like many another reputation based on infallibility.

Through the same dingy passages and vaults, along the identical mouldy yards and lurid squares, which had frowned a few months ago on Mortimer and Madame Françoise in search of Paolo, now Paolo and Madame Prudence toiled in search of Thornton. The prefecture was to Prudence a *terra incognita*. In fact, she had never been there, and knew no more about the different offices, their names and attributions, than about Troy or Tyre. The best course, in her holy state of ignorance, seemed, and was, to apply to a sergent de ville — there were many about — and ask for direction; but the moment she tried to shape her question, she found it far from easy, considering that in order to ask one's way somewhere, one must know, or thereabouts, the name at least of one's place of destination. Nothing remained in this dilemma, but to put the police agent on the scent of what she wanted, by briefly stating her case, which she did. It was a case for the *Bureau des Renseignements*, said the man, and he forthwith took her to the foot of the staircase, which led to the office of information on the first floor.

A great stillness prevailed in the room, into which, after a discreet knock at the door, and an answer from within to "come in," our visitors ventured with a beating heart. Two gentlemen were busy writing at a desk, and to the one of them who raised his head in mute interrogation, Prudence explained her errand.

“Was she, or was the gentleman in her company, related to the person they inquired for?” asked the official.

“Neither were related to the gentleman they sought after,” replied Prudence; “but her companion was a great friend of Mr. Thornton.”

“Had they a written order from the prefect of police, authorizing the inquiry?” asked the official again.

They had nothing of the sort. Well, then, let them procure one, and come again with it. It was indispensable.

As our discomfited couple issued on to the little piazza facing the office, they met at the very spot where they had left him, the identical policeman who had directed them, and who now asked of the lady, if she had found her man.

“Alas! not,” said Prudence; “we must have an order from the préfet.”

“I thought so,” said the man, walking along a little way with them. “You needn’t apply in person, you know — the préfet wouldn’t receive you. Send in your request in writing.”

Prudence thanked him for the information. They were standing now in front of the *Bureau des Passeports*.

“Did not you say, that your friend that’s missing was an American?” asked the policeman.

“An Englishman,” rectified Prudence.

“Ah! yes — a foreigner at all events. Suppose he had set off? Had you not better see at the *Bureau des Passeports?*”

The hint was sensible, and appeared good to follow,

so, with many thanks to the prompter, Paolo and Prudence walked in.

The passport office was to the office of information what a surging sea is to a stagnant pool. In the month of June, Paris, like London, begins to move out of town, and consequently great was the concourse of applicants, and lightning quick went the employés' pens and tongues, taking down descriptions of, and cross-examining, we were going to say, the accused; for there is something suggestive of a criminal court, and a witness-box, in the calling up of persons, and then subjecting them to interrogations, the answers to which are written down. As the half-bewildered Prudence, with a rueful face, was contemplating a gap in the thick human wall standing between her and the official's desk, the municipal guard on duty stationed in front of the rails, noticing her distress, bade her come forward, and, gallantly making way for her, observed to a tall by-stander, who grumbled about being beforehand, that the fair sex always took precedence in France. Thanks to this seasonable succour, she was enabled to make known her request to the nearest employé, who directed her to another part of the room, where there were more desks and more men at them.

The one to whom she addressed herself proved of a very humane disposition, and showed an interest in her and her companion. Maybe he had a mother or sister, not better off in the world than poor scantily dressed Prudence, or perhaps he had once had a brother looking as emaciated and careworn as Paolo. Sympathy, however, is to be gratefully accepted without prying into its origin, and gratefully it was received in this case, when the kindly disposed individual,

depositing his pen behind his ear, took himself out of
the room with a scrap of writing containing the name
and last address of the person inquired after, and presently came with the little consoling intelligence, that
"*Sir*" Mortimer Thornton had had his passport *viséd*
for the United States on the 16th of May.

"He is gone to look after me, I am sure," said
Paolo, as he walked away slowly and with tears starting into his eyes.

"Well, when he does not find you there, he'll come
back, and seek you out here," replied Prudence with
a show of confidence and cheerfulness which did not
go farther than the surface. They reached home before
Prosper's state of distraction had entirely disorganized
the service of his line of omnibuses; for the little man
had been so frightened out of his wits by the visions
of dungeons, bagnios, and scaffolds, which friendly
Benoît had evoked for his comfort, that for the last
quarter of an hour he had been sending the passengers
for the Jardin des Plantes to the Pantheon, and *vice
versâ*, heaping blunder upon blunder.

Prudence slept little that night, and thought much,
and the upshot of her reflections was, that it would be
worth while to apply to the English Embassy; "for,"
reasoned Prudence, "Mr. Forton" (such being her pro-
nunciation of Thornton's name), "Mr. Forton has been
gone now, if he went at all, for nine-and-twenty whole
days, and even I know that nine-and-twenty days is time
enough for going, staying, and returning from New
York. He may then be back already, and if he is,
ten to one but they know it at his embassy."

Madame Prudence told this to Paolo next day, as
the fruits of a counsel held with her pillow, and, un-

like most counsels, it was favourably received by all, and eagerly grasped at by the young man; and with renewed hope Prosper's wife and her *protégé* started on this new expedition after Thornton.

As directed by the concierge of the British Embassy, they turned into the consulate office, where the simple statement of their wish to know whether an English gentleman of the name of Thornton was actually in Paris, drew forth a volley of questions as to who they themselves were — if they had any pecuniary claim against this Englishman, or were related to him — and what had put it into their heads to come to the English consulate. These queries answered, and the nature of the interest prompting the inquiry clearly and fully explained, then, and not till then, the secretary or clerk, by whom they were received, informed them that Mr. Mortimer Thornton had solicitors in London, whose address he would write down for them, if they wished it. Meagre as was the proffered service, it was accepted with thanks, and Mr. Secretary accordingly presented them with a bit of paper, on which was written, "Messrs. Henstrid and Co., 14, Golden Square, London," whereupon the two applicants walked out very little wiser than they had walked in — Prudence, with feminine perspicuity, suspecting the consul's clerk of knowing more about Thornton than he chose to say, a suspicion which, however, with feminine kindness, she forbore to impart to poor Paolo.

Paolo despatched without delay a letter to Messrs. Henstrid and Co. in London, and one to Mortimer Thornton, addressed to Via Babuino, in case his friend should have returned to Rome. He also wrote a few lines to Angelo Gigli — that being the real name of

our funny little friend, Salvator Rosa — to recollect
which cost Paolo not a little thinking. This last epistle,
sibylline enough, simply stated that Thornton had disappeared, but without the least reference to any of the
attendant circumstances, asking, should any clue to him
happen to reach Salvator, that the intelligence might
be immediately sent to the writer in Paris, care of Mr.
Prosper, Quai Montebello, 77.

To his illness or to his money difficulties, Paolo
made no allusion whatever. Why should he give the
good little painter the pain of knowing his friend to be
in distress, when he had no power to help? For well
did Paolo know that not all the money Salvator and
his other companions could scrape together, would be
half sufficient to take him from Paris to Rome.

We may as well mark here that Paolo, on quitting
Rome, had, in the anticipation of a long absence, taken
with him all the money he possessed in the world, and
that the French bank post bill representing this sum,
had been left with Thornton; also that the half-dozen
pieces of gold he had had about him when he set off
on the unlucky expedition to the Hôtel de Ville, had
also gone, purse and all, comprising the scrap of paper
with the address of the Rue de Rohan, probably dropped while he was either scuffling with or trying to
bribe the guards to let him in as one of the ball guests.

In due course of post Messrs. Henstrid and Co.,
with business-like alacrity, acknowledged Paolo's letter:
they regretted not being able for the present to furnish
Mr. Mancini with the address of their esteemed client,
M. Thornton, Esq., whose absence abroad they had
every reason to suppose would last a considerable time.

This letter, however unsatisfactory, had in it a drop

of consolation for Paolo. It assured him that, wherever
Thornton might be, he was safe and uninjured.

Messrs. Henstrid's letter was quickly followed by
one from Salvator, to say that Thornton had not been
seen in Rome since he had left the city with Paolo.
Salvator's letter, naturally enough, teemed with questions and conjectures about the mystery of Thornton's
disappearance, and asked to be told what were Paolo's
plans for the future. Paolo wrote back that he had no
other plan than to be back in Rome as soon as possible, and
would delay all explanations about Thornton and himself until he could give them *vivá voce*. Paolo had two
motives for this postponement of confidence — one, his
unwillingness to make known his present embarrass-
ments to his friend, which he could not avoid if he
entered into any details of what had occurred; the other,
his repugnance to accuse Lavinia, which it would be
difficult not to do, if a real statement of the case was
to be given.

CHAPTER V.

Himself again.

MESSRS. HENSTRID AND Co.'s concise and well-
written letter had extinguished Paolo's last hope of
reaching Thornton for the present, even through the
medium of the post, but had in no way diminished the
young man's confidence, that wherever that good friend
was, he was in search of him. In the meantime he
must depend on himself, that is, he must work not
only for his daily bread, but to gain wherewithal to
make his way back to Rome.

Paolo did not disguise from himself that it was easier to wish for work than to procure it; more peculiarly so for one in his own situation — a stranger in a foreign land, imperfectly acquainted with French, with no possession but a threadbare suit, a solitary change of linen, and the good-will of three kind-hearted creatures, poor as rats, and without a right to claim kindred with any other human beings. But when necessity gives us a gripe of her iron claw, it is said that she communicates to us invention. Paolo consulted his confidant, Prudence, or rather reposed his confidence in her motherly heart. A good woman, whatever her station, is the earthly providence of the men about her. Prudence shrank a little from the idea of the delicate-looking invalid working for his daily bread; he must get stronger first, indeed he must.

"I am strong enough," said Paolo, "and I cannot afford to go on idling. I have been already too long a burden to you — I hate to think how long; but I have not been myself till to-day."

Prudence scorned the notion of his having been a burden to them. The little they had been able to do was more than repaid by his having put up so willingly with their poor accommodation, so far below his station and habits.

"Pray," said Paolo, trying to smile, "don't seek to diminish the benefits you have conferred, by fancying me some prince in disguise. I wish I may never have worse accommodation than what you are pleased to disparage. I have not been brought up in lavender, I assure you. At seventeen I was left naked as a worm, with no other capital than my two hands. Had I twenty lives to spend in your service, I should still never be quits with you — never."

If it be true, as it certainly is, that we must do good for its own sake, and not for any thanks it may bring us, it is not the less true, that a warm acknowledgment of what we meant as kindness, is, next to the testimony of our own conscience, the very sweetest reward we can receive. The grateful enthusiasm of the young Roman went to her heart the more, that Prudence was less accustomed to anything like demonstrativeness on his part. Only now had his benumbed feelings suddenly awoke to life, showing him, in their full extent, the obligations he was under to his kind hosts. Paolo had spoken the literal truth when he had said, that till this day he had not been himself.

"Well, then," said Prudence, briskly, "we'll do our best to find you work; and — *à la garde de Dieu* — is there any one thing you can do better than another?"

"I can draw and I can paint," returned Paolo. "I was brought up as a painter."

"Painting and drawing are rather out of my way," and the Frenchwoman, with her forefinger on her lips, fell to musing. "Playing on the piano and singing would have been better; there's the daughter of the porter next door, she wants a singing-master, I know."

"I can teach Italian, or copy papers," said Paolo. "I don't care what it is; I am ready to be a street porter and carry loads, if I can get nothing else to do."

"We shan't come to that, I hope," said Prudence; "but you must give me time to think."

Prosper, when he was apprised of Paolo's wants

and wishes, racked his brain, but found nothing there
except omnibuses, and what belonged to omnibuses;
and he was keen for applying to his company for a
vacant place of conductor for his *protégé*. Benoît got
frightfully excited at the thought that here was Signor
Paolo, actually a painter, and a painter in want of work,
and not a fortnight ago all the baths of his establishment had received a fresh coat of green. More practical Prudence passed all her neighbours in a mental
muster; the review did not take long, and the result
was, that "if Mr. Perrin did not help him out of this
trouble, why he'd have to stick in it."

Mr. Perrin accordingly received a visit from Madame
Prudence, and the dilemma was made known to him
with a circumlocution and diplomacy, that would have
been creditable in quarters to which Prudence and Co.
looked up with the awe due to principalities and arch-
angels. Mr. Perrin, having, with glasses on his nose,
succeeded in penetrating into the subject on which he
was being consulted, now took off his spectacles, twirl-
ing them between his thumb and first finger — the
ordinary sign with him of contention of mind.

"He is a painter, is he? a noble calling, no doubt;
but for practical purposes I had rather he had been a
musician. But all these Italians can sing and play,
can't they?"

"Just what I said to him," sighed Prudence; "but
it's just another of his misfortunes that he can't do either
the one or the other; and I see no help for it."

"None, indeed, that way," said the doctor; "we
must think of something else — we must think; when
I have thought, I'll call and tell you. Adieu."

By the time Prudence got home, a placard, written

in Prosper's best hand, was already on the window
shutters of the office, announcing to all passers-by, that
drawing lessons by a first-rate master were to be had
on moderate terms; for the terms and address to apply
within. From that day, Mr. Prosper, whenever his
avocations called him momentarily out of his premises,
and that was pretty often, we know, never failed, before recrossing the threshold, to stop and read his own
placard with the utmost attention, giving himself all
the while, to the best of his ability, the air of an ama-
teur meditating upon the benefit to be derived from the
union of a first-rate and cheap master.

Poor Prosper! his kindly artifice had no effect.
Luckily, however, after two days of heart-sickness, Mr.
Perrin appeared in the waiting-room of the establishment, his spectacles particularly bright and clear; he
came to leave the address of a gentleman, on whom he
requested Mr. Paolo Mancini to call next day at eleven
in the morning. The gentleman in question was a savant
of much renown, named Pertuis, one who had brought
to bear upon Rome and the Romans of yore a pro-
digious amount of knowledge and of critical acumen,
and the patience of a Benedictine monk. In all likelihood, Mr. Pertuis knew more about both subjects than
most of their own contemporaries.

Mr. Pertuis occupied an old and rather quaint-
looking house in the Place Royale, a quiet nook in
busy, worldly Paris; and Paolo, while traversing a
suite of lofty rooms on his way to the study of the man
of learning, had his eyes and heart truly gladdened by
the sight of many a dear, and once to him familiar,
object. On the walls were finely engraved views of
Rome; some good copies from Raphael — on pedestals,

casts from *chefs-d'œuvre* of sculpture.   Paolo found Mr.
Pertuis busy comparing different authors, with a view
to establishing a contested date, and the wide writing-
table before him having proved incapable of accommo-
dating the number of open volumes of all sizes, to which
he wanted to refer, the savant had ranged on either side
of the arm-chair he occupied two lesser tables, also over-
loaded with books.   It was in this state of circumvallation that Mr. Pertuis was surprised by Paolo, who,
according to orders, had been ushered in without any
previous announcement.   The archæologist, therefore,
in order to get out of his entrenchment without en-
dangering the equilibrium of his tables, and the rank
and file of his books, a work of trouble and time, had
no other alternative but to push his chair backwards
out of risk of upsetting his allies, and to meet his visitor by a flank movement, which he dexterously accomplished, laughing heartily, and apologizing at the same
time.

This trifling incident saved Paolo much of the awkwardness that invariably attends a first visit, particularly
when the visitor is very shy, and comes to ask a favour.
Mr. Pertuis's cordial reception and amenity of manners,
without mentioning his fluent Italian, soon put Paolo
at his ease.   Rome and Art were the exclusive topics
of the conversation, and Paolo spoke of both like
the warm-hearted patriot and devoted artist he was.   If
Mr. Pertuis, as was more than probable, aimed at drawing out his companion, his wish must have been fully
gratified.   After the lapse of a good half-hour, Paolo
felt it incumbent on him to rise; shaking hands, Mr.
Pertuis begged the favour of another call in a few days,
when he hoped to have found some opening for him.

This was all the allusion made to the circumstances, which had been the motive of the young man's introduction to the savant.

After a week, Paolo considered he might venture again to seek an interview with his patron of the Place Royale. Mr. Pertuis received him cordially, and handed to him the address of a Mr. Boniface.

"An excellent friend of mine," added Mr. Pertuis; "and an astronomer of much repute. I fear the occupation he may have to offer you may not be very acceptable, as it has nothing whatever in common with your profession. Nevertheless, I would not advise you to refuse it, for you remember the old saying — a bird in the hand is worth two in the bush."

Paolo eagerly assented, and lost no time in seeking out Mr. Boniface. This gentleman was a retired employé of the observatory, who, by dint of having been perpetually on the look-out for new planets, and new or old comets, had nearly lost his eyesight. He was now using his forced leisure in arranging his former notes and observations, and preparing them for publication; but, as he was unable either to read or write for any length of time at a stretch, he wanted a secretary who could do both for him, and had for some time been in quest of one, without ever having been able to decide on any of those who had offered to take the situation. For Mr. Boniface, simple and naïf as a child in all other respects, in what concerned his MS., distrusted the entire bulk of mankind, being convinced there was a general permanent conspiracy on foot to rob him of his theory on the formation of comets, and of the glory that must accrue from it. A foreigner and a stranger to science, such as Mr. Pertuis had guaranteed the person he recommended to be, was, under the circumstances, a godsend to the old astronomer.

"Sir," began Mr. Boniface, a tall bony man past sixty, rather bent, and with a green silk shade over his eyes — "sir, I must warn you at once that I am very fidgety in my ways."

Paolo thought it polite to make a deprecatory gesture.

"Indeed, I am," continued Mr. Boniface; "my sister here present will tell you that I am so, and not easily to be satisfied — and — an early riser to boot. Marie, my dear, if I forget anything else I ought to say, be so good as to remind me. Well, then, if what I have confessed does not serve to deter you, sir, well, then, I shall be glad if you agree to come, and we will begin work to-morrow." Here Mr. Boniface stopped and gazed vacantly at the space before him.

"About the hours," whispered sister Marie, into his ear.

"Ah, yes — about the hours," resumed Mr. Boniface; "thank you, Marie, my dear. I had forgotten about the hours. If you can be here by eight in the morning, sir, at eight precisely, you will oblige me greatly."

Paolo bowed assent.

"Very well, at eight in the morning; then it's all settled;" and all being settled, Mr. Boniface gave a nod, and relapsed into what seemed a trance.

"My brother's hours," said Mdlle. Marie, now taking the conversation into her own hands, "are from eight in the morning to mid-day, and again from one o'clock to six in the evening. Will they suit you?"

"Perfectly, madam," said Paolo.

"Now for the terms," cried the sister again, into her brother's ears.

"Ah, yes — for the terms," repeated Mr. Boniface, awakening; "very kind of you to remind me of the terms — I had forgotten all about them. Well, then, we say from eight in the morning till noon; will that do?"

"It is not that," interrupted the sister, "it is not that."

"How not that?" said the brother; "I am sure I thought it was from eight till twelve."

"Bless me — yes, brother; but we are speaking about money now, not hours. Shall I arrange it for you, my dear?"

"Precisely, precisely," reiterated Mr. Boniface, suddenly relieved.

"My brother, sir," said Mdlle. Marie, turning to Paolo, "offers four francs a day, or, to be more exact, sixty francs a fortnight, always payable in advance; each party remaining free at the expiration of the fifteen days to break or renew the agreement. This clause," added the lady, remarking the disagreeable effect it had upon the young man, "means nothing further than that my brother is, or fancies himself, over particular, and consequently is unwilling to bind you for a longer period than a fortnight to duties which might prove unpalatable to you."

Paolo stammered forth a few words, expressive of confidence in his employer's indulgence, said that he hoped to make up by zeal for his want of knowledge, and withdrew, not at all enlightened, and considerably alarmed as to the nature of the employment he had un-

dertaken; which, however, proved on the morrow, as
far as one day's experience might be trusted, far less
trying than he had anticipated. His hours were thus
divided: from eight o'clock to twelve, he had to put in
chronological order a good many notes, and then reading
them aloud, to retrench or add to them under Mr. Boniface's direction and dictation; from one to six in the
evening, to make a fair copy of the morning's work.

As a neighbouring clock struck six, Mdlle. Boniface
appeared to announce to her brother that dinner was
on the table, and to Paolo that his task for the day
was over. Paolo took his leave, and was already in
the passage, when he was overtaken by Mademoiselle,
who put a small packet in his hand, explaining that it
was the fortnight's salary, as stipulated. The young
man reddened, as if he had been caught in the act of
stealing the famous theory, and hurried away without
a word of thanks.

The first thing he did, even before allowing himself
the meal, of which he stood in great need, was to go
and hire a furnished room in the garret of a house in
the Rue du Four, a street close to Rue Cassette, where
Mr. Boniface lived; the second, to buy some toys for
the children, and then for himself a hat, to replace
Prosper's old greasy cap. This done, he entered a
third or fourth rate restaurant, and indulged in what had
become a luxury to him, viz. a *bouillon*, a beefsteak *aux
pommes-de-terre*, and bread *à discrétion* — all enjoyed
for the modest sum of fifteen sous, one sou for the waiter
included.

Great was the impatience with which Mr. Prosper's
household waited to know how Mr. Paolo had passed
his day, and great was the excitement produced by his

account, and the presentation of the sword and gun for
the little ones: but there was almost a tumult when he
announced that he had taken a lodging, and meant to
go and sleep there that night. Benoît especially was
so overcome by his feelings, and by something else to
boot, that in an attempt to vent them on the wall, he
lost his balance, and would have fallen flat on the ground,
but for the "boy's" catching him in his arms — an embrace from which Paolo could not extricate himself
short of many solemn vows never to forget his "vieux."

By ten o'clock that night Paolo was established in
his attic, busy with his accounts. Eight francs paid in
advance for a fortnight's rent of his room, five francs
for his hat, fifteen sous for the toys, ditto for his dinner,
made up a sum of fourteen francs fifty centimes, an
enormous amount for one day, which, deducted from the
sixty he had received, left a balance of five-and-forty
francs, and fifty centimes. Paolo reckoned that, by
exercising the strictest economy, with the proviso that
Mr. Boniface continued satisfied with him, he might be
able to realize within two months wherewithal to defray
his journey back to Rome. Two months seemed long
in prospect, but they would pass as so many others had
passed, and with this consolatory reflection he jumped
into his bed, which gave a succession of cracks, like the
bursting of a rocket. A rap on the thin partition wall
immediately followed. Paolo rapped back, and a voice
so near that it seemed to be in the room, said, —

"*Bonne nuit, voisin.*"

"*Bonne nuit, voisin,*" returned Paolo; and then all
relapsed into silence.

"A neighbour of a kind disposition," thought Paolo.
"I'd bet any wager that he is just such another poor

devil as I am. Poverty is a good conductor of kindliness. Were this a palace, and my neighbour and I
millionnaires — save us, ye gods — what introductions,
and notes, and cards it would need to bring us together."

Paolo could think no further, for he fell asleep. We
will leave him in this satisfactory condition, and take
a trip across the Channel to see after the fortunes of
one, whose claims on our sympathy are scarcely, if at
all, inferior to those of our Morpheus-stricken friend.

CHAPTER VI.

The Alternative.

NOTHING could prevail on Miss Lavinia to leave the
house in which her aunt had died. The very reasons
urged by Mr. Jones against her remaining there, its sad
associations and utter solitude, for the surrounding villas
were emptying apace for the London season, only served
to endear Holly Lodge to her. What Lavinia wished
above all things, was to be let alone. Hers was not
one of those griefs, which seek to be diverted, or eva-
porate in visits of condolence and idle demonstrations.
Mr. Jones did not insist. There was that about Lavinia
— a something new and imposing, the majesty of sorrow — which enforced acquiescence. In all the bloom
of health and spirits, in all the splendour of her gay
attire of yore, she had never impressed him as being
half so commanding and queen-like, as she did now
in her plain mourning dress, with her pale face and
dejected looks.

Nor was she sorry to be separated from Mr. Jones

at this period. Her uncle had gained nothing in her
eyes of late. The deceit he had practised on her, and
imposed on his wife, the perfect indifference and unfeel-
ingness he had displayed throughout the whole of Mrs.
Jones's illness, were little calculated to increase the
esteem or affection of his niece for him. Nor had she
forgotten a confidence made to her in a moment of
anguish, at Rome, viz. that Mrs. Jones had married without a settlement, and that consequently all she possessed
had become Mr. Jones's property. Arguing upon the
strength of her recent impressions, Lavinia came to the
conclusion that Mr. Jones's sole aim in marrying the
widow Jarman, had been to get hold of her money,
and that he had done so by taking advantage of her
simplicity and good faith. The prospect, therefore, of
residing with, and indeed of being entirely dependent
on, a man so unscrupulous and selfish, alarmed her
moral sense and revolted her honest pride. Had she
but been wiser, she would not have lacked a firm friend
and protector in this crisis. Much did she now dwell
on Paolo and on his love for her, and oh! how she
wished from the depths of her soul that she could recall the past. Vain longings! vainer regrets! she had
wilfully thrown away, past hope of recovery, that which
would have been a strong stay alike in happiness or
sorrow. She was alone in the world — no, not alone
— she had a father.

And then she resolved on having an explanation
with her uncle about this unknown father of her, and
anxiously waited for an opportunity. This, however,
did not occur for some little time. Mr. Jones wrote
frequently to her would-be kind and consolatory notes,
asking after her health, and whether she wanted for

anything, but he stayed away a whole fortnight. When he at last made his appearance, it so happened that Lavinia was too unwell to venture upon a topic so trying to her feelings, and she was fain to put off her inquiries until a more favourable moment.

The next Sunday morning brought Mr. Jones again to the Lodge, and this time Lavinia at once told him she was glad to see him, as she wanted to know all that he could tell her of her father. Mr. Jones grew black in the face, which was his way of blushing, and with an oath, —

"So the old woman peached, did she; never mind, it is all the better that she broke the ice for me. I had made up my mind to tell you all, but you must curb your impatience. You will require, I know, tangible proofs of what I have to say, and you shall have them on my next visit."

Not another syllable on this subject could Lavinia draw from him.

The day of the longed-for explanation at length arrived; it was on the Sunday following that on which Lavinia had asked for it. Mr. Jones's statement was full, minute, consistent in all its parts, leaving nothing to desire in point of clearness of evidence. We give its substance in as few words as possible, though with some touches, which Mr. Jones's modesty suppressed about himself.

Mr. Mark Jones had, as we already know, a brother older than himself by some years, who went to seek his fortune in London, and had been established there for some time as a wine merchant, when the younger brother set out for the capital, bent on a similar errand. Nay, it even clearly resulted from some of our Mr. Jones's reluctantly made admissions, that this elder brother had been of some use to the younger, on his *début* in the vast theatre of the metropolis. However this may be, it came to pass that in proportion to the rise of the younger's fortunes, was the decline of those of the elder, owing to his addictedness to drink. The issue was bankruptcy, and the bankrupt drank the harder to console himself, and became what all drunkards become, a pest to society.

The younger brother, who had just married the widow Jarman, felt the presence of this near relative to be a disgrace, and fearing that the discredit it reflected on himself might injure the profitable and genteel business he was now carrying on, agreed to secure a small annuity to the ex-wine-merchant, on condition that he should quit the fashionable West End, and banish himself to one of the most distant and obscure suburbs. The bargain was at once accepted, and the bankrupt retired to Whitechapel, where he found some one willing to help him to bear his troubles. So he married and had a daughter, who received the high-sounding name of Lavinia. Though forbidden any, whatever intercourse with his lucky relative of the West End, the exile of Whitechapel repeatedly applied, both in writing and in person, to Mr. Mark Jones for an increase of his annuity, which he alleged to be scarcely enough for one, and starvation for two. Mr. Mark said he should have thought of that before he took a wife, and obstinately resisted all importunities until this child was born; when, more out of fear of further disgrace from an exposure of family circumstances than from compassion, he consented to a small augmentation of the allowance.

After this, the written demands and personal requests for money grew rarer, but did not wholly cease for all that, and it was upon the occasion of one of these interested visits, that Mrs. Jones first noticed and was captivated by the little Lavinia, who had accompanied her father. Lavinia was then seven years old, and a miracle of beauty, gentleness, and intelligence. Even matter-of-fact Mr. Jones was not insensible to her infantine grace, and precocious witty sayings; so no wonder Mrs. Jones, to whom Providence had denied the boon of children, should have earnestly desired to adopt and bring her up as her own child. It is not to be supposed that Mr. Jones yielded at first, or with a good grace, to his wife's wishes, but he did so at last; and after much mean haggling, that bargain was entered into between the two brothers, the clauses of which have been already hinted at by dying Mrs. Jones. When Lavinia was made over by her willing parents to their rich relations, she was immediately consigned to a first-rate boarding-school to receive a brilliant education. Together with this act of adoption, Mr. Jones took another important step; he parted with the Italian warehouse. He had capital enough to insure his being a man of some importance anywhere, and self-conceit enough to match his capital.

A couple of years after Mr. Jones's name as a tradesman had been erased from the *General Directory*, he received by post a note, entreating his attendance without delay at the residence of a Mary Holywell, who had important revelations to make with respect to Miss Lavinia Jones, without doing which, she did not dare to face death. The appeal, earnestly worded enough, might, as the experienced Mr. Jones was aware, be a snare to draw him into an ambush, from whence no escape without undrawing his purse; it might even be one of his worthy brother's stratagems to force from him a few more pounds; and Mr. Jones had fifty minds to throw note and request to the winds. But there is fascination in a mystery, and so after wasting some hours in wise pros and cons, Mr. Jones ended by proceeding to the address given by the *soi-disant* Mary Holywell.

It was one of those haunts of vice and misery, which a beast of the field would not have chosen for its lair; one of the foul excrescences, not unfrequently met with on the smooth stuccoed surface of the proud, rich, and prudish metropolis of Great Britain. At the house, to which he had been directed, Mr. Jones found a woman evidently in the last stage of consumption, on whose death-stricken face still lingered the traces of great past beauty, and who in a husky voice painfully gasped out the following strange tale.

She had known the elder Mr. Jones and his wife well, having occupied for years a house in common with them in Whitechapel. She herself had at that time been living with a man, a Spitalfields weaver, who was not her husband, and she and her fellow-lodger Mrs. Jones, had been confined within a week or two of one another, and admiring the name given to the Jones's baby, she had called hers also Lavinia. Lavinia Jones, always a puny, sickly child, died before it was quite a twelvemonth old, a great distress to the father, who became alarmed that the increase of allowance, made on account of his child, would be withdrawn by his brother, as soon as he knew of the poor little creature's death. Under this pressure, Jones proposed to her to let the deceased child pass for hers, and to give him up her living infant, for the consideration of a weekly allowance. She was sickly, pleaded Mary Holywell, unable to work, and otherwise utterly destitute. The man she lived with had left her and gone to California. God forgive her, but she was sorely tried and yielded to Jones's tempting tongue. She did not feel much what she had done, as long as her girl lived with her fellow-lodgers, but her heart had begun to trouble her, when Mr. Mark Jones took the child, believing it to be his own blood, and now she couldn't die with the lie on her conscience.

Well, we have not recorded much good of Mark Jones: he was compassionate in this instance, he sent a medical man to attend on Mary Holywell; but the poor troubled spirit, relieved from its burden of a bad secret, passed away on the very following day.

Mr. Jones was a man of business habits, therefore he went at once to the registrar's office for the parish of Whitechapel, to seek confirmation of the allegations made by Mary Holywell. There he found, and had copies taken of the certificates, which he now laid before his present wretched listener, — one of Lavinia Jones's death, and one of Lavinia Holywell's birth. His next act was to go to his brother's, with the two damnatory documents in his hand, and there he swore a frightful oath, that if the guilty wretch ever breathed a syllable of this foul transaction, or even showed his face again in his (Mark Jones's) neighbourhood, he would try what punishment the law awarded for such knavery. This done, he debated with himself what his own course should be, and he came to the conclusion — half from liking to the child, half from dread of the scandal which might arise — that the wisest thing to do was to hold his tongue, and keep his knowledge to himself, even to the exclusion of his wife; and this determination he had steadily adhered to, up to this moment of revelation to Lavinia herself.

A thunderbolt does not carry stronger conviction of its reality to the senses of the terror-stricken wayfarer, at whose feet it falls, than did the truthfulness and authenticity of Mr. Jones's statement to the almost stunned mind of Lavinia. She took in, nevertheless, at one glance and for ever, its whole purport, and was spared at least the struggles of suspense. All failed her at once — the past, the present, the future, even her own identity. The very affection, which from the other side of the grave cast a ray of light into the *camera oscura* of her life, was no longer hers — she had no right to it. Her inner as well as her outer world reeled and crumbled about her. Despair clutched the poor girl's heart, and hiding her face with her hands, she burst into a passion of tears.

Mr. Jones tried to console her in his way. There was no occasion for her to put herself in such a state; it was mere folly; for what, after all, was there changed in her situation? — nothing but a name. Had he not known of her real condition for these eleven years past, and yet had he not gone on with her education, just as if she had been his real niece; made her the thorough lady she was, and which she might remain to the end of her days, if she only trusted to him? His house was hers as before, his fortune at her disposal, as it had been, and so on. Lavinia sobbed out her thanks as best she could, but said, the shock had been too sudden, had taken her so unawares, that

she must have time and quiet to think, and to regain
composure. Certainly, poor thing, agreed Mr. Jones.
He showed himself, under the circumstances, both discreet and attentive. He called to see her the next day,
and the next, but only stayed a few minutes, as he
explained, to satisfy himself that she was not ill, and
wanted for nothing. By and by, he relapsed into his
usual Sunday visit.

Thus two months passed by — two months full for
Lavinia of anxious consultations with herself. One
point was perfectly clear to her perception. She could
not go on with any propriety living under the same
roof with, and eating the bread of one to whom she
was no kin, who had been, in fact, by a fraud, forced,
as it were, to become her benefactor. Independently
of her innate self-respect, which forbade such a course,
she would, so she felt, at least, by continuing to occupy
a place which was not hers by right, be a party, passive
indeed, but still a party, to a deceit upon the world.
But where was she to go? how was she to support
herself? She had none from whom to ask advice and
guidance; because to none had she the courage to
reveal the shame of her birth. None but Mr. Jones.
Why then not trust him? He had correspondents, con-
nections, interests in every quarter of the globe; of all
people he was the best able to help her, and having
the power, why should she doubt his good will? He
had shown himself to her a real friend. Thus arguing
with herself, she came to the conclusion that she would
make him the confidant of her wish to find some situation — abroad.

Mr. Jones's conduct well justified his claim to the
title of friend, that she had bestowed on him. She had

surely misjudged the man. He was unobtrusively attentive, kind, at times almost tenderly so. He brought her newspapers, books, and the choicest flowers; he never interfered with her wishes by word or deed, even seemed quite reconciled to her plan of seclusion. He availed himself of every opportunity to encourage and reassure her as to her future. He had even repeatedly hinted at a something in store for her — a something that might greatly surprise, but he fondly hoped would not be displeasing to her. She knew not what to make of this innuendo, unless it was an allusion to some offer of marriage he had received for her. If so, the moment, in her opinion, was ill chosen, but it would be a reason the more why she should let him know her intentions.

One afternoon, before dinner, she summoned all her courage, and told him she wished to speak to him about herself. He did not look at all disturbed — of the two, rather pleased. He said that, though he was not her uncle, that did not militate against his being her friend — a tenderer friend than perhaps she surmised, and as he spoke, he took one of her hands in his.

"I am sure you are my friend," replied Lavinia, "and indeed I am grateful to you for your kindness; at the same time you must acknowledge, that your being only my friend, and unfortunately not my uncle, must prevent my remaining with you on the same footing as if I were in reality your niece."

"Well, I allow it," replied Mr. Jones, and added quickly, in a would-be passionate tone, "why may I not become to you something better than uncle or friend?"

She did not seize his meaning.

"Is there not a more sacred and dearer title that you can bestow on me?" asked he, in a still tenderer tone; "a title which will confer on me the right to protect you in the face of the whole world?"

She looked alarmed and perplexed, like one who cannot take in the sense of earnest words, spoken in an unknown language.

"I am healthy, and strong," went on the tempter, "and many a younger lady than you are, has married an older man than I am, and not rued the bargain; quite the contrary. What do you say to it, eh?"

She remained as if made of stone for a while; then violently disengaging her hand, and recoiling from his effort to repossess himself of it as from the touch of a serpent, she sprang to the other end of the room, saying, —

"Oh! never — never — rather die!"

Mr. Jones turned the colour of lead, and strode towards her with a menacing air — all the worst passions which degrade man's nature flashed from his eyes.

"Don't rouse the devil in me," he shouted, "or by ——"

He made an effort to control himself, retreated a step or two, and burst into a coarse laugh.

"I am a precious donkey to take your big words seriously; you'll not find it easy to bully me, I warn you. I mean to have you for my wife, and, will you, nill you, my wife you shall be. I give you a night and a day for meditation on the difference between abandonment, beggary, starvation, and every luxury of life, a jolly husband, and lots of friends. You'll say 'yes' to me with a good grace, I dare say." And he left her.

Lavinia locked herself into her room, watching with a throbbing heart for the sound of wheels, to let her know that he was gone. Sooner than she had hoped, she heard his gig drive away. Then she threw herself on her knees, and first prayed long and fervently, then putting a few articles of clothing into a small carpet-bag, she glided out of the house, and walked as fast as she could to the nearest railway station. Within another hour she was at the London terminus. There she took a cab, telling the coachman to drive to Camden Town. The name had slipped involuntarily from her lips, in the effort to remember some out-of-the-way place. She had never been in Camden Town, did not know whether it was a single street, or a suburb consisting of many streets.

The coachman asked where abouts he was to stop in Camden Town; "it were a loose sort of direction."

"I will pull the check-string," said the perplexed girl.

She was made aware of having reached her destination by the obstinate turning of the cabman to peep in at her. She stopped him at once, paid him his demand, took her carpet-bag, and walked straight on, not quite sure whether she was awake or in a dream. The cabman stared after her, shook his head, then set his horse again in motion, satisfied that it was no business of his to care what became of his out-of-the-way passengers.

Lavinia's legs tottered under her, as she looked to the right and the left, trying for the courage to knock at one of the many houses, in the windows of which

were notices of apartments to let. No bench near for
the tired, yet rest she must; she was ready to drop
on the pavement — still wandering on, wandering on.
She was now in a row of two-storied, neat little
houses; looking over the railing, she could see the
four walls of the front parlours; anything so diminutive
must be cheap. She knocked at one of these small
dwellings, and said she wanted a room. It was the
landlady herself who opened the door; after a close
and suspicious inspection of the inquirer, she answered
that she never let rooms to single ladies. A second
application farther down the row met the same fate.
The third time she was permitted to see a room, but
when, in reply to the query of what luggage she had,
she allowed that she had nothing but the carpet-bag in
her hand, she was told, civilly enough, that the room
was already all but let to another party, and that she
had better try elsewhere. A fourth attempt succeeded.
The landlady of No. 25 was either more needy or less
distrustful; to be sure, she required an assurance that
the young lady received no visits, and was willing to
pay a fortnight's rent in advance. Lavinia drew out
her purse, and paid the money immediately — not
without difficulty, indeed, everything round her reeled
so. After this preliminary, she was admitted into a
clean, tidy room, surprisingly cheap to the poor tyro
in poverty. If she wanted for anything, there was a
bell, said the landlady. Nothing; Lavinia wanted nothing, only rest, she said, as she laid herself down on
the horse-hair sofa.

CHAPTER VII.

Found and Lost again.

THE reader may perhaps owe us a grudge for having so long kept Mr. Thornton out of sight, and for having left unsolved a riddle or two connected with that gentleman. Had he really gone to the United States in search of Paolo, as the last visa of his passport, entered at the *Bureau des Passeports*, would lead one naturally to believe? And, if so, what could have been his motive, and that of the clerk of the consulate, and of the solicitors in London, for making a mystery of his destination? We are going to meet categorically, and we hope satisfactorily, this double query; our only reason for not having done so before, being that we cannot relate the history of several people at one and the same time.

Mortimer had, after leaving the Rue de Rohan for the Rue Neuve des Augustins, still continued to receive communications connected with his advertisement about Paolo, most of them unworthy of notice, but which he persevered in forwarding to the police. One letter, however, dated from Havre, alike from its feeling tone, and the quarter from whence it assumed to come, commanded his attention. The writer, who styled himself the agent of a company for emigration to the United States, and who professed himself to be a philanthropist, explained how his sympathy had been aroused by the perseverance of the advertiser, and how consequently he had set on foot an inquiry in his own office, with the view of ascertaining whether any one answering to the description of the person missing had applied for a

passage in any of the company's steamers. The result
of the inquiry was, that, in fact, a young man whose
appearance tallied with the description given of Signor
Paolo Mancini, had called at the office on the 26th of
March last, and had secured a second-class berth for
New York in the *Atalanta.* The name of this person,
as appeared from the books, was Paolo Manni, and not
Mancini; but the slight difference in the surnames might
be, perhaps, owing to some incorrectness of the clerk
who had registered the passenger. Unfortunately, wrote
Thornton's unknown correspondent, he had not himself
seen the Italian, but should the advertiser think it worth
his while to follow out this clue, and come to Havre,
the clerk above mentioned would be too happy to impart
all his recollections as to the personal appearance of the
gentleman booked as Paolo Manni. Here followed the
signature of the writer, and the street and number of
the office at which application was to be made. A
postscript further intimated that the steamer *Nonchalant*
would leave Havre for New York on the day after the
morrow.

Mortimer thought the indications too precious to
allow of a moment's hesitation. He went straight to
the police, had his passport *viséd* for the United States,
in order to be ready for instant embarkation, if necessary, and then set off for Havre, where he was not long
before he ascertained that he was the victim of a heartless hoax. The signature, the street, the number, and
the office, were one and all a fabrication. Thornton
came back utterly discomfited, and more sombre and
dejected than ever. He took to going frequently to the
Morgue. The ill-omened spot, and the lurid sights it
presented had a sort of savage fascination for him. The

impression, which he had had from the first, that Paolo
had thrown himself into the river, returned again and
again with the pertinacity and vigour of mania, and his
diseased fancy could not help speculating upon how
Paolo's dead body would look, stretched on the lugubrious flagstones of the sinister establishment. Thornton
was there one morning when a body, just dragged out
of the river, was being carried in. It had lain in the
water but a few hours, and was not at all disfigured.
It was the corpse of a young girl, not yet twenty,
middle-sized, slender, and strikingly handsome. The
wet masses of her rich auburn hair adhering to her
temples and neck, brought out in strong relief the
alabaster delicacy of her complexion. She was dressed
in white. Great was the concourse of people round the
beautiful dead girl, unanimous the pity, and loud the
guesses as to the cause of her untimily end. A
disappointment in love was, of course, the solution
given.

Long and wistfully did Mortimer gaze at the solemnly
quiet face, and lo! as he gazed, a strange work of transformation, such as we have examples of in our dreams,
slowly accomplished itself in the solemnly quiet face,
until the unknown features shaped and settled themselves into those familiar ones, which had been for the
last nine years engraved in outlines of fire on his brain
and heart. All notion of time was obliterated withal,
and it seemed but yesterday that she, whom he identified
in the corpse now lying on those cold stones before him,
was hanging, a happy, confiding girl, on his arm; and
he had had the heart, madman that he was, to fling her
from him, and consign her to despair. And here was
his work! and so then he was standing a convicted

murderer before his victim! Under the sway of this horrible delusion, Mortimer rushed forth and precipitated himself into the Seine!

In large and crowded cities, a man may drop from sheer exhaustion, and breathe his last on the unfriendly pavement little heeded; but if he takes to the river for his death-bed, he is sure to be interfered with by the very persons who would have shrugged their shoulders, and passed on the other side, in the first case. The reason of the difference is obvious; the inhabitants of large towns are *blaséd* and fearful of being imposed upon; a man writhing and foaming at the mouth in the street may he an impostor, whereas he who plunges into running water cannot but be in downright earnest; and once the possibility of a trick removed, human sensibilities reassert their rights and get fair play. No sooner was Thornton in the water, than a double shout was raised from a multitude of anxious spectators lining both banks of the Seine, and several boats and swimmers put off to the rescue. A barge full of timber was coming up the river; the man at the helm manœuvred, so as to place the barge sideways. Thornton, borne swiftly down the current, was stopped awhile by this impediment, then sank under it. A loud cry from the shores testified to the universal horror; a boat shot forward to the spot where Thornton had disappeared, and one of the men in her jumped into the water and dived. There was a moment of thrilling silent suspense, and then the brave fellow reappeared, and not alone. A real shout of triumph and admiration rent the air. With a stroke or two of the oars, the men left in the boat brought her close enough to preserved and preserver to lift them safely in, and in five minutes more the still unconscious

Englishman, followed by the excited multitude, was being carried to the nearest *corps de garde*.

A commissioner of police was already there, who, as soon as Mortimer recovered his senses, proceeded to an interrogatory. Mortimer's replies were at first collected and to the point. He said who he was, and where he lived, and cautioned the functionary not to interfere with the liberty of a British subject. But when questioned as to what had impelled him to attempt self-destruction, he began raving that he was a murderer, and that he had passed sentence of death upon himself. He referred the commissioner to the Morgue, where he would see his (Thornton's) victim. The commissioner, though strongly impressed with the belief that he had to deal with a person in a state of insanity, sent one of his staff to the Morgue, who brought back information which completely proved the groundlessness of Mortimer's self-accusation. He was accordingly conveyed in a carriage to his lodgings, and left there under the strict surveillance of two police agents in plain clothes, lest he should renew his attempt against his life. In the meantime, the English embassy was officially informed of what had occurred, and a clerk of the British consulate, the very same to whom Paolo and Prudence had applied for information about Thornton, was sent to the Rue Neuve des Augustins.

Mortimer answered all this gentleman's inquiries rationally; said he had no near relations that he knew of; and when asked to do so, made no difficulty to give the address of his solicitors in London; but once put on the track of his late rash act, immediately accused himself of murder, launching forth in the same wild strain as before. As Thornton seemed to have no friends

about him, the best thing to do was to telegraph to
Messrs. Henstrid and Co. information of the state of their
client.

One of the firm from Golden Square came at once
to Paris and had the unfortunate gentleman examined
by the English physician of the embassy, and by the
eminent Frenchman, Dr. Ternel, whose specialty was
the treatment of mental diseases. Both these gentlemen
agreed that Mr. Thornton was labouring under delusions,
and could not with safety to himself be left without
restraint. Upon this a sort of family council was held,
composed of the commissioner of police, the clerk of
the consulate, and the representative of the firm of
Henstrid and Co., and attended by the two physicians,
who had already examined into the case. It was then
unanimously decided on, that the best course to pursue,
was to place the English gentleman under the care of
Dr. Ternel, and for that purpose to have him removed
to a *maison de santé*, immediately under that celebrated
man's direction. Owing to the infinite tact and persua-
sive ways of Mr. Ternel, no difficulty or demur was
made to the carrying out of this plan, by him whom it
chiefly concerned.

The nature of Thornton's malady, one of those which
relations and friends strive to conceal to the very last,
accounts for the evasive and ambiguous answers of
Messrs. Henstrid and Co. and of the clerk of the consulate.

It is scarcely necessary to add, that Mortimer's seclusion put an end to all further advertisements, or inquiries about Paolo. More than this, one of the strangest
symptoms of Thornton's derangement was the dread and
terror, with which the recollection of Paolo was attended.

He was often busied writing out petitions for protection against the persecution he endured, and claiming from Dr. Ternel the promise that he would prevent Paolo from having access to him.

Madame Françoise had felt keenly for her lodger, nor did she desert him in this his time of need. She was frequently at the *Maison de Santé*, striving to comfort him with a woman's ingenious kindness. But a month having elapsed without any apparent improvement in his condition, and her questions as to the probability of a speedy recovery meeting with no more explicit answer from Dr. Ternel than a doubtful shake of the head, the good lady lost heart and went to Evreux to redeem her long-made promise to be with her daughter during her approaching confinement.

Dr. Ternel did not shake his head in despair of Thornton's case, but in despair at not being able to seize on the indispensable clue for handling and mastering it. Such details as Madame Françoise had been able to relate of Thornton, previous to his outbreak of madness in the Morgue, though of service in forming a partial diagnosis, were of too scattered a nature, and too disconnected with the immediate cause of Thornton's disorder, to afford the doctor a good standing ground. Material evidence it was that Dr. Ternel wanted, in order to counteract effectually the lunatic's delusions. Till he could lay hold of that, and there was little likelihood of his doing so, he had scarcely any hope of a favourable result to his treatment. The unlucky Englishman seemed an isolated being. Apart from the quarterly payments made regularly for him, no one inquired about, or cared for him. Poor deserted Thornton!

CHAPTER VIII.

On the Left Bank of the Seine.

WAS Paolo really in gay, turbulent, noisy Paris, or had he fallen from the clouds into some convent on the top of Mount Lebanon? Such was the question that he often put to himself during the first days of his new employment. The house inhabited by Mr. Boniface was the quietest of a quiet collection of houses, through a court, down an alley, between another court and a garden, in quiet Rue Cassette; and the quietest nook in this quietest of houses, was allotted to Paolo for his daily avocations. The cell of an anchorite, as far as silence and retirement go, could alone stand a comparison with his little study. Not the faintest echo of the noisy world without found a way to it, and within, no sound but that of the scraping of a pen against paper. The maids who shook carpets out of the opposite windows, did so with a care; the very sparrows which lighted on the solitary tree in the centre of the noiseless court below, seemed impressed by the stillness that reigned, and chirped *sotto voce*.

Paolo had never come in contact before with a real devotee of science, and for the first time had an idea of that tranquil, unremitting race after knowledge, which the life of an intellectual pioneer can be. The specimen he had under his eye interested him the more. Scientific speculation was with Mr. Boniface a process as natural, indispensable, and continuous as respiration. Shut up as in a coat of mail in his world of thoughts and calculations, the only realities for him, he forgot

the external world and its exigencies, and would have
dropped exhausted over his volume or his slate, without a surmise of the why and the wherefore, had not
his sister been at hand to warn him that it was time to
breakfast or to dine. A fish out of water was not more
helpless than he was, when summoned from the lofty
regions in which his spirit soared, and forced to take
into consideration any detail of common life — such, for
instance, as the being measured for a coat — then he
would search after something sensible to say, and invariably miss it; but set him on any of his favourite
themes — and all scientific subjects were so — or ask
an explanation of his own speculations, and he would
warm up and develop the most ingenious theories with
true eloquence.

Of an afternoon, Mr. Boniface often had visitors,
and as his study was contiguous to that of his amanuensis, and the conversation, owing to his deafness,
was carried on in a loud voice, Paolo had naturally his
share of it. Mr. Boniface's friends were for the most
part men of science like himself — naturalists, archæo-
logists, orientalists, mathematicians — each having a
particular hobby of his own. Mr. Pertuis, of the Place
Royale, he who had introduced Paolo to Mr. Boniface,
was one of the most assiduous visitors at Rue Cassette.
Often would Paolo lay down his pen to listen, and
derive the greatest gratification from what he heard.
Not that he could understand or take in the hundredth
part of what was said on these occasions — he would
have been quite another and a more accomplished man
than he was, had he been able to do so; it was the
lofty standard of their callings, the entireness of their
devotion to the interests of the mind, the all-absorbing

character of their pursuits, the depth of their convictions, their enthusiasm, their patience, their simplicity, which commanded Paolo's sympathy and admiration. Paolo felt instinctively that these were the salt of the city, and that to the patient investigations of such men might be traced the germ of all the great discoveries that honoured and benefited mankind. Thus Paolo, in his humble capacity of copyist, had a revelation, and a bird's-eye view, of the world of intelligence.

In other and more personal respects also, he had every reason to be satisfied with his present lot. Setting aside the difficulty of quick communication with one who was half blind, tolerably deaf, and always absent in mind — a difficulty, however, which each day's habit lessened — his duties were easy enough; and the regard shown him by brother and sister soon made them pleasant. Mr. Boniface never came to him with a change to make, of which he had bethought himself after more pondering, without offering an apology for being so tiresomely particular, and without uttering many self-reproaches for thus taxing Mr. Mancini's obligingness. Mademoiselle on her side never let him depart at six o'clock, without expressing her own and her brother's thanks for his kind attendance. Mr. Pertuis also was very civil, and rarely called without slipping into Paolo's study to shake hands with its inmate. Thanks and smiles and handshaking, you will say, don't prove much regard: agreed; but they do good all the same, and go far to sweeten dependence. Nor were these outward signs of good-will the only tokens of satisfaction received by the *pro tempore* secretary. At the end of the second fortnight, his salary was raised, from sixty to seventy-five francs, an item of some importance to one whose heart was bent on amassing funds as fast as possible for a journey from Paris to Rome.

In spite of this augmentation, however, and of the strictest economy, Paolo's savings at the end of the mouth proved much less than he had anticipated. More claims than he had reckoned upon had drained his purse — the cobbler's wife opposite, who blacked his shoes, and cleaned his room, had to be paid, and there was an occasional wax-candle, and his washing. This last expense was a very heavy one. Besides, manage as best he could, it was, after all, an impossibility to go on decently with a change of linen, and a worn-out pair of boots. And a pair of shoes, at the lowest price, was seven francs, and three shirts, at three francs and a half each, had made altogether a large outlay. If one could only do without eating; but no, one must eat every day, and several times a day. Truth to say, Paolo had reduced this necessity to its simplest ex·pression. A hot roll — poor Salvator's breakfast, minus the roasted chesnuts not to be found in Paris at that time of the year — a hot roll munched on his way to Rue Cassette in the morning — two other rolls at twelve, swallowed before a book-stall on the quays, his usual and most economical circulating library; or while walking in front of yonder noble pile, the Louvre — and at half-past six in the evening, such a luxurious dinner as we have described already — constituted his daily food, at the cost of eighteen sous *per diem*. It is possible that some of the materials of the last-mentioned repast were not always unimpeachable, but the condiment of hunger seasoned them. Neither bitters, nor absynth, nor vermuth render the stomach of a youth of twenty-

four so optimist as a fast of ten hours broken only by
three halfpenny rolls.

Paolo had taken a local affection for the old-fashioned
and comparatively tranquil part of the town in which
chance had thrown him, and seldom went out of its
precincts. The Seine was his Rubicon. He liked to
stroll of an evening over the half-deserted quays, and
watch, from one or other of the bridges, the setting of
the sun behind the heights of Chaillot, to contemplate
the imposing silhouette of Notre Dame by moonlight,
and follow the reflection of the lamps in the dark rolling waters below. His rambles and his admiration were
not unfrequently shared by a companion, his neighbour
of the "*Bonne nuit, voisin!*" a young student from
Evreux, as he afterwards proved to be, who was supposed to be accomplishing his *droit* at Paris — equiva-
lent, I fancy, to keeping Law Terms in Lincoln's Inn
— and, under cover of that convenient legal fiction,
sowing his wild oats.

A more sociable, sanguine, thoughtless, and original
Bohemian than Théophile Courant had never pitched
his tent in the Quartier Latin. As long as his quarter's
allowance lasted — which, when he was most prudent,
might be a fortnight — he had a merry life of it, re-
fusing himself nothing; the rest of the time he shifted
as best he could, living on fried potatoes and credit; a
change of diet which in nowise affected his humour:
merrily and carelessly as he had gone through his seven
years of plenty, to use his own phrase, merrily and
carelessly he traversed his seven years of famine.

The Frenchman disapproved of the Italian's somewhat ascetic ways and retired habits of life, and would
fain have enticed him into forming acquaintances among

the *grisettes* frequenting the *Marché aux Fleurs* close by. It was to that humble stage, that the *soi-disant* student, weaned for the time being from the joys and conquests of the *Chaumière* and the *Closerie aux Lilas*, confined his exploits, seeking there thrice a week easy *bonnes fortunes*. He had, in truth, plenty of them, and was fond of relating his triumphs. The mixture of a Sardanapalus and a Diogenes in him, not to speak of the attractions of a *pâté de foie gras*, and *rognons sautés aux truffes* in his days of abundance, took amazingly with the fair and loving spinsters of the Quartier Latin. Paolo did not envy him his successes. Love, to his mind, meant something better, he would say, than a temporary association for the sake of pleasure; upon which Théophile nicknamed him *farouche* Hippolyte, favouring him with much ridicule and laughing at his own jokes. Courant was a clever fellow, full of talk, of wit, of paradox, boldly flying at all subjects, and agreeing with Paolo on none, save that of politics. All epicurean and sceptic as he boasted himself to be, the young Frenchman had strong' political convictions of the same decided hue as those of his new friend.

As usual during what he termed his temporary eclipses, Courant was in a concentrated literary mood — had, in fact, on the stocks, at one and the same time, a poem, a comedy, and a novel — and spiced his pennyworth of fried potatoes with visions of the Cross of the Legion of Honour, and a seat at the Institute. He loved to dilate on his plots, especially on that of his *Prédestiné*, a novel of passion. According to · him, passion was the only field in which Balzac had left anything to glean. All other forms of fiction, whether of wordly life or private life, whether of morals or philosophy, that great dissector of the human heart had exhausted.   Balzac was Courant's prophet, and the *Physiology of Marriage* the book of books with him.

Well, then, to return to the student's favourite theme. The "Prédestiné" was a Parisian poet, young, handsome, rich, and highly gifted withal, intensely unhappy from the absence of that sister soul, caressed in dreams, and which was to complete his existence. Stormy had been his youth, an Ixionlike race after his half-ball; he had demanded it from the aristocratic salons of Europe, from the workshop, the thatched cottage, from the pampas of America, and the orgies of the *salon doré*. All in vain: the "Prédestiné" walked through life gloomy, incomplete, alone. One day, as he emerged from the depths of a forest, he heard a merry peal of bells from a little village church. He enters it — there is a wedding going on. The clerk to the notary of the village, a common-looking personage enough, is being married to the daugther of his employer, a slender, pale, and far from handsome blonde. The "Prédestiné" — mark this — objects, always has objected, to blondes in general; but the more he looks at this one, strange to say, the more he feels attracted. Surely there is something fatal in the fascination she exercises over him. His whole soul flies towards her as to its centre. In short, as the benediction is pronounced, he has received a full irrefragable revelation, that the bride of the notary's clerk is his the "Prédestiné's" heaven-destined better half.

"How was it revealed to him, the fool?" interrupted Paolo.

Courant, unmoved, continued: —

"Like a wolf who does not lose sight of his prey, he follows the bridal party to the little country inn, where the modest family banquet is to take place. As he does so, contending thoughts sweep over his brain, like wind-driven clouds over the sky. No, he will not be defrauded of his own — his rights, registered in heaven, are anterior to those of that paltry *épicier*. She shall be his. Acting upon this resolve, the 'Prédestiné' forthwith procures a quantity of a narcotic; hires a small chamber contiguous to the dining-room, where the wedding repast is to take place; pours some of the soporific in the champagne glasses, ten in number, and lies in wait for the effect. The dinner proceeds slowly and prosily, at last he hears the report of the champagne corks — toasts are drunk — and then little by little the murmur of voices subsides, one head after another drops on the table, and the whole company is fast asleep. The 'Prédestiné' seizes the moment, pounces upon his prey, lifts her up in his arms, and carries off his precious charge to his retreat."

"An infernal trick, worthy of ten thousand guillotines," cried Paolo.

"Rather so," said Théophile; "'strike hard to strike home,' is my motto. I see my plot is a taking one. I have not done yet — there's something still more spicy in store. Hearken to this:". "After a time, the bridegroom, awaking, misses his bride, seeks her with tottering steps, notices a door ajar, pushes it, and enters. The door was that of the chamber of the 'Prédestiné,' which he had forgotten to lock. A tiger disturbed in his den is not more terrible than the 'Prédestiné' at sight of his rival; the clutch of a tiger's claws not more deadly than the grasp of the 'Prédestiné's' fingers round the intruder's throat. A struggle of ten seconds, a stifled groan, and there lies the morning's bridegroom — a corpse." "What do you say to that, eh? I hope it is lively and passionate enough for a first chapter," chuckled Courant.

"I say it is unnatural, absurd, abominable, nonsensical. What is the use of this string of impossible horrors? *Cui bono?*"

"He asks *cui bono?*" retorted Courant, laughing. "Why, to carry away the reader from the first, to lay violent hands on his attention, to have a sale of twenty thousand copies; in a word to succeed."

"You will never do so by means of giving people nightmares," said innocent Paolo; "there are other and purer sources of interest, thank God, than treachery, murder, and such like amenities. Listen to this;" and enthusiastic, and overflowing with recollections, as all true Italians are, of the *Promessi Sposi*, Paolo gave his friend on outline of Manzoni's celebrated novel; namely, the simple story of two obscure existences, a poor silk-weaver and his affianced bride, momentarily brought in contact with, and dragged along by, the current of the evil passions of a rude age, and making their way out of the turbid whirlpool through humble faith and love, and landing in safety after many trials, wiser, better, humbler, happier.

"I daresay it is all very fine," observed Théophile; "but it has a radical defect; it might compete for the *prix Monthyon* — it is too moral."

"Too moral!" exclaimed Paolo, his eyes widening with amazement.

"Yes: far too moral, and tame in proportion," averred Courant; "no cloves and pepper; no *chic;* no touch of what I call *real* passion in it; none of the *positions risquées*, in which the public delight. The author had a precious gold vein within his reach, in the love affair of La Signora with Cavaliere Egidio — the passion of a nun; a capital hit, if properly developed. But no; he did not see it."

"He rejected, he spurned it," said Paolo, with warmth; "never would Manzoni have so lowered himself."

"So much the more stupid. Morality, as a rule, is unbearable in a work of fiction. The very reviewers, who praise it professionally, laugh at it in their sleeves. The palate of the public is blunted, palled, my dear friend; it requires, and must have, stimulants. Every nose turns up at your boiled beef; no — no! you must give viands with *sauce piquante;* game that is high; stuffed with truffles into the bargain; plenty of cayenne, — that is what is wanted."

"Rather than gratify such tastes, I would throw away all pens, and black shoes for ever," cried uncivilized Paolo.

"I am more of a philosopher than to do that," said Courant. "History teaches me that every age has its crotchets. I am of my age, and accept it as I find it without discussion. Such of its foibles as can help me up, I take advantage of; that's my philosophy."

"Your scepticism, you mean. And the dignity of letters, the eternal moral, the right divine of the beautiful and the true; what becomes of them, pray, in your system?" interrogated Paolo.

Courant looked at him with compassionate interest, and said, —

"I never saw such fly-swallowers as you Italians,

with your inexhaustible stock of enthusiasm. There's something in it, though, artistically speaking, and I have a mind to put you in my next novel. In sober truth, let me tell you, that you drivel — *tu patauges.* The high-flown theories about Art of a few visionaries, a few fanatics, are no gospel. My theory is far simpler, all summed up in that famous verse of the great master: *Tous les genres sont bons hors le genre ennuyeux.*"

"Down to the cynical," expostulated Paolo.

"And why not, so long as the form is good, and success attends it? Did not Horace skirt it, Ovid dive into it, Longus, the sophist, revel in it? and don't we admire them to this day?" asked Courant.

"But they were pagans, my dear friend. And so then you reduce literature to an affair of style?"

"And success," quoth Courant.

"And the Venus de' Medici, and the Hottentot Venus, provided they attract the crowd, are equally welcome in your eyes."

"*Dixisti.*"

In spite of these disagreements, or perhaps owing to them, the two neighbours were on the most friendly terms, sought after each other, and regularly spent the Sundays, Paolo's only holiday, in walking through the galleries of the Louvre and Luxembourg. Théophile was even introduced to Mr. Prosper and his wife, at whose establishment Paolo generally ended his evening strolls.

Thus time wore on up to the middle of August, when our Roman painter, who had almost forgotten that he was one, found himself master of the round sum of a hundred and twenty-two francs. This, according to his calculations, was more than sufficient for his journey to Rome. His economies of the fortnight just entered upon, and which he reckoned would amount to some forty francs, were destined for an object, on which his heart had long been set; for the purchase of some useful article for the self-denying Madame Prudence. Nor must it be supposed that Paolo had been remiss in showing gratitude in substantial ways towards Prosper's family — many a franc had been spent on the little ones, which otherwise would have accelerated his hour of hoped-for freedom. We have done as Paolo himself, laid no stress on what was so immeasurably below his wishes and their claims.

Such being the satisfactory state of his affairs, it occurred to our Roman, that it might be as well to go betimes, and look after his passport. Accordingly, one morning, instead of indulging in his habitual lounge between the Pont Neuf and the Pont des Tuileries, while he made his noonday repast of the two halfpenny rolls, he took them and himself through the Rue de l'Université, his road to the residence of the Pontifical Nuncio in Paris. Introduced to a gentleman in black, he gave his name, calling, and address at Rome, explaining that he had come to Paris in the preceding March, had lost his passport, and wanted to replace it in order that he might go back to Rome.

The affair seemed a very simple one to the applicant; not so to the gentleman who received the application. He did not mince the matter, but said at once that what was asked was impossible. Before furnishing any one with a passport, it was indispensable, the gentleman in black explained, first, that it should be clearly ascertained that the applicant was the person he represented himself to be; secondly, that he did not be-

long to any of the categories of refugees, who were
excluded from the Papal States. The first desideratum
might and would be, he had no doubt, in the present
instance, satisfactorily fulfilled by unexceptionable
guarantees; but none could supply the second, save the
government of·his Holiness, to which it would be his
duty to submit the case, and apply for instructions.

A poor devil who has been living for two months
on a hope, and sees it torn from him at the very moment he expects its realization, may well be pardoned
a moment of impatience, when he asks, rather snap-
pishly, as Paolo did, what possible length of time this
weighty affair of State was likely to require. The
patient answer was, that no time could be fixed, but if
Signor Paolo Mancini would give himself the trouble
to call again at the end of three weeks, or a month,
there might probably be some communication to impart
on the subject of his application.

This conclusion of the interview having ·by no
means improved Paolo's temper, he made his exit
chewing something between his teeth, which was not
precisely a blessing, and it may also be that he did
not shut the door, but allowed it to close itself with a
smart bang. The gentleman of the Nonciatura received
from these petty incidents a decidedly sinister impression of Mr. Paolo Mancini, which impression he hastened
to convey to his superior, who, in his turn, transmitted
it to his chief at Rome. A circumstance, which at first
sight would seem as if it ought to have told in Paolo's
favour, on the contrary. strongly militated against him
— it was, that his name did not figure on any of the
lists and reports forwarded to the Nonciatura by any
of its Paris agents; a proof as clear as day to every

one belonging to the Nonciatura, that he must have
been skulking elsewhere than in Paris, most likely had
been to London for fresh orders and watchwords of in-
surrection.

No one but philosophic-tempered Théophile could
have stood the porcupine mood of Paolo, after this
mishap. Beyond calling him now and then *massacrant*,
and lecturing him on the excessive absurdity of wishing
to go anywhere else, when one had the luck to be in
Paris, the student never evinced any symptom of impatience. Perhaps his equanimity was sustained by the
metamorphosis he knew to be near at hand, and which
occurred with the arrival of his quarter's allowance.
The caterpillar rose up a butterfly, which took its
flight to higher regions, after vainly urging Paolo to
send Bonifaces and passports to Hades, and learn what
life might be.

CHAPTER IX.

Surprise upon Surprise.

As Paolo, one-and-twenty days after his first application for a passport, was walking at full speed down
the Rue Jacob, towards the Nonciatura, his progress
was suddenly checked by an omnibus crossing the street
in a diagonal line. Without waiting for the huge obstruction to leave the road clear, Paolo glided round it,
and found himself face to face with the tall horse of a
tilbury coming in the opposite direction from the omnibus, and concealed by the big machine. The driver
of the tilbury, shouting "*Gare, maladroit!*" reined in
his horse quickly enough to prevent any more serious

mischief than the rash passenger's hat being knocked off by the head of the horse.

Paolo picked up his hat, and was proceeding on his way, when a voice cried after him, —

"By the Capitol! it is that enraged Telemachus in search of the Ideal."

Paolo stopped, and in his turn cried, —

"By Jove! it is Du Genre."

"The very same, at your service," said Du Genre; "get in, there's a seat for you, my fine fellow," stretching out his hand to Paolo; and as soon as he had him by his side, bestowing on him a fraternal *accolade*. "Since how long in Paris? And you didn't seek me out, you false friend! Where is Mentor? You look as pale, and thin, and shaved as if you came out of a convent of Trappistes. Lucky that the horse knocked off your hat, or I should never have recognized you under that monument; no wonder you run against carriages with that Babel structure on your caput."

"Always the same," said Paolo, smiling. "First of all, I must tell you that I am bound for the Nonciatura, and if out of your way —"

"I'll drive you to Mecca if Mecca is your destination," answered the realist; you are not going to get rid of me so easily, I can tell you. May I, without indiscretion, ask what business takes you to the Nonciatura?"

"To get a passport, if I can, to replace the one I have lost."

"You are not going to leave Paris, are you?" asked Du Genre.

"Most positively so," said Paolo.

"At any rate not yet, for I lay an embargo on you

for at least three weeks. You shall not leave Paris without tasting some of its sweets under my direction."

"I have had quite enough of its bitters," said Paolo.

"You talk and look as mysteriously as one of Byron's heroes. Paris, I told you often, is exactly the place for such as you. It will cure you of many of your crotchets; it will send you back to Rome a new man, a wiser man."

"Thank you," said Paolo, "but I have no wish to part with my old skin, or old crotchets. I have an affection for one and the other. But here we are at the Nonciatura."

The two friends alighted and went up to the office. On giving his name, Paolo had a letter handed to him by the same gentleman in black, whom he had seen on his previous visit three weeks before; and who said, that the letter had been waiting there for some time, as, Mr. Mancini's address not being known, there was no possibility of forwarding it. Taking it for granted that it was a written answer to his former application, Paolo broke the huge black seal, looked at the signature after glancing at the first few lines, then exclaimed, in a tone of disappointment, —

"But this has no reference whatever to my request. What about the passport, I have applied for?"

As to the passport, replied the urbane gentleman in the black suit, he was sorry he was obliged to say that it could not be granted. Strict injunctions to the contrary had been received from his government at home.

If ever man was provoked, Paolo was. He fretted and fumed and demanded to know the why and wherefore of this order: a usual weakness in those smarting under injustice; they are always wanting reasons, as if those who inflicted injustice always knew the why.

The business of the gentleman in black was to see orders executed, and not to inquire into their cause. If Signor Mancini considered himself aggrieved, he was at liberty to forward a petition.

Paolo, wishing petitions and petitioners at a certain place not usually mentioned aloud at the Nonciatura, bolted out of the office.

"A precious state of things," he said, getting into the tilbury after his friend, "and for which we have to thank your country, Du Genre."

Du Genre hung his head.

"A famous *boulette* it was," said he, rather sulkily; "nothing like clever people for getting themselves and their friends into a mess. Where do you want to go?"

"Can you drive me to Rue Cassette?"

"Willingly, if you will direct me. I thought I knew the town well, but I never heard of that street before. It must be at the antipodes of Paris, out of the pale of the habitable world. Are you in search of the fossil remains of antediluvian megatheriums."

"I am going to Mr. Boniface, my employer, who lives there."

Du Genre opened his eyes wide. There was no help for it now. Paolo had to explain, and in so doing, he had necessarily to touch on some of those circumstances — Thornton's disappearance among others — which had rendered a search for means of gaining his daily bread imperative.

Du Genre looked like one fallen from the clouds, but he was not slack in offering his purse, which Paolo declined at once. They were still deep in interesting topics when they reached Mr. Boniface's door.

"Here is my address," said Du Genre; "but can't I see you again to-day?"

"At a quarter past six on the Pont Neuf," said Paolo, laughing.

"The impressive silence of Pompeii," said Du Genre, looking round him; "the air full of the odour of mummies." Then he called out, as Paolo alighted, "Mind, old fellow, you have dropped your big despatch; by-the-by, you have never read it."

Paolo picked up the letter, saying —

"As far as I could see, it was the notification of Bishop Rodipani's death. It is signed 'Guarini,' a name quite unknown to me."

"Guarini?" repeated Du Genre; "why, that is the name of a celebrated lawyer in Rome. Allow me to observe, friend Telemachus, that it is always an injudicious act to read any letter partially, especially so when it is one announcing the decease of a relation. Who knows but that you are down in the bishop's will for a handsome legacy."

"The most likely thing in the world," said Paolo, shrugging his shoulders.

"More unlikely events have happened," said Du Genre. "Come, I wager two to one that it is so now; read it, or let me read it."

"See for yourself," said Paolo, giving Du Genre the letter; "I can't wait, I am already behind my time."

Du Genre, throwing the reins to his little groom, followed Paolo through the *porte cochère*, the first court, the alley, and the second court, taking in the contents

of Signor Guarini's communication the while; then gave
a jump as if a mine had exploded under his feet, —

"It's true, by Jove! I have won; you were born
with a silver spoon in your mouth. Hail to Bishop
Rodipani's illustrious heir!"

"Chut, nonsense," said Paolo, looking back.

"Believe your own eyes. *E-re-de u-ni-ver-sa-le.
Excusez du peu.*"

Nothing less than the evidence of his own senses
could convince young Mancini of the truth of his friend's
assertion. Strange, unlikely, almost unnatural as the
fact was, there it was, the clear statement staring him
in the face. Who can fathom the mysteries of a death-
bed?

Paolo stood mute and blank, as if confronted by
the head of Medusa.

"What is the matter with the man now?" cried
the Frenchman; "a fortune has fallen at your feet, and
you look as if you saw a ghost."

"I wish Bishop Rodipani had made another will,"
was Paolo's answer. "I feel as if I ought not to accept
this fortune."

"That's a little too *cocasse*," cried Du Genre, in a
sort of comic despair; "the man's lunatic. And pray,
why is it incumbent upon you to refuse such a godsend?"

"Because it comes from the persecutor of my
parents."

"Listen to him," ejaculated the Frenchman. "Never
mind the instrument Providence employs, my Telemachus. Money never smells bad from whatever source
it comes, was the remark of a Roman emperor, who
was far from being considered a goose. If the donor

has given you cause of complaint, reason the more for accepting the peace-offering meant in reparation; would you have him broil in purgatory to all eternity?"

"I will think about it," said Paolo, one foot on the stairs; "I must leave you now."

"I shall go with you," said Du Genre, following; "I am not going to forsake you in this dangerous frame of mind; you are not *compos*, you are not indeed."

"You can't come in with me; it is against all rules," expostulated Paolo, on the landing.

"You'll see whether I can or not," said the realist, pulling the bell. "I tell you, you are not fit for work just now. I'll ask this employer of yours to give you a holiday."

Mr. Boniface's lucky star ordained that the bell should be answered by Mdlle. Boniface, who, to spare her brother all contention of mind, graciously took upon herself to grant Du Genre's request; she was sure, was Mdlle. Marie, of her brother's approbation. Upon this assurance Paolo thanked the lady, and the two friends drove to Du Genre's notary, a fine old gentleman, with white hair and a mild, benevolent countenance, which did any one good only to see. Nor was the face wanting in caution, still less so in acuteness; you might see the one in the slightly pinched lips, and the other in the quick glance of the clear eye.

He listened to a translation of the letter from Rome, and to the comprehensive statement which Du Genre afterwards gave him, with the utmost attention, his eyes half closed, which he opened wide enough, however, when he heard the nature of Paolo's scruples; and looked so searchingly at the young man, as to make him redden and cast down his eyes.

"Had the testator any other relation than this young gentleman?" inquired the old lawyer.

His query being answered in the negative, he added, —

"The question at issue is one that scarcely comes within the domain of a notary; it is nothing more nor less than a case of conscience, the solution of which had better have been asked of a priest. However, as men of my profession have often been styled, and are, in a certain sense, the directors of the consciences of their clients — as to worldly affairs I mean — I think I shall not be passing beyond the boundaries of my own calling, if I give an opinion about this matter. It will be done in a very few words."

Turning himself round so as to address Paolo in particular, he continued, —

"To spurn a fortune, my dear sir, may be, according to the circumstances, a very wise or a very foolish thing. To the enthusiastic and the unreflecting, self-abnegation may seem a virtue, *quand même*, but it is not so. An act, for being generous — for entailing, I mean, a sacrifice on him who does it — is not essentially good; what makes it so, is its consonance to reason. It is consonant to reason, that to avert a great evil or to effect a great good, which cannot be averted or effected otherwise, one's fortune, or even one's life, should be imperilled or renounced; but it is contrary to reason that any such sacrifice be made — for what? — for the mere pleasure of making it. Now, the more I think of the step you are meditating, sir, the less I see what rational purpose it can answer. It confers no benefit on any one else, while it deprives you of the power of good which resides in money; that's what your sacrifice would accomplish, and *ad quid perditio hæc?*"

"But," faltered Paolo, considerably abashed, "the person who has left me his property, was cruel to my parents in a way and to a degree you cannot realize; and whatever reason may say, my feelings make me shrink from accepting from Bishop Rodipani dead, a benefit that I most surely would have scorned from Bishop Rodipani living."

"Allow me to tell you," replied the notary, "that a feeling which is in itself a sin, cannot be received as your justification. All earthly resentment should cease before a tomb; this liberality from one formerly little friendly to you or yours, is evidently intended as an amends."

"Did I not say the very same words to you?" broke in Du Genre.

"It is a token of reconciliation proffered to you from the grave," wound up the old gentleman; "you ought no more to refuse it than a pardon to the dying."

"I must be honest," said Paolo; "I cannot say that my heart is softened to forgive when it is not."

"It will soften in good time," said the notary. "One token of the forgiveness of trespasses commanded to us all you can give at least — respect the will of the dead, it ought to be held sacred."

"Let it be so then," said Paolo, conquered, if not convinced (Du Genre drew a long breath of relief); "I'll abide by your decision, sir."

The letter from Rome contained simple, but minute

directions for Mancini's guidance. If the heir could not or would not return to his own country for the present, Signor Guarini informed him that he had but to send a power of attorney to one of Mr. Guarini's friends and colleagues, whom he named, and that gentleman would, in his capacity of Paolo's legal representative, see to the taking off of the seals, the drawing up of the inventory, &c.; in short, would go through all the forms incumbent in such a case. This power of attorney was drawn up then and there by Du Genre's notary, signed by Paolo, attested by Du Genre and the notary's head clerk, and finally sent to the proper quarter for the necessary legalization.

Paolo then rose to go.

"Stop a minute," said the realist: "since that pearl of lawyers, Signor Guarini, volunteers to advance any sum you may require, which I consider very handsome on his part, had you not better draw on him for a thousand scudi or so?"

"A thousand scudi, and what for?" cried Paolo. "I have got plenty of money at present — more than a hundred francs."

"And how far will five napoleons go in Paris? Well, say five hundred scudi."

"A hundred is more than is necessary," replied Paolo, sitting down to write.

"I insist on five hundred," said Du Genre. "You need not spend them; money costs nothing to keep. Then there's that little fellow — what do you call him? — and his wife, who nursed you; you must deal handsomely by them."

"You are right; what was I thinking of to forget that debt?" and without hesitation he drew a cheque

for five hundred scudi, which he left with the notary to
be forwarded with the power of attorney. They then
took a cordial leave of the old gentleman.

"Ouf," said Du Genre, as soon as they were in the
street, "what hard work you have given me. Pythias
and Damon, Pylades and Orestes, put together, never
stood as much for one another. I am ready to drop
from exhaustion; and imprudent that I was, I sent away
the tilbury. Half-past four — scarcely a decent time to
ask for dinner — but sit and eat I must, or there's no
answering for the consequences. Are you for a *supréme
de volaille* or a lobster salad?"

Paolo would have preferred to either of the dainties
proffered, a quiet *tête-à-tête* with himself, to probe, if
possible, a certain uncomfortable feeling, touching the
resolve he had been induced to take, and which still
lurked somewhere in his heart or in his brain; but this
being out of the question without rudeness to his friend,
he answered that he left the dinner to Du Genre. They
proceeded to the Boulevards des Italiens, and entered
a *café*.

"Not considered first-rate," explained the Frenchman, "but the cookery is excellent, and the *dame du
comptoir* adorable. Come close and look at her."

But Paolo would not comply, and with his usual
shyness, stood aloof from the red velvet shrine at which
his companion was offering his devotions. At any rate,
Paolo did not share Du Genre's enthusiasm for the
divinity of the counter; on the contrary, he found plenty
of defects in her — her eyes wanted depth, her complexion transparency, her head character.

"Of course," said Du Genre laughing, "she is but
a woman, and not a picture."

"As to that, I am not quite sure," retorted the Roman.

"*Mauvais farceur!* I assure you she is not painted. Not a bad hit, however. What was I saying? Ah, she is but a beautiful specimen of flesh and blood woman, without an atom of the ideal Madonna in her, and this is what constitutes her fault in your eyes. By dint of cultivating the ideal, you have lost the sense of the real. But never mind, it will return to you by and by."

Paolo shook his head incredulously.

"A little patience and a trifle of good will," persisted the Frenchman, "and you'll recover from your mania. *Il n'y a que le premier pas qui coûte.* It is like eating oysters," continued he, the simile suggested by the very thing on the table. "You object to them without knowing yourself why; the moment you taste them, your scruples vanish and you ask for more."

"But supposing I do *not* taste them," said Paolo, sending away his plate untouched.

"Why, in that case — *que diable* — you are prejudiced; that's my opinion at least."

Du Genre was in mourning for that uncle of his who had had the triple indelicacy of summoning him to Dauphiné on the eve of Armida's *début*, of lingering on for months, and of leaving his affairs in a substantially good, but very confused state. The care of putting them in order — Du Genre was a man of method — had kept him in Dauphiné much longer than he wished, and it was only late in June, that is, long after all advertisements for Paolo had ceased, that he had been able to come and settle in Paris. While these explanations were being given, the room was filling

apace, and not a table, right or left, opposite or behind, was unoccupied. Paolo felt ill at ease among so
many strangers, and hardly opened his mouth, except
to eat, during the rest of the dinner. Du Genre talked
for two, was quite at home alike with waiters and with
customers, exchanging salutations and shakes of the
hand with many of the latter. It seemed to Paolo an
age before the good-natured rattle proposed to go.

From the *café*, Du Genre led the way to a tobac-
conist's on the other side of the Boulevard. As they
were going in, he said, —

"Here is another bit of reality, which I recommend
to your special notice."

Paolo looked and saw a richly attired lady behind
the counter, who, with the delicate tips of her fingers,
carefully guarded from pollution, by neatly fitting gloves,
dropped pinches of *caporal* into one of the small scales
erected before her. She was good-looking in her way,
with a face which the French designate as *minois chif-
fonné*, which translated, means a turned-up nose, hair
drawn back *à la Chinoise*, *accroche-cœurs* on the temples,
and mutinous dimples. "Would she be so amiable,"
asked Du Genre, "as to give him some *panatelas?* he
wished to choose them from a fresh box." The lady,
with great affability, sprang up on a chair, stretched
her arms up at full length to reach the box, and in so
doing displayed a remarkably elegant shape. Du Genre
was nudging Paolo during this exhibition.

"And, monsieur," she said, turning to Paolo, and
offering him the *panatelas*, with a bewitching smile.

The monsieur addressed declined at first, saying he
did not smoke; upon second thoughts, however, he chose
one, and lighted it. This second thought — and it

came with a sigh — was, what was the use of putting any constraint on himself? whether he smelt of tobacco or not, was a matter of indifference to every body, himself included.

And so, cigars in mouth, and arm in arm, the friends lounged up the Boulevard, and down the Boulevard; sat down outside a *café* to sip their Mocha; in course of time got on their legs again for a new lounge, limited as before by the Rue de la Chaussée d'Antin on the one side, and by the Rue Richelieu on the other.

"Are these two streets your Pillars of Hercules?" inquired Paolo.

"Exactly," returned Du Genre. "I never go beyond them; no Parisian, worthy of his birthplace, ever does, without some extreme cause. The Boulevard des Italiens is a compendium of Paris — it is Paris seen to its greatest advantage. Every comfort and elegance of civilized life is compressed within its narrow compass. Not a pretty woman, not a man of note, but pay their daily homage to it. Our lions in politics, in literature, in art, in fashion, in finance, gravitate hither as towards their natural centre. What the Lyceums were to the ancient Greeks, and the Thermes to the Romans, the Boulevard des Italiens is to the Parisians. Here it is that statesmen, writers, singers, actresses — that everybody and everything are judged, and sentenced without appeal. Paris is the world's brain, and the Boulevard des Italiens is the brain of Paris."

"I am unwilling to throw cold water on your lyrical effusions," said Paolo, with a little irony; "but to me, one of the uninitiated, your brain of Paris, after two hours' enjoyment of it, begins to savour a little of monotony."

"It is another of the realities, which with cultivation will improve on you," said Du Genre. "Let us go to the flower market of the Madeleine."

"To look after grisettes?" questioned Paolo.

"A notion from the left bank of the Seine. For your information, the grisette, as a class, has no existence on this side of the water. Such stray specimens as may emigrate hither, soon soar into the lorette. Lorettes rule supreme here. Let us go."

They were at this instant standing in front of the Chaussée d'Antin. But for the growing dusk, Paolo might have distinguished the windows of the house where *she* had lived on the Boulevard des Capucines. A deep gloom fell on his countenance, and he answered, —

"No, thank you. I care neither for grisettes nor lorettes. I feel out of my place in this quarter of the town. I'll bid you good-bye, and go back to my penates."

"Go home at seven?" remonstrated Du Genre; "scarcely time even for hens to go to roost."

"It will be nearly eight when I reach my street, and I have to be up early in the morning."

"Early — and what for?"

"To go to my employer!"

"Your employer? What a ridiculous notion for a bishop's heir."

"Your pardon; my altered circumstances do not, I presume, allow me to dispense with common honesty. I have been paid in advance for a fortnight, and a fortnight more I shall work."

7*

"Upright as a post — inflexible as an iron bar. You are a capital fellow, and if I were not Felix Pélissier, I would willingly be Paolo Mancini. The 500 scudi will just arrive, I calculate, at the end of your semi-monthly engagement. Should you want any money in the meantime — No; well, then, no be it. I wonder what your income will be — I hope something handsome."

"I wish you would spare me your calculations just now."

"And why so, most austere of youths?"

"Because they give me pain — because I loathe the subject."

"Upon my word, this sounds like insanity; and after all the trouble, too, that the notary took to clear the matter of all clouds."

"Clear or not," said Paolo, impetuously, "is nothing to the purpose. Not all the arguing in the world can argue away a feeling when it exists; and I feel that I am wrong in accepting this inheritance. You will see that it will bring me ill-luck. Good night."

"That which will bring you ill-luck," Du Genre cried after him, "if you don't gain wisdom before it is too late, is your false point of view of life. You look upon it as a tragedy, when life is but a farce — but a farce! Good night."

CHAPTER X.

Self-Discipline.

Twilight had superseded broad day, and darkness twilight, and there on her couch still lay Miss Lavinia, apparently in a heavy slumber, yet half conscious, a dead weight on her chest, a dead weight on the crown of her head. If the widow who had let her the lodgings, went once on tiptoe to her sitting-room door, she went twenty times, listening in vain for any, the least sound indicative of life within, returning to her parlour after every disappointment with a still more elongated face, and resuming her knitting with more trembling fingers.

"Are you sure, Molly, that the new lodger has not rung for candles?"

Molly was ready to stake her life that no bell had so much as stirred in the house. Bless her heart, it was quiet enough to hear a pin drop, let alone a bell ring.

Mrs. Tamplin had no eyes but for the gloomy side of life. Of a lymphatic temperament, and anything but sanguine, even when young, independent, and on the whole happy, she had had all her little stock of spirits squeezed out of her by the simultaneous loss, in her fortieth year, of husband and fortune. "Despair and die," had become her motto ever since. To moan over the past, and tremble for the future, to create difficulties where there were none, and magnify into impossibilities those which existed, to fancy dangers everywhere and to anticipate misfortunes from every quarter, — such was the unfortunate lady's bent of mind and occupation.

All new lodgers were objects of suspicion for Mrs.

Tamplin, and the days on which she received any such,
were fraught with particular terrors, lest, if a man, he
should be a housebreaker, come with intent to rob and
murder her; lest, if a woman, she should be one of a
gang of thieves, sent for the purpose of admitting her
associates. Miss Jones, however, it must be allowed,
had so far found favour at first sight with the morose
widow as to be spared the degradation of such an hypothesis. But if tolerably free from uneasiness as to
any conspiracy against her person and property, Mrs.
Tamplin very soon found a cause, and improved it, for
alarm and gloomy speculation on another score. This
cause, obviously enough, was the continued deathlike
stillness of the new comer, as repeatedly verified by
her own observations. "People did not engage rooms,"
reasoned the low-spirited landlady during the intervals
of her stations at the ominous door — "people did not
engage rooms to sit still in the dark, as if for a wager;
it wasn't natural; people moved about, coughed, sneezed,
called for candles, in short, gave signs of being alive;
if they didn't, why, then, they must be in a fit, or —"

At this point of her argument with herself, Mrs.
Tamplin recollected having once read in the newspaper,
of somebody — was it a lady or gentleman? she rather thought it had been a lady — well, of somebody,
hiring lodgings for the purpose of taking poison, or
cutting his or her throat, whichever it was. Such things
had happened, and why shouldn't they again? The
young lady looked flurried enough for anything. That
she, Mrs. Tamplin, of all the landladies in the world,
should have the luck of such lodgers, where was the
wonder? It would only be in keeping with all the rest.

The mine was rich, and the miner indefatigable.

She pursued a fancied lugubrious scene through all its details, from the first finding of the corpse to coroner and jury sitting on the morrow in the little back-room — pursued the theme with the minuteness and zest peculiar to the habitual dealers in horrors. The excess of her self-inspired terror at last gave her the courage, she had hitherto lacked, to go and confront the incubus she had conjured up. She seized a candle, hurried across the short passage, opened the little back-room with resolution, and went in.

Miss Lavinia, startled into full consciousnees, sprung to her feet, and asked, —

"Is that you, Grace? What a fright you gave me."

"Bless me! she is wandering in her mind," thought Mrs. Tamplin, this fresh alarm swallowing up her satisfaction at the groundlessness of the old one. She said aloud, "It's only me, Mrs. Tamplin, with a light. Are you ill, miss?"

"Oh, no! not ill, thank you, only a little giddy and sick," answered Lavinia, reseating herself.

"You haven't taken anything to make you so, have you?" eagerly inquired the landlady.

Lavinia shook her head.

"Are you sure, quite sure?" urged Mrs. Tamplin.

"Quite sure," repeated the poor girl, looking up at her questioner with some amazement. "What makes you ask me that?"

"Sometimes, you know," stammered the widow, nearly reassured by the frankness of Lavinia's face, — "sometimes what one eats or drinks — one's food, I mean, disagrees with one's stomach — and, no headache?"

"A little."

"Your eyes told me so. I am a bit of a doctor; not a complaint that has ever been heard of, but I have had it; I am a perfect martyr to ill health. Will you allow me to feel your pulse? Gracious goodness! why, what's the matter with you? your hands are as cold as death."

Those of the affrighted lady, if not cold, were manifestly trembling from the contact.

"I am only chilly," said Lavinia; "I'll lie down quietly for a little, and then, I dare say, I shall be well again."

But Mrs. Tamplin was of a different opinion. It was a chill, according to her, not to be trifled with; the best thing to do was to send for a doctor. This proposition Lavinia opposed with all the little strength she had left; while Mrs. Tamplin held to her idea with the energy of despair.

"Just to satisfy me, miss — being both of us strangers to one another. I dare say it is nothing, only it makes me fidgety, when I don't see clearly into things. It isn't much of a sacrifice to see a good gentleman just for five minutes. We have a doctor next door. Dr. Duncan will see what's amiss at a glance. We call him doctor, but he is only a surgeon; but it would take a dozen doctors to make the like of him, though they are not ashamed to charge a guinea. His visit is but half-a-crown, medicine included. Half-a-crown won't ruin any one. Ah! I see. I may send for him. There's a good girl. I'll be back in a minute."

Poor Lavinia, sick and faint, with her head splitting with pain, was no match for the excited widow; and to get rid of her teasing, gave at last a reluctant consent.

Mrs. Tamplin's vehement burst of eloquence, the reader has already guessed, was produced by a new fit of terror, which had seized on her. She had noticed in the last week's return of deaths for London, a few in the hospitals arising from cholera, and had been ever since in dread expectation of an outbreak of this fearful malady. Now, finding to her dismay, that her lodger's hands were stiff and cold — it being hot weather, mark, and well knowing that cold hands were one of the first symptoms of cholera; and considering further, that if there was to be a visitation of cholera, it was but natural that it should begin at her house; on the strength of these premises, we say, Mrs. Tamplin rushed to the conclusion that she had a case of cholera before her, on her very own couch.

Mr. Duncan must surely have had a presentiment that his services would be required, and have accordingly been prepared, for in less than five minutes after the landlady's exit from the little back-room, a short, thickset, bull-headed, goggle-eyed personage, with shaggy eyebrows and tufts of hair at the root of every finger, bolted in with a grunt, —

"Is that the person? Ah! how are we?"

Lavinia looked at the assemblage of grimacing, squinting, topsy-turvy, unnatural features hanging over her, in a frightened wonder, tempered, however, by a sense of their ludicrousness, and began an account of her sensations; but was instantly stopped. No need of that; he did not care a bit for symptoms. What he wanted was to go to the root of the evil at once. Had *we* had the measles? Yes, very well; he thought so; he would bet a wager that *we* had had the hooping-cough also. To the best of her recollection, she had

had the hooping-cough, said Lavinia. Very good; and
he should not be surprised if *we* had been suffering
from low spirits lately? He might have guessed that,
without being a prophet, from the careworn face, and
mourning dress of the patient. And what did *our* tongue
say? The recondite meaning of this query, as explained
by Mrs. Tamplin, who had gone through the process
passim, was that Lavinia was to put out her tongue for
inspection. As Lavinia obeyed, Mr. Duncan exclaimed, —

"All right; he saw it as plain as daylight: a trifle
wrong with the great *sympathetic*. You needn't be uneasy, nor you, Mrs. Tamplin; *we'll* soon be on our legs
again, and as jolly as ever. Just desire Molly to come
to my house, and I'll send you a powder — to be taken
in half a tumbler of hot brandy-and-water — very hot,
and the stronger the better. And you," turning to Lavinia, "mind you send all blue devils to Coventry; do
you hear?"

After this witty sally, heightened by a broad grin,
the facetious Esculapius withdrew, escorted by the
gloomy landlady.

The short palaver in whispers held in the passage
between the surgeon and his escort, must have been
greatly to the satisfaction of the latter, for she returned
to Lavinia in high 'spirits enough, to hint at the possibility of a speedy recovery — in a week or two.
Mrs. Tamplin saw to the literal execution of Mr. Duncan's prescription, not sparing her charge one drop of
the beverage. If the surgeon meant it as a practical
means of enforcing his recommendation about blue devils, his success was complete. Miss Jones at once fell
asleep and slept all night like a post. She awoke next
morning refreshed, and wanted to get up, but Mrs.

Tamplin would allow of no such imprudence. Mr. Duncan, when he called, said Mrs. Tamplin was perfectly right. Two days after, the medical practitioner paid another visit, and still ordered rest. Miss Lavinia had to keep her bed for a whole week.

This forced leisure was not lost upon her; no lack of subjects, Heaven knows, had she for earnest and anxious speculations, wherewith to beguile the long hours. Her old self to unlearn, as it were, and a new one to create in keeping with her new circumstances — a particularly knotty point connected with the past to settle; some course of action to decide upon, with a view to earning her bread — these were the salient subjects principally engrossing her mind during her imprisonment in her bed. Nor without some good results, she hoped, save, indeed, as to the means of gaining employment. All was mist and gloom to her vision in that direction; not that she anticipated any difficulty in this respect; she was far too ignorant of the hard realities of the world, far too strongly imbued with one of Mr. Jones's favourite axioms, that "where there is a will there is a way," for any fear of that kind; but she was in want of any practical data to go by; she must be put on the right road by some one with more experience in the matter. All she knew was through having heard it mentioned *à propos* of some recommendations made to herself, that ladies of education in reduced circumstances turned governesses. But was she qualified to teach? She was rather afraid not. Governesses were expected to know everything, and she hardly knew any subject that she could venture to say she was capable of teaching — music, perhaps, and French and Italian. Would that be enough?

In her honest endeavours to bring her spirit down to the level of her low fortune, Lavinia arrived at a more satisfactory result. The trials she had gone through during the last few months, and the reflections they had induced, had ripened her reason, and awakened her to the sense of the duties and moral responsibilities which life implied. Even when steeped in all its vanities, and untouched by grief, she had had many a sudden qualm of conscience at Paolo's earnest appeal to those duties and responsibilities. The life she had hitherto led, what a poor figure it now cut, viewed by this new light — if, indeed, such a worthless fluttering of childish impulses and aimless pursuits, as had filled her days, were worthy to be called by the name of life. Happy still, if by it, she had wronged no one but herself; but she dared not thus console herself; she knew she had wronged others, one, at least, most cruelly, perhaps irreparably. And could she for a moment regret having lost a position, the recollection of which filled her with shame, and alas! with remorse. Had she not, on the contrary, every reason to thank Providence for having hurled her from it — even by a thunderbolt? for forcing her to begin life anew? for granting her the means of atoning for the past?

We alluded to a knotty point which greatly perplexed her; but this also she managed to settle. It related to Lady Augusta, the friend to whom her confidential letters from Rome were addressed. Their friendship had begun in girlhood, at the fashionable boarding-school to which both were sent, and had afterwards continued unabated. Out of a rather numerous circle of nominal friends, Lady Augusta was the only one who had not contented herself with sending cards or conventional letters of condolence, but had gone to see her former playmate after Mrs. Jones's death, and shown real feeling for her bereavement. It seemed but natural, under the circumstances, that Lavinia should have no secrets with Lady Augusta, nay, should throw herself for sympathy and support on so staunch a friendship. Her first impulse had been this; but further thought made her question the wisdom of such a course. That Lady Augusta would befriend her in spite of everything, she had no doubt — but would it be in her power to do so? Would not that perfectly polite, but cold and formal countess, discountenance her daughter's doing so? nay, probably, put an absolute veto against any further intercourse with Lavinia? It was more than likely from one, who had no more than tolerated the friendship between the young girls, and though courteously condescending to the niece, had maintained a frigidly patronizing manner to the uncle and aunt.

After long weighing of the pros and cons of her anticipations with regard to the countess, Lavinia came to the conclusion, that, having doubts on the subject, she would not be justified in running the risk of becoming an apple of discord for parent and child — at all events of entailing upon her friend a painful struggle between duty and inclination. Having most conscientiously made this resolve, Lavinia felt freed, as from a load, from the necessity of making a confession of what she looked upon as a disgrace, but which was, in fact, a misfortune. To one person alone in the world could she have told all without dying from shame. Not to Paolo; no. She recollected very well his once treating the notion of the transmission of a badge of honour or dishonour, to one who had done nothing to deserve it, as most absurd. But she remembered also — with what confusion, God knows — the contempt with which she had treated such a notion, and the warmth, she had displayed in her arguments against it. He whom she could have made her confidant of all men, he from whom she could anticipate receiving sympathy and pity, was Thornton. He had been to her, while himself sorrowing, so forbearing, so generous, so fatherly, that her heart melted at the recollection.

Some disaster must have occurred to him, she was sure, or he would have written. His last letter, in which he told her of his change of abode, and gave his address to the Rue Neuve des Augustins, was dated as far back as the beginning of May. She had written twice to him since then, but had received no replies. Surely, this silence foreboded no good. It seemed to her as if she brought misfortune on all those she loved.

This sad and long monologue with herself was, oftener than she might have wished, interrupted by Mrs. Tamplin, who, under the thick coating of morbid selfishness and vulgarity, forming the staple of her character, had a vein of kindliness, which she showed after her manner. She would of an evening bring her knitting into the sick chamber, and by way of raising the spirits of her young lodger, give her the benefit of the newest "mysterious disappearance," "frightful loss of life," or "shocking suicide," as the case might be, found in the day's paper.

Mrs. Tamplin delighted in horrors — would willingly dine, and sup on them. She was ever ready to welcome the most marvellous amount of misery, whether produced by fire, shipwreck, self-murder, or legal executions. Not a casualty occurred in the year, but she noted it down, stored it in her mind.

At other times, she reverted to the better days she had seen, and would enter into a minute explanation of the how, and the why, and the when of the wreck of her fortune, winding up by expressing some doubts, whether the lady who kept three servants in her house at Pimlico, was identical with the woman who let lodgings in Camden Town, with a servant of all work.

Lavinia was determined not to lose patience with her querulous vulgar hostess, and to show herself gentle and sympathizing. Rather a difficult task at first, but it grew easier after a time, until she even felt thankful for the opportunity thus offered of testing her powers of self-control. The effort was not without its reward — it secured her Mrs. Tamplin's good graces, who had never before lighted on so complacent a listener as Miss Jones. And by Lavinia, in the utter isolation to which she was reduced, even the good will of so helpless and low-spirited a creature as her landlady, was not to be disdained.

CHAPTER XI.

Hard Apprenticeship.

THE first thing that Lavinia did on being at last released from her bondage of bed, was to write to Lady Augusta and to Mortimer. It was not easy to justify the extreme step she had taken in quitting Mr. Jones's house, without bringing an accusation against him, nor was it easy to establish the impossibility of any further intercourse between her and her friend, without making any allusion to the quarter from whence opposition to the continuance of their intimacy might be apprehended. However, she managed to make her meaning clear without bringing in third persons, choosing rather to appear rash, over-sensitive, or even ungrateful, than to injure others in Lady Augusta's estimation.

The account she gave of herself was of course entirely conformable to truth. She had lately discovered that she was not Mr. Jones's niece, in no way related to him or to Mrs. Jones. Her mother had died many years ago in very poor circumstances; her father had gone abroad when she was an infant, and had never been heard of since. She hinted at some disgrace in her case, which she said was as unnecessary as painful to relate. Professions of faithful, unvarying attachment, warm from the bleeding heart, traced amid a shower of tears, closed the letter. It consummated her divorce with the past.

That to Thornton contained but two lines. They were simply to say that she had written twice, but had received no answer; that she had much to say, but dared not write explicitly until a word from him, which she entreated for, came to relieve her from the uncertainty of whether the present letter would reach him. It did reach him, but alas! was like all others, either unread or unheeded. She had signed only Lavinia, both to Lady Augusta and to Thornton — her Christian name was her own still. The surname which she intended henceforth to bear, was that of her mother — Holywell.

Her next thought was of something to do, of some work to begin immediately. Not a minute of her time could she afford to lose. Drawing or painting, with any view to making a livelihood by either, was, she knew, out of the question. Landscape, she was aware, sold best, and she was unable to paint landscapes. She might have copied figures tolerably well, but not invent; and how was she to obtain originals to copy? besides, how meet the dreadful outlay for brushes, colours, canvasses, &c.? Needlework would do better, it required no capital. Hers were not very clever fingers, truth to say, as far as needlework was concerned. Still she was a tolerable adept at crochet, embroidery and worsted work. Which of the three, she wondered, would sell best? Not being competent to solve this question, she went and put it to Mrs. Tamplin.

On hearing it, the worthy matron's face lengthened considerably, and she gave it as her opinion that none of the three had any chance of a fair price, if sold at all. The market was glutted with such articles, competition kept prices down, and tradesmen turned the screw very hard upon the poor workers.

"Then I will put my question another way," said Lavinia. "Which — crochet, embroidery or worsted work — is the most likely to find a purchaser, whatever the price given?"

"I should say embroidery, if neatly done, and according to the fashion," said Mrs. Tamplin; "but it so soon destroys the eyes, and gives so little profit, that for my part I had rather break stones on the road than work muslin."

"But, how much do you think a tolerably good worker might realize by it in a day?" asked Lavinia, not to be daunted.

"Why, from eight to tenpence at most, and working

twelve hours. I have heard of first-rate hands making as much as a shilling, but they are exceptions."

"But can a workwoman support herself on a shilling a day?" was perplexed Lavinia's next inquiry.

"It's a miracle when they can," answered Mrs. Tamplin; "and as miracles don't happen every day of the week, that's why so many young women starve or do worse. There's such a competition, you see. The men, though, God knows, often badly off enough, have more ways than one of turning an honest penny; while a woman has but one, you know — her needle; and the consequence is, that there are more needles than work for them. A firm in the city, I miss the name now, advertised the other day for fifty hands — guess how many applied? Seven hundred, my dear young lady, seven hundred, fourteen times as many as were wanted."

Apparently, Miss Lavinia did not look particularly cheered by this intelligence, for Mrs. Tamplin said suddenly, —

"It is not, I hope, on your own account, that you are asking for information about these sort of things?"

Lavinia did not speak, but nodded her head despondingly, in the affirmative.

"Oh! my poor lady, is it as bad as that?" exclaimed the widow, with more feeling than might have been anticipated from one so utterly wrapt in self. "So young, so — genteel-looking; what will become of you?"

"He who clothes the flowers of the fields, and feeds the birds of the air, will provide for me also," said Lavinia. "None of God's creatures perish for want."

"Goodness me! where do you come from?" cried Mrs. Tamplin, clasping her hands. "I cannot be responsible about the sparrows, but this I know, that in the last year alone, as many as 358 of God's creatures did perish in this blessed metropolis from absolute want of the necessaries of life. You look as if you didn't believe it. I'll show it you in print. I can prove it. Where has it gone now?" muttered Mrs. Tamplin, as she fumbled in a drawer, one of her many repositories of lugubrious facts. "Ah! here it is, cut out of the *Weekly Dispatch:* Mortality from privation, want of breast-milk, neglect and cold in 1853—358. Read it yourself."

Lavinia was fain to drop the conversation, she felt that she must have a little fresh air, so she asked for a direction to the nearest place where she might get the materials for her embroidery, and went out in quest of them. Mrs. Tamplin had given her facts enough to startle her out of all her preconceived notions. Well might her landlady ask, with hands clasped in wonder, from whence she came. It is astonishing how little the young lady of the fine world knows of another world, which, for not being fine, is not the less real.

Screened from all rude contact by her carriage and servants, meeting everywhere the ready deference that wealth commands when abroad, smiled upon by all that is comfortable, elegant, and pleasant at home, finding in every house in which she visits, a counterpart of her own, what can a young lady do but argue from the known to the unknown, and pronounce this world to be the best and happiest of worlds? The greatness, the riches, the unparalleled prosperity of the land, are freely dwelt upon in her presence; but all disagreeable topics which might cast a shade on the bright picture, are studiously avoided. The papers and novels she is allowed to read, or rather to turn over — for our fine young lady is always at a loss for time — are most of them strongly impregnated with "high life" musk, calculated to enhance her delusions; and such bits of hard reality as she may chance upon in Dickens or Thackeray, disagree so entirely with her habits of thought, and feeling and experience, that she puts them down either as claptrap, or exaggerations for the sake of effect.

Such was in the main the state of mind out of which Lavinia had been aroused by the awful revelations of that morning. As one tries to get at an approximation of the number of the wounded, from the ascertained number of those slain on the battle-field, so did she start from the ghastly cypher just learned, to speculate upon the amount of misery which it presupposed. It was frightful, and an immense pity for those who were suffering, an immense yearning to be of service to them, took possession of her heart. Oh! that she had known of this in time, — when she had the means of being useful! How much evil she might have prevented! how much good effected! Oh! that an occasion would offer to call into action the newly-born power of charity which stirred within her!

There was a something in Mrs. Tamplin's manner and voice, when she greeted her lodger next morning, which gave Lavinia courage to say at once:

"Will you bear with me while I put to you a few questions, and will you kindly give me the benefit of your experience?"

Who refuses to give advice? The permission asked having been willingly granted, Lavinia began: —

"I can draw a little, I know French, German, and Italian pretty well; I am considered to play and sing better than most ladies. Do you think these things are sufficient to qualify me to be a governess?"

"Enough, and to spare, if you fall in with reasonable beings; but people have grown so exacting of late; and then it's the same affair about governesses as about needlewomen. For one that is wanted, fifty offer; a good situation as a governess is a prize in the lottery, 99 to 1 against getting it, and the salaries are so small. You have to pay your own washing, and always to be well dressed — fit, as they call it, to go out with your pupils, and to appear in the evening in the drawing-room. Then the drudgery of a governess's life — all work and no play; always wanted if they ask for an hour's holiday; and the holes they have to sleep in!— no fireplace often; and the tea they have to drink! — it's awful," concluded Mrs. Tamplin. "I knew a lady who had a governess; dear me! I never shall forget the sort of resigned, haggard look of the poor thing's face; it used to make my heart sore every time I saw her."

"Is there nothing else I could do — no other situation for educated young ladies?"

"I know of none other except that of being companion to a lady; but, oh, dear! I would not wish my worst enemy to be a companion. The ladies who want companions are generally old, infirm, and irritable; you would be more of a prisoner even than as a governess, for you would not have the daily walk you are sure of with the young people. You would be expected to read aloud till you had no voice left, to be constantly amusing her, for ever doing something for her — nothing better than her shadow. I would rather be a sick nurse, they manage pretty well to have their own way."

Lavinia was silent for a while; Mrs. Tamplin's last speech had touched a spring in her memory; slowly and with difficulty she recalled some account she had heard or read, of an institution for nurses.

"You have given me a good idea, Mrs. Tamplin; I will learn to be a nurse."

"Dear me, I am sure I never meant to put such a preposterous plan into your head."

"A very good one, and not preposterous at all. There are training institutions for nurses — I remember hearing of them; and then the pupils, or whatever they are called, have to go through several ordeals to see if they are fit for the vocation, and if they are, they are sent into hospitals or wherever they are most wanted."

"An hospital nurse!" exclaimed Mrs. Tamplin, in consternation; "no one in their senses would accept of you for one. First of all — excuse me, I mean it friendly — you are too handsome to be safe in an hospital; this world isn't heaven yet, dear lady; in the second place, if you were ever so ugly, you are not strong enough for all the rough, dreadful work that goes on in hospitals."

Though far from seeing the link of connection between her being handsome and the world not being heaven, Lavinia felt too diffident now of her own judgment to have any inclination to contest the point.

She resumed instead the train of thought abandoned for the moment, and said, —

"You really think, then, I am capable of being a governess?"

Mrs. Tamplin emphatically decided that she was.

"And you will be so good," continued Lavinia, "as to tell me how to set about trying for such a situation?"

"Really," Mrs. Tamplin could not help saying, "you seem as ignorant of the doings of this earth as a baby. The most natural course would be to apply to your friends and relations — to anybody, in short, likely to have an interest in you — and ask them to look out for some place of the kind among their acquaintances."

"And if I have no friends, no relations — no one to take an interest in me," said Lavinia, big tears gathering in her eyes.

"But that is impossible; every one belongs to somebody," cried Mrs. Tamplin, beginning to be agitated. "Human beings don't grow at the foot of a tree, like mushrooms. Compose yourself, and try to recollect."

Lavinia shook her head dejectedly, forlornly; two large tears were running down her cheeks.

"Pray don't," entreated Mrs. Tamplin, who, much addicted to the melting mood, knew the danger of example. "There is no earthly use in crying, you know. My dear lady, you must see the truth of what I say; without a little interest, nothing is done in this world of ours. Besides, you must have references, you must; without a reference, not a soul will employ you."

Lavinia wiped away her tears, and with them every trace of emotion, and said quietly, —

"Excuse me for troubling you with a last question. Is there no agency through which a person, situated as I am, can make known her want of employment?"

"There are the newspapers," returned Mrs. Tamplin. "You can advertise in them for the situation of a governess; but I would not advise you to do so, as advertising comes very expensive, and in your case it would just be money lost, or I am much mistaken. You had better take a reading of a daily paper, and look through the advertisements till you see something you think might suit you, and then you can apply for it either in person or by letter, as the advertiser directs. But without references, my dear lady, it is scarcely worth while trying."

However, Lavinia was determined to try. Not that she did not feel the full force of Mrs. Tamplin's objection; her efforts would, in most quarters, she was convinced, be foiled by it; still she did not despair of lighting on the right person — some pitying woman, some kindly mother, for whom the knowledge that she was an orphan, one alone in the world, would be sufficient reason for befriending her. She sent for *The Times* next morning, and had not gone far down its advertising columns, when she discovered what seemed the very thing for her: "Wanted a governess in a quiet family, residing in the country, &c. Apply by letter." She had made up her mind from the first, to seek for no situation but in the country or abroad. She was known to far too many in London not to dread disagreeable encounters there. The very idea of meeting Mr. Jones again, turned her blood cold. She applied at once by letter for this situation in the country, and waited the result divided between hope and fear. Every double knock in the street reverberated through her heart. Nothing came of this application, however; days wore on, a week passed, and no answer was vouchsafed to her letter.

She resolved to answer another advertisement. A family setting out on a tour abroad wanted a governess who could speak German, Italian, and French; apply every day, from three to five P.M., Hyde Park Place. From Camden Town to Hyde Park Place is quite a journey — one undertaken by Lavinia in a great flutter of spirits. Excepting those who have had a similar experience, few can realize to themselves what must be the feelings of a girl who has scarcely ever set foot on the streets before, and then always well accompanied; few, we repeat, can form an idea of what her physical and mental discomfort, on finding herself for the first time alone, having to thread her way through a motley throng.

Lavinia's courage rose, however, on perceiving the streets to be quieter than she expected. But when she reached the New Road, an obstruction of carriages, and its natural accompaniment, a crowd, enjoying the fun, forced her to stop. A lively quarrel was raging among the several drivers; their looks, words, gestures, would have been more in character for cannibals than for Christians. They cursed, swore, shook their fists and whips at one another, until the terrified Lavinia expected to see them fly at each other's throat; but as soon as their wheels were in safety, they passed on as if nothing had been.

Was it a delusion originating in her troubled mind,

or was it a fact, that the farther she advanced towards the West End, the keener her impression that the passers-by took more notice of her than was consistent with good breeding? No, it was not fancy; they certainly did so — not the artisans, but the gentlemen, or whatever they were, who were dressed like gentlemen. One and another, as they went by, peered curiously through her veil, some, to do so more conscientiously, leant forwards, or raised their eye-glass. Five out of ten who were going down the street in the same direction with her, would linger by her side, stare at her over their shoulders, and when they had passed on, turn their heads again and again. In spite of her thick veil, and keeping her eyes on the ground, Lavinia could not help being aware of these manœuvres, so openly and audaciously were they carried on. Presently, near Regent's Circus, a tall, fair, whiskered dandy stopped so directly before her, that in order not to stop also, she had to make a circle round him. She had scarcely time to breathe, when there he was again at her side; she hurried on — it was no use, he kept the step with her, or went before, halting and turning round to wait for her. A mist rose before her eyes, she crossed the street, without caring for cart or carriage, and ran on with the speed of despair. She hardly knew whether her terror or indignation was the greatest. Where had they all gone, those highly-bred gentlemen she used to meet at parties, the pink of courtesy, whose deferential manner she had considered the perfection of refinement, so flatteringly obliging at dinner, concert or ball, so chivalrous in protecting her from all inconvenience in crowds, darting furious looks at the chance contact of some unruly elbow — where had they all gone? Surely none of them trod the pavement that day. To see London from the height of one's carriage, or from the height of one's legs, makes a rare difference, I can tell you.

Lavinia reached her destination with the wan looks and jaded feelings of a remanded culprit, brought to the bar to hear sentence passed on him. The consciousness of innocence is but a poor shield against the utter dejection, which protracted anxiety, such as she had gone through, carries along with it. Fortunately, the lady who received her spoke kindly and encouragingly — with that good-natured, motherly sort of face, she could not speak otherwise. Lavinia stood in great need of encouragement; a frown, or a harsh word would have sent her into a violent fit of tears. In answer to the lady's inquiries, she stated with modesty her accomplishments, said she could play on the piano and harp, and sing.

"Very nice," said the lady; "isn't it, James?"

"Very," said the gentleman addressed, never looking up from the newspaper. Clara, her eldest daughter, explained the lady, had just begun the harp, and Miss Holywell could carry her on perhaps, without a master for the present. The lady then mentioned the salary she was accustomed to give. Lavinia made no difficulties, the sum was quite satisfactory. "Of course," resumed the lady, "I expect you to give me good references." Lavinia faltered out that she had none to give. "None in London, perhaps, you mean," kindly suggested the lady.

"Neither in town nor in country, madam," said Lavinia, now ashy pale.

"Surely, you are known to some one in England, who would answer for you."

"Pray, madam," cried Lavinia, so choked with emotion that she could scarcely speak intelligibly, "pray, be not prejudiced against me by what I am going to say. Indeed, I have done no harm. God is my witness, I have injured no one, but still there is no one I can give you as a reference."

The lady looked fixedly at the speaker all the while, but there was nothing hard in her look, rather the contrary. She mused for an instant, then said, —

"Strange, almost incredible, as your statement may seem, if you could only account satisfactorily —"

"Mary," said the gentleman, never looking up from his newspaper. The tone in which these two syllables were pronounced must have lowered the thermometer.

"All things considered," said the lady, rising, "I am sorry I cannot engage you."

"God bless you the same for your kindness," said Lavinia, bowing low, and departed.

Poor thing! so near the port, and wrecked.

CHAPTER XII.

On the Right Bank of the Seine.

WHILE Lavinia was thus hunting for some charitable soul who would employ her, and found none, Paolo, on his side, was looking out, with no better success, for some one who would relieve him of a portion of the 500 scudi he had received from Rome. Let us hasten to add, lest the reader should be tempted to laugh at this statement, that the young Roman's application for such a service was restricted to a very narrow circle of persons, whom it is almost useless to name — in fact, to the group of good Samaritans who took him in, and nursed and tended him in his sickness and poverty.

Youth is so happy to give for the mere pleasure of giving! It was the only gratification Paolo anticipated from being rich. How keenly he enjoyed in thought the agreeable surprise he would one day manage for his little friend Salvator, and his betrothed Clelia! But to do so as generously as he wished, he must be no longer dependent on the complaisance of a man of business, he must be in the actual possession of his own. In the meantime, however, here were those at hand, who had stretched their small means to the utmost to help him in his distress; and it was lucky that he had it in his power to show his sense of the services he had received. But in this, as we have just hinted, he had reckoned without his host. Save Dr. Perrin, who, when made to comprehend the change in his patient's circumstances, did at last consent, though with reluctance, to receive a moderate fee for himself, and a contribution for his more indigent patients, none of the young man's other friends would hear of anything like cash.

Fortunately for Paolo's peace of mind, they proved less intractable on the chapter of *souvenirs;* and many were the useful household articles, *soi-disant* trifles for the children, and little comforts for the table, which, under that commodious nickname, were smuggled from the neighbouring shops into Mr. Prosper's establishment, and into Mr. Benoît's den. Among these last contribu-

tions figured a collection of black bottles, of whose contents Benoît could never hereafter speak without *quois*
of enthusiasm, and repeated thrusts at the nearest wall;
and also a magnificent meerschaum, which he seemingly disdained to use for smoking, but of which he
must have been pretty vain, as he constantly wore it,
inserted daggerwise, in the strings of his apron. After
all, it might have been a better feeling than vanity
which prompted his carrying it; as to the manner he
had no choice — Benoît's costume admitted of no such
thing as a pocket.

Paolo had given up his secretaryship at the end of
the fortnight, and, for having plenty of money and
time at his own disposal, he was none the happier;
quite the reverse. He positively knew not what to do
with himself — he thought once of hiring a studio,
and settling himself to his painting again. But then,
à quoi bon? Even should he succeed in acquiring
fame, beyond what was probable in a foreign country,
was the end worth the trouble? With Lavinia — his
only incentive for wishing to arrive at greatness — had
vanished every spark of ambition — his enthusiasm for
art — as he believed, for ever. Who has not laboured,
more or less, under such dispiriting influences? who has
not, on the newly covered grave of some dear being,
or not less dear dream, pronounced all pursuits worthless? The soul takes long to recover the shocks of
such bereavements.

Du Genre was not slack in proposing a method of
cure for his friend's ennui; it consisted of a series of
measures, the first, the most urgent, the *sine quâ non*
of which, was to pass what he styled the Rubicon; by
which he meant that Paolo should cross the Seine, and

remove his quarters to the habitable part of Paris, viz. the right side of the river. To this Paolo said neither yes nor no. He had already made up his mind to leave his garret, and seek for a more eligible lodging; but he had, as was natural, a strong prejudice against the Boulevards so vaunted by Du Genre. Nor was he particularly inclined for the present to take a stall twice a week at the theatre of the Palais Royal, or to canvass for admission to the club of which his French fellow-painter was a member. The only one of Du Genre's various devices for killing time, which at all tickled Paolo's fancy, was that of taking riding lessons at a *Manège*, to which the realist, himself a subscriber, volunteered to introduce him. Riding was a manly and healthy exercise, and Paolo saw no reason why he should not devote a few of his idle hours to that, as well as to walking. It was, therefore, settled that this introduction should take place as soon as Paolo should have fulfilled the indispensable preliminary of making himself fit, as far as personal appearance went, for so fashionable a lounge.

"For, indeed," observed Du Genre, "your dress and hat are quite anachronisms in this part of the world, though they might cut a tolerable figure in a museum of antiquities."

Paolo took a survey of his threadbare black coat and trousers, smiled assent, and in less than eight-and-forty hours, thanks to the combined exertions of Du Genre's tailor, hatter, and bootmaker, he was in a fit condition, though rather an absurd figure in his own eyes, to be presented at the *Manège*.

Being Du Genre's acquaintance, his admission met with no difficulty, one of the old members being easily

found to stand sponsor for him, according to the rules.
To this ceremony, and a few other conditions and limi-
tations, submitted to by all those entering, the establishment owed its character rather of a riding-club than of
a riding-school, the appellation usually, however, given
to it.

The riding-master augured well of him from the
first day. Light hand, quick eye, strong, supple limbs,
and plenty of pluck, Paolo was wanting in none of the
natural gifts which go towards the making of a fine
horseman; he had, moreover, what is more rare, that
intuitive perception of the best means to an end, which
is to all undertakings what a good ear is to the mastery
of music. He took to the saddle *con amore*, and made
rapid progress. A few days sufficed, Du Genre aiding
and abetting, to establish between the new pupil and
the *habitués* those relations of *bonne compagnie* so easily
formed in France; but none of these ever ripened into
intimacy. The men he met there were most of them
jovial young fellows of Paolo's own age; some, however, mere boys; but one and all were deep in the
"hausse," and the "baisse," and in the scandalous
chronicle of the day. The way they spoke of women
was alone enough to distance our idealist.

Among the patrons of the *Manège*, who from time
to time came thither, and even occasionally joined the
youths in a ride, was the Vicomte du Verlat — we
have heard this name before — a peculiarly good-
looking elderly gentleman. His tall stature, and grey
beard, which he wore long; his elegant, yet simple
style of dress; the ease and distinction of his manners,
reminded Paolo of his English friend, Thornton. Erect,
supple, and active as any of the young men, Vicomte

du Verlat maintained intact at fifty his well-earned reputation of being one of the best riders of the day;
and great was the excitement in the riding-house, when
the tyros felt the keen glance of the master on them.
The vicomte had noticed Paolo as a promising pupil;
had given him several useful hints; came to the school
more frequently than he had lately done, as if drawn
thither by some new interest. Paolo, flattered and
pleased by the attention of one so generally looked
up to, met Mr. du Verlat's advances gratefully and
warmly.

Meanwhile the whereabouts of the new quarters for
Paolo remained, notwithstanding Du Genre's advice and
persuasions, an open question. One day the viscount
said to Paolo, —

"I never meet you on the Boulevard; I suppose you
do not reside in this neighbourhood?" (The *Manège* was
in the quarter of the Madeleine.)

Paolo turned red as he replied that he lived at some
distance, but that he was intending to come nearer to
the Boulevard.

"Allow me to say that the sooner you do so, the
better," said the vicomte. "Come nearer to us; you will
find it more cheerful; at least, I, for one, will try to
make it so to you."

From this day, Paolo felt discontented with his attic
on the left bank of the Seine, and made up his mind
to pass the Rubicon. Du Genre, delighted with this
resolve, gave the most unwearied help towards its
realization. A good many apartments were looked at
by the two friends fruitlessly, for some days; those
patronized by the Frenchman being objected to by the
Italian as too luxurious and expensive; those the Italian

would have chosen being rejected by the Frenchman as
shabby and unfit for a man with any self-respect.   At
length, as usual in such cases, each party conceded
somewhat, and the matter ended in a compromise.   A
snug *entresol* in the Rue St. Georges was selected as
neither too cheap nor too dear, neither too showy nor
too plain; and when Paolo had satisfied the porter that
he was possessed of neither children nor dogs, and that
he had wherewithal to pay a month's rent in advance,
the keys of the apartment were delivered to him.
Cerberus, moreover, condescended, for an additional sum
of twenty francs a month, to clean Mr. Mancini's shoes,
and look after his rooms.   Paolo scorned the notion of
having a servant all to himself.

And so possession was taken *ipso facto*, and the two
friends, each lighting a cigar — Paolo had become an
habitual smoker — intended as a votive offering to the
familiar Lares, proceeded to make arrangements for the
removal of what moveables Paolo had on the other side
of the water.

"You are probably not aware," said Du Genre, as
they walked down the street, "that you have given yourself a master and a tyrant in the shape of this porter
of yours. Remember, however, never to call him *Portier*,
but always *Concierge*, or he will call you to severe
account.   You had one real advantage in your hole in
the Rue Dufour, and that was having no porter. Porters
with our absurd style of houses are indispensable, but
not the less a scourge.   They are the natural enemies
and persecutors of their proprietors' tenants, whom they
look upon, and justly so, as the cause of their own
bondage.   It is perfectly logical, for if there were no
lodgers, there would be no porters. They have a thou-

sand ways of embittering your life: they can stop your letters; forget to give you the cards left for you; say you are at home to the visitors you dislike to see; say you are out to those you wish to receive; keep you in the rain *ad libitum* of a night, — and woe to you if you seek redress. Either the landlord will back them against you, and you are at their mercy; or he will reprimand them; and then, farewell to peace, — the house will soon grow too hot to hold you. So, let it be your constant policy never to resist, or have the slightest difference with, the gentleman you have just engaged to clean your rooms and your shoes. Propitiate him at all costs. You laugh. I am speaking in sober earnest, I assure you. Let me see; there was something else I meant to say. Ah! you must not be quite unprovided for visitors. Order in a dozen of Madeira; yes, that and Vermuth will do for the stronger sex; the softer will prefer champagne or maraschino."

"But I have no intention of receiving ladies," said Paolo, with some surprise.

"Nonsense! you are too well launched now, to be able to stop midway. Now you have got a decent apartment, the next thing you must provide yourself with, is a fair companion."

"Thank you," said Paolo, blushing like a girl; "but I shall do no such thing. Let us act like Christians."

"Why should we act like what we are not?"

"Are we not Christians?" said Paolo.

"Certainly not, save in name," returned the Frenchman. "Show me any, the least spark of the spirit, which made a stable the cradle, and a cross the throne of a humanized god, and I will follow you into the

desert, and live upon locusts. Christianity, to most
people, is an ingenious theory, with no more practical
bearing on men's actions than the theory of colours, or
that of the formation of hail. Look around you," continued Du Genre, pointing to the throng of men on the
Petite Bourse, blocking up the pavement on both sides
opposite to the passage de l'Opera. "Here it is where
it is decided whether the *Rente* shall rise or fall; here
plenty of bargains with the devil are made; the single
aim and passion of all these so-called Christians here
assembled, but one — money — to get rich — make
a fortune. Step on that bench and tell these Christians
that there is written in a book, which they have accepted
as their rule of life, that, 'It is easier for a camel to
pass through the eye of a needle, than for a rich man
to enter the kingdom of heaven,' and see how they will
receive the intelligence; it will not anger — oh, no!
but amuse them vastly. Christians forsooth! The religion
of our age is a mitigated Paganism; its gods, Plutus,
Venus, and Bacchus. Take away the Bourse, the
Dames aux Camelias, and the wine-shops, and society
will collapse like a balloon out of which the hydro-
gen has escaped. You see I can moralize when I
choose."

"With a vengeance," said Paolo. "But then, if
the world be so wicked as you make it out to be, rather
than seek pleasure, we ought to put on sackcloth, and
cover our heads with ashes."

"The conclusion of morose Heraclitus," said the
Frenchman; "laughing Democritus knows better, and
says, Let us wreathe our temples with roses, and do as
others do. Take my advice, Telemachus; choose your
Eucharis."

"Never," said Paolo; "every principle, every feeling, the very foundation of my soul, rises up in arms
against the notion. There is a gulf between your ideas
of woman and mine."

"Aye!" sighed Du Genre; "the gulf that separates
sober reality from wild fancy. What do you know about
women? Living like an anchorite, you have made for
yourself, and *bonâ fide* worshipped, an ideal type, which
no more resembles a flesh and blood woman, than the
brilliant plant of the tropics reared in a hothouse resembles the common flowers of the field. Experience
alone will cure you of your delusion; it will come. In
the meanwhile, condescend to open your eyes, and
comtemplate the stream of inflated ladies, who pour out
of the church of the Madeleine. Mark me, they are
most respectable; examine them, and reconcile, if you
can, your high-flown sentiments with their frivolous appearance. Do they answer best to the description of
the angels and muses you dream of, or to that of the
thorough-bred daughters of Eve that they are? The
fool's cap, I know, does not make the fool; but when
wilfully worn, it is not the less indicative of a certain
frame of mind. Can you think of the respectable mother
of a family stepping into her steel cage, and help laughing? And why should we be in earnest, and bruise our
hearts to a jelly for those who are not in earnest about
themselves? They do not expect it of us."

During the last part of Du Genre's speech, Paolo's
attention had been divided between it and a group of
three artisans, who had stopped to watch awhile the
passing of some of their fair, so styled, superiors. He
could not hear what they said, but judging from their
curled lips, and half-angry, half-sarcastic survey of

waving hoops and flounces, he could guess pretty well at the nature of their opinions and comments. Paolo nudged his friend, who, following the direction of the Roman's glance, said, —

"When those in authority on board the vessel condescend to play the fool, no wonder the crew take them at their own valuation. After all," added he, with a shrug, "it's no business of ours — *après nous le déluge.*"

Mr. du Verlat's was the first visit Paolo received in his new abode. "A snug comfortable *pied-à-terre,*" remarked the vicomte, approvingly; no gingerbread show about it. Looked like common sense, and the vicomte valued simplicity of all things. And what was his young acquaintance doing? Beginning to dabble in the wickedness of the world? Too late in the year for Mabille or the Château aux Fleurs; but there was Valentino, and the Concerts de Paris. Not been there yet! Was he an ascetic? Very agreeable rencontres might be made there. Parisian belles, the vicomte was aware, could not stand comparison with Roman beauties, but they had the *brio,* the *entrain,* the *je ne sais quoi.*

Paolo shook his head despondingly, as though he would say he made as light of Roman beauties as of Parisian belles, or that it was not that he looked for.

"A! I understand — I feel for you," resumed the vicomte. "Early love, disappointment, deception. We have all gone through it. I have been young and romantic as you are; I have pursued my *beau idéal* as fervently as any one, have wept bitter tears on its flight, and — I have ended by *me faire une raison.* Follow my example, sir; try a little homœopathy — *similia similibus.* Life is too short to spend it in dreams, and youth comes but once — *carpe diem*. Believe me, life has realities not to be disdained, and with your physical powers —"

"Perhaps it is a fault in me," said Paolo, smiling, "but what if I prefer my dreams to your realities?"

"Pardon me; that proves nothing more than that you are in a morbid state of mind, out of which it is the duty of those who wish you well to arouse you. You cherish your disease, and that's the worst feature of it. I did much the same when similarly afflicted. What would you say of that person — excuse the triviality of the simile — what would you say of any one, who, disappointed of the woodcock he had relied on for his dinner, would rather not dine at all than do so on a pigeon pie? Make an effort, sir, and shake off your trammels. True wisdom consists in asking of life no more than life can give. Constancy, you see — I could prove it to you both on anatomical and physiological grounds — is a virtue incompatible with our faulty organization. Have you read Balzac? Well, read him; there is great philosophy in Balzac. If you will permit me, I will send you some of his works. Adieu."

Du Verlat was sincere in saying he felt for Paolo; he felt like a compassionate physician, who sees his patient refuse the medicine that would restore him to health, or rather like one who sees his friend labouring under a painful hallucination, and strives to reason him out of it. The good-humoured viscount was not a common *roué*, nor had nature intended him for one at all. He was born generous, confiding, tender-hearted. A coquette he had met with at twenty had made him what he now was, an elegant sensualist. There are men who cannot resist the deleterious effort of a first deception; and in that of which he had been the victim, there were peculiarly aggravating circumstances. Mr. du Verlat had spent some of the best years of his life in inoculating himself with the belief — nay, had erected it into a sort of system, backed by anatomy and physiology — that women were irresponsible agents, and ought to be treated as such. This belief it was that had kept him a bachelor, in spite of the urgent entreaties of all his family that he would marry.

But his scepticism had nothing in it either malignant or aggressive. The vicomte did not make it his profession to go about slandering the fair sex, nor did he treat them cavalierly; quite the contrary. The systematic view he took of them, together with the inborn elegance of his mind, inclined him rather to that deferential indulgence which is shown to infants. It was from pure good-nature, that he had so far gone out of his usual routine as to catechize Paolo; but possessing, as he believed he did, an infallible antidote against the malady, which, according to his own guesses, and Du Genre's confidences, afflicted his Italian acquaintance, could he keep it from one so young and interesting?

Days and weeks passed, and Paolo saw with amazement, as he looked back, the alteration in his habits, which his simple change of residence had stealthily brought with it. Somehow or other he had, since passing the Rubicon, with difficulty found time for a couple of visits to his friends of the Quai Montebello; and Mr. Boniface, or Mr. Pertuis, on whom he used to call once a week at least, he had entirely neglected. Somehow or other, he was rarely in his bed till an hour after midnight, rarely out of it before ten in the morning, and yet he had not been to the theatre more

than five or six times during these three weeks, and as
to balls or concerts, he had never set his foot in one
of them. He had besides lost his great dislike to the
Boulevard; he would loiter there with much equanimity,
exchanging greetings and cigars with other loiterers,
having become by this time on speaking terms with
most of the frequenters of the *café*, at which he took
his meals.

Perhaps, had he scanned the inner man as closely
as the outward, Paolo might have noticed modifications
in the former, as well as the latter. Not that he had
come the length of being in the least disposed to ex-
change his gods for the gods of others — not at all;
but his holy horror of what he considered idolatry had
much abated, and instead a new spirit of tolerance was
springing up within him for tenets distant as pole from
pole to his own. Balzac's philosophy, Arnal's *double
entendres*, Rosati's *entrechats*, and evening walks on the
Boulevard, are not exactly calculated to strengthen spi-
ritualistic tendencies. The atmosphere in which Paolo
lived, notwithstanding his attempts to neutralize it,
began to tell on him, imperceptibly, but steadily.

CHAPTER XIII.

Despair.

THERE was, at the time of the events in course of
narration, an extensive linen-drapery establishment in
the vicinity of Camden Town. Miss Lavinia walked
into this shop one morning, a little basket in her hand,
containing some embroidery of her own working — a
chemisette with sleeves to match — the labour of many

scores of weary hours. Had her countenance been clearly visible, instead of only indistinctly through her thick veil, it would have betrayed the great effort which the step she was taking cost her.

The eager politeness of the counter official, who stepped up to her side soliciting the honour of her commands, on hearing the nature of her request, and the tone in which it was made, vanished; he pointed in silence to the farther end of the room, wheeled round, and left her to herself. Her request was to the effect that she wished to speak to one of the gentlemen of the firm; and she had to repeat it twice over to two different young men, before she could make out which was the person she was in search of. It being not yet nine in the morning, business was more than languid, and the master, seated a little apart from his shopmen, was diligently trimming his nails with a penknife. All that was visible of him in his semi-reclining posture, was a big bunch of crisp black hair carefully brushed to one side of his head, and a profile view of a chin and mouth of that deep blue hue, indicative of a strong black beard.

Lavinia went up to him, and, leaning over the counter, which half hid him from view, said, in a timid whisper, ——

"I beg your pardon, sir; I have come to offer some work for sale," and she produced her embroidery.

The partner of the firm rose, looked at her, noticed the small gloved fingers, took in at a glance the fine proportions of her figure, and conveyed the satisfactory impression he had received from the *tout ensemble*, by a wink and a grin full of meaning to some one standing behind the lady. The smart, bandy-legged little fellow, thus telegraphed to, no less a personage than the head clerk, stole on tiptoe to Lavinia's side, and tried to peep under her veil; caught in the act, he assumed an air of unconsciousness, took the embroidery handed him by the gentleman of the firm, examined it, and asked if it was for sale. Being answered in the affirmative, he said, "by your leave," and without waiting for it, he pretended to measure the sleeves to Lavinia's wrist, and in so doing, managed, with *malice prepense*, to touch the fair hand and arm more than necessary. She drew it back hastily.

"Heyday, you needn't be afraid of me; my skin is as clear as yours, ma'am," said he; "if we are to have dealings together, you must be a little more agreeable."

Lavinia took no notice of him, but repeated her question to the partner.

"Will you purchase these things, sir?"

"Certainly," he replied, with another wink to his subordinate; "but you are aware, ma'am, that we cannot buy articles without identifying the seller."

"I can leave you my name and address," said innocent Lavinia.

"That's not enough, miss. Suppose some lady comes in half an hour hence, sees this chemisette and sleeves, and says that they belong to her, that she has lost them? I know what you are going to say, and I don't doubt you are speaking the truth, when you tell me they are your own work; I have no doubt you would appear to prove them to be so; but pray, how could we swear you were the person that sold them—"

"Unless," added the head clerk, with a very grave face, "you would be so kind as to remove your veil—just for an instant."

His too well preserved gravity was the ruin of the joke. The partner could not resist it, and burst out into a roar of laughter. Bandy-legs took the infection and roared also. Lavinia now saw they had been amusing themselves at her expense; she silently picked up her work and walked away. Her tears for not gushing forth were not the less bitter; only the more heavily did they fall back on her heart. What coarse, mischievous men these were, thought she. She had never guessed at the existence of such beings.

Mrs. Tamplin comforted her in her way.

"And so they made game of you! the more shame for them. I might have known as much. You are not the sort of person to be going from shop to shop on selling errands; you are too handsome and too good. They wanted to see you without your veil, and so they trumped up that ridiculous story about identification. A parcel of saucy scamps. Beauty is a sad gift to the poor and modest. They think they have done wonders, when they buy the worth of a sixpence from you, and expect no end of complaisance in return — and they get it in most cases. And how can it be otherwise? If you knew what it was to be hungry! A wicked world I can tell you. All the effect of competition, that's what it is."

Mrs. Tamplin, to her honour be it said, did not confine her consolations to worse than sterile theories about human wickedness. She did better than that — she did something practical — namely, took the embroidery and went about with it herself. Lavinia could the better appreciate this effort in one so low-spirited as her landlady, after her own recent personal experience. The effect upon herself had been to blight

that most precious and most tenacious flower of youth
— confidence in mankind. She now shrank from them.
Not to gain the world would she a second time have
gone through the same ordeal as that she had passed in
the Camden Town linen-draper's shop.

The embroidery sold after all — sold for a higher
price than Mrs. Tamplin had supposed probable. Even
the gloomy widow, elated for a moment by her success,
found some chords within her which sounded like hope!
The flower withering in Lavinia's breast revived, and
her want of faith filled her with shame and remorse.
She felt as if, in doubting her fellow-creatures, she was
doubting Providence! How ungrateful of her! Was it
not more than she deserved, her having already secured
an active sympathizing friend? If instead of desponding
at her first disappointment and crouching down like a
coward, she had put on patience as an armour against
all rebuffs, had she been strong in the knowledge
that she was doing well, her failure must have been
followed by success. It was her pride, her faint-hearted-
ness, that she ought to find fault with, and not her
neighbour.

Impressed with a deep sense of her unworthiness,
she shut herself into her little room, knelt by the side
of her poor couch, and prayed and wept as only those
can pray and weep, who have no proper stay but Our
Father that is in Heaven. And then, fairly worn out
by emotions of many kinds, and want of rest for the
last two nights, she fell asleep like a little child and
dreamed that she was driving in the grounds of Villa
Borghese with her aunt by her side. There were
numerous loungers strolling in the gardens; one with
his back to her reminded her of Paolo. She knew in

her dream that she had not seen him for very long, and an earnest desire arose in her to tell him how much she had changed, and that she cared no more for those things he cared not for. And presently the gentleman turned, and she saw that it was Paolo, and he had a large rose in his button-hole, and she beckoned to him. He came to her hurriedly, and stretched his hands, holding his beautiful rose, towards her. In her eagerness to grasp it, she leaned far out of the carriage, and felt that she was falling, which she was doing in right earnest. As Paolo, the rose, the gardens disappeared, she found herself lying on the floor by the bed, fortunately without any hurt.

There are moods of the mind which predispose one to receive strong impressions, however unwarranted by reason, from causes almost puerile. Lavinia was in one of these moods, and, silly as it may seem in her, drew so happy an omen from her dream as to amount to a certainty of Paolo's safety. We will not grudge her this superstitious feeling, considering the great comfort she derived from it, and her great need of some comfort.

Renewed trust in God, in the good-will of His creatures, and a strengthened purpose to keep herself, to the best of her powers, in the spirit of one who is sure to be helped, such was the revulsion of feeling with which Lavinia arose from her momentary fit of discouragement. As to the means of earning her bread, she had no choice but to persevere in the old course — applications for the situation of governess and her needle. Answering advertisements, whether in person or by letter, occupied but little of her time; all the rest was devoted to her embroidery. She grew so chary of every moment, that she grudged herself even the quarter of an hour for her dinner — and such a dinner! If the few sparrows whom she had tamed to come to the window-sill and peck crumbs from her hands, were at all slow in coming to her call, she would chide them for keeping her idle. Yes, even the very poorest have their superfluities. She had her luxury also, something to tend, and watch, and think of, and hope in, and love — a hyacinth growing in its long blue glass. That poor root represented all the external poetry of her life.

To see her pretty lodger slaving from early dawn till late at night, ought to have afforded Mrs. Tamplin an occasion for many a comfortable moan about the misery that always dogged her life; but she neglected this precious opportunity, setting her wits to work instead, to devise some means of forcing Lavinia to enjoy a second's respite; her cunningest trick being reserved for the evening, when, pleading the sad state of her eyes, she would entreat the young lady to read to her from the day's paper the account of the man who smashed a pane of glass that he might obtain a lodging in a prison; or that of the family of four persons who spent most of the night in taking down bills from the walls, and made from the sale of the paper thus obtained as much as sevenpence a day, upon which the four persons contrived to exist.

One day Mrs. Tamplin had an idea — a bright idea. The young lady played on the piano, she believed; could she not give music lessons? Lavinia thought she could, only —

"Wait a moment," said the widow; "I don't mean that you should seek to give lessons at the pupils' own homes. I know very well it would be the old story over again about references, and good-day to you as the wind-up. Nothing, however, hinders you from opening a class for the piano; very cheap, of course, at the beginning — a class for the piano, here, in this house. I will very willingly let you use the drawing-room for it."

"Thank you very much, kind Mrs. Tamplin," said Lavinia. "But to give lessons on the piano, I must first have a piano and —"

"Wait a moment," interrupted the widow. "I know all you are going to say. There is no occasion to hire a piano before we have secured pupils enough to pay for the hire. Here's my idea: we'll put a card in the window, on which we'll write as clearly as possible: 'A pianoforte class for young ladies three times a week, by a pupil of —,' and then the name of whoever was your master; it will sound very well, I daresay. 'For further particulars, apply within.' Now, either pupils come or they do not. If enough of them appear, we hire the piano; if no one comes, well and good, then we do not hire the piano, and the class is unavoidably postponed to the first of next month; do you understand now?"

The scheme promised well, in so far that it was feasible and necessitated no outlay on mere chance, and Lavinia eagerly embraced it. A card was written and hung up in the front parlour window; then came the calculations; supposing only six pupils could be got; six pupils at ten shillings a month each — what happiness! Why, after deducting the hire of the instrument — and Mrs. Tamplin was sure one was to be had for sixteen shillings — there would remain forty-

four shillings, and it would be independence, riches.
And surely in this interminable Babylon of London it
was not very improbable that she might find six pupils,
or five, or at the least four.

Alas! days and weeks crawled on, and the card in
the window availed nothing. The piano scheme went
to pieces. Many persons applied, asked questions,
wanted to see the class-room, wanted to see the music
mistress's certificates from her master, wanted to hear
her play, and were disgusted when they found there
was no piano in the house. One volunteered to bring
three pupils, provided her own daughter had the benefit
of the class gratis, and after the bargain was agreed to,
took her leave, and never reappeared. Of all the in-
quirers one lady alone accepted the terms as they stood.
The same unlucky issue attended all Lavinia's personal
or written applications for the situation of a governess.
Once, only once, since her failure with the lady at Hyde
Park Place, had a ray of hope entered her sinking
heart. A lady commissioned by one of her friends in
the country to look out for a governess, had received
the poor girl most courteously; had begged to hear her
play on the piano; had expressed warm admiration of
her fingering and style of playing, and great gratification at having fallen in with a person so calculated to
satisfy her friend; but the moment the question of
references was mooted, clouds quickly obliterated the
sunshine. Lavinia did not hurry away in despair as
in the instance above alluded to; she pleaded her cause
earnestly and simply. The lady was touched, went so
far as to say that, were she acting for herself, she might
perhaps trust to her feelings, and overlook the irre-
gularity of the want of a reference, but acting as she

was for another person, the mother of several young daughters, the thing was impossible.

The little stock of money Lavinia had had about her, when she left Mr. Jones's country seat, was long since exhausted. Of the few costly ornaments, chosen from among the many she owed to the generosity of Mrs. Jones, and which she had felt justified in taking away with her, on account of their particular character of keepsakes, and of their having been intended as such, one, a bracelet, had already been sold, — with what a pang, God knows; the rest must soon follow — and then? what then? For the produce of her indefatigable needle scarcely sufficed for her shoes and washing. Well might the lovely face grow wan, and the youthful figure waste away, as she tried to work out some answer to the terrible question of what was then to become of her.

Mrs. Tamplin, more and more drawn out of her selfishness by the patience of her gentle, uncomplaining lodger, was once more racking her brains for some fresh expedient; and seeking, she found one — and a capital one it was this time. Mr. Duncan, the surgeon, their next-door neighbour, was the person to turn the scales in Lavinia's favour. Mr. Duncan had both the will and the power to do so, at least, so Mrs. Tamplin affirmed. Naturally obliging as he was to every one, she knew he was particularly favourably disposed towards Miss Lavinia; she could see that, by his civility on two or three occasions, and by his having dropped in unprofessionally after the young lady was well again, and by his never meeting her (Mrs. Tamplin) without inquiring for her interesting lodger. As to

friends and interest, few men could equal him. Why
not confide in him?

If Mr. Duncan could be induced to recommend Lavinia as a governess or companion — and Mrs. Tamplin
was certain that he would do so — and also take upon
himself the responsibility of being a reference for her,
every difficulty now in her path would vanish like
mist before the noonday sun. Was there any objection
to Mrs. Tamplin sounding the surgeon? The gentleman,
judging from the little Lavinia had seen of him, had in
his nature a rich vein of coarseness, which made him
unpalatable to one of her refinement and delicacy of
feeling; but was she, merely from perhaps dainty
squeamishness, to reject the hand, rough indeed, yet
perhaps the only hand which could and would rescue
her from utter shipwreck? These blunt, rude-spoken
men were often the truest and best, she had heard it
said; in short, Lavinia ended by accepting this new
project with thanks, and Mrs. Tamplin went forthwith to open negotiations.

Mr. Duncan fully justified the most sanguine expectations of his melancholy admirer — nothing could
surpass his obliging kindliness. He called to see Lavinia that evening, and exhaled good-will from every
pore.

"And so," said he, "*we* were at a rather low ebb, were
we? No occasion to despair. *We* should be afloat
again in less than no time. He had set to rights many
worse cases than this, eh, Mrs. Tamplin? Stooping over
embroidery wouldn't do, it hurt the chest, it spoilt the
shape. Away with it, and with drooping mouths, and
faded cheeks. Let roses and lilies and that sort of
thing be the order of the day."

10*

Mrs. Tamplin, good soul, for once chuckled with un-
mixed delight, and gave it as her decided opinion, that
one might go far, and not find Mr. Duncan's match.
Lavinia's conclusions, without going that length, travel-
led, however, in the same direction. A rugged exterior,
but a kindly heart, thought she, and her spirits rose.

Mr. Duncan took the habit of frequently dropping
in at Mrs. Tamplin's now, and his interest in his fair
protegée waxed warmer, and more demonstrative at
every visit. He began to call her his "little pet," and
"still waters," find fault with her pale cheeks and thin
wrists, pinching both with much the grace an old bear
might display in toying with a rose. Lavinia would
willingly have dispensed with these familiarities, indeed,
they were positively odious to her; but taking into account the coarse grain of the man, his kindness to her,
and his age — young ladies of twenty are apt to look
on a green quinquagenarian as upon a Methusalem —
she saw in his newly-adopted ways, merely the odd
expression of a fatherly interest, and endured them with
patience.

One evening Mrs. Tamplin was called out of the
sitting-room. Mr. Duncan, who happened to be there,
immediately twisted his face into a would-be agreeable,
reassuring grin, and said, in a confidential whisper, —

"I have found a first-rate situation for you."

"Have you, indeed? how very kind of you!" cried
Lavinia, with a burst of joy and gratitude. "Is it as
a governess?"

"Faugh! a governess! Something far better. You
come and stay with me."

"With you?" she exclaimed, and her face lengthened.

"Yes, with me; the ill-combed monkey is growing oldish, and wants somebody to look after him and his house; come you, and be my housekeeper; not a bad offer, let me tell you."

Lavinia looked at him in great perplexity, not free from some alarm. Mr. Duncan's countenance was not exactly formed for the display of tender feelings; all his efforts to produce insinuating smiles only gave him a greater resemblance to a mischievous terrier. The astonished girl said at last, —

"But you are a single gentleman, sir."

He laughed his coarsest laugh.

"Yes, thank God, I am — reason the more for you to come; you will have everything your own way, don't you see? — eh? — plenty of the best that's to be got to eat, and to drink — plenty of fine clothes — plenty of money."

Lavinia could bear no more. She jumped up, cast on the grinning knave one look of infinite contempt, and walked away without deigning even a word of rebuke.

"Oh! merciful God, save me from my despair; oh! merciful Lord, take me to Thee."

Such was the agonized cry of the heart-broken girl as she threw herself down — her face on the floor of her bed-room, as if she would bury it for ever from the sight of all mankind. It seemed, indeed, as though the God of the afflicted, the God of the fatherless, had in His mercy listened to her prayer, for all consciousness left her.

CHAPTER XIV.

A Bachelor's Supper, and what came of it.

ABOUT the middle of the month of November, Paolo received intelligence from Rome, of the transfer of Bishop Rodipani's fortune to himself, according to the terms of the will. The solicitor regretted to say that the bishop proved to be less wealthy than had been expected; in fact, that Signor Mancini's legacy would exceed little more than a hundred thousand scudi, half of which, as detailed in the annexed statement, was vested in various foreign stock, realizable at a short notice. Prudent Monsignor Rodipani, in the choice of his investments, had evidently had an eye to the mutability of earthly things. There was, besides the sum of money above mentioned, another of eighteen thousand scudi lying at the bankers, about the disposition of which the solicitor asked for directions.

Paolo very curiously examined the several items of the statement furnished to him, and far from any astonishment or regret at the modicity of his inheritance, he felt a kind of bewilderment at the idea of being so rich. Positively, it was more like a fairy tale than a reality, his being able to fulfil one of the most earnest of his wishes, namely, the securing of the independence and happiness of his two friends, Salvator and Clelia. A really happy morning he spent in writing, first, a very long and affectionate letter to the little painter, then one less long, but not less affectionate, to Clelia, which was enclosed in that to her betrothed, together with a cheque in favour of Salvator for a thousand scudi.

By the same post he wrote to apprise his man of business of what he had done, desiring that henceforth, without any further advice from himself, the sum of sixty scudi should be paid monthly to the person named in the cheque. This done, Paolo went in search of his breakfast, and a hearty meal he made of it; for his satisfaction at the good turn he had been able to do for his friends, was overshadowed by none of the misgivings, as to the source of the wealth of which he disposed — misgivings which had so obstinately haunted him two months ago.

At the Manège he met the Vicomte and Du Genre; they were waiting expressly for him, said M. Du Verlat. One of the *habitués* of the school was on the point of marriage, and according to an established custom, the bridegroom elect was bound to give a *souper de garçons* to the best riders. The choice of the guests had been left to the Vicomte, in his capacity of honorary president, and Paolo naturally had a right to a high place on his list. It would have been difficult, even for one inclined to do so, to decline an invitation so flatteringly and so courteously given; but Paolo, in his present mood, was not likely to run the risk of disobliging any one of his acquaintances; so he accepted the compliment paid to himself and his equestrian powers, with thanks. M. Du Verlat looked much pleased as he said, —

"We are to meet at twelve to-night at Barruel's. You know where I mean; if not, Pélissier is of the party, and will show you the way. Adieu, till then, and remember there is no need to dress."

"A few hours of *ennui*," thought Paolo to himself, as, on the stroke of midnight, he walked, arm-in-arm

with Du Genre, to the place of rendezvous — at most
a few hours of *ennui* — to listen to how some lucky
speculator won a fortune within an hour by the *hausse*
or the *baisse*, or to hear the apotheosis of the legs of
La Petra Camara. Other danger or dangers he could
not see, unless indeed from the bottle; and against that
he felt fully armed. Of the possibility of there being
ladies among the guests, he never once thought, or his
natural shyness would have been on the *qui vive* at
once. A bachelor's supper, as he in his innocence
understood it, meant a supper of men in the blessed
state of celibacy, to the entire exclusion of the other
sex. Fancy then his consternation when, on being
ushered into the *sancta sanctorum*, he confronted a bevy
of ladies — he would have sworn to there being fifty
of them, though, in fact, there were only eight, the
same number as of gentlemen. Paolo's first instinctive
movement was to draw back, but this probability had
to all appearance been foreseen, and provided against
by Du Genre, who gave his friend a gentle push forward, and a gentle warning not to make a fool of himself. The consciousness which now dawned upon
Paolo, of having been intentionally decoyed into a
trap, gave him a finishing stroke — his heart thumped,
his ears tingled, his head swam. All this was the
affair of a few seconds.

"Mdlle. Celina," called the vicomte, as he hastened
towards the Italian, and took him courteously by the
hand. A graceful, impish figure sprang to her feet at
this summons, fluttered across the room on the points
of her toes, came to a full stop, and suddenly describing
a parabola in the air, alighted on her right foot, with
the whiz of a bomb, between Paolo and Du Verlat.

"Mdlle. Celina, of the opera ballet corps," explained the vicomte. "Mademoiselle is all impatience to make your acquaintance, Mr. Mancini, and to hear of the wonders of Rome. I confide her to your gallantry as your partner for the evening, or rather for the night. I leave you to each other."

While the introduction was taking place, Mdlle. Celina slowly waved herself about, crossed her arms upon her bosom, and curtseyed in full choreographic style. She was in the costume of her calling, bare neck, bare arms, plentifully rouged, with a fabulous circumvallation of white muslin around her. She might have figured to advantage in a picture of the temptations of St. Anthony. Her well-cut eyes, and cherry-round lips — the only beauty about her, except her youth — were as saucy and provoking as any of Propertius' odes. A girl hardly past sixteen, with the figure and manner of that age, hers were the set features, the assurance, the knowing look of a coquette of thirty. Little fit to observe, and to reason out his observations as Paolo was at this moment, he felt intuitively this glaring want of harmony, and was repelled by it. An old soul in a young body, as he defined her afterwards.

Dropping all that was professional for the nonce, Paolo's partner for the night passed her arm within his, and said abruptly, —

"Art thou a prince, a marquis, or what?"

Rather wincing under the infliction of the quaker-like form of address, he replied that he had no title at all.

"Not a little bit? what a pity; particularly for

a *joli garçon*. I doat on titles. I will dub thee chevalier."

"I beg you will commit no such folly," said Paolo.

"Papa vicomte," called out the miss, "fine my partner; he has called me *you*."

A general burst of laughter welcomed the accusation. Every eye brought itself to bear on the Italian.

"Pardon him for this once," said Du Verlat; "besides, we are not yet at table."

If what he had already seen and heard by this time had not revealed to Paolo the nature and the purpose of the surprise prepared for him by his friends, a very little further observation of what was said and done, soon fully opened his eyes. The curious, though carefully guarded attention, of which he was the object, marked him out plainly enough for the hero of the *fête*, and what the nature of the *fête* was to be, was as clearly intimated by the look of the *lionnes* convened — the look of Bacchantes in repose, ready to rush forth in their real character at the first call of the *systrum*. A few months ago, when he was a thorough savage, neither stratagem nor force would have kept him from breaking loose, and, come what might, quitting the company; now, that he was half civilized, the fear of ridicule was a potent spell, and rooted him there. Yet to breathe that stifling atmosphere, to face for any length of time that odious little imp by his side, to sit a witness, if not an actor, in the revel — all this he felt to be a moral impossibility.

An irruption of waiters with trays, and the bustle that followed, aroused him from his brown study. He did what he saw the others do — led his allotted partner to a seat, sat himself down beside her, and —

Don't shut the book, fair reader, in fearful expectation of our being about to shock your feelings. If anything improper took place at the convivial board, neither Paolo nor the muse of his historiographer — a teetotaller muse, by the way, and one who wears high dresses — know anything of it. For no sooner had Paolo dropped into his chair, than he had an inspiration — yes, a positive inspiration as to how effectually to isolate himself from his surroundings. He deliberately gulped down a glass of Madeira, then a second, a third, and a fourth, and being little used to libations, was out of harm's way, that is, dead drunk, before the initiatory oysters were disposed of; and had to be removed from the room, conveyed to his entresol, consigned to his bed, and left to the care of his portress. A headache of three days' duration, and, if possible, a greater horror than ever of that particular kind of orgies, into which he had been entrapped — such were for Paolo the immediate results of his having made one at the bachelor's supper. It was, unluckily, destined to have some further consequences.

Pique and champagne are dangerous counsellors. Mdlle. Celina, of the opera ballet corps, was brimful, at all events, of the first, and must, and would have her revenge. In what had Paolo offended her? Paolo had done more than spurn, revile, trample her under foot; blessed with the promise of her society, he had, to get quit of her, wilfully parted with his own reason, making her thus a butt for the quizzing of the whole party. There was no room for the shadow of a doubt; for Du Genre, who saw no cause why he should keep

his convictions secret, frankly declared his belief that
Paolo's intoxication was an intentional, predetermined
act.   His sober, nay abstemious habits, together with
the fulminating character of the drunken fit, left room
for no other explanation.

And so it came to pass that the spiteful little imp
hatched a plot against the poor absent youth, and then
and there chalked it out before her wine-heated com-
peers — amid frantic acclamations and promises of unconditional support, more especially from Du Genre,
whose patronage was regarded as peculiarly necessary
to the success of the scheme.

Du Genre, and most likely the other men, had forgotten all about Mdlle. Celina and her projects by the
morrow, but Mdlle. Celina had an excellent memory.
A few days after, in fact, when her preparations for
action were complete, the piquant young lady, with the
well-cut eyes, and cherry-round lips, paid Du Genre an
unexpected visit; she came to summon him to redeem
the pledge of assistance he had given. Du Genre would
rather that his pretty friend had not asked this, but
he did not dare to withdraw from his engagement. He
had promised — he well recollected having done so —
and must abide by his word. Men have sometimes odd
notions of duty. I have known some who never paid
their tailor's bill, hold a gambling debt sacred, and
starve themselves to meet it. On the other hand, Du
Genre reflected that, after all, little was asked of him
— very little — merely to furnish a few indications of
Paolo's where-abouts and habits, and he gave them.
Paolo greatly frequented the Boulevard des Italiens,
drove or rode almost daily to the Bois de Boulogne,
and had just taken the stall No. 22 at the "Italiens"

for the season. After all, philosophized the Frenchman, since Telemachus must needs go through his
apprenticeship and pay for it sooner or later — as well
with a Mdlle. Clarisse as with any other.

Mademoiselle Clarisse, the intimate friend of Miss
Celina, and who was to act for the latter in this affair,
was a *lionne* of some renown. She had walked the
boards professionally, and could personate all characters
to the life, both on and off the stage,. but her triumph
was in that of the *Ingenue*. Sentiment was her *forte:*
to see her gaze pensively before her, as she would often
do for mere frolic, her head slightly bent forward, her
chin reclining on the palm of her hand, her cheek
against her stretched-out forefinger, was to see the
image of an Ophelia. Nature had blundered in Mademoiselle Clarisse; given the outward distinction, the
reserve, the dignity of a Lucretia, to a humbug.

A few evenings later, Paolo was in his stall at the
"Italiens." The *Somnambula* was the opera; he knew
it by heart, and yet he was all eyes and ears. Who
can ever have enough of the *Somnambula?* Everything
about it — the story, music, and feelings — so simple,
so true, so fresh. Paolo's soul swam in a bath of
delight. At the end of "*Cari luoghi,*" a few exclama-
tions of unmitigated enthusiasm drew his attention from
the stage to those about him; on his right sat a lady
of the age of chaperones, and by her one of the age of the
chaperoned, both of whom, but especially the younger,
seemed to enjoy the performance keenly. The latter
had positively big tears in her lovely eyes. Paolo was
charmed to see his own emotion shared by others, and
naturally felt an interest in those doing so. The ladies
were richly but simply and soberly dressed; the fea-

túres of the elder one were rather commonplace; those of the younger, fine, noble, even haughty, had they not been softened by her present emotion. Her pure white complexion, hazel eyes, and acorn-hued hair, gave to her beauty that subdued and mellow tone, so dear to poetic dreamers; rather suggestive of violets and moonlight, than of sunshine and roses. Paolo could discern about her eyes and temples traces of early suffering; or, of late hours and hard libations, as the case might be. But he only thought of the former.

Occasional remarks were interchanged between him and the elderly lady, his immediate neighbour, but the younger did not join in the conversation, though her eyes and his met often in sympathetic communion. She addressed him once though, and in this way: He overheard her whisper to her *chaperone* that *he* must be an Italian. Paolo looked at her, and smiled assent, when she suddenly leaned forwards, seemingly incapable of controlling the impulse, saying to him, —

"I was certain of it, only an Italian can feel this music as you do."

Then she blushed scarlet, and said no more for the evening.

When Mario sang *Il piu tristo dei mortali*, the sentimental lady fairly gave way and sobbed aloud; she knew it was very foolish, but she could not help it. It was all Paolo could do not to follow her example. The curtain fell, too soon for Paolo's pleasure; the ladies withdrew, not without a gentle inclination of the head to the stranger, who bowed low and even sighed, as the lovely vision disappeared. How long it was, since he had sat at such a feast! Here was a woman worth knowing and caring for! What a soul she had! Ten to one he should never meet her again in this Babylon of Paris; though, perhaps, they might come again to hear Bellini's masterpiece. Whether they did or not, a sweet recollection was his, nobody could rob him of that; and his thoughts rested long and fondly on the fresh oasis he had discovered.

Apparently it was written somewhere, that he should have something more substantial than recollection to feed upon. The next day but one — what a piece of luck! — he met her most unexpectedly in the Bois de Boulogne. She was in an open carriage — the weather being uncommonly fine and mild for the season — looking passively before her, her head slightly bent forwards, in short, in the *pose* that we already know of. Du Genre's tilbury and her *coupé* brushed past each other; the hazel eyes met the black eyes. Paolo blushed and bowed.

"Heyday," cried Du Genre; "it seems that we have been making fine acquaintances."

Paolo, who had kept his adventure to himself, now made a clean breast of it, and did so with a warmth of tone and feeling, which gave the Frenchman quite a qualm of conscience. He pursed up his lips, and answered, —

"As a general rule, never take the measure of a woman's sensibility from the tears she may shed in public. Some women look beautiful in tears, and they know it."

"Nonsense; hers gushed from her very soul," averred the enthusiast.

"Are you sure she has such a thing as that? Plato denied souls to women."

"Then Plato was a fool; and you have a perverse pre-determination to depreciate all that is exalted."

"Holy patience!" cried Du Genre. "I disclaim any blacker purpose than to put you on your guard."

"This is, indeed, quite a new sort of mission you have undertaken; hitherto, you have rather endeavoured to throw me off my guard."

"True enough," said Du Genre; "but then, it was with a view to something defined — it is the vague, the unknown, that scares me for you."

A little opposition was just the ingredient wanting to give zest to the pursuit. Du Genre's disparaging hints had no other effect than that of raising the owner of the hazel eyes. That a materialist of Du Genre's calibre, should misjudge, nay feel an instinctive antipathy to her, where could be a clearer proof of her superior nature?

Paolo returned to the Bois on horseback — alone; gazed at her, raised his hat, sighed, but kept at a respectful distance. Encouragement came in the shape of an embroidered handkerchief, inadvertently dropped; he dismounted, picked it up, returned it to the fair owner, and withdrew. This was provoking discretion on his part — the fine weather could not last for ever. On the morrow, the fairy was suddenly seized by an immoderate wish for a walk in a solitary alley — by a strange coincidence Mr. Mancini happened to be passing at the moment, he stopped irresolute — a smile and a glance invited him to dare. He alighted, tied his horse to a tree, and joined the lady with such a beating heart. She did not look offended, thank God — spoke of the charms of solitude — there was nothing like nature. Could he sketch or paint? A little; he said, but not landscape. Was he acquainted with Troyon's pictures? they were so beautiful, so real — she possessed two of them. Did she really? he should so much like to see them. No; would he? as a rule she received no company — hers was a life of retirement; but for once she would make an exception. Her address was 101, Rue Breda, if he dropped in some day after one o'clock, he should be shown her two gems.

He went, und was ushered by a man in livery into a small but gorgeously fitted apartment — soft carpets, and endless mirrors. Madame received him in her boudoir — in her pensive *pose*. How stupid of her to have forgotten that she had sent her Troyons to have new frames. He had actually come for nothing. For nothing! when he enjoyed the blessing of her presence. Time flew on its swiftest pinions in her society. She was full of enthusiasm about all that was grand and noble, Italy, of course, included. She was a widow, had had her affections horribly trifled with — believed men to be invariably false and fickle. Such was the precious information gathered on his first visit.

A second and a third followed — then came a full stop. Madame de Saint Victor was not at home; was not to be met at the Bois — the weather had veered to rain und mud — nor yet was she to be seen at the Italian Opera. Poor Paolo was a living image of disappointment. What could be the meaning of this eclipse of his sun? The explanation was vouchsafed in the following note left with her porter one morning.

"DEAR SIR, —

"Pray, do not call any more. My door is shut against you by *my* orders. To no living man but your-

self, would I condescend to account for any of my
actions. I am sure you will feel for me, and not mis-
understand me, when I say that the course I have
adopted is the only one consistent with my future peace.
I have been too cruelly wrecked on the sea of passion
to venture on it again. Do not think me bold when I
am only frank. I wish to see you *once* more — when
and where I have not yet decided; but not here, in my
own house. Farewell till then.

"C. de S. V."

Every syllable of this rigmarole, down to the very
dashes, and pallid-hued sealing wax, wrought the young
recipient up to white heat. Paolo took to staying much
at home, he expected a second note, which would fix
the time and place of the heavenly *last* interview, and
was in mortal fear lest it might reach him too late to
allow of his obeying the summons. Paolo's fancy at
its utmost stretch did not go beyond a letter.

One morning he was poring over a letter just received from Rome, in which his man of business informed him that no cheque for a thousand scudi had
been presented by Signor Angelo Gigli, and that he
had moreover ascertained, that that person was no
longer in Rome — his present abode no one knew.
Where the deuce can Salvator be? was Paolo thinking
to himself, when a great pull at the bell startled him.
He went to open the door and lo! there *she* was. His
heart alone told him it was her, for the thick folds of
her black veil quite concealed her features. She walked
past him into the salon, there with trembling hands
raised her veil, and showed him the adored face, ashy
white with emotion.

"Oh! what have I done! What must you think of me!" and with this cry of despair, she threw herself on the sofa in an agony of tears. Paolo dropped on one knee, and wiped away her tears with his lips. Celina was revenged.

The Boulevard knew Paolo no more for the next ten days. Vague reports to the effect that he had been met with at Fontainebleau, and at St. Germains accompanied by a lady, reached Du Genre, who, pushing his inquiries further, learned that his Roman friend had hired a small *pied-à-terre* in the Avenue Montaigne, together with a carriage and men-servants. Du Genre felt uneasy, and grew still more so, when unexpectedly called upon by the Italian, at the request he received, and the excited manner in which it was made. Paolo wanted five thousand francs within three hours. Du Genre had not the sum himself, but hoped he could manage to find it — at the same time, he could not help hinting at the danger of raising money. Paolo winced and said bitterly, he rather expected to have been congratulated than remonstrated with. Was he not making a fool of himself, just what his friends had wished him to do from the first. Du Genre's conscience smote him, and in his heart he wished Miss Celina at the devil. He would willingly have made a full confession, but he saw that Paolo was in no state to listen to anything like reason — and then — to what purpose now. The evil was done, and could not be undone.

The required money was had, but not without difficulty. Paolo gave his note of hand for the sum at a month's date, six per cent. interest being guaranteed per month. The five thousand francs were equally

11*

divided between Miss Celina and Clarisse. There's
nothing like honesty in trade.

We have at least this consoling intelligence from
Paolo's own lips, that he knew he was making a fool
of himself; let us add for our own satisfaction that three
weeks had not gone by, before he also knew that he
was being made a fool of by quondam Mdlle. Clarisse.
She was not the woman long to play an uncongenial
part to please anybody, and her inherent tastes for
champagne, extravagant dress, and bank notes asserted
their existence little by little, and then blazed forth the
more vigorously for their momentary repression. In
short, Paolo saw much, endured much that jarred with
his nature, endured it, partly from timidity and a scarcely
conscious desire not to write himself down an ass so
soon, partly also from the base spell which held him
captive. But endurance has limits even for a man —
bewitched. Among the host of male and female cou-
sins, with whom she had made him acquainted, there
was a young scapegrace, particularly offensive to him
on account of his coarse manners, and unbecoming tone
of familiarity with her. Paolo asked Mdlle. Clarisse
one day to forbid this fellow's visits, and received a
flat refusal. Paolo insisted and said she *must*. To hear
her laughter at this! She improved the occasion to let
him hear a bit of her mind. To oblige a dear friend,
she had condescended to act a little comedy with Signor
Mancini, she said; but not for twenty, such as he was,
would she give up her Désiré — the cousin on whom
she doated.

Paolo was confounded by her cynicism, at the parade she made of her own deceit, at the naïve pride
she evinced in her own infamy. He left her to see her

no more. But thoroughly as he despised her, he despised himself still more — for missing her as he did. Yes, he missed her — or rather missed the excitement that followed in her footsteps. Not knowing how to fill up the vacuum she had left in his life, he took to haunting the public balls — the carnival was just then at its height. A very handsome man such as he was, and known in certain quarters to be rich and generous, Paolo was offered consolation, and accepted it, accepted it without illusion, and for what it was worth.

Let us turn aside from viewing him wallowing in this mire. Who knows but that from his own debasement, he may leave a lesson of forbearance for the weaknesses of others!

CHAPTER XV.

A Plank of Safety.

BROUGHT back to consciousness and helped to her bed by the affrighted widow, who, on learning the cause of the young lady's distraction, kept on assuring her that Dr. Duncan could not have meant what she suspected him of, and that it was all a mistake which would be cleared up on the morrow, — Lavinia at last found relief in tears; and after indulging in a hearty fit of crying, she recovered something like composure and begged to be left alone — to sleep. Not that she entertained the least hope of sleeping, but she had reached that stage of wretchedness, at which even sympathy becomes importunate, and complete solitude is the only boon craved for.

In this desolate mood she turned her misery round

and round, looking at it from every side, and mused and mused upon it till her head grew quite bewildered, and her thoughts ungovernable; and feeling greatly afraid of her own excitement, she bethought herself of the Word which never fails to calm, and soothe, and comfort. She took up a New Testament lying on her dressing-table — a gift from Lady Augusta's mother — it opened of itself at these words: "Come unto me, all ye that labour and are heavy laden, and I will give you rest. Take my yoke upon you, and learn of me, for I am meek and lowly in heart, and ye shall find *rest unto* your souls. For my yoke is easy, and my burden is light."

She read long, and as she read the whiz and buzz in her brain subsided, a sense of repose stole alike over soul and body. Hoping to be able to sleep now, she put down the book, and in so doing caused a slip of paper to drop from it on the floor. She took it up, it was a card, on the back of which were written in pencil these words: "Ask, and it shall be given you; seek, and ye shall find; knock, and it shall be opened unto you." The quotation was in the large bold angular handwriting of Lady Augusta's mother. On the other side of the card was engraved in minute characters — "Countess Willingford." The merciful sentence endorsed as it were by the countess, struck Lavinia as a prompting from heaven. The very voice of Lady Augusta's mother seemed to call to her and say, "Ask and it shall be given you." Why had Lavinia not asked of her old friend? It would have been so natural to have done so from the very beginning of her troubles. Had it been some lurking pride, which had held her back? If so, reason the more to humble herself now.

Lavinia rose from her bed, and wrote a long better to the countess, describing all her attempts and failures; the utter sinking of her heart but a few hours ago; and related the circumstance under which her hopes and her confidence in her, whom she was now addressing, had revived; freely accused herself of ingratitude, and begged to be pardoned; acknowledged her readiness to accept of even the humblest situation, and the impossibility in which she stood of procuring any, unless a word from one so high in station as her ladyship, came to the assistance of her own efforts. This and much more that we leave out, Lavinia wrote, signing herself Lavinia Holywell. This outpouring of pent-up feelings lightened the heavily-burdened young heart; she slept a sound refreshing sleep, and rose next morning with renewed elasticity of spirit and body. Her first act was to drop her letter into the box of the nearest post-office.

At nearly four o'clock of the same day, a hackney coach stopped opposite Mrs. Tamplin's, and a tall lady, whose age and countenance were concealed by a thick veil, stepping out of it, knocked at the door, and in a clear voice asked for Miss Holywell. At the sound of the well-known tones, Lavinia rushed from her room to meet the visitor, and —

Let it be understood that Lady Willingford had started on her present mission, very much in the mood of an old diplomatist going to take a part at a congress; namely, in a spirit full of reservation on many a point. The mystery she had made of Lavinia's letter to her daughter, the hired coach, the rather shabby attire, and the closely-drawn down veil, were all so many guarantees to herself of a pre-determination to keep strictly within certain limits braced by prudence — to go so far, and no farther. But at sight of the sweet pale face — oh! how much changed since last seen — at the sound of sobs which involuntarily broke from the stooping form — at the feeling of the hot tears on her hands, the woman swallowed up the countess; and raising the humbly bent face to her own, she pressed the poor girl to her heaving bosom with a tenderness which, had Lavinia been the daughter of the mightiest duke in Great Britain, instead of the friendless orphan she was, would certainly not have been warmer or more sincere.

"Here I am, your old friend! Let us have done with tears," said her ladyship, her own voice choked by emotion.

"It is not grief," sobbed the girl, smiling amid her tears.

"What you must have gone through, my poor child," said the countess, taking a long look at Lavinia's haggard countenance. "Augusta and I have been really alarmed by your obstinate silence. Every day for these last three months have we been expecting and hoping to hear again from you. My dear, why did you not write?"

"I was wrong, very wrong," and again Lavinia's tears began to flow.

"Come, come, I do not mean to scold you."

"Oh yes, do scold me, pray do. It was so ungrateful, so heartless of me; I deserve that you should be angry."

"Well, if it will be any comfort to you," said the countess smiling, "I shall call you a very naughty child," and a hearty kiss softened this not very sharp rebuke.

"And now that my scolding is over," continued Lady Willingford, whose own usual composure had by this time returned, "let me praise you for the care you took to spare Augusta's feelings; it was so sensible, so considerate in you to write to me and not to her. Charming as your letter is, there is much in it that might have pained one of her quick sensibility; that is the reason why I have kept it from her for the present: you must not consider it as an unkindness."

"Oh! Lady Willingford, could I ever think you unkind? No, indeed; whatever you decide to be best for me, I shall believe to be best."

"Thank you, my dear," said the countess, much pleased; "however, do not imagine that I purpose long to deprive her of the good news that our Lavinia is found — only for a few days — until I see my way as to how I can best be of use to you. To speak frankly, I rather fear being hampered by Augusta in my measures, she is so hasty and vehement. Of course, I expect and wish you both to meet — how glad she will be to see you — previous to your leaving London, as you say you wish to do. We shall discuss this plan of yours by-and-by, but first will you not give me your entire confidence that I may be able fairly to judge whether there is no choice for you, except this extreme one of being either a governess or companion?"

Lavinia was quite ready to confide in Lady Willingford. Not a single particular of the sad narrative related by Mr. Jones was withheld from the eager listener, who now learned how the real Lavinia Jones had died when a baby, how, in a sordid view of gain, the little Lavinia Holywell had been substituted in the deceased infant's place; and how, to ease her conscience, one of the accomplices in the fraud, Lavinia's mother, had sent for Mr. Jones and made a full confession to him. Nor was the squalor of the dying woman's condition, nor the fact of her being unmarried, passed over in silence, but simply and unhesitatingly stated.

Peremptorily as all this established the absence of any relationship between Lavinia and Mr. Jones, it still left unaccounted for and unjustified the extreme step she had taken in breaking of all intercourse with him. Pressed on this point, Lavinia said for all answer, —

"Indeed, I had no alternative but to do so."

The countess must have had in her disposition some of her daughter's impetuosity, so emphatically did she exclaim, —

"The villain!"

"He wanted me to marry him," added Lavinia, who saw the expediency of correcting the erroneous impression she had given.

"Oh! the old wretch," said her ladyship, by way of variation.

The ground was now clear for taking into consideration Lavinia's future prospects. They afforded indeed little room for discussiou; the necessity of some situation, which should assure Lavinia the means of existence, and the desirableness of finding such a one in the country, where there would be less risk for her of disagreeable meetings, stared her ladyship in the face. She accordingly promised to set about this search immediately, and bade her *protégée* be of good cheer. The countess had too much good sense and good feeling, and was, besides, too deeply impressed by the girl's gentle dignity, to venture on any offer which would have made Lavinia dependent on her bounty.

"We shall find some snug home for you after all, where you may enjoy comfort, even happiness," said Lady Willingford. "Station and riches, believe me," and here came a sigh, "do not always secure either; it is the spirit in which we accept our lot, great or humble, which renders it a happy or unhappy one."

The parting was as affectionate as the meeting had been. Patroness and patronized might have been easily mistaken for mother and daughter, so tender was the former, so dutiful and confiding the latter.

Kind and encouraging notes, and little presents, after this red-letter day, began to pour in on the young recluse of Camden Town. Those best know the value of these priceless nothings, who have been long sequestered from all interchange of the small coin of courtesies. Be it only a bunch of violets, or an inquiry left with a card at your door, how sweet the assurance thus implied that you are something to somebody! The countess herself came now and then. Doubly lucky was it for Lavinia to have this fresh supply of sympathy from abroad, for scanty indeed was that she met just now at home.

Mrs. Tamplin's milk of human kindness, we are very sorry to say, had waxed rather sour ever since the impeachment of her matchless surgeon. Mr. Duncan was the widow's last illusion, the only sunny spot in her mental perspective, and no wonder she clung to him with the tenacity of despair. His right to be heard and explain, which she was sure he could do most satisfactorily, was as clear in the eyes of the landlady as was in those of her lodger the utter uselessness, nay, the positive degradation, of anything like an argument with a man who had so indubitably insulted her. This

contrary point of view, in spite of all Lavinia's efforts
to divest her opposition of any asperity, could not but
create between the two parties concerned a little jarring,
which the jealousy fermenting in Mrs. Tamplin's breast
all this while did not tend to allay. How could she,
who had hitherto played the first part, not wince at
being reduced to the second?

Happily, this disagreeable state of affairs was not
to be of long continuance. When the powerful of this
world set their hearts on anything, it is rare but that
the realization should quickly follow the wish. Service-
ableness is certainly a virtue far from uncommon, but
never so effectually exercised as when they who draw
bills upon it can be drawn upon in their turn. A fortnight had scarcely elapsed from the day of the countess's
first visit to Lavinia, when a little note came to announce that the much-desired situation was found. Lady
Willingford put off all particulars till the morrow, when
she would call as early as eleven in the forenoon, and
Lavinia was desired to have her trunk packed, and to
be ready to accompany her friend — whither? The
note did not explain; probably to her new home; at
least our heroine argued as much from the circumstance
of being told that she was to be prepared to leave her
lodging.

She did not take long to pack. Her wardrobe had
dwindled to the smallest compass, and she might have
said, with the ancient philosopher: "I have all my be-
longings about me." The whole of this, her last day
under Mrs. Tamplin's roof, Lavinia spent in propitiating
that worthy matron, but for whose kindly advice, and
help, and motherly care, the grateful girl protested she
knew not indeed what might have become of her. Low-

spirited Mrs. Tamplin, who had no heart of stone, was quickly mollified, and ended by forgetting her grievance as to the charge against matchless Mr. Duncan. And when Lavinia pressed her to accept a simple ring, which she' begged Mrs. Tamplin to wear in remembrance of the good she had done to a poor friendless orphan girl, the widow was fairly conquered, and the two amicably mingled their tears; that great luxury of rich and poor alike.

By ten minutes past eleven the next morning, Lavinia was driving with Lady Willingford to the station, from whence they were to go by railway to her lady-ship's country seat near Southampton, where Lady Augusta was impatiently waiting for them. Fancy our dear girl's agreeable surprise at this prospect, when she had been thinking she was to go directly to the family who had engaged her! On the contrary, it had been arranged that she was to spend three days with the countess and Lady Augusta, and to start on the fourth to join Mrs. Ennerly, the lady whose companion she was to be. Mrs. Ennerly was just now, and would be till after Christmas, at her country house, near Moreton in Dorsetshire, and she had desired that Miss Holywell should come to her there; but Weymouth might more probably be considered Lavinia's ultimate destination, as it was in that watering-place that Mrs. Ennerly resided the chief part of the year. She was a person of good family and fortune, and, Lady Willingford had been assured on all sides, also of very kindly disposition and not difficult to please. She was passionately fond of poetry and music; and reading aloud, and playing and singing would be the principal duties exacted from her companion. Fifty pounds a year was

the salary agreed on, considered as a tolerably fair re-
muneration out of London. Altogether, the countess
hoped that the situation was one to suit her young
friend; if not, Lavinia had only a word to say, and
another should be sought out for her. Lady Willingford also exacted a promise, that no notions of false
delicacy should prevent her young friend from frankly
confessing if she were uncomfortable. Lavinia must
learn to trust her friends. Lavinia gave the required
promise, fervently kissing the white hand held up in
playful menace, and said simply, —

"Good bless you, Lady Willingford!" words spoken
in a way that made the object of that blessing feel
really blessed.

If we were to say that Lady Willingford did not
feel a little nervous on reaching the station, and that
the five minutes she had to spend in the waiting-room
did not seem very long to her, we should say that
which is untrue. It was only too probable, well known
as she was on the road they were about to travel, that
she might meet some one she knew, and be asked
questions inconvenient to answer, as to her lovely companion. However, the train departed, and in due time
deposited the travellers safely at Southampton, without
her ladyship's incognito having been once endangered.

Though the beginning of December, the weather
was uncommonly clear and fine, and the forty minutes'
drive from Southampton to Willingford Castle was more
keenly enjoyed by Lavinia than any drive she had ever
taken. After long seclusion in dreary, foggy London,
every picturesque spot, every patch of green, every
glossy-leafed holly, were welcomed by her as old friends
lost and found again. But how her heart fluttered, and

how dim grew her sparkling eyes, when they caught sight, far up the long avenue of stately oaks, of a lovely, familiar figure tripping quickly towards them! The carriage stopped at the sound of a sweet voice, calling to her joyously by name; she jumped out to find herself clasped in the arms or her dear faithful friend, Lady Augusta.

Let us be as discreet as the countess, and leave the young people to an uninterrupted three days' *tête-à-tête*. Lavinia had, as we know, plenty to relate, and it is easy to fancy the one rehearsing the eventful history of the period of their separation, the other building castles for the future. We all live chiefly on memory and hope; the present, a fugitive point no sooner possessed than gone, occupies but little room in the flying mirage of life. On this we may rely, that amid the evocations of the past, the days at Rome, and true-hearted Domenichino, were not forgotten on one side, as was not, on the other, among the anticipations of the future, the hope of a speedy and long reunion at Weymouth. Weymouth would be a far more agreeable place to go to than Brighton.

Perhaps Lavinia might have been inclined to shake her head a little disconsolately at this anticipation; perhaps she might even have spoken out some of her fears; but at sight of a sweet mouth beginning to droop, kept her wisdom to herself, and even paraded a confidence as to their meeting, which she did not feel. What was the use, in fact, of throwing cold water on illusions originating in the warmest affections? Surely enough, the realities of life would assert themselves in due time, and dispel all such fond dreams.

Lady Augusta's preoccupations as to the future,

however, did not blind her to some of the urgent ne-
cessities of the present. She had detected at a glance,
insufficiencies in her friend's wardrobe, glaring enough
indeed to attract the notice of less friendly eyes, and
immediately set to work to supply what was wanted
with what she had best of her own. With so much
delicacy was this done, that not even the most irritable
susceptibility could have been wounded. Lady Augusta
must have Lavinia dressed like herself, as they used
often to be in former days, and under this pretext a
black dress and cloak were procured from Southampton.
Lavinia must have furs like Lady Augusta.

"And now," said her young ladyship, "if you don't
captivate Mrs. Ennerly, she must have the heart of the
dragon that attacked Andromeda; though, after all,"
she added, fondly, "you would look charming with a
brass pan on your head; unlike some other people, not
a hundred miles away, who require fine feathers to be
fine birds."

How could Lavinia have refused any gifts so offered?
She was almost as happy to receive as Lady Augusta
to give.

Longer than a three days' meeting comes to a close.
Early on the fourth morning since her arrival at the
castle, mother and daughter accompanied Lavinia to
the Southampton station. Sad and silent was the drive,
sad and silent the ten minutes spent at the terminus.
The countess placed in Lavinia's hand a handsomely
embroidered purse, and said hurriedly, —

"Keep it in remembrance of me; it is my own
work, and I had meant it for Augusta; I know it will
be doubly precious to you on that account. There is
a little money in it, which you must not refuse, as it

will make my mind easy about you. I am only treating you as I would my daughter; it is requisite always in travelling to be prepared for unforeseen contingencies.

Lavinia took the purse, kissed it, and the hand which bestowed it, but did not venture to speak.

By this time the warning bell rang. The two girls fell into each other's arms, holding one another in a long, long embrace.

"Oh! must it be really so?" cried Lady Augusta, with an appealing glance at her mother.

"It must," said Lavinia, firmly, "because it is plainly the will of God. He knows best, who cast my lot among the lowly; and my clear duty is to accept my portion humbly and cheerfully; help me to do so, dearest. God bless you, Lady Willingford! God bless you, my own dàrling!" And Lavinia was hurried from the platform into a carriage.

Oh, fatal platform! how many dramas, not the less heart-rending for being compressed into a few minutes, have you not seen!

CHAPTER XVI.

The Rose Unique.

LAVINIA, as she took her seat in the carriage, let down her veil, and — We have had so much of the melting mood in our last chapter, that we dare not say what she did. After all, it is not our fault if, dealing as we do with the realities of life, we stumble oftener on tears than on smiles. It is not, we should say, without good reason that the world has been styled "a valley of tears."

Whatever Lavinia's occupation on first entering the
carriage, she was soon roused from it by the novelty
and responsibility of her situation. The mere fact of
finding herself travelling alone amid strangers, on her
way to an unknown place, a fact unprecedented in her
life, was sufficient to inspire her with some vague uneasiness, and keep her nervously awake to the present,
without taking into account the incubus of her luggage
to look after, and the dread of passing Wareham; the
station at which, being bound for Moreton, she had
been told she would have to change carriages. Suppose
she were to be carried on, and find herself at Exeter,
what would become of her! Such preoccupations, ridiculous as they may seem to practised travellers, did
not weigh the less heavily on the mind of one so
thoroughly unpractised and unpractical — and how
could she be otherwise — as our poor heroine?

However, all went smooth with her; when Wareham
was reached, passengers for Moreton were warned
audibly enough, God knows, to alight; and she had the
further satisfaction of seeing her trunk safely deposited
in the luggage van of the train for Moreton. Much
eased in her mind, Lavinia had leisure to feel hungry;
she ventured into the refreshment room, and bought
some buns, and, searching out an empty carriage, got
in, ensconced herself in a corner seat, and amused
herself with watching the coming and going of passengers.

One in particular attracted her notice, a lady of
middle height, who was carrying a flower-pot large
enough to require her to use both hands. Had it been
a baby, the lady could not have hugged her burden

more carefully and tenderly against her bosom. The railway porters vied with each other as to who should free her of her flower-pot; but she defended it against all officious offers, with as much determination as graciousness. There is no surer conductor of sympathy between gentle natures, than the care bestowed upon gentle and delicate things, be they even inanimate. Lavinia felt an interest in this lady, and followed her movements with kindly curiosity. She saw her stand still to speak to one of the officials, and for an instant obliged to take her right hand from her charge, in order to receive a newspaper this person presented to her; he, standing all the while with uncovered head, in spite of her signing to him repeatedly to put on his cap. "A lady of consequence, unassuming withal and most good-natured," thought Lavinia, as the object of her survey was moving forward in quest of a carriage. "How I wish she would come in here!" The wish was scarcely formed before it was gratified. The stranger installed herself in the corner opposite to Lavinia.

"Is it not beautiful? a real rose unique," said the new comer, in answer to the glance of admiration cast on her roses by her *vis-à-vis*; "they smell so sweet too," and saying this, she held them towards Lavinia.

"Thank you — they are delicious," said Lavinia, burying her face in them; "they are doubly beautiful so late in the year."

"Yes, I managed to preserve them in bloom, by keeping them in the greenhouse," added the lady, placing the flowers on the bottom of the carriage in order to be at liberty to unfold *The Times*. She turned the enormous paper over and over, evidently in search

of something special, which having found, she began
earnestly to read. Her attention, however, was speedily
diverted from her perusal, for, the train being now in
motion, the flower-pot danced about most ominously.
She tried first to steady it by the help of her feet, then
put it on the seat by her, then finally took it in her
lap; but this last device interfered terribly with her
reading: the unruly flower-pot requiring one hand to
make it maintain its perpendicular, the other proved
sadly insufficient to manage the huge printed sheet.
Seeing this, Lavinia begged that the care of the rose
might be confided to her; a proposal which was
naturally objected to on the plea of the trouble it
would give, but Lavinia assured her it would be no
trouble.

"I really should be glad to be of some use to
you," she said, and so feelingly, almost entreatingly,
that the other, with a look of pleased surprise, gave up
her perplexing charge, and returned to the perusal of
her paper.

Meanwhile, Lavinia was studying the sweet little
face before her. It was still young and pretty, but its
charm lay 'elsewhere than in youth and loveliness.
Sprinkle with grey the auburn hair as much as you
like, and print with wrinkles the soft transparent skin,
and yet the suavity of expression which comes from
within would remain the same, and go straight to your
heart. It was one of those faces which do good to
look at, inasmuch as they convey at once an impression of moral worth, and win immediate confidence.
There was something of quaker-like simplicity in the
make and material of her dress: a gray gown, a dark
waterproof cloak, and a gray beaver bonnet; the snow-

white border of a closely fitting cap, with no ribbon or ornament whatever, giving to the pure oval of the face a somewhat austere grace. Lavinia was greatly puzzled by this cap, which had nothing of the character of what is styled a bonnet cap, but resembled a mob cap, singularly unsuited to the age of the wearer. Was it worn in obedience to some hygienic prescription, or in a spirit of renunciation of the vanities of this life? Really, the wearer seemed to attach so little importance to personal appearance, that this second hypothesis was not unlikely. And if so, what could have detached one so young and good-looking from the world? Do what we will, there are countenances about which we cannot help speculating, nay, having an irresistible longing to know the history of their owner. Lavinia would have given a good deal to know something about her fair travelling companion — would have also given a little to know the subject and kind of interest which fixed her attention so engrossingly to the newspaper.

That the interest, whatever it might be, was of a painful nature, was evidenced by the cloud which overspread the reader's fine features as she read on. At one moment, she changed her posture, with a sudden jerk, as if to give vent by physical motion to the pressure of inner feelings. Presently the lips drooped, and from that moment the tide of anxious emotion flowed continually, until at last it overpowered the reader, who, letting the paper fall on her knees, leaned back, and shut her eyes like one in bodily pain.

"I hope you have not seen any bad news?" asked Lavinia, kindly, when her *vis-à-vis'* eyes opened again and encountered her own.

"Dreadful!" replied the lady, and without another word, she handed over the paper to the inquirer, laying her finger on a certain passage. It formed part of a correspondence, headed "Siege of Sebastopol," and told a heart-rending tale of multiform misery — snow, rain, hurricane, cholera, wrecks; tents blown down, or no better shelter from the inclemency of the weather than so many sieves; trenches turned into ditches of mud; sick soldiers driven out of the hospital marquee by the winds, seeking refuge in sheds, shivering and moaning; able-bodied men killed by cold and wet, or dying by scores of disease — a scene of utter desolation. The mere description made Lavinia's heart bleed; the sad picture took her by surprise. Too busy with her needle for months past to read the newspaper herself, never told by her general informant of the world's disasters, of these Crimean sufferings, which apparently were not in Mrs. Tamplin's line, all that she knew about the great contemporary event was, that England and Russia were at war, and that the seat of that war was in the Crimea.

In a voice of anguish, she exclaimed, —

"Can nothing be done for these poor creatures?"

"What can avail against the elements?" replied the lady, with a despairing shake of the head.

"But why is it more impossible to house the soldier now than in other wars?"

"We know little of the details of other wars, whereas one of the features of this age, is the information we have of all that is going on at a distance; however, huts are now building in England to be sent out to the Crimea, and some have been sent already. Charity is astir throughout the land, large sums are being subscribed, quantities of clothes and medicine-chests are preparing, bands of nurses for the sick and wounded are already gone, and more will soon follow."

"God bless them," said Lavinia, "that is indeed the highest charity. May anyone go as nurse who wishes to do so?"

"Yes, I believe so; that is, any one who is not only willing, but strong. Surely you must have heard of Miss —," and here the speaker pronounced the sweetest name of our century, a name which future generations will record with benedictions, even when those of the conquerors of the Crimea are forgotten. Yet Lavinia had never heard of it.

"Is it possible!" exclaimed the other; "a name which is on every tongue."

"Mine has been for some time past a very retired life," pleaded Lavinia, in extenuation of what seemed her unpardonable ignorance.

"I understand," answered the lady, with a compassionate glance at Lavinia's black dress, and then she proceeded to give her eager listener a full account of that "angel in human shape," to use the relator's enthusiastic words, who had initiated the female crusade of mercy, and who had herself gone at their head to the east.

Amid such interesting talk, Moreton was reached, and the two ladies alighted.

"Can I be of any use to you?" asked the owner of the roses, as she took back her flower-pot.

"Thank you," said Lavinia; "perhaps you can tell me how best to reach the house I am going to — Ivy Lodge."

"Ivy Lodge?" repeated the lady in gray, in a

voice of pleased surprise. "I am going there myself, I am Mrs. Ennerly's niece."

"Are you? how glad I am. You have been so kind to me that I was really sorry to think we were going to part for ever."

"No chance of that, for the present at least, you see; since we are both bound to the same place, we will go there together. Are you going to pay my aunt a long visit?"

"The time I stay will entirely depend on Mrs. Ennerly's pleasure," answered Lavinia.

"Surely, you cannot be Miss Holywell?"

"Yes, indeed, I am the person engaged as companion to Mrs. Ennerly."

"I am very glad I have met you; you and I are old acquaintances, as it were, so that I can have the pleasure of introducing you to Mrs. Ennerly. Does she know that you are in mourning?"

"Really, I cannot tell," said Lavinia, a little surprised at this question; "I have had no communication myself with Mrs. Ennerly; a lady, a kind friend of mine, managed the business for me. Will my being in black be an objection against me?"

"I hope not; indeed, I am sure it cannot be; the first impression may not be agreeable, but one look at your face will set everything right. My aunt is an excellent woman, but rather over-partial to what is gay-looking."

"If so, my chances with the lady are small indeed," thought Lavinia, but she kept the thought to herself.

This dialogue, begun on the platform, had ended outside the Moreton station in front of some public conveyances, large and small, waiting there for fares.

Lavinia, as desired by her companion, followed her into one of these. Mrs. Ennerly's niece, to all appearance, was as well known here as at Warcham; no railway official passed her without lifting his cap, even the omnibus and fly-men behaved respectfully to her, and contrary to tradition, offered their services without the least trace of their habitual roughness. Little was spoken by either lady during the short drive. The approach of so decisive a moment for Lavinia, even without the hint that had been given as to the possible bad effect of her lugubrious garments, easily accounted for her abstraction. Neither was the current of thought of Mrs. Ennerly's niece difficult to guess, from the glances she bestowed now and then on the lovely girl by her side. She who had been the object of Lavinia's study, studied Lavinia in her turn with compassionate interest. What concatenation of circumstances could have brought one so evidently of the upper class to accept of the painful situation of a lady's companion? This was the enigma, the effort to solve which, kept Lavinia's fellow-traveller silent.

Ivy Lodge justified its name. The porch, and all that could be seen of the dwelling from the approach, was one mass of ivy. Ivy also covered the massive stone pillars on either side of the gate, and seemed to threaten with suffocation the two cat-like caricatures of lions which mounted guard on the tops. The sound of wheels brought out an old woman from the lodge at the gate, and a man-servant to the porch, while a person with a superlative cap loomed in the background of the entrance hall. Miss Schmaltz, Mrs. Ennerly's housekeeper, was a rather ill-favoured masculine specimen of German spinsterhood, whose immoderately

gaudy and huge caps were famous both in Dorchester
and Weymouth.

"Good morning, Miss Schmaltz, I hope you are
well; this is Miss Holywell whom my aunt, I suppose,
has told you to expect."

"I am quite well, thank you, Miss Clara, and much
obliged to you for your kind inquiries. What beautiful
roses you have got! Dear me, I believe they are the
rose Unique."

For her share of notice, Lavinia had only a stiff
curtsey, coupled with a formal inquiry if she had had
a good journey.

"How is my aunt?" asked Miss Clara, walking
towards one of the room doors. A large spaniel here
rushed upon the scene, nearly upsetting Lavinia, who
could not restrain a little scream, more of surprise than
of fright.

"Down, Turk, down," cried Miss Clara, seizing the
dog, now in a paroxysm of barking at the stranger;
"be quiet, Turk;" and she tried by mingled coaxing
and threatening to quiet him.

"Shall I fetch Miss Holywell a little hartshorn or
sal volatile?" asked Miss Schmaltz, with sarcastic
politeness.

Lavinia felt the intended sneer, but replied in a
propitiatory tone, "Oh, dear no, thank you; it was
very silly of me to be so startled, I am not in general
afraid of dogs."

This little incident had prevented Miss Clara's
inquiry about her aunt being answered. When they
were all three in the drawing-room, she asked again
for Mrs. Ennerly. Mrs. Ennerly was quite well, Miss

Schmaltz hoped and trusted, and at Exeter by this time.

"At Exeter?" cried Miss Clara.

"Yes, at Exeter, as I have the honour to tell you. Mrs. Ennerly got a letter yesterday, begging her to go at once to Exeter for the christening of her friend Lady Amelia's grandchild, which is fixed for to-morrow. It was settled some time ago, as you may recollect, Miss Clara, that Mrs. Ennerly was to be godmother, when the little one came, and Sir Timothy Livingston, of Holly Park, godpapa. Somehow or other, the ceremony is to take place sooner than had been first decided, and Mrs. Ennerly had to start this morning by the nine o'clock train; and, as it couldn't be helped, she desired me to say that she hoped Miss Holywell would excuse her absence."

"How long do you think my aunt will be away?" asked the niece.

"Mrs. Ennerly was not sure how long — three or four days — perhaps it might be a week."

"It is really provoking," murmured Miss Clara, "really provoking."

"Miss Holywell's room is ready for her," said the housekeeper. "Miss Holywell will be made as comfortable as I can make her; though," added she, with pinched lips, "of course I understand that a young lady will have but a dull time of it with an old woman like me."

Here was the sting again, the instinctive protest of a vulgar nature against the claims, felt, though unacknowledged, of a refined one. It went deep into poor Lavinia's heart, as her blanched cheeks and quivering lips testified. Nothing so entirely upsets inexperienced youth, as the marks of an hostility, that they cannot account for. Miss Clara observed all this, and made up her mind not to leave her new acquaintance alone, at the mercy of the jealous housekeeper. She accordingly said, —

"I have no doubt that you would make Miss Holywell very comfortable, and very happy, Miss Schmaltz, but it occurs to me that, since my aunt is away, I might just as well take the opportunity of doing now what must be done some day or other — I mean the introducing Miss Holywell to my sister. What do you say to going home with me, Miss Holywell?"

Lavinia had to put a strong curb on herself, not to betray, in a manner offensive to her fresh enemy, the immense relief afforded her by this proposal of her new friend. Instead, therefore, of giving way to a spontaneous outburst of joy, she expressed her thanks and willingness in what seemed to herself a very cool and commonplace way.

"Don't thank me yet, for I have an interested motive in asking you to come to our Hermitage for a few days," resumed Miss Clara, smiling, "which, like a postscript to a letter, though last is not least. The fact is, I have a quantity of needlework on hand, destined for the Crimea — a whole lot of flannel jackets to make, and I don't think you will refuse me your assistance."

Lavinia did not look as if disposed to refuse any aid Miss Clara might require, and so it was settled that the young ladies should start immediately to catch the two o'clock train for Wareham, which would enable them to reach Owlscombe, the name of Miss Clara's home, by four. At Miss Clara's desire, Miss Schmaltz ordered round Mrs. Ennerly's pony-chaise, hoped to see Miss Clara soon again at Ivy Lodge, and wished Miss Holywell, in a rather prim manner, a pleasant visit.

Miss Schmaltz was not really an ill-natured woman — the *personnel* of the household over which she ruled, and even most of the poor cottagers in the village, would have given her quite a different character. She was simply jealous and imperious, and might have well adopted as her motto the famous *parcere subjectis et debellare superbos*. Had Lavinia been a common-looking girl, arriving at Ivy Lodge alone, ten to one but that Miss Schmaltz would have patronized and befriended her; being, on the contrary, beautiful and unconsciously distinguished looking, and, to boot, already known to, and a favourite with, Mrs. Ennerly's niece, the new companion was endowed with all the requisites to be a successful rival, and must, therefore, be crushed. *Delenda Carthago*. We begin to tremble for the poor girl's situation at Ivy Lodge.

The return to Wareham, and the drive to Owlscombe did not take altogether more than an hour and a half. This time was not lost by our travellers in improving their acquaintance with one another. They had a good deal of talk upon different subjects, and unconsciously drew each other out, and to their mutual satisfaction. Though treated and addressed by Miss Clara on a footing of perfect equality, Lavinia never departed for a moment from that modest reserve of manner, which suited one in her inferior position.

Owlscombe was just what Lavinia, judging by Miss Clara, had fancied her home was likely to be; a modern, unpretending building, with nothing showy, or

even picturesque about it, but with a look of homely
simplicity, for those who could appreciate it, better felt
than described. Miss Clara led Lavinia to a small room
on the second floor, saying, —

"I give you twelve minutes, just time enough to
get ready for dinner, and not to take cold. A fire
shall be made while we are at dinner. I'll send you
your trunk directly."

CHAPTER XVII.

Owlscombo and its Inmates.

LAVINIA was received by the master and mistress of
Owlscombe, as if she had been an old acquaintance.
She saw at once that family union reigned supreme in
the house, and that she need have no fears that Mr. or
Mrs. Aveling should consider that her new friend had
taken any liberty in bringing her thither, an unexpected guest. Mrs. Aveling was fairer, taller, and some
years older than Clara, but in features and expression,
the sisters were the living portrait of each other. Mr.
Aveling was tall, swarthy, and gentlemanlike, with a
profusion of iron-grey hair tossed back, and falling in
weeping-willow fashion on both sides of his temples.
His forehead was high and broad, but furrowed; his
countenance fine and intellectual, but wanting in softness. Such, at least, was Lavinia's first impression,
an impression confirmed by his vehement manner of
speaking.

The topic of conversation was, naturally enough,
the hardships of the troops then besieging Sebastopol.
Mr. and Mrs. Aveling had evidently also read the cor-

respondence from the Crimea, which had so affected Miss Clara during the morning's journey. The women, like true women as they were, had no eyes nor feelings but for the fact, the heart-rending fact, that thousands of their fellow-creatures were suffering and perishing miserably far from their homes. To take their share of these sufferings, as it were, by a vivid representation of all their dire variety, and to devise methods how best to alleviate those which could be helped, and prevent their recurrence for the future — such was the circle out of which the sisters never for one moment strayed.

Mr. Aveling, on the contrary, true to the combative ingredient in his sterner sex, was less full of pity for the terrible suffering, than roused to wrath by what he believed to be the cause of it; and this cause, according to his judgment, was the utter want of forethought, nay, the gross neglect, of those he termed the red-tapists. If there be any truth in de adage of the tingling of ears when we are being evil spoken of, how must these gentlemen's ears have tingled at the loud denunciations of carelessness, incapacity, &c., which irate Mr. Aveling hurled at their heads. Above all, he would hear of no allowances being made.

"No one," he cried, "has any right to make allowances where the lives of our soldiers are at stake; the life of the youngest of our drummers in the Crimea is more precious to the country than that of a dozen such hirelings at home, who, by their guilty negligence, leave our fine fellows to rot and starve amid mud and rain. I say it is a shame, a crying shame, and that they ought to be hanged for it," and with a portentous jerk of the head, Mr. Aveling sent his long hair flying about his face.

"How fiercely you talk this evening, George," said Miss Clara.

"Do I — now really?" and he gazed round him with much the look of one just emerging from under water.

"Yes, indeed, you are very fierce; and Miss Holywell, who does not yet understand your ways, will take you for a regular fire-eater, if you go on in such a strain."

"Well, then, as I don't wish to give myself out for anything but what I am — a peaceable member of society," said Mr. Aveling, with a queer mixture of contrition and comicality, "the sooner I leave off, and beg Miss Holywell's pardon, the better. The truth is, that I have a strong and a weak point, Miss Holywell; my strong point is to hate all that is bad with the whole intensity of my reverence for all that is good; my weak one, to express my detestation of what is bad intemperately, without measure, in a sort of a mad bull way, offensive alike to reason and good taste."

"It is only natural that those who feel strongly," said Lavinia, rather puzzled, but wishing to say something conciliatory, "should express strongly what they feel."

"But not violently, not rashly, not uncharitably," urged Mr. Aveling, warmly.

"Now, George, you go too far against yourself," protested Miss Clara.

"I cannot bear to hear you blackening yourself so unwarrantably," said Mrs. Aveling. "Don't believe him, Miss Holywell."

"Just listen to them, Miss Holywell," cried Mr. Aveling; "they will swear next that I am a lamb."

"So you really are," cried both sisters together.

"You be my witness, Miss Holywell," said Mr. Aveling, half cross, half pleased. "Here is a man who passes a sweeping condemnation on a number of his fellow-creatures, on no other foundation than the allegations of a newspaper — a man who gets into a passion and talks of hanging — and that man is not rash, oh, no! — not uncharitable, oh, no! — not unjust, oh, no!"

"Not a word more, pray — to please me," entreated Mrs. Aveling.

"So be it, to please you, Eleanor, and you too, Clara. Miss Holywell has heard enough to draw her own conclusions without further comments of mine."

Lavinia truly had heard enough to be aware by this time that Mr. Aveling was a simple-minded, warm-hearted fellow, with just such a proportion of impulse in his nature as to keep constantly alive his sense of justice and moral responsibility. And as she gazed on his now smooth brow and smiling face, she inwardly called herself stupid and blind for having fancied she discovered in either a want of softness. She was anxious to atone for this inner hasty judgment, and succeeded pretty well in ingratiating herself with him. The task was not difficult, for Mr. Aveling had all the simplicity and the *laisser aller* of a big boy. Even physically, there were glimpses of youth in his eyes, and in the tones of his voice, more suited to a lad of twenty than to a man past forty.

On adjourning to the library, which was the general sitting-room, the ladies took their seats round a table,

and set to work immediately on the flannel jackets for
the Crimea, of which there were three bulky heaps
lying already cut out upon three chairs. Mr. Aveling
took up a review, and occasionally read snatches aloud
from it. After a little, he put down the book, and
began pacing up and down the room in a fit of musing.
Now and then, as he passed the table, at which the
ladies were busy, he would stop and gaze at his wife
and sister with infinite complacency, sometimes play
them some childlike trick, such as stealing the thimble
of the one, or hiding the scissors of the other, pretending the while with the utmost gravity to know nothing
of the missing articles, but sure to end by betraying
himself with a laugh.

There was, of course, no lack of "For shame,
George." "Did you ever see such a harum scarum,
Miss Holywell?" even of bodily struggles to recover
by force thimble or scissors, out of which conquered
and conquerors came equally well pleased. At last the
harum scarum grew composed, sat down at a small
table on one side of the chimney, and began writing.
The scratching of the pen on the paper, the hissing of
the thread, and the ticking of the French clock on
the mantelpiece, were the only sounds audible in the
room.

"All is so still," said Mr. Aveling, after some time;
"I wish the little birds were chirping, it might help
me to my simile."

"The birds are too busy to chirp," said Miss Clara.
"What simile are you hunting for?"

"A simile for the Coliseum; the image ought to be
grand."

"Difficult to find one both grand and true, except

on the spot itself," observed Miss Clara. "You must go to Rome, George."

"So we will, by Jove," cried Mr. Aveling, with enthusiasm, tapping on his writing-desk. "It is monstrous that a poet — one, at least, who writes and publishes poems — should know nothing of the Eternal City, save by hearsay. But I cannot wait for my simile till I go to Rome."

"I have been there," joined in Lavinia, timidly, "and seen the Coliseum."

"What a piece of good luck!" cried George, delighted. "Did you see it by moonlight, Miss Holywell? I hope so."

"Yes," said Lavinia, "as every one makes a point of doing since the days of Byron."

"And what was the impression you received?"

"I will give you that of one whose ideas are better worth repeating than mine," said Lavinia, with a little sigh, as she recalled that evening. "A young Roman painter, who was of our party, likened the Coliseum, looked at sidewise, remember — and the image struck me by its justness — to the carcase of a gigantic ship, stranded —"

"Stranded on the shore of Time's ocean," concluded Mr. Aveling, with a flourish of his right hand. "That's it: simple, grand and true. I am much indebted to you, Miss Holywell."

"I am afraid you will have little rest now, Miss Holywell," observed Mrs. Aveling, laughing, "for I must tell you that the scene of the poem my husband is writing is precisely in Rome. I tremble at the thought of the demands that are in store for you."

"And not without cause, and not without cause,"
affirmed the poet, with mock gravity.

Lavinia expressed, of course, her willingness and
readiness to give all the help in her power, and on went
the pen and on went the needles, this time not without
a brisk accompaniment from the tongues of the needlewomen. Lavinia's kind hostesses were full of curiosity
about Rome and the Pope and the events of the siege
in 1849, on all of which topics, especially the last,
Lavinia possessed and could give, thanks to her friend
Domenichino, authentic and entertaining information.
Miss Clara wanted particularly to know all about the
persons who had volunteered as nurses, and from whom,
as stated in the newspapers at the time, the sick and
wounded during the siege had met with such unremitting
care. Were they chiefly ladies or women of the people?
Lavinia stated what was the fact, that all ranks and
stations of life had united in this work of charity. She
remembered a young and handsome princess having been
pointed out to her, who had been one of the foremost
assistants in and out of the hospitals; and she had herself known a most interesting girl, only a poor worker
in cameos — but what a rich heart she had — who
had also been one of the pious sisterhood. The enthusiasm with which these nurses were spoken of by all
who had seen them at their task, concluded Lavinia,
was a voucher for the devotedness and efficiency with
which it was done.

"It seems," said Miss Clara, with gentle gravity, "as
if suffering, both in oneself and others, is an indispensable stimulant to noble exertions here below — absolutely necessary to develop in human nature what it
has of divine. Troubled times are always the richest

in heroism. Only think what incalculable amount of power of self-sacrifice would lie dormant and waste, but for such occasions of being called into action, as, for instance, that direst of all calamities, war."

"Who speaks of war?" said a doleful voice from the writing-table; "I am sadly at war with myself at this minute. Doubts rush upon me like the Balaklava charge of cavalry."

"We'll bring up an auxiliary force," said Miss Clara; "I'll ring for tea."

"I want help and not tea, you unfeeling jester. I am in a bog, Nelly."

Nelly rose and bent, supple, graceful and loving, over her husband's desk. One of her arms lay coiled round his neck, and supported her delicate frame, her long ringlets fell in golden streams over his shoulders and face, and he, while explaining his difficulty, caressed the flowing curls, twisting them round the fingers of his left hand, the only one he had free — for his right arm encircled his wife's waist in a chaste embrace.

"I hope you will give us some music, Miss Holy-well," said Miss Clara, while this little conjugal scene was going on; "I am sure you sing and play well."

"I ought to do so," replied Lavinia, "considering the time I have wasted on singing and playing."

"Wasted!" repeated Miss Clara; "that is a very severe word to use upon what seems to me one of the most elevating and beneficial influences in this world."

"I quite agree with you," said Lavinia, "in your high estimate of music, yet I cannot but regret having made it the chief occupation of my life. There are so many other things that one ought to learn; and then music in amateurs is generally a temptation to vanity and display."

"Sometimes, perhaps, but not necessarily," returned Miss Clara, kindly; "and in a family circle it may be a great source of good as well as pleasure. George is very fond of music; and whenever something goes wrong — I do not mean at home, thank God — we have the blessing of being all of one mind in the house; but whenever some injustice, or some sad occurrence, such as that which ruffled him before dinner, puts his soul, as he expresses it, out of tune — music charms away his irritation, and —"

An intimation that she was wanted at the writing-desk, interrupted Miss Clara's confidences for the nonce.

"A full cabinet council! — some mighty question to solve," said she, laughing; "you must excuse me for a minute, Miss Holywell," and she joined her sister, and listened gravely to the matter in dispute. Her answer came quick and decided — she spoke loud enough for Lavinia to hear — she said, —

"Yes, a woman actuated by love would do it" (whatever it was, that Mr. Aveling doubted), "and remain true to her nature." Upon this, the council broke up, and the sisters resumed their seats at the work-table.

"Can you keep a secret, Miss Holywell?" asked Mr. Aveling.

"I hope I can — really, I don't know," returned Lavinia, taken by surprise.

"I am determined to run the risk of your reservation," said he, "and take you into my confidence. Here it is — I am a humbug."

"Oh, sir! oh, George!" protested three voices at once.

"I knew there would be a unanimous outcry against me; unvarnished truth always is repulsed, but — *amicus Plato, amicus Cicero, sed magis amica veritas* — I will give you my reasons for what I state, Miss Holywell, for it is to you I appeal as to an impartial judge. The verses which I send forth into the world under my name, and of which I get the credit, are none of mine."

"How can you tell such fibs, George?"

"What stuff and nonsense are you —"

"Attend to me, Miss Holywell, if you please," went on Mr. Aveling, overpowering both his opponents by his sonorous voice. "The verses which the reviewers criticize as mine, or praise as mine, belong by right of authorship to the two blessed women who are sewing by your side."

This declaration met a stout, almost angry denial, from the sisters.

"I protest to heaven and earth, Miss Holywell, that not one deep feeling or striking thought, not one felicitous image or expression, ever dropped from my pen, whose filiation I cannot easily trace to some feeling, thought, image, or expression of theirs; that not one of those gentle personations, which have given some little fame to my name, but is their work, their creation, the very essence of their souls crystallized. In short, they are at once the poet and the poem, and I but the amanuensis. Now that I have made a clean breast of it, I feel more comfortable."

"The best refutation of George's libel against himself," said Miss Clara, addressing Lavinia, "is this very poetic effusion — not his best performance, though — in which he has just indulged as to Eleanor and to me. Who but an *inborn* poet —" she underlined the word by the emphasis she laid on it — "could discover and colour as he did a flimsy paradox?"

"Specious, but unsteady at the base," parenthesized George.

"Miss Holywell," said Mrs. Aveling, "George published his first poem when he was seventeen: I don't think we knew each other at the time."

"Rather incorrect as to chronology," observed Mr. Aveling, quietly. "Evelina, if I remember, the heroine of my first production, was no other than Mrs. Aveling."

"A heroine of ten years old," retorted Mrs. Aveling.

"What matters the age? I can answer for it that I was just as much over head and ears in love with you at seventeen as I am at fort —"

"Be quiet, George; how dare you!"

"Miss Holywell, I appeal to you again; is it improper in a husband to say that he is in love —"

He could not say, or rather he chose not to say, "in love with his wife," for the little hand, which by this time was pretending to close his mouth, was more of a virtual than a formal impediment to utterance. He shut his eyes instead, crossed his hands over his breast, and otherwise intimated his helpless condition under overwhelming force. The entrance of a maid-servant with the tea-things put a stop to proceedings which, however little dignified they may look on paper, had a charm of their own in action, and were suggestive of much to the credit of human nature.

All work of every kind was put aside, and the party drew round the tea-table. The sisters made use of their leisure to retaliate on the poet; they recalled with merciless circumstantiality every one of his literary triumphs, from the letter of encouragement he had received when quite a lad, from the laureate of that day, down to the *furore* of tears created by his last poem.

"Fears were entertained of an inundation," said Mr. Aveling, gravely, "and boats were at a premium."

"And bad jesters at a discount," retorted Miss Clara. "I must warn you, Miss Holywell, that my brother professes the superbest disdain for the melting mood."

"But at the same time," added Mrs. Aveling, "indulges in it with sufficient zest."

"Oh, Nell! *On n'est trahi que par les siens*," exclaimed the husband.

"Listen to me, Miss Holywell," said Miss Clara, in her turn; "listen to an illustration of his masculine fortitude. He took it into his head, while writing his last poem, that the heroine, a perfect darling, should die."

"Oh, Clara! and you also!" deprecated Mr. Aveling.

"We entreated, we implored her grace, all in vain," continued the implacable narrator. "It was an absolute necessity that she should die, he affirmed. Authors are among the worst of tyrants, they destroy the flower of their flock; though justice compels me to own, that being determined to kill her, George did so in some of the most magnificent verses that ever welled up hot from his heart. Well, he came and read them to us, as is his wont — I ought rather to say that he attempted to read them, for, at the middle of the second stanza, he began to blubber dreadfully; this gentleman, who does not look very like a baby, sobbed like one, I assure you."

"I plead guilty, but with extenuating circumstances," said Mr. Aveling. "Of all my creations, Bianca was my favourite —"

"There!" cried his wife, with a little shout of triumph, "he is caught. I appeal to all present, has he not confessed to being the creator of *all* his heroes and heroines?"

"You take advantage of a mere form of speech, used to avoid circumlocution," explained Mr. Aveling. "What I meant to say was this, that of all the personages, of which you were the sun, and I only the photographic machine —"

"No, no, that won't do — too late for recantation."

"Well, Bianca was the one I loved best. She had become for me a thing of flesh and blood; it was not without a long and hard struggle that I made up my mind to sacrifice her. No wonder if, at the moment of striking the fatal blow, my hand trembled a little."

"No equivocation," cried both ladies. "Trembled, indeed! you wept like a fountain."

"I don't deny it, I was completely upset, there never were tears more pleasant than those I shed. Through them I had the revelation that my Galatea had the breath of life in her; through them I could say to myself, *Anch' io son pittore.*"

"Now, I am satisfied," said Miss Clara. "Spoken like a man and a true poet."

Mrs. Aveling said nothing, but looked the proudest of wives.

"Now for the end of my story," resumed Miss Clara. "When he was disabled, Eleanor took up the MS., read three lines, and broke down shamefully. It was now my turn. I screwed up my courage, steadied my voice, got through a line and a half, and joined in the wail. Jane came in with the tea-tray at that critical moment, and found us all dissolved in tears. She stood aghast at the sight, desperately inclined to scream and run away, as she confessed afterwards. The ludicrousness of the situation struck us so forcibly, that we all three burst into a Homeric fit of laughter, which, however, only half reassured Jane as to nothing dreadful having happened. We wasted a good deal of time and ingenuity in trying to explain to her the cause of the emotion she had witnessed, but we succeeded very ill in making the case clear to our country maiden; and to this day she looks with suspicion on George's manuscripts, which, to use her own phrase, can play such tricks with master and mistress."

Amid such pleasant talk the evening wore on. Lavinia, when again pressed, went to the piano and sang, to the delight of her audience, some popular Italian songs she had learned at Rome. At ten the family party broke up, and Miss Clara accompanied her guest to her room, to make sure that everything there was comfortable; and all being as it ought to be, she wished Lavinia good night and pleasant dreams. If dreams are but the reflex of the impressions received during the day, it was difficult indeed under that hospitable roof to have any other than pleasant dreams.

CHAPTER XVIII.

A new Link clinched by an old Name.

Miss CLARA did not appear at breakfast next morning, nor did she for several days running join the family circle till near dinner-time. Lavinia was consequently thrown on the hands of Mrs. Aveling, and was no loser by it. Miss Clara herself could not have done the honours of Owlscombe with greater cordiality and friendliness. No corner of the house or grounds was left unexplored; the conservatory, the aviary, the Alderney cows, the Cochin China fowls came in each and all in their turn for a share of notice and admiration. Lavinia's attention was especially claimed for a particular plot of ground in the garden, at which Mr. Aveling used to work every morning, as if for his daily bread; and to a little summer-house, of which he made his study in the hot season. Mrs. Aveling also pointed out, not without a little look of pride, two full grown fir-trees, which overshadowed the summer-house, and which she and her husband had planted with their own hands, and christened with each other's name, on the day of their marriage, now more than fifteen years ago.

"What a nice idea!" said Lavinia; "they have grown the very image of their namesakes; so straight, so vigorous. It must do your heart good to look at them."

"Yes, indeed; though at times it saddens me to think," said Mrs. Aveling, with a sigh, "that they will pass into strange hands when we are gone. After all," she added, waving her head as if to throw off some

annoying burden, "it is worse than foolish to indulge
in regrets for what one has not, when one has so much
— oh! so much as I have."

Lavinia needed no clearer hint to show her the
nature of the regret, which had wrung a sigh from her
cheerful hostess. Passing lovely and sweet as was the
picture of the interior it had been her good fortune to
have a peep of, she had missed in it a feature which
would have given it completeness; a group of rosy
cherubs gambolling on the hearthrug, and filling the air
with their infantine voices. Yes; even Mrs. Aveling was
no exception to the rule, that there is on earth no absolute felicity; even she, the proudest and happiest of
wives and sisters, had a wish unfulfilled, an ambition,
the most legitimate of ambitions, unsatisfied.

Let not the reader, however, imagine that this longing proved the bane of her life; not at all: there was
sweet enough in her cup to drown this drop of gall.
Such passing clouds of melancholy, as the thought might
evoke now and then, were lost in the sunshine of love
in which she walked. The Roman conquerors of old
were not the worse for being reminded in their day of·
triumph, that they were but mortals. Perhaps, without
this remembrancer of the disappointments to which all
flesh is heir, Mrs. Aveling's flow of gentle sympathies
for the unfortunate would have run less abundant and
active. Certain it is, that this trial, if such it was, had
rather tightened than otherwise the bonds of affection
and reverence, which bound the two sufferers from it;
for the consciousness in each of a wish ungratified in
the other, acted on both as an ever fresh stimulant to
that endless interchange of little tendernesses and en-

dearments, which said, in their own peculiar language, "Know that I have *nothing* to wish for."

With such, and other little confidences, Mrs. Aveling enlivened the long mornings, when they sat, needle in hand, in the cosy oak parlour at Owlscombe. What other subjects could she broach, but those of which she was full — her husband and her sister? They were all the world to her. Clara was an angel, Mrs. Aveling averred. She had refused every proposal of marriage in order to stay with her brother and sister, and do good. Doing good was Clara's passion. Her life was an uninterrupted succession of errands of charity. No needy or afflicted ones, within a circuit of ten miles, but she carried comfort and assistance to. The sick were pre-eminently her favourites. Just at this time she was the centre and soul of a movement throughout the county, for collecting funds and clothes for our soldiers in the Crimea. It was this which kept her so much from home. Clara neglected herself for the sake of others. She was far from strong. No doubt Miss Holywell had remarked the mob cab she always wore. She had been advised to wear it as a preventive against the severe headaches, from which she suffered so constantly. And yet she was never satisfied that she did enough, and yearned for a wider field of usefulness and self-immolation. Another and a deeper sigh at this place seemed to point to some special cause of uneasiness, which was left a mystery for Lavinia.

Mrs. Aveling looked upon her husband as the *beau idéal* of a hero and genius. She worshipped his very shadow. Young, handsome, gifted beyond all men, the very essence of all goodness, as he had appeared to her girlish vision, when he came, a printed author al-

ready at seventeen, to spend the holidays at Owlscombe
with her father, so he stood in the eyes of the wife
woman now, after the lapse of nine and twenty years,
and the same he would remain for ever. Had there
ever been a friend like George? If she and her sister
had a roof over their heads, were they not indebted for
it to George? After the death of her father, Mr. Aveling, then only beginning his career as a barrister, had
spent five of the best years of his youth, had devoted
all his energies, and his little fortune as well, to save
such wrecks of theirs as could be saved. Thank God,
he had succeeded — not till this happy issue had been
secured, had they married. How sweet to owe everything to him one loves!

These, and similar disclosures, were not made, of
course, in the compressed and uninterrupted form in
which they are here given, much less given in one day;
they oozed out in intermittent streamlets under the pressure of scarcely appreciable agencies. One of these
was unmistakeably Mr. Aveling's visits to the ladies'
sitting-room. His presence left a glow after it, which
was favourable to confidence. Truly, he had always
something affectionate to say or do. It seemed as if
he could receive no agreeable impression without
enhancing it by sharing it with his Nelly. Now it was
a fresh bud which had opened on some favourite plant
she had placed in his study, and which she was requested to admire; now a piece of news in a newspaper,
or a striking passage in a book which he knew would
interest her.

When he came in with no such apparent message,
which was pretty often the case, he was always saluted with the question, "Do you want me, George?"

This afforded an inexhaustible fund of merriment, for then he would wonder at the self-conceit of some better halves, who thought they were for ever wanted, and pretend that he had come to see that Miss Holywell was not being canvassed against him behind his back. At other times he would answer, —

"Well, suppose I wanted to have a peep at your sweet face, where is the harm?"

"The harm is in the saying so," would say his wife, and, "Oh, the hypocrite!" be the laughing retort. "Do you hear her, Miss Holywell? I put it to you. Is it so very shocking in a husband to say he wished to look at —"

Probably Mrs. Aveling here rose with such a threatening aspect, that the gentleman was fain to take to his heels, concluding in his flight the obnoxious phrase, to the increased wrath of the offended party, who would run after him, and disappear in the chase.

On the fifth morning of Lavinia's stay at Owlscombe, Miss Clara breakfasted for the first time with the rest of the family. The day was clear and fine, the ground dry and frosty.

"Just the day and the ground for a good walk," observed Miss Clara. "Will you go out with me, Miss Holywell?"

Lavinia answered in the affirmative, and away went the two young ladies. They walked on in silence for some time. Miss Clara looked grave.

"I hope you are not suffering from one of your bad headaches," said Lavinia.

"Oh, no! I am pretty well, thank you," replied Miss Clara, "only vexed and puzzled."

"But nothing seriously wrong, I hope?" asked Lavinia, with interest.

"No; only disagreeable; and I am sorry to say it concerns you, Miss Holywell."

Lavinia started.

"I have heard from Mrs. Ennerly," continued Miss Clara. At the mention of that name Lavinia's face lengthened. "There is no cause for alarm," hastened to add Miss Clara; "you are among friends, you know, who will take care of you, whatever happens."

"Then Mrs. Ennerly refuses — to — receive me," faltered Lavinia.

"Not exactly so; but she objects to your being in mourning — you know, I rather apprehended as much from the first — not that I believe such an objection would have weighed a straw, had she seen you. As it is, I perceive with pain that my aunt has received an impression — You see what a poor hand I am at diplomacy," wound up Miss Clara, with a little embarrassed laugh. "The short and the long of the matter is," she continued, resolutely, "that my aunt hints at a wish to annul the engagement she entered into with you, to annul it in a way, you understand, honourable and agreeable to both parties, if possible; but, rather than give offence to anybody, she would abide by her agreement purely and simply."

After a moment's reflection, Lavinia said timidly, "I could not take advantage of Mrs. Ennerly's considerate scruples, to force myself, as it were, into her house contrary to her wish."

"Surely not, if it were not next to a certainty that that wish would be altered the moment she saw you," said Miss Clara. "It is quite on other grounds I feel

disposed to influence you to accept of the overtures
Mrs. Ennerly makes towards the cancelling of your engagement.   Listen to me, Miss Holywell.   I have not
the least doubt but that my aunt, did I advise her to
do so, would receive you immediately and kindly, and
also come to like you in a very short time.   I have as
little doubt, but that any hostile influence, if such there
were, which you might meet in her establishment,
would be eventually conquered by your gentleness and
candour.   My doubt and fear is as to your happiness.
I do not believe that, with your tastes and habits, such
as I judge them to be, you could easily accommodate
yourself to those of Mrs. Ennerly. For instance, she is
in a constant whirl of company and entertains a great
deal.   During the Weymouth season, her house is the
gayest of the gay.   Now, would that suit you?"

"Oh! no," was the hurried answer, "I have had
quite enough of gaieties; I literally thirst after retirement and obscurity."

"I guessed as much," said Miss Clara; "I am glad
I have consulted with you on the subject.   You will
oblige me by writing to Lady Willingford so as to exonerate my aunt as much as you can from blame."

"I shall exonerate her entirely; and I will also
write to Mrs. Ennerly herself," said Lavinia, "if you
do not disapprove."

"Yes, do, it will be very kind of you; let us make
a golden bridge for her to escape from reproaching herself too much.   Of course, she owes you a handsome
compensation —"

"Will you think it presumptuous of me to say," interrupted Lavinia, "that I would rather have no compensation?"

"Why not?"

"Because you have been so kind to me, all of you so very kind, that it would mortify me very much to accept of anything like money from one of your family."

Miss Clara saw Lavinia struggling with her tears, and said, —

"Well, well, I shall not press the matter further for the present; and now let me see you look cheerful again. You need not be uneasy about the future," concluded Miss Clara; "we shall not have any great difficulty in finding a situation suitable to your disposition. In the meantime we shall detain you at Owlscombe, as a most skilful needlewoman. Perhaps, I may even have to beg of you to prolong your stay at Owlscombe for an indefinite period — beg you to fill my place while I am absent."

"Are you going away?" asked Lavinia, in painful surprise.

"Yes, and for some time; but I do not go immediately," replied Miss Clara, with a little reserve of manner. Lavinia said nothing further, and they walked on, both thoughtful and silent.

Lavinia was the first to speak.

"Since you are so good as to take an interest in my fate," said she, "I will venture to tell you of a wish I have, which my engagement with Mrs. Ennerly being at an end, I may perhaps be able to realize. I am so ignorant of all practical things, that I need advice and help. Can you tell me if fifty pounds would be sufficient to take me to the East?"

"To the East?" echoed Miss Clara, in the greatest

wonder. "Do you really and positively mean that you wish to go to the East?"

"Yes; to serve as a nurse in one or other of the hospitals there," said Lavinia. "I have thought of little else ever since I had the good fortune to meet you. I should be so happy, oh! so happy to do something for my fellow-creatures."

"I can understand and sympathize with your wish," said Miss Clara; "at the same time, do not take it ill, I beg of you, if I counsel you to be on your guard against any precipitate and rash resolution. Your vocation for such a service being of so fresh a date, had you not better test it a little first?"

"Perhaps," said Lavinia, meekly, "though what you name my vocation dates much farther back than you imagine. Months ago, had I known how to manage it, I would have gone and served in the hospitals of London; from the very day, indeed, on which I learned what an amount of misery there was in the world — I was ignorant of it once and so thoughtless — from that day, not a very distant one, after all, I have begged of God each morning and evening that I might not die without having been of some use."

"Have you no family ties?" asked Miss Clara.

"None, I am an orphan."

"No one on whose judgment you ought to depend, whose sanction you ought to have?"

"None, except Lady Willingford, without whose consent I would take no decisive step."

"Well, then, if Lady Willingford consent, and if within three weeks from this you are still of the same mind, your wish shall be gratified. At the end of January we will start for Scutari together."

"'Together? you are going there?" cried Lavinia, at the acme of astonishment.

"Yes; when I spoke of being away from home for awhile, I alluded to my intended journey to the East; it has been a settled thing for more than a month past."

"I understand now," said Lavinia, "what Mrs. Aveling meant the other day, when mentioning all the good you were accomplishing at home, she added that you yearned for a still wider sphere of usefulness and self-sacrifice."

"Mrs. Aveling looks upon my poor exertions in this neighbourhood, with the eyes of a partial sister, that is, she looks upon them through the magnifying glass of affection. By-the-by, I must warn you, that to spare ourselves as much pain as we can, we have tacitly agreed at home to avoid all reference to the subject of my departure. It preys heavily enough on our minds as it is," added Miss Clara, with a sigh. "We love each other so dearly! we are so happy together, that sometimes I am tempted to ask myself if I am justified in taking the course I am bent on; and yet I feel impelled to it so strongly, in so unconquerable a manner."

The subject being one of too peculiar a nature for Lavinia to venture any remark upon, they both again fell into a silence, which was unbroken until they emerged from the intricacies of a small wood into a road which ran across some downs, and commanded a full view of the surrounding country. The prospect was rather dreary as long as the eye dwelt on the naked, slightly undulating spread of upland; but to the south the hills sloped gracefully down into little valleys, which lay, as it were, folded at their feet; smiling nooks, sprinkled with coppice, hedgerows, meadows, farms, country-houses, and hamlets. A little farther off, the steeples and church towers of the old town of Wareham, rising behind leafless trees, cut sharply against the sky. A broad expanse of sea extended beyond to the horizon.

"This is a favourite spot of mine," observed Miss Clara; "I hope you admire my Dorsetshire."

"Indeed I do," said Lavinia, "lovely as it is even now in its austere winter déshabille, how charming it must be when decked in its summer mantle of green!" and as she was surveying the numerous country-houses, which dotted the landscape far and near, her gaze was arrested by one in the foreground, which reminded her, she said, of an Italian villa, less owing to its noble proportions and vast portico, than to the two stately cypresses standing in front of it, a picturesque feature very common in Italy near any dwelling of note. The closed windows and other signs of neglect clearly pointed out that the mansion was empty; and Lavinia wondered how such a lovely place should be un-inhabited.

"Poor Cypress Hall!" said Miss Clara, with a sigh; "it has been forsaken for nine years. Its owner lives abroad."

While Miss Clara was speaking, a misgiving arose in Lavinia's mind, that Cypress Hall was fraught with painful associations for her friend, and she therefore dropped the subject.

On their return to Owlscombe, the first thing Lavinia did was to write to Mrs. Ennerly and Lady Willingford, as she had promised to do, and to show both letters to Miss Clara before despatching them. It will be as well to state at once, that she received satisfactory replies by return of post; Mrs. Ennerly enclosing a cheque for twenty pounds, which Lavinia was persuaded to accept; and thus this mighty negotiation ended to the contentment of all parties.

. After this, Lavinia became Miss Clara's inseparable companion in her errands of charity, and a very docile and clever aid she proved in the art of tending and relieving the sick. Like all charitable ladies living in the country, Miss Clara had a considerable smattering of medicine, and into all that she knew herself, she initiated her pupil, who soon became as great a proficient in prescribing as her instructress.

Never had Lavinia been so busy and so happy. Her shyness and sense of social inferiority had gradually worn away under the warmth of cordiality she met from her hosts. They treated her as though she were one of the family, and she soon felt like one. And thus days and weeks rolled away, quick and full in their sweet uniformity. Here is a little incident, however, which we have obvious reasons for recording.

One evening, some chance observation of Lavinia's brought the siege of Rome again on the tapis, and among other facts she was relating, she said that one of the stanchest defenders of the Eternal City in 1849 had been an English gentleman of the name of Thorntorn. This mention was immediately followed by one of those awkward silences, which are so painful to all present, and more especially to the person who is their unwilling cause. The sudden hush was the more striking from the conversation having been more than usually animated. Miss Clara was the first to recover

herself, but no efforts of hers sufficed to dispel the
chill which had so suddenly fallen on the whole party.
It was a relief when bed-time came, and they separated
for the night.

Miss Clara, however, went with Lavinia into the
latter's room, saying, —

"I have something to explain, and to apologize
for."

"Apologize for?" repeated Lavinia, in surprise.

"Yes, for sitting like a dumb goose, instead of
having presence of mind enough to prevent your being
distressed by such a mysterious change of manner in
my brother and sister. To explain it, you must know
that the name you pronounced this evening, has not
been heard by the walls of Owlscombe for years, and
is one, I must add, unwelcome to everybody here but
me."

"How unlucky that I should just hit upon that
particular one!" exclaimed Lavinia.

"How could you know?" said Miss Clara, adding
hurriedly, and with a good deal of agitation, — "A
gentleman of the name of Thornton was once our neighbour and friend, in fact he owned that Cypress Hall
which you admired so much the other day. In an ill-
omened moment a misunderstanding arose between him
and my family; mark, it was my fault — yes, my
fault — and he went away, and has never been heard
of since. Appearances were against him, and in their
blind tenderness for me, George and Nelly threw the
whole blame on him. I, who knew better, was in duty
bound to take his defence; and this difference of opinion
led to some little discomfort at home, to avoid which,

by a mutual tacit agreement, all mention of the subject, even of the name connected with it, was dropped."

"I am so sorry — so very sorry," exclaimed Lavinia, "to have been the unconscious occasion of this revival of bitter association in your mind."

"Not so bitter as you think; there is also some sweet. If there is any good in me, I owe it chiefly to having been thrown back on myself — to the recoil of the event alluded to. It was from the throbs of a noble heart that I had wounded, that a timely warning was conveyed to me. But no more of myself; tell me about this Thornton you met at Rome — was he tall and very good-looking?"

"Yes; and I should think about fifty," added Lavinia.

"Oh, no; then he must be another person. Mr. Thornton of Cypress Hall cannot be more, let me see, than seven-and-thirty at most."

"The one I knew is certainly much older than that; though, now that I think of it, perhaps it was his almost white hair and beard which made him appear so. By the by, my Mr. Thornton's Christian name is Mortimer."

"Then it is he," said Miss Clara. "Only to think of his hair being white! and when he was twentyeight he did not look his age."

"Nearly white," again repeated Lavinia. "He must have suffered cruelly; indeed, I know he has, for he told me so himself — not while I was at Rome, I could not endure him then. He was so grave and reasonable, took everything so in earnest, and I was so unreasonable, so giddy. It was not till the day of trial came that I found out his worth: ah! he is one of the noblest and kindest of men. Without him, I do believe, I should have gone mad. And yet he was sorely tried himself at the time, and through my thoughtlessness. Shall I tell you how it was? Oh, yes, if you will allow me — if only that you may know how much I owe to him, and how much I have to atone for."

And, Miss Clara readily accepting this offer of confidence, the repentant Lavinia related her poignant recollections of her last stay in Paris, beginning at the untoward circumstances that had attended the arrival of the young Roman painter there, describing the fatal ball at the Hôtel de Ville, the distraction, and subsequent disappearance of Paolo, down to Mrs. Jones's sudden illness, winding up her narrative with a violent fit of crying.

Miss Clara evinced the keenest interest in the sad tale, and was not chary of words of comfort to the afflicted girl.

"You have been more unfortunate than guilty," said she. "Cruel as it is to be in any way an instrument of suffering to others, there is consolation in the consciousness of not having meant it, at least."

"Ah! but the injury done remains no less an injury," said Lavinia.

"Alas! too true," said Miss Clara, with the deep feeling of one who speaks from painful personal experience. "All we can do is to try and make atonement. You have never heard more, then, of this Italian gentleman?"

"Never; nor had Mr. Thornton, up to the date of his last letter to me, which is as far back as May. Since then all my letters to him have remained unanswered; and when I try to imagine the reason of this silence, I grow frightened."

"Let us hope for the best," said Miss Clara. "As we pass through Paris, you will have an opportunity of inquiring about Mr. Thornton at the place from which he dated his last letter to you; and probably you will be able to obtain some clue to his present whereabouts. If so — and something tells me it will be so — he will give you tidings, either by letter or by word of mouth, as to his Roman friend, which may set your mind at rest. The ways of Providence are inscrutable, my dear Miss Holywell. Who would have believed that through you, an utter stranger to me a few weeks ago, I should receive, after a blank of nine years, such cheering news of the dear friend of my youth? Cheering in this sense, I mean, that whatever alterations his trials may have brought in the flesh, his soul remains unchanged, that he is the same upright, noble, and tender specimen of mankind I knew him to be, and that I have persisted in reverencing to this hour. He had faults, certainly — who has not? He was morbidly sensitive, exacting, exclusive in everything; but the richness of his heart made up for all his faults. He had experienced much early injustice and harshness. His stepmother hated him, his guardian deceived him, and to recover what was his own he had to fight a hard battle for years. What wonder if a man so circumstanced should have had his temper soured, and looked less at the sunny than at the shady side of human nature!"

Thus, led on by invisible threads, the two kindly souls drew closer and closer together, and the seeds that pity and sympathy had sown, by a fresh community of interests and feelings, grew up fast and vigorous into a blessed flower of sisterly friendship.

CHAPTER XIX.

The Discovery in Paris.

THE departure of Miss Clara and Lavinia was fixed for the 25th of January. They were two of a large batch of accepted nurses — all female England would have gone *en masse*, if allowed — who were to start from Marseilles on the 3th of February, by the steamship *Vectis*, weather permitting. The general rendezvous was to be at the English embassy in Paris, on the 31st of January at latest. Having some particular business of their own to transact in Paris, viz., to make inquiries about Mr. Thornton, our two young ladies had naturally determined to give themselves a few days in advance, in order not to be straitened for time.

We must not forget to say, before proceeding further, that Lavinia had written beforehand to Lady Willingford, and had not only received her ladyship's consent to her intended journey, and her sanction to apply her gift of fifty pounds to it, but another sum of equal value, accompanied by praises, and blessings innumerable. Lady Augusta's half-a-dozen sheets of the largest note paper were scarcely legible — not so much on account of the very small, close writing, and crossings and recrossings, as of certain patches here and there as if it had rained upon the paper.

Their last week at Owlscombe was a great trial to every one there. It was a pitiful and a touching sight to watch the looks of assumed unconsciousness and cheerfulness with which each of the sisters practised upon the other a pious deceit, which deceived no one. Never had Miss Clara gone her rounds of charity more regularly, never had she been more indefatigable in her attentions to the conservatory, the poultry yard, the dairy, and the aviary; never showed a keener interest in the calf that was expected, or the bud of the rare camellia, which was about to open, as if such were to be for ever her engrossing occupations. Never had Mrs. Aveling been more lively and more suggestive of improvements in this or that department of the little household, or Mr. Aveling more talkative and sportive, or more assiduous in his devotion to his poem, which, nevertheless, somehow or other, did not progress very rapidly. But there were now and then sudden silences, sudden exists, and as sudden returns with red eyes, which no one perceived, of course.

Let us draw a veil over the scene of parting. It was cruel, as all partings are; more cruel than most. If the path of duty were strewn with roses, where would be the merit of walking on it? The dear sister did not go alone, there was comfort in this; she had by her side a dear and loving friend, one who would stand by her, and take care of her if — oh, may God avert it! — any evil were to befall her. Affection is always full of fearful anticipations. Nothing untoward happened, however, as far as the journey to Paris was concerned, where our two travellers were safely housed by ten in the evening of the morrow.

Though from the Hôtel de Hollande in the Rue de la Paix, where they had rooms, to the house in the Rue Neuve des Augustins, from whence Mr. Thornton had dated his last letter, the distance was scarcely more than two hundred paces, they drove thither in a coach, in which Miss Clara might wait for the result of Lavinia's inquiries. Lavinia was shown into a parlour, where two respectable-looking women were sitting, one of whom came up to the young lady and begged to know in what way she could be of use to Mademoiselle. Lavinia, with many apologies for her intrusion, stated as briefly as she could the object of her call. On hearing which, the other, a good-natured, middle-aged, buxom woman, who had not yet spoken, came forward, saying, —

"You must be Miss Jones, who lived last year on the Boulevard des Capucines."

"Yes, and you, I am sure, are Madame Françoise, whom Mr. Thornton mentioned so often as the very best of landladies."

"Just so," answered Madame Françoise, curtseying; "the proverb is right which says, that only mountains do not meet. As to the being kind to Mr. Thornton, there was little merit in that. I never met a gentleman so easily satisfied, or so considerate and good-natured — pity he was so queer; all the English are so, I know; but he, particularly the last time he came to Paris — well to be sure I always expected he would end so."

"End how?" asked Lavinia, in mortal fear.

"Is it possible that you do not know? Mr. Thornton is —" The end of Madame Françoise's phrase was in dumb show; she lifted her right hand to the level of her forehead, and gave it a rotatory movement.

"Not — out of his senses?" cried Lavinia, looking aghast.

"No doubt of it," returned Madame Françoise, with a very sonorous "Alas!" and she would have immediately entered on a full history of the circumstances preceding, accompanying, and following the sad catastrophe, had not Lavinia, with many apologies, stopped her, saying to the one who appeared the mistress of the house, —

"Will you allow me, madam, to go and fetch a friend of mine, who is waiting down-stairs in a coach, and who, as an old acquaintance of Mr. Thornton, is equally anxious to hear about him?"

As may be supposed, this request was easily granted, and Lavinia, running down the stairs, in her agitation hurriedly revealed the whole extent of the sad intelligence at once, which so overpowered Miss Clara, that Lavinia was for putting off any further disclosures. But Miss Clara, regaining her self-command by a strenuous effort of will, would hear of no delay.

"You understand that time is precious," she said; "perhaps we may yet be of some use to him." And a minute after, the two friends were seated in the Frenchwoman's little parlour, listening, pale and mute as two marble statues, to the distressing tale.

"That ce cher Monsieur Thornton should give himself out to be a murderer," wound up the loquacious matron, "he who would not have willingly hurt a fly — that is what passes my comprehension. To know what a heart he had, one ought to have seen him as I have done, taking care of that young friend of his — more like a mother than a father, so anxious always: 'Won't you take a crust of bread and a glass of wine, Paul, or a bouillon, or a cup of tea: suppose we take

a drive, it will do you good;' — always something to
pleasure Mr. Paul. And how often, in the night as
well as the day, did he go to listen at the young gentleman's door. And no wonder, for poor Mr. Paul was
an object of pity, if ever there was one, as white, and
haggard, and distracted looking as if he had come out
of his grave. Oh dear! I am sure I for one don't wonder at his being lost — not I, indeed."

This was, perhaps, the twentieth time that Paolo's
name had been mentioned, and each time a question
had been trembling on Lavinia's lips, which the terror
of the answer it might elicit had frozen on them.
Guessing at the cause of her friend's silence, Miss Clara
at last ventured on the perilous query, —

"Was Mr. Paul ever heard of again?"

"Oh, yes! thank God, he turned up in the course
of time," answered Madame Françoise. (Lavinia joined
her hands, and raised her eyes — oh! what a look
that was!) "A young man of Evreux, that I know
very well, called Courant," continued Madame Françoise, "who studied law in Paris, met him in the month
of July or August, somewhere in the Quartier Latin.
Mr. Paul was just rallying from a serious illness, and
was very feeble and melancholy, poor as a rat, and
longing to be back in his own country. When Mr.
Courant saw him last, he was busy about getting a
passport. I hope he got it, and is long ago safe at
home. He was an excellent youth, not like our young
men — no balls, no *cafés*, no — never mind what.
That Courant, who, by the way, is one of the scape-
graces, though a good boy at the bottom, used to quiz
him mightily, and call him sentimentalist. Better he
had been more of a sentimentalist himself — Mr. Cou-

rant, I mean — and then he would not be ill at Evreux
as he is, and at daggers drawn with his uncle, who
swears he will disinherit him."

As soon as Madame Francoise stopped for breath,
the visitors rose to take leave, whereupon both Mr.
Thornton's ex-landlady and her friend poured forth a
perfect torrent of offers of service, begging the English
ladies to call again, Madame Françoise taking care to
explain that her time was her own till the middle of
March, she being on a visit to the mistress of the *maison meublée*.

Furnished with the address of Dr. Ternel, the director of the sanitary establishment where Thornton was,
Lavinia, by Miss Clara's desire, directed the coachman
to drive thither at once. Little was spoken during the
long drive. One is not told of the safety of the long
lost, nor of his illness, his goodness, his sadness; one
does not go to meet a dear and esteemed friend, un-
heard of for nine years, at a lunatic asylum, without a
revival of feelings too deep and tumultuous for utterance.
A sympathizing pressure of the hand by which they
held each other, was a mute language thoroughly understood by the two friends.

Dr. Ternel's *maison de santé* stood at the western
extremity of Paris, on the outskirts of the Champ de
Mars. We use the past tense purposely, for it is a
thing of the past. Even that tranquil and out-of-the-
way corner, with its shady walks and centenary cedars
of Lebanon, has been engulfed and swept away by the
successive encroachments of the pickaxe, which have so
completely transformed the face of Paris within the
last few years. High wooden boards painted green,
entirely lined the iron railings of the gate of the esta-

blishment, thus securing the interior against any indiscreet glance of the passers-by. A porter's lodge on the right hand, a snug little *chalet* on the left, and in front, beyond a trimly kept lawn, an elegant villa overshadowed by trees — such was the agreeable prospect which met you when admitted within the premises. Lest the appellation of villa should seem out of character, it may be as well to explain that the dwelling had been intended for the summer residence of the governor of the Invalides, and had served as such at no distant date. The extensive grounds attached to it stretched from the Rue St. Dominique, in which was the principal entrance, to the Rue de l'Université, not far from the banks of the Seine. Our two visitors crossed the court, as directed, and entered that of the two lesser side doors, which was on the right. A servant met them in the passage, and immediately introduced them into the study of the doctor.

Dr. Ternel was a little spare gentleman about fifty, in the neatest professional costume, and whitest of cravats and frilled shirts. There was nothing remarkable either in the details or the ensemble of his person, save a mouth full of finesse, and a general expression of good nature. Perhaps, despite the courteous frankness of his manner, a keener observer than our English ladies could be at the moment, might have noticed in his looks, and in the whole carriage of his person, something collected and guarded, something like an armed neutrality, the result most likely of a long experience of the often dangerous customers with whom he consorted, and of more than one narrow escape. A ten seconds' inspection of the two fair faces however — just the time to rise and offer seats — brought with it a general disarming both of body and mind, and there was nothing in the clear grey eye, as it fell upon the visitors — absolutely nothing but a plain interrogative point.

Miss Clara, who was quite unprepared with any form of speech to make clear the object of her visit, felt awkward at this tacit summons, and said at haphazard, —

"We are English, sir —" (an acquiescent nod and a half-smile from the doctor, intimated that she might have dispensed with this preliminary), "I mean, that we are the countrywomen of an English gentleman, who, we learned only this morning, is one of your patients, and —"

"And as such," said the doctor, coming to her help, "take a natural interest in your compatriot. I have several English patients. Pray, what is the name of this gentleman?"

On hearing that it was Thornton, a glow of pleasure lighted up Dr. Ternel's face.

"May I inquire without indiscretion if Mr. Thornton is related to you?"

"No, not exactly; he is a friend, only an old family friend," said Miss Clara.

"It is not mere curiosity makes me put that question to you. In Mr. Thornton's case it is most important for me to ascertain whether the malady under which he at present suffers is hereditary or not."

"I cannot speak positively; but to the best of my belief, it is not," was the answer. "I never heard him make any, the very least allusion to anything of the kind. His father, and indeed his grandfather, I am

15*

certain, were of perfectly sane mind to the last day of
their lives."

"'This is good news," said Mr. Ternel, pondering.
"Did this Mr. Thornton ever, to your knowledge, show
any signs of particular eccentricity — anything that
attracted general attention?"

"Never that I heard of. He was perhaps at all
times — somewhat different to other men — more
earnest, more thorough-going; always slightly melancholy, even subject to fits of depression, but never, never
the least unreasonable. I speak of nine years ago."

"I beg your pardon for appearing so inquisitive; do
not answer me if you have any objection to do so; but
am I to understand that you lost sight of Mr. Thornton entirely for nine years?"

"Yes, sir."

Dr. Ternel had another fit of musing, then looking
Miss Clara fully in the face, said, —

"I suppose, then, you are not acquainted with the
sad circumstances under which Mr. Thornton's present
derangement broke out. He had been for some time
labouring under great despondency, consequent on the
mysterious disappearance of a young man, to whom he
was greatly attached. It had become his habit to visit
the Morgue, with a vague terror of some discovery of
this youth's untoward fate, and it was the accidental
sight there of the corpse of a girl, who had drowned
herself, that brought on a fit of madness, and, in fact,
he attempted suicide. From that moment, his former
constant preoccupation of mind about his lost friend,
which was the root of his morbid disposition, vanished
entirely, and its place was taken by a new one, the
links of which with reality, if any such exist, it has

been out of my power, or that of any of his acquaintances with whom I have communicated, to discover. This shifting of fixed ideas is a not uncommon phenomenon in mental maladies. Mr. Thornton's present monomania consists in this, that he identifies the drowned girl he saw at the Morgue with a person, real or imaginary, whom he has, or fancies he has, wronged; this it was which led him to try and destroy himself, and this is why he accuses himself of being her murderer. He sees, argues with, and entreats for pardon this person, whom he calls Clara." Here the doctor made a full stop. "In every other respect, Mr. Thornton speaks and acts as a man of sound mind; but his interest in every thing which is not his delusion, is extremely languid and fugitive."

By the time Dr. Ternel had finished speaking, he knew what it mattered him to know. Miss Clara's feelings, struggled against in vain during the doctor's explanation, had fully confirmed a suspicion, which had crossed his mind the moment she had mentioned Thornton's name. No doubt, he had found the lever he had for the last eight months been seeking.

"Can you hold out any hope of Mr. Thornton's recovery?" asked Miss Clara, after a silence of some minutes.

"Certainly I can. I seldom despair of any of my patients, least of all of those like this one. I have witnessed such wonderful cures. I could almost answer for it if" — (every syllable of the next phrase came out in an earnest *staccato*) — "if the person he mourns over as dead, were a woman of flesh and blood, and would help me in the task."

The scarlet flush that rose to Miss Clara's face, told

the doctor plainly enough that his appeal had found an echo in the right quarter. Determined, therefore, to pursue his advantage, and strike the iron while it was hot, he continued, this time, however, addressing himself more particularly to Lavinia, —

"A task well worthy of a woman, nay, such as only the boundless devotedness of a woman's heart can accomplish. And then think of the result," added the doctor, his features bright with enthusiasm; "to call up harmony from chaos, to rescue a noble mind from the worst of bondages, to new create a man, as it were, in God's image. Really, it is a task almost divine."

"You speak of it with the feeling of one who has seen and brought about such effects," said Lavinia, with sympathizing warmth.

"Thank God, I may say I have," said the doctor, with elation; "but, alas!" he added, with a sudden change to grave sadness, "for a few successes how many failures — oh! how many."

"Doctor," exclaimed Miss Clara, "will you allow me to call again to-morrow?"

"Certainly; with the greatest pleasure."

"I have another request to make. Could I — I think it would be best so — see the gentleman, myself unseen?"

"Oh, yes," urged Lavinia; "pray, if you can, let us have a sight of our friend."

"That can be easily managed, if he should be in his garden, as is probably the case," replied the doctor; then turning to Lavinia, he asked, "Is there any reason why you should wish not to be seen by him?"

"None at all," said Lavinia; "I should be too glad to shake hands with him."

"Very well; however, it will be wiser that I should mention your visit to him beforehand. What name shall I say?"

"Lavinia Jones," answered the young lady, "one whom he knew both in Rome and Paris."

The ladies drew down their veils as they were desired to do, and, under the guidance of the doctor, issued through a back door into the park attached to the establishment. As they advanced, every now and then their attention was attracted by some lonely figure flitting among the trees, or gravely pacing up and down the well kept gravel walks. One of these, a tall man, closely followed by two others, hurried up from a distance towards the doctor, who whispered to his companions, —

"This patient is going to speak to me; do not be afraid, he is quite harmless, and, besides, his two servants are at his heels."

A tall, handsome young gentleman with a flowing beard bore down upon the doctor, as if he meant to run over him, but stopping suddenly, cried in an excited manner, —

"How long are you going to keep me in a madhouse?"

"Until you remember to behave like a gentleman," said the doctor, stepping briskly forward, a pace or two nearer to the speaker. "Gentlemen and reasonable persons, Mr. Marcel, show themselves to be such by treating with due respect the head of this establishment and the ladies whom they see in his company."

Mr. Marcel's eye quailed under the keen glance of the doctor, and he almost instantly turned his back, but presently wheeled about again, and said, with much composure, —

"The ladies, at all events, shall have the benefit of this meeting; here are some of the finest emeralds which ever graced the crown of an emperor. I am making a necklace of them for Queen Victoria. Here is one for you, madam, and one for you," and as he presented a pebble to each of the ladies, he muttered, in a low voice, "Beware! you are in a madhouse," and hastened away.

"That is one of my saddest cases," sighed the doctor, "a most gifted young man, an only son, the pride and delight of talented, wealthy, fond parents; and scarcely any hope left, for his malady is hereditary. He lives in that little cottage on our right, and Mr. Thornton in that with the green jalousies and the small walled garden in front. He seldom comes into the park, he prefers solitude. I will go in first," said the doctor, as they reached the gate of Thornton's residence, "and should I think the moment favourable, I will send a servant to conduct you to a good post for observation, and then I will come myself to fetch Miss Jones, when I have prepared the gentleman for her visit."

The two ladies were shortly joined by a man-servant, who led them up to a room on the first floor, and having drawn the muslin curtain of a window which looked into the garden, left them there.

Thornton was sitting on a bench by the side of a big hole he had been digging in the earth. A spade and shovel lay at his feet. A shade of unspeakable sadness clouded his gentle features, as he sat pensively resting his chin on his right hand, and looking into the hole. Nothing in the outward man announced the disorder of the inner one; on the contrary, everything about him, his beard and hair, now entirely white, his loose dressing-gown, his linen, were all clean and properly attended to.

"You see what I am doing," he said, in answer to the doctor's inquiries, "I am acting the grave-digger."

"Indulging in your morbid fancy, you mean," observed Dr. Ternel. "Graves are dug to receive corpses. I see none here."

Thornton shook his head, and answered nothing.

"Mr. Thornton, I say," cried the doctor aloud, "where is the corpse?"

"It was here when you came — lo! there it is," and Thornton pointed to a corner in the little enclosure. The doctor went to the spot indicated, and, sawing the air with his arms in every direction, kept saying, —

"There is nothing here, don't you perceive that there is nothing; how could I toss my arms about as freely as you see me doing, if there were any obstacle in the way?"

"No one saw the spectre of Banquo, save he who *was* to see it — the murderer," groaned Thornton.

"A spectre!" exclaimed the doctor; "but that is unsubstantial — how can you expect to bury that which has no substance?"

Thornton smiled, and hung down his head without answering.

"Oh! Mr. Thornton," resumed Doctor Ternel, passionately, "how can you, a gentleman, a scholar, and, above all, a Christian, allow yourself to be made the sport of such idle dreams?"

"Dreams!" repeated Thornton. "Let me tell you that there are more things in heaven and earth, Dr.

Ternel, than you dream of in your philosophy. There! now! don't you see her?" and the monomaniac started up, clasping his hands imploringly, his eye fixed in the direction of a tree.

"Come, then, let us follow and force an explanation from her," said the doctor, laying hold of Thornton's arm.

"No, no, no!" cried the Englishman, in an agony of terror, and grasping at the bench he had been sitting on.

After a pause, Dr. Ternel said, —

"There is a lady here who wishes to see you. Are you listening to me, Mr. Thornton? A countrywoman of yours, a friend of yours, is come to pay you a visit — Miss Lavinia Jones."

Not a muscle of Thornton's face moved.

"Do you not remember Miss Lavinia Jones, a tall, handsome young lady, whom you knew at Rome and also here in Paris?"

"I may possibly have met her," said Thornton.

"Allow me to tell you that it is not very amiable of you to receive the news of a friend's visit so coolly."

"What matters who comes or who does not come — now?" returned Thornton, with great dejection.

"Shall I tell her to come to you?"

"As you like," was the reply.

The doctor went for Lavinia.

"How glad I am to see you again, Mr. Thornton," faltered the young lady, with assumed glee, as she came in; "my good and excellent friend, do you not remember me in the Palazzo Morlacchi at Rome, and in the Boulevard des Capucines, here in Paris?"

The cloud rolled from the cast-down countenance,

which cleared for a second, but in a twinkling the deep shadow overspread it again, the lustrous eyes wandered from the beautiful face down to the black dress, and there remained riveted.

"It is well and right that you should wear mourning for her," he said, slowly; "all the world ought to wear it; there is not left a creature like her."

"I am in mourning for my dear aunt, Mr. Thornton — poor Mrs. Jones, who was so kind to me; you must remember her — she is gone from this world," and Lavinia's eyes filled with tears.

"Don't cry, don't cry, poor thing," he said, compassionately; "it is worse than useless. All the tears in the world could not make another Clara; but what we can do for her, is to give her Christian burial," and he took up his spade.

"I have been staying in Dorsetshire, and seen your house, Cypress Hall — what a delightful place it is. You will go back there some day, Mr. Thornton, won't you, to live," but he paid no heed to her. Lavinia persisted in her efforts to gain his attention. "And Signor Paolo is found, and safe in Rome; blessed news that, is it not?"

"No news to me," replied Thornton, with a start at the mention of the name. "I knew he would reappear one time or another to bear witness against me."

"Against you? Oh! Mr. Thornton, he would stand by you against all the world, and love you, and comfort you, as he did at Rome."

"Pshaw! everything is changed now; he is sworn to tell the truth, and tell it he will — he said so himself to me here. But now, excuse me, I must go on with my work, or I shall be behind my time."

A glance from the doctor warned Lavinia that the interview had lasted long enough.

"Well, then, good-bye, my dear, dear friend," said Lavinia, scarcely able to restrain her tears, and stretching out her hand; Thornton withheld his.

"Will you not shake hands with an old friend?"

"Better not," he said; "no good can come of touching my hand; the smell of blood is on it still. You recollect that line, 'All the perfumes of Arabia will not sweeten it;' very true, too true," and he recommenced his digging.

Miss Clara had not lost a syllable nor a look of what had been passing in the little garden.

Not a word was exchanged between the three, as the ladies, pale and mute as shadows by the doctor's side, were reconducted through the park back to the entrance gate.

"*A demain*," said the doctor, as he handed Miss Clara into the carriage.

"*A demain*," she answered, and the long and warm shake of the hand which accompanied the words, gave them a significancy, which a man of Dr. Ternel's penetration could not mistake.

CHAPTER XX.

The Result of the Discovery.

THE result was — all that the reader foresees. Startling events are not our province; on the contrary, nothing gladdens our heart like the seeing what is to follow, anticipated from what has preceded. Let Miss Clara tell her own story: —

"DEAREST ELEANOR, DEAREST GEORGE,

"WHAT should we have said to any one, who, when I parted from you only a week since, had ventured to predict that my journey to the East would end in Paris! I see from hence Nelly's look of amazement at this piece of news, answered by an ominous shake of George's mane; not altogether unwelcome the announcement, I fancy. Now or never is it a case for quoting, "Man proposes, God disposes." Yes, I hope and believe that I am not indulging in a superstitious feeling, when I allow myself to trace the finger of God in the course of events which have led to this issue. The way in which it has been brought about does seem marvellous when I recall its several steps. Had I not delayed my going to Scutari for two months in deference to your wishes — had I not during that interval met Miss Holywell on her way to my aunt — had it not so happened that my aunt was from home, Miss Schmaltz unusually cross, and Miss Holywell in so sore a puzzle what to do with herself, that she enlisted my sympathies in her behalf, and that I carried her off to Owlscombe, why — But it is really cruel in me to be retracing at my leisure every link of a chain of events, while your curiosity is on the rack. To make my story clear, I must, however, go back a little.

"Miss Holywell, you must know, while at Rome, had become acquainted with Mr. Thornton, and circumstances followed which caused the acquaintance to become intimacy. The last time she had seen him was in Paris, some nine or ten months ago. He had promised to write to her, but as, after her return to England, she never received any letter, she had some misgivings, and one of the first things she did on her arrival here was to try and find out what had become of him. I cannot now enter into some details, principally because doing so would involve the disclosure. of other people's affairs — suffice it to say, that once informed of Lavinia's anxiety, I fully shared in it.

"Our inquiries were successful, and we have found him — if a man can be said to be found whose better and nobler part is missing. Dear sister, dear brother, the gay beginning of my letter will not have prepared you, I am sure, to hear that we found him the inmate of a lunatic asylum. Oh, my dear ones, what a sight! I cannot tell you what a mingling of agony and tenderness swept through my heart, when I looked at the sad wreck of my former friend. I used to think I knew what it was to feel for others. It was a mistake — no, never till that moment did I learn what active charity was like. Thank God, I am here; thank God, I can be of service! At first I could scarcely identify him — his hair quite white, his noble figure bent like an old man's, yet nothing haggard in his countenance; the same gentle and mild expression as of yore; but so thin, so pale, so sad! My heart —: no, I can't write what I felt. He was digging a grave — his habitual employment — a grave for a woman he had wronged and killed; that is, for me, whom he fancies dead through his fault. In this fancy lies the root of his madness. The misgiving of his past injustice has been his crown of thorns for these nine years, a crown of thorns that has pierced to his very brain. Oh! my dearest brother and sister, what woman worthy of the name could stand the appeal conveyed by such a fact?

"Need I, after this, plead his cause with you? I am sure I need not. I know that, as you read this, all leaven of resentment passes away from your hearts. But I owe it to him to say, that if he sinned against me — and he did wrong me — I was not myself exempt from blame. Indeed, I was not. The subject is disagreeable to you, but bear with me while I tell you now the whole truth; nor must you imagine that I am wilfully blackening myself, because I refuse to be thought better of than I deserve. You were not with me when the circumstances I allude to occurred.

"I had gone on a visit to my aunt at Ivy Lodge, for the purpose of attending one . of the Moreton assemblies. It was my first ball, and I was quite carried away by the gay scene, and the lovely music. What girl of nineteen but is fluttered on such an occasion. Among the company, more than usually numerous and brilliant, aunt singled out, and introduced to me in a very marked manner, a young officer. Aunt, I must say, had neither eyes, nor ears, nor smiles for anyone but this gentleman, who was neither prepossessing in manner nor appearance; but then he was the son of an earl. His attentions to me became, during the evening, so pointed and assiduous as to attract general notice. Probably, he was not aware that I was an engaged girl, nor that my future husband was at the ball; and I, with the stupid bashfulness of my age, and country education, lacked both the courage and the tact that would have enabled me to check this young coxcomb of a lord. He laid regular siege to me, prevented any but himself from approaching me, insisted, in a way I knew not how to resist, that I should dance every dance with him — (Thornton, as you are aware, never danced) — and when I expressed a wish to sit down, led me to a corner, and sitting down by me, cut me off from all communication with the rest of the company. Now, believe my confession, that, annoyed as I felt at this sort of persecution, still I was not insensible to the honour done me by the principal person in the room.

"Thornton, and in this he was wrong, did nothing to help me out of my awkward predicament; on the contrary, kept aloof. I remarked this with pain, as well as the vexation his looks betrayed, but soon forgot everything in the excitement of a new quadrille. I had a glimpse of Thornton at the door of the supper room, as I was going in with my lord. I did not see him again that night. He called at Ivy Lodge the next day but one; he was cold and grave, and I read reproach in his eyes. I received him peevishly. Aunt's taunts about what she called his neglect of me at the ball, had influenced me to believe that I had rather received than given offence. I need not remind you that aunt was anything but friendly to Mortimer. His measured remonstrances called forth ungracious answers. What had I done? I had been civil to those who had been civil to me; I had danced with those who had asked me. Where was the great harm? Why had he not danced with me himself? I knew, he said, that he never danced. That was no reason why I should not, was my repartee. For what did a girl go to a ball, but to dance? Ah! for what else indeed? echoed he significantly.

"My lord came in at this instant. He was full of the races, the dinner and the ball, which were to take place at Weymouth on the day after the morrow. His present visit was to make sure that we had received invitations. I assured him that we had our tickets, and should certainly be there. Mortimer went away without another word. Next day brought me a short note from him: —

"'Will you give up, for my sake, your Weymouth ball? The request may seem unreasonable, but you are so good and so indulgent to my whims, that I venture to make it."

"I made up my mind to comply with his wish, and showing aunt the note, told her I should not go to the ball. Aunt was incensed with the note and with me; the note was absurd, ridiculous, odious, my complying with it an impossibility, and she gave me plenty of reasons why it was so. The end of it was, that I wrote in answer, that much as I wished to humour even his whims, aunt declared that I could not do so in the present case, without infringing every rule of good breeding and of good society. The ball was given at the barracks, and as we approached the gate, I perceived Thornton standing there; he bowed low, but did not make the least attempt to accost us. I believe he was in the ball-room for some time, but I did not see him.

"You know the rest. The next evening I received a letter from him dated London — the letter in which he told me he released me from my engagement to him; that he did so, not in anger, but in the sad conviction that, being such as he was, he should be unable to make me happy. Was the punishment disproportioned to the offence? Strangers might deem it so; but I, who had had a twelvemonth to judge of his peculiarities, who had accepted him for better and for worse — oh! no, I could not think it so. The scales fell from my eyes, and I at once measured to the full the extent of my fault, and the worth of the heart I had wounded. That letter marked a new era in my life, and I may say without exaggeration, that if there is any good in me, I owe it to the man who penned it. Thus far I have thought it my duty to unbury the past; and now let us consign to everlasting oblivion all that relates to that ill-omened transaction.

"The sanitary establishment of which Mortimer is an inmate is under the management of Dr. Ternel, an eminent physician, and a most worthy man, who has a passion for his calling, and better still, infinite devotion to his patients. Our friend could not be in better hands. With what might well be taken for divination, Dr. Ternel at once detected that I was the very person he had been longing for all these eight months. For you must understand this, that nothing but reality can dispel Thornton's morbid delusion; nothing but a Clara of flesh and blood can obliterate and put to flight the shadowy Clara, which haunts him by day and by night. So, you see, that I am the only person in the world, who can effect a cure — if a cure is to be effected — and Dr. Ternel is sanguine of success. God grant that his anticipations may be realized! As mine is to be no small part in the pious task, in fact, the chief one, under the doctor's guidance and direction, I have, of course, no reserve with him on this matter; while he, like the true-hearted and plain-spoken man that he is, is above all things anxious that I should not be the dupe of what he calls my generosity. Consequently, he has kept from me, not only none of the difficulties of the present, but also none of the responsibility of the future. 'For,' says the good doctor, 'even in case of success, don't imagine your task to be over. To confirm that success and render it definitive, your constant presence will be indispensable for a length of time; without that, a relapse would be inevitable. In a word, my dear lady, you must learn to consider yourself the guardian angel of this gentleman, and stick to his side as closely as his own shadow. Unfortunately, we live in a sceptical age, and even the part of a guardian angel, when enacted by a young and handsome lady, might be liable to misconstruction.' (The doctor is short-sighted, which accounts for his calling an old maid of eight-and-twenty, young.) 'There is a way, however, of getting over the difficulty. I beg your pardon for my seeming audacity, but my motive must be my justification. If you could take upon yourself to do now for Mr. Thornton, in the event of his recovery, what you promised and intended to do nine years ago, I could almost answer for there being no return of his present attack.' I answered, that if indeed my presence was of such vital consequence to Mr. Thornton, and he should ever express the slightest wish that I should become his wife, I could and would consent. So do not be surprised, my dear George and

16*

Eleanor, if one of these days you are pounced upon by a jolly couple. Speaking in earnest, the situation of a wife-nurse to a man, whom of all men I respect, has nothing in it that repels me — quite the contrary. Ours would be a sort of joint-stock association, to do a little good in this world, and Thornton's ample means would go far to secure the prosperity of the association.

"For the present, my only occupation is to go every day to the doctor's *maison de santé*, and hear progress reported, for the patient is now undergoing a sort of preparatory training. All Dr. Ternel's indefatigable ingenuity is brought to bear on a single point, that of impressing upon Thornton the notion of my existence. The doctor refers constantly to many particulars connected with our days of courtship, and which I communicated for this purpose. The doctor represents me as full of life and affection, quite bent upon finding Thornton. It is painful, yet at the same time curious, to hear their conversation respecting me, for most of these discussions I overhear, according to the doctor's wish, in order that I may become familiarized with Thornton's aspect, ways, and habit of thought. A Madame Françoise, a kind old soul, with whom he lodged for some time, is the most useful auxiliary in this part of the affair. In a little while, I shall have to write a letter to Thornton, and another to the doctor, fixing on a certain day for my arrival, and on the effect of these letters the doctor greatly counts. A piano is to be put near the doctor's private room, and I am to play once familiar airs, and sing the songs of the merry days, when we were young. Ah, me! and the doctor will manage to bring Mortimer somewhere within hearing.

But neither letters nor music will be resorted to, until the present preparatory discipline has given some favourable result. Then, should the plan so far succeed, I am to show myself; and I pray to God to give me courage, and to inspire my words, for much, if not all the cure, will depend on my presence of mind, and unwavering resolution.

"But even should we fail in the first trial, we shall not despair. Dr. Ternel has a second scheme in reserve — an *en cas*, as he calls it — which he thinks would be worth the trying. It will be to take Thornton to England, to Cypress Hall. His native air and the sight of familiar objects may, so the doctor avers, produce a favourable crisis, when all other measures have failed. In that case, a young physician, one of the most skilful of Dr. Ternel's pupils, is to accompany us to England, and we are implicitly to obey his directions. Should things come to this, then, my dearest brother and sister, we shall indeed require your kind assistance, and I know we may depend on that. Let us, however, hope that there may be no necessity for any call upon you.

"I enclose a note from Miss Holywell. She starts to-morrow morning for Marseilles in excellent company. I cannot tell you how much I regret to part with one, who has proved to me a sincere and affectionate friend. By a strange coincidence — providential might be a better word — she also has had tidings of a person she was much interested in, and whose disappearance, under very suspicious circumstances, had been a source of wearing anxiety to her, and also to poor Thornton. This person was a young Italian artist, to whom Thornton had much attached himself at Rome; and

from what Miss Holywell has said, I can understand
that Thornton was also once of much use to her in
trying circumstances, here in Paris — I mean before
this illness of his. You see the man was born to do
good to everyone he had to do with. Miss Holywell
always speaks of him as the best of men. Without
him, she declares, she should have gone mad.

"Do not be uneasy about me, or my whereabouts.
I am in capital health and spirits, and very comfortable
in this *maison meublée*. The landlady is quite respectable, and Madame Françoise is on a visit to her, and
both of them take every possible care of me. You
must not, therefore, think there is any necessity for
your coming over here on my account. If I want you,
believe that I will write to summon you. And now,
good-bye, dearest brother and sister, and believe me,

"Your ever affectionate,

"CLARA."

Among the several letters despatched that day by
Lavinia, was one addressed to Signor Paolo Mancini,
Rome, of which we shall hear at some future day.

CHAPTER XXI.

Awakening.

PAOLO in the meantime had little joy of his halt in
the mire. The longer his body stuck in the bog of
sensualism, the less his soul got acclimated to the foul
atmosphere. A being organized to soar, cannot crawl
without suffering from the violence done to its nature.
How could he, who had dreamed all his life, and for a

short while had tasted of the ambrosia and nectar of re-
quited love, how could he be satisfied with the food of
swine of which he was now partaking? And yet, loath-
some as it was, he lacked the strength to turn from
Circe's proffered cup. He who wonders at this incon-
sistency, knows little of human nature. The *video me-
liora, deteriora sequor*, has been a phenomenon common
to all times. Exuberance of youth, idleness, force of
habit, and last not least, that most tremendous of bars
to a good resolve, "For whose sake now?" were the
enemies which kept Paolo balancing himself uneasily
on the slippery slope. But whatever the blandishments
used, they could not silence the inner witness, who cried
to him now and then, "You debase your immortal soul,
you give the lie to every precedent of your life, you
are a contemptible wretch — shame, shame upon you!"
With so sensitive a patient there is room for hope. The
sick man who does not feel his disease, is past recovery;
for one who groans and laments himself, there is the
chance of a favourable crisis.

Our sinning young hero had gone to bed at four in
the morning. Not, however, in the Rue St. Georges,
where we left him; his friends had decided, not himself,
that apartment to be too shabby and mean for him; besides, there was no coach-house or stable attached to it
— too great an inconvenience for a man, who no longer
hired, but kept horses and carriages of his own. Paolo
then had rented a second floor in the Rue de la Chaussée
d'Antin, capacious, gorgeously fitted up, and extra-
vagantly dear. Well, then, he had gone to bed about
four in the morning, after a night as ill-spent as may be.
He had played and lost a round sum of money — lost
it certainly to very gentlemanly persons, but, as he had

every reason for believing, sharpers into the bargain.
Money, in general, was the least of his troubles, indeed,
he squandered it with a sort of rage. In the present
instance, it was the way in which he had been tricked
out of it, that galled and provoked him. A man does
not find himself enacting the part of a dupe, without
wincing a little, and, to render Paolo justice, the strings
of conscience had also something to do with his sleep-
lessness. On what he had staked and lost, two families
of honest artisans might have lived in plenty for a whole
year. Prosper did not earn a quarter as much in a
twelve-month by his unremitting labour. Then he began to wonder what had become of the little man, of
Prudence, of the children, of Benoît and Dr. Perrin, of
Mr. Pertuis and Mr. Boniface. They might be all dead
for anything he knew. He had not only not seen any
of them, or sought to see them for ages; but he had
literally forgotten them, ungrateful wretch that he was.
It was not till the dawn began to peep through the
silken curtains, that something like calm stole over his
senses, and allowed him to sleep — a heavy unhealthy
sleep.

He was dreaming of a violent ringing of bells, when
what was in reality a most formidable pull of his door-
bell, succeeded in thoroughly awakening him. He sat
up in his bed and listened; the faint echo of an angry
debate in the room preceding his salon, reached him.
What could it be? He jumped out of bed, slipped into
a brocade dressing-gown, and shouted through the
salon, —

"What's the matter, Victor?"

No answer being vouchsafed, and the noise of the
scuffle without, continuing unabated, Paolo pushed open

the door leading to the hall, and saw Victor, with his
back to him, defending the approach to the salon, par-
rying, with a chair held in front of him, the attack of
a smart little fellow, brandishing a broom twice as long
as himself, by which he was striving to brush Victor
out of his way. At first Paolo was struck dumb by
surprise; the next instant, little disposed to merriment
as he was, the ludicrousness of the scene was too much
for him, and he burst into a glorious fit of laughter.
Salvator — for Salvator it was, threw down his broom,
and, holding his sides, sunk on a chair, convulsed;
while Victor, his face as red as his waistcoat, looked
on in grim expectation of what was to happen next.
Naturally, this was that Paolo and Salvator fell into
each other's arms, giving and receiving the hearty hug
of brotherhood, on seeing which, Victor relinquished his
chair, and withdrew in undisguised disgust.

"By Jove!" cried Salvator still laughing, "you are
better guarded than the Pope; it is no metaphor to say,
that one has to fight one's way to your presence. I
may well sing with the libretto, *A pugnar m' accinsi,
o Roma —*"

"Hush!" said Paolo leading the way to his bed-
room, for he began to wish for more covering than even
his wadded dressing-gown.

"Why hush? — is singing forbidden in private in
the classic land of *chanson?*"

"Certainly not, but it is so early."

"Early? my fine fellow, do you call eight o'clock
early? You seem not to be aware of the fact, that, *Da
tre ore il sol ris-ple-ende.*"

"The fact is, it's the fashion about here to keep
rather late hours," returned Paolo, a little abashed, as he

drew aside the curtains, and opened the jalousies. The flood of light he let in was like a reproach.

"The saints preserve me!" cried Salvator; "you are lodged like a cardinal, and habited like the Grand Signior."

"Or like a fool" said Paolo, with a side glance at the sky-blue cachemire pantaloons he was even then donning. "But never mind me just now; rather tell me about yourself and Clelia, and all my old friends. Are you married? and how is it you are here? why did you not answer my last letter?"

"Your letter of the beginning of November, with the one for Clelia, enclosing the cheque for 1,000 scudi, you mean? — for the simple reason that I never got it until our return to Rome from Palermo, a fortnight ago. Clelia and I, you must know, spent the winter with the marchioness, at Palermo, or rather, to be precise, near Palermo, at a villa belonging to a sister of Prince Rocca Ginestra. As there were to be operatic performances, and acting, and tournaments, Clelia and I were, of course, articles of absolute necessity to the marchioness. As it turned out, she might have dispensed with us, as, instead of gaieties, we had nothing but jealousies, quarrels, and confounded confusion, as of old. But all that is nothing to you, nor yet to the post, who did not forward my letters, because, not expecting any, I had taken no precautions to have them sent on. Thus it was that, returning to Rome in the middle of February, I thought myself a favourite of fortune to find your letter of November still awaiting me — and then it was I learned, for the first time, that difficulties were raised by Government to your return. Finding also no letters of a later date, I grew uneasy about you. Why should I not do like Mahomet, and go to the mountain, since the mountain could not come to me? Clelia encouraged the idea; money I had in plenty, without touching the 1,000 scudi, which, indeed, are intact. So I put myself *en route*, and, after a week's stay at Turin, to satisfy myself from what quarter the wind really blew there, I arrived in Paris yesterday morning. My first visit was to Rue St. Georges, the address marked in your last letter. I was told there that you had long left, they no longer remembered for what neighbourhood. I then went to Mr. Prosper's, Quai Montebello, the address you gave me in your first letter. Mr. Prosper sent me to Rue du Four; nobody there knew of your whereabouts; and, in short, without that excellent Madame Prosper, I never should have discovered you. We spent the whole of yesterday in tracking you, with the genius and patience of a policeman, from Rue du Four to Rue St. Georges, from Rue St. Georges to Avenue Montaigne, and from Avenue Montaigne here. I called three times last evening, but the porter said you were not at home, and would not let me in. Very grim personages these French porters. But your jackanapes in red sleeves beats them all. *Midi* and *midi*, and *midi* again — I could wrench from him nothing but *midi*. What could I do under such circumstances but drop all parley, and push forward a reconnaissance. Red sleeves bars the way, and skirmishes with a chair in defence of the approach.

> 'Ah canaglia vuol battaglia,
> E battaglia ti darò.'

sing I, and at him with a broom. Luckily you appeared, like a *Deus ex machinâ*, in time to prevent further hostilities."

"My good friend," said Paolo, half touched, half amused, "what a deal of trouble I have cost you! It was like you to come, and it is, I assure you, like a providential interference to have you here. I have so much to say, oh! so much."

"And I such an impatience to hear all you can say; but tell me first about Thornton — no, first about Miss Lav — By the by," and Salvator bounded up from the sofa like an india-rubber ball, and began fumbling in his pockets: "if I am not mistaken, I myself am the bearer of news of *la Diva*. Where is it got to now?"

"Where is — what?" asked Paolo, in great agitation.

"A letter addressed to you, which I found at the post-office in Rome, and I had no end of discoursing to do, before I could rescue it from the officials there. Ah! here it is, in my very last pocket."

Paolo seized the letter, broke the seal with shaking fingers, and literally devoured the contents. This was what Lavinia wrote, —

"Paris, 31st Jan. 1855.

"MY DEAR SIGNOR PAOLO,

"Passing through Paris, I have heard from Madame Françoise of your safety, and indeed that, in all probability, you are at this moment once more in your dear Rome. I feel so happy and thankful at this news, that I cannot resist the temptation of telling you so. But when I try to find words adequate to my feelings, nothing comes but tears — sweet tears, and inarticulate blessings. Accept them — not the less for being unspoken — accept them, though they are from one who has rendered you evil for good. Most sincerely and humbly do I entreat your forgiveness. Indeed, indeed,

I knew not what I did. I saw without understanding, and mistook the semblance for the substance. I was intoxicated with prosperity and flattery. Since we parted, I have become acquainted with that stern, but friendly monitor, adversity. I needed humbling, I needed sobering, and this austere friend has done both for me. The trial has been a hard one, but blessed be the day which brought it to me; blessed be the day which opened my eyes to the knowledge that life has duties, and that in the performance of duty lies true happiness; and, so help me God, I will do my part. How many other truths you tried to impress upon me, and which, passing unheeded at that time, now rise up and people my memory! Believe me, my recollection of you is indissolubly associated in my mind with all that is good and noble, while when you think of me —- Oh! Signor Paolo, how you must have despised me! and I deserved it well. But now you may give me back your esteem; you may, indeed; I am entitled to it. Not for my eternal salvation would I impose on you. The only claim I impose on you is for your esteem; every other I can and do entirely give up; let the past be in every other respect as if it had never been, but your esteem I must have. It is, I feel, the staff on which I rely, to support me on my thorny path. It is not likely that we shall ever meet again in this world. I am setting off on an expedition from which I may never return. But wherever I am, you will have my earnest prayers for your welfare, and for that of your country also. May its destinies be what your patriot heart desires; and now, good-bye. All good be around you.

"LAVINIA.

"P. S. — Don't imagine I wish to justify my past folly, but one thing I must state in my defence. It was not my fault, that I inflicted that last disappointment on you in Paris. What I said in my hurried note was the exact truth. I went to the ball against my will. I was positively forced to go. From thence date all my troubles. · Mrs. Jones was taken ill there, and never recovered. She is dead. Sickness, estrangement, and death followed in the wake of that night. Surely you will forgive me. Mr. Jones and I have parted for ever. Adieu."

Paolo threw down the letter with a gesture of despair, buried his face in the sofa cushion, and sobbed desperately.

"What is the matter? Good heavens! is the news so bad?" cried poor Salvator, in an agony of sympathy. Paolo pointed to the letter. Salvator took it up and read it. "Upon my word," said he, after the perusal, "though I don't understand it quite, I cannot see anything in it to put you into this state. There is a horrible hint, to be sure, about her never coming back, but she may, you know; it's only mountains that never meet."

"It is not that, it is not that," sobbed Paolo, swinging his buried head from side to side, like an obstinate child.

"If it is not that, I don't see what vexes you," pursued Salvator; "perhaps it is that the dear old lady has departed this life."

Still the head oscillated in sign of denial.

"If it is not that either, I give up trying to guess what it is," continued Salvator, with just a shade of impatience. "All the rest, to my common-place vision, at least, reads well and promising. She confesses to have done wrong, like a brave, honest girl, asks for pardon, and begs for your esteem."

"My esteem," groaned Paolo.

"Well, well, the word is rather icy, but in the dictionary of lovers, you may take it as a rule," added the little man, wagging his head with a great air of wisdom, "that esteem stands for love."

"Don't say any more, don't say any more," exclaimed Paolo.

"I assure you I am right; why, any one with a grain of sense can understand what she means; just look at the way she speaks of you; everything you ever said or did, quite right in her eyes; every one wrong but you."

"That is exactly what I cannot bear; that is what is enough to drive me mad," burst forth Paolo, standing up, in a whirlwind of passion. "Praising me! I tell you it is horrible mockery, a downright profanation; every word she writes cuts me like a knife. My esteem! I have none to spare for myself; my virtues are those of swine; my goodness! hell is full of such. I wish I were dead!"

"Paolo!" shouted poor Salvator in new-born terror; and taking hold of Paolo's hand, he raised himself to the level of his friend's eyes. "Paolo!"

"Don't be afraid. I am not out of my senses," said Paolo more composedly; "it would be better for me, perhaps, if I were. I am not mad, but a degraded being, who recoils, horror-struck, from his own degradation. You yourself are the mirror in which I see it in full length."

"I?" exclaimed Salvator, in increasing perplexity.

"Yes, you. There you stand, in your manly simplicity and innocence, the living reproach of my effeminacy, my profligacy. Those ridiculous coxcombs we used to call women-men, and make sport of at Rome, I am one of them, nay, worse. A glorious figure I cut in my Turkish morning costume, don't I? Look at my collection of whips, canes, cravat-pins, wrist-buttons, and scent-bottles, and be lost in admiration. Worthy property for an artist, is it not? By and by, the hair-dresser will he here, and elaborately arrange and curl my hair. How manly! ha! ha! Why don't you laugh too? Open the safety-valve, or, by Jove, you will be choked by contempt."

"Come, come," expostulated Salvator, who now began to have some inkling of the state of the case, "you take things too tragically, a moment of weakness is soon retrieved. For a man of your spirit, to shake off any worldly shackles requires but the will."

"And the inward bonds, friend Salvator! Samson pulled down pillars; did he free himself from inward bonds? His ideal dragged in the mire by Dalilah, was he ever able to raise it again on its pedestal? My soul is a sink of pollution."

"Nonsense!" here ejaculated the little man.

"Such a life, such orgies I should rather say, as I have revelled in for these last three months, you cannot imagine; to tell you of it, would be to contaminate you; but there, in that escritoire, lie materials for the history — scented documents signed by names renowned in infamy. Foulness, foulness, foulness, has been my daily pittance. Everything respectable, everything holy — chastity, patriotism, disinterestedness, honesty — I have heard quizzed, lampooned, cursed — heard it without wincing, until, by G—, I have come not to know right from wrong."

"Fibs!" exclaimed Salvator. "If that were the case, you would not talk as you are doing."

"And now that I have sunk so low as to be past any hope of ever rising again," pursued Paolo, without heeding his friend's interruption, "here comes my finishing stroke — a glimpse of Paradise to madden me on my dunghill. Purified through suffering, restored to her angelic nature, she who was the embodiment of my ideal of a woman, lays her innocent heart open before me, prays for peace, and lavishes blessings on me — O heavens! on me, a lump of corruption! The fate of Tantalus — the draught of happiness within sight, and yet never to be reached. My own doing — that's the comfort I have — my very own doing. Do you understand what Tantalus may feel in such a predicament, Salvator? That he'll not go on for ever suffering, I should say."

"Hush!" cried Salvator, "this is the raving of a Pagan; we are Christians, Paolo, and, as such, must think, speak, and act. Suppose yourself in the next world, have you escaped from yourself there? Be a man."

Paolo for all answer covered his face.

"Besides," continued Salvator, descending from his unusual altitudes to the level of an argument *ad hominem*, "besides, allow me to observe, that it is but a sorry welcome to a poor devil who has come all the way from Rome to see you, to tell him —" Here Salvator came to a full stop. "I say to threaten —" The good little fellow could not finish his remonstrance.

"Forgive me, Salvator," said Paolo, wringing his friend's hand; "I am not the unfeeling wretch I may seem. It was that letter which upset me — that letter, with the associations and memories it evoked — it sets old wounds bleeding afresh."

There are emotions which admit of no utterance but tears.

After a while, Salvator exclaimed, —

"It's just one of the tricks of this nasty Paris."

"Not at all," said Paolo. "Paris is a place like any other, it is within one's option here, as elsewhere, to live simply, reasonably, and yet agreeably. I question if there be any other capital in Europe where there are so many opportunities for self-cultivation and honest recreation. Everywhere public monuments, picture galleries, libraries, lectures, gardens, and what not, accessible to the public gratis. Temptations also of all kinds there is no lack of in Paris, nor is there in any other huge metropolis; but their high price here, as elsewhere, acts as a safeguard for the great majority. Money has been my bane. But for it, I might still be the honest fellow I was when I came here, and look every man in the face without a blush. Talk to me of the corruption of Paris! Misery threw me among the hard-working class. There, in that humble sphere, my friend, you may find all the virtues inculcated by the Gospel in action — Charity first and foremost. Later again, benignant fate brought me acquainted with the studious of Paris. My employer was a savant, simple as a child, learned as a Benedictine. Good Mr. Boniface! — his mind in a constant state of contention lest he should overtask me. No scarcity of good examples there, for his friends were cast in the same mould

as himself — living rather in the spirit than in the
body. All the elevating influences which can improve
a man, I breathed in that atmosphere. About that time
I met with a wild young student, a good fellow at
bottom, but a Voltairian *quand même*, who took to
hectoring me, to drag me down from my height of
spiritualism. In vain; I was firm as a rock. Poverty
and constant occupation kept me out of temptation.
Then, I received that fatal legacy, and ere long, idleness aiding and abetting, I was low enough in ma-
terialism. My guardian angel whispered warnings to
me to refuse it, but my evil genius prevailed. The
moment I was rich, I was transformed from my old self
to another being, and from weakness to weakness I
sunk to what you find me — a grovelling sensualist.
There is a curse in money, Salvator, believe me."

"Well, if it be so," replied Salvator, "the remedy
is easy. Cast from you that curse, and begin life anew
on bread and cheese."

"And so I will, by all that is holy," cried Paolo.

"At it at once," urged Salvator; "put on your shab-
biest coat and hat, to be in keeping with mine, and let
us go out. Do you know of any place where we are
likely to see any blackbirds?"

"Possibly in the Tuileries, or Bois de Boulogne;
but, to tell the truth, I know nothing about birds, or
trees, or flowers."

"Well, let us take our chance with both places."

"My good fellow," said Paolo, with a very signi-
ficant unwillingness, "the Tuileries and the Bois have
been the theatre of more than one of my follies, and
besides, I am sure to meet at either the one or the
other, hosts of people I know."

"Hm! can you think of no retired nook, where there are turf and trees, and none of your acquaintances?" pleaded Salvator.

Paolo mused a little, then said, —

"Yes; though it is ages since I was at the place, I remember being struck by the number of blackbirds in the cemetery of Mont Parnasse.

"A cemetery!" repeated Salvator, with a grimace indicative of anything but gratification.

"You must not be alarmed by the name. A burying-ground in Paris is a fresh, verdant, quiet spot. You will like it well, I promise you."

"Here then goes for the burying-ground," pronounced Salvator.

Paolo was ready in a few minutes. Victor listened grimly to an intimation that the room off the *salle-à-manger* was to be got ready for the new arrival.

"Is the hairdresser to wait for monsieur?" asked Victor, solemnly.

"No! tell him not to come any more till I send for him."

"Is the carriage to be sent to meet monsieur?"

"No; and tell Pierre I shall not want him to-day, and that he may consider himself at liberty for the whole of next week."

"And should any visitor come for monsieur?"

"I am out of town; let the concierge know."

"Is monsieur absent even for — the person who breakfasted yesterday with monsieur?"

"Even for that person," and monsieur shut the door with a bang.

Victor looked despondent for a second or two, then rallying his spirits, he lifted up his right leg, leant his head to one side, stretched forth both arms, and gave to all limbs concerned a vibratory motion to and fro in the direction of the door — a sort of blessing *sui generis* to his master.

The only precise idea Paolo had of the whereabouts of the cemetery of Mont Parnasse was that it lay somewhere on the other bank of the Seine; but thanks to that thread of Ariadne, which in the person of "commissionnaires" is ready for use at almost every corner of every street in Paris, the friends were not long in being put in the right track. Prejudiced as he was against Paris — most foreigners are so on first coming thither — disposed as he was to find fault, Salvator was nevertheless too fair not to acknowledge the usefulness of this provident institution; and when he espied in a bye-street the familiar sight of a vendor *sub dio* of roasted chesnuts, Salvator's heart relented for good and all, and he openly allowed France to be a civilized country, whatever her shortcomings. Incredible how far these imponderables go in determining our estimate of objects and places! Salvator improved the occasion, and stuffed his pockets full of his favourite eatable — horribly dear though, as he said — and then he held a little conversation with the seller, and discovered him to be a native of Italian Switzerland.

Another and agreeable novelty to the small painter were the number of shops with flowers and funeral-wreaths, garlands, statuettes, and mementoes of many kinds, which studded the immediate neighbourhood of the cemetery. Paolo bought some garlands of evergreen, which he intended for little Annette's cross, if he found it, which he did not; nor did his conscience reproach him in the least, that by so doing he was en-

couraging an immoral traffic ou the holiest sympathies
of mankind, as is urged by some people. Would to
God that the spirit of commerce were never applied to
worse purposes!

The cemetery of the Mont Parnasse is one of the
humblest of the French capital, yet not the less impressive for that. Few and far between are the pompous
monuments — vain protests of posthumous vanity against
the stern equality of death — many the modest slabs
of marble — innumerable the anonymous crosses, suggestive alike of obscure lives, and Christian humility.
Not one but had a wreath hung round it, or a tuft of
flowers carefully reared at its base. Go thither at what
hour of the day you will, and you find pious hands
are busy — many of them the horny ones of artisans,
or the sorely needle-pricked ones of seamstresses —
clearing away, embellishing, propping up or watering
the silent home of their departed ones. It is in this
assiduous care of the living for the dead, that lies the
great charm of the Paris burying-grounds.

Salvator could scarcely understand the scene at first,
and when he did, he nearly vented his pleased wonderment in a profane *ut de poitrine*, which he checked, however, in time, declaring instead most emphatically, that
if the respect for the dead was to be taken as the measure of the worth of the living, the Parisians certainly
were superior to their reputation.

"Let us sit down here," said Paolo, "and enjoy the
prospect from this mound."

The view before the friends had a melancholy charm
of its own. Not a tint, not a sound, not a movement
in the vast enclosure at their feet, but was subdued to
harmony with its destination. The mellow light of a pale

March sun, the gentle undulations of the plain, the twitterings of birds, which filled every ivy-bush and cypress, the tender green of the new shoots on syca-mores, acacias and pendent willows, were the soft notes, if we dare use the expression, from whose *ensemble* arose a full chord — a chord which struck home to the heart, inclining it to reverie.

"A beautiful spot, and full of blackbirds, I declare," said Salvator at last.

"Did I not tell you, that even though a cemetery, it was beautiful?" replied Paolo, as if awaking. "Sweet must be the rest under this verdant turf, and in these quiet shades."

"True — but not before a journey, let us say of fourscore years in search of some grand object," returned Salvator spiritedly.

Paolo shook his head despondingly, upon which Salvator thought the moment a fitting one to remind his gloomy friend, that for him, Salvator, Paolo's his-tory, since his departure from Rome, was still a mys-tery. Salvator knew nothing of Thornton, nothing of Lavinia, and was still in the first wonderment as to what had caused so complete a severance between the three friends. Paolo, not unwillingly, consented to re-late the particulars of a tale, which had lain long heavily hidden in the depths of his heart. He now poured forth his sorrows, told of his fit of frenzy on learning that Lavinia had gone to the ball at the Hôtel de Ville, his subsequent illness, his useless search after Thornton, and the conclusion he had come to, that Thornton had gone to the United States in search of him; and last but not the least momentous event to

him, his accession to his uncle's fortune, and his subsequent dissipation.

Salvator was so moved by this narrative, a real
romance he declared, and which as such, must end well
sooner or later, and then so dreadfully excited by the
sight of a blackbird perched just below where they were
sitting, whistling and trilling, as if in defiance, that
he protested he must either give way to his singing
propensities, or choke. To avoid one or other extremity, it was better to beat a timely retreat; in effecting
which, a savoury smell which exhaled from a small
wineshop by the roadside, a smell suggestive of cutlets
on the gridiron, and of potatoes in the act of frying,
came to remind Salvator of one of his idiosyncracies —
viz. that any strong emotion infallibly made him hungry.
A halt was accordingly decided on, and the young men
entered the humble eating-house. It was without effort
as without repugnance that Paolo seated himself at a
small table with a coarse cloth — he was at bottom
still as simple in tastes, notions, and habits as when at
Rome; and riches, thank God, had not inoculated him
with any of that fastidiousness, which teaches people to
turn up their noses at everything not set in gold, or
bearing on it the stamp of fashion. Paolo did ample
justice to the frugal meal. A stomach of five and twenty
will assert its rights, whatever the mental frame of the
owner.

After this they walked to the Luxembourg, strolled
leisurely through the gardens on to the Pantheon, which
concluded their walking tour of Paris for that day. It
was eight in the evening when a cab put them down
at Paolo's door in the Chaussée d'Antin — it was the
only drive they had had, and that was necessitated by

Salvator's portmanteau having to be fetched from the fourth-rate hotel, to which he had gone on his first arrival. No wonder they were ready to drop with fatigue, they had been nearly nine hours on their legs.

CHAPTER XXII.

Tedium Vitæ.

WELL might red-waistcoated Victor, and his colleague of the whip, deplore the degeneracy of the age, and indulge, glass in hand, at their quasi-fashionable wine-shop over the way, in ominous forebodings how all this would end. Ever since the advent of little *saute ruisseau*, as they styled Salvator, the life they led had become sorry and unprofitable. No more *billets doux* to carry, no more mysterious visitors to introduce, no more cases of champagne and Strasbourg *pâtés* to order, no more *parties fines* to superintend; and naturally no more little douceurs to realize out of these several items. The snug little establishment which they had served with such complacency, was turned, alas! into a desert. How else designate a house, the master of which sallied forth at seven in the morning, returned at dusk, and was in his bed at ten!

Such was, in fact, the course of life adopted of late by Paolo, under the influence of his friend and guest. They went out early, spent most of the day in visiting public galleries or other remarkable places — when tired of being on their legs, jumped into the first omnibus they met, stopping where it stopped, most frequently at a barrière, occasionally in a suburb — took their dinner at the nearest restaurant, and then returned home, either by the same omnibus or a similar conveyance, Paolo having laid it down as a rule never to hire a cab.

Nor had he wished to do so, would Salvator have allowed of it. Salvator delighted in the omnibuses; he considered them as the most wonderful, instructive, and amusing contrivances of modern times. His power of observation, which was of the scantiest, and his propensity to communication, which was of the largest, both found full scope in those rolling stages, whose actors were for ever changing. Nothing deterred by his ignorance of French, he spoke freely and good-humouredly right and left, making friends among his fellow passengers — rarely leaving the vehicle without being on intimate terms with the benevolent gentleman — thank God, there is one at least in every batch! — who assists in and out the aged and infirm, the children and the ladies, and is for ever on the stretch, with danger to himself of a twisted neck or spine, in-his readiness to collect the fare of those in the farthest off seats, for the conductor. Even within the small compass of a public carriage there is a plenty of room for the exercise of the smaller charities of life. Unfortunately — and our little friend was not long in making the discovery — there is space also for selfishness and harshness — and your active, good-natured, kindly disposed gentleman finds his contrast too often in yonder gruff individual, who looks upon every newcomer in the light of an intruder, nay, of an enemy, and would not for any consideration move an inch to accommodate a delicate woman or child, and snarls when inadvertently brushed against — a living negation of all human fellow-feeling.

This half-artistic, half-nomadic existence was the very one for Salvator to enjoy, had not Paolo's increasing gloom cast a shadow upon it. Paolo grew more self-absorbed, less sociable every day; the very topics nearest his heart, Lavinia, Thornton, Clelia, Rome, seemed to have lost their hold on him; he dismissed them with monosyllables. If he spoke at all, it was to agree with Salvator's praise of picture or statue, of the weather, or the scenery, or living creature, in a strain far too high-flown and exaggerated not to betray a pre-determination. But even such kindly effort was too much for him in the evening. Neither self-control nor self-reasoning could soften or stem the paroxysm of dejection, which after dark seized on him, crushing body and soul in its cruel grasp. He would plead fatigue, stretch himself at full length on a sofa, and lie there for hours with closed eyes and lips. All Salvator's attempts to rouse him — and God alone knows the ingenuity, the patience, the gentleness, displayed by the little fellow — proved unavailing. The only result was a "Don't mind me, I am tired to death; I am past entertaining now," or such like phrase; which made Salvator droop his head and look grave and anxious.

Gravity and anxiety sat ill at ease, almost unnaturally, upon Salvator's childlike brow and cheery features. One evening — it was the fifth the young men had thus spent together — one evening, Paolo awaking, as it were, from one of his trances, his eyes met those of his friend riveted upon himself, and the change in the familiar face, once so mirthful, now so forlorn, gave him a qualm of remorse, rousing the latent warmth of his heart.

"Oh! my poor Salvator!" exclaimed Paolo, "what a selfish, unfeeling, ungrateful wretch I am!"

"Heyday! what a luxury of adjectives," said Salvator, brisking up; "may I inquire their drift?"

"It is my destiny to bring misfortune on all those who love me. I am killing you by inches."

"Stuff!" laughed Salvator. "I am of too tough materials to give way so easily; you grieve me deeply, I don't deny it; but as for killing —"

"My only excuse is that I cannot help it. I am not a free agent. The axe which inflicts death is not more responsible than I am. Indeed, Salvator, I cannot help it."

"Try as much as though you could," replied Salvator; "perhaps your distemper lies in this same morbid impression of your helplessness. Perhaps there is nothing more required to cure you, than a manly effort to shake off the incubus. Make it, summon up all the energy of your will."

"Ah! my will — forsooth! you have thought of a mighty lever. My will is like a worn-out key, which doesn't bite any longer. Bid a man, stung by a cobra cabello, exert himself; he has neither the power nor the inclination; hot pincers won't make him stir. All that survives of him is a desperate craving for rest. So it is with me. I am stung by a serpent whose name is *tedium vitæ*."

"At it again!" groaned Salvator, with a sort of shudder.

"If you knew what it was to be sick of life," continued Paolo; "if I could describe the feeling to you! On our journey hither we had to pass through a long tunnel. It must have been somewhere between Lyons and Paris. My recollections of that journey are dim and confused; I was restless in body and mind, and my feelings were undoubtedly morbid. Nevertheless, I remember that tunnel well, and the effect produced on me by the passage from broad daylight to pitch darkness, and the shrill, fiendish yell with thousands of yells compressed in it, which, as we tore madly along, seemed to cheer us on to destruction. Then all sense of motion onwards ceased, and there we were, as I fancied, oscillating in the vacuum, suspended over the abyss. Oh! the horror of that moment. It was more than I could stand, I was ready to jump out of the carriage window. Well, what that tunnel was, life has become to me, it is unbearable. I long to be out of it."

"Nothing of the kind. Away with such feelings," burst forth Salvator with an energy and vehemence the more startling, as nothing hitherto in his look or manner had given any warning of the direful impressions he was receiving from Paolo's words. "A thousand times no, I say, unless you choose to have to answer for another life as well as your own, for the ruin of two Christian souls."

"Salvator!" exclaimed Paolo in a subdued voice.

"Yes, your life and my life, your soul and my soul. We'll have no equivocations between us; play false to yourself, my good fellow, and here I solemnly swear to follow your example."

"O Salvator!" groaned Paolo, "I did not expect this of you."

"And I, poor fool, who left house, country, friends in the fulness of my affection for you, do you think I expected such a welcome as you have given me? Te-

dium vitæ must be a precious selfish disease, if it blinds you for a moment to the monstrous part you would have me perform — the part of a mute confidant in a living tragedy, which is to snatch from me my best friend, the friend in whom I prided and delighted." Here the speaker was obliged to stop, for his voice had grown dreadfully husky; but at sight of Paolo's eyes glistening with tears, he cleared his throat in a hurry, and pursued his advantage. "To die is to surrender; far nobler to fight against all odds. Take example by Miss Lavinia. Did she despond under her trials? Not she, but took her staff, and started on the Lord knows what errand, like the sweetest of pilgrims. And why should you not do as she did? Look out yourself for some such noble task, as I am sure hers must be. To those who have a country to free, there can be no lack of scope for action. There is the Crimea, for instance. Will you go to the Crimea?

"Go to the Crimea?" repeated Paolo, with the most undisguised astonishment.

"Just so; why shouldn't you help to take Sebastopol?"

"You mean, that if I am so desirous of death, I might perchance find a glorious one there. True, that would be a certain benefit to myself, but I see none to my country."

"Apart all other considerations," replied Salvator, "methinks he is doing good service to his country who contributes his best to uphold the honour of its arms. Piedmont is sending some thousands of her soldiers to the Crimea — join them. That is the spot where a man may live or die with credit."

"I don't dislike the idea," said Paolo; "but could

I, a republican, consistently with my creed, serve under a royal banner?"

"Why not, if that banner be an Italian one, and floats wherever a blow is struck for the independence of Italy? Take my word for it, Sebastopol is the first stage of the journey to Milan."

"If I could only believe that!" said Paolo.

"Why should you doubt what all Europe believes by this time? If it were not so, why should the Piedmontese meddle with the war at all? Be so good as to follow my argument. Sardinia has no interests of consequence to look after in the East, she has no old grudge against Russia to gratify; Sardinia is still bleeding from the wounds she received in 1848 and 1849; her debt is heavy, her credit indifferent, her exchequer all but empty. For a kingdom in such a condition, there would seem but one course left, that of neutrality. If Sardinia discards this self-evident policy, and takes upon herself the chances of a war, depend upon it, she must have a mighty inducement for so doing; and what other inducement could tempt her, but a promise from the Western powers, a formal promise that if Sardinia lends a hand towards the reduction of Sebastopol, England and France will lend her two towards ridding her of Austria in Italy?"

"Seeing is believing," said Paolo, sententiously. "You spoil a plausible argument, by trying to make it comprise too much, my friend."

"Not a bit," affirmed Salvator, who had his own reasons for colouring richly: "I tell you it is all settled, and set down in black and white. When a cup is full, a drop is sufficient to make it overflow. Austria has been fooling France and England in this Oriental business for many a long day, and their cup of patience is fairly running over. They wish to humiliate her — they tell her so in so many words. Down with Austria, and long live Piedmont, is the burden of the song of their newspapers, and the newspapers after all represent the opinion of a country."

Paolo shook his head doubtfully.

"I know the objection you are about to make," went on Salvator, "that the press is not unfettered in France. Reason the more, if it be not, to believe, that it expresses at least the views of the government; for, what the government might, yet does not prevent, it indirectly sanctions. That is plain enough, is it not? However, let us lay aside the French press, if you will not believe in it, and turn exclusively to the English. If ever there was a free press in the world, that is one, you allow that — very well. Open any of its public journals, and what do you find? Columns teeming with sneers, denunciations and threats levelled at Austria, and with praises and encouragement for Piedmont. You look surprised at my knowledge, my dear fellow; all these articles are translated into Italian, and re-published in the Turin papers; and there, in that nest of Italian liberty, I feasted my eyes on them. Yes; you should read the comparison drawn between the selfishness and sluggishness of the huge empire, the backwardness of its ruler, the crooked ways of its statesmen, with the pluck of the little kingdom, the chivalrous spirit of Victor Emmanuel, the daring of its premier. Austria is set up as a scarecrow, and Piedmont as an example."

"Very possibly," returned Paolo; "but have you forgotten our proverb: *Dal detto al fatto, ci corre un gran tratto?* (From word to deed, there is far indeed.) I re-

member Thornton warning me against trusting to such
ebullitions of feeling. In 1849 there was something
similar to what you now describe, which, nevertheless,
did not hinder our being left to our fate. The immense
majority in England, Thornton bid me believe, do not
consider the Italian cause worth the sacrifice of a drop
of English blood, or the out-lay of a single English
guinea. Their real sympathies, he said, were all with
their old ally, Austria."

"*Were* so, I allow," cried Salvator, "but *are* not so
now. You confound the days of Pitt with those of Lord
Palmerston; you overlook the Concordat with Rome,
that dealt the death-blow to Austrian influence in England. Side with Austria, forsooth! Why, Austria is the
negation of all that makes Great Britain great." And
the little painter went on to prove mathematically to
the incredulous Paolo, that the English to a man were
against Austria, and for Italy. Poor, innocent, simple-
minded Salvator!

Much more than we choose to relate was added on
either side, still no immediate practical result came of
this conversation. However stringent Salvator's arguments, however tempting the prospect they opened to a
man afflicted with *tedium vitæ*, they failed because a
participation in what he called a kingly war, involved
in Paolo's eyes, as a first consequence, the abandonment
of the principles which, right or wrong, he had always
held. Salvator must rest content with carrying to his
bed the consoling assurance, that his friend was far less
dead to the interests of this world, than he himself believed. Night brought him no sleep, but it did counsel.
About three in the morning, he went and knocked at
Paolo's door.

"It is only me; are you acquainted with Manin?"

"Not personally," was the answer given so readily, that it showed Paolo must have been already awake. "Why do you ask?"

"I mean, do you consider him a leader to be trusted?"

"Entirely; who doubts it?"

"And," pursued Salvator, "were he to say that a course of action was right that you deemed wrong, would you abide by his decision?"

"I think I should," replied Paolo.

"Very well; that is all I want to know. Good night."

Ten seconds after the active little fellow was in his bed again, and his mind at rest, in another ten seconds he was snoring placidly.

During his short stay at Turin, Salvator had heard much about Manin, and of the conciliatory line of policy adopted of late by the great Venetian. Manin in fact, not long before, had published his new programme of "Independence and Unification," that programme which, whatever may be said to the contrary, did so much towards preparing that unanimity of purpose and of action, which a few years later, was to form the admiration of all the friends, and provoke the despair of all the foes of Italy. Thrice happy in this, that he did not live long enough to see the worse than useless issue of his work of conciliation for the heroic land, alas! which had given him birth, the land he had loved so well, so wisely, so valiantly — alas! for his own Venice! Well, then, it so happened that Salvator had had given him at Turin the address of the illustrious exile in Paris. This circumstance, almost forgotten amidst his constant preoccupation about Paolo, now returned to his memory in this hour of need, and he resolved to turn it to account.

When, next morning, Salvator proposed a visit to Manin, Paolo raised no objection, only regretted their not having a letter of introduction to make their access to the ex-dictator more easy.

"Never mind that," said Salvator, "you know the proverb as to good looks; your face must serve to recommend us; and great men, you know, are the property of the public."

Manin occupied a small and more than modest lodging in the third story of a house in the Rue Blanche. His reception of the two young men was full of that frank cordiality, which is a distinctive trait of the Italian character. Manin had his hat on, evidently ready to go out, when his unexpected visitors appeared; nevertheless he would not permit of their going away, as they wished to do, but said he had a quarter of an hour at their service. Paolo, therefore, after giving his own and his companion's name, their calling, and their country, stated in as few words as possible the case of conscience he had come to submit to Manin's judgment. Could he, without betrayal of his republican faith, join the Sardinian ranks in the Crimea?

"Which do you care most for?" asked Manin, "the Republic or Italy? Italy, of course. To be either a republic or a monarchy, Italy must first exist as a nation — that is, be independent — and form one body. Every act which tends towards that end — to make a united Italy, I mean — deserves the support of all patriots, whatever their creed. Is the co-operation of Piedmont in the Crimean war to be considered an act of this sort, a step in the right direction? I do not hesitate to say it is so, inasmuch as it widens her circle of influence in Europe, and strengthens her hands for good, inasmuch as it places her in manifest antagonism with Austria, inasmuch as it furnishes a precious occasion to add to the prestige of Italian arms. Those who go to fight under the three colours of Italian redemption, are not the soldiers of the Piedmontese State, but the soldiers of Italy. Would to God that I were young enough and strong enough to be one of them."

As soon as he ceased speaking, Paolo and Salvator rose to go, but he detained them, adding, —

"I have been subjected to much obloquy lately for being too favourable to Sardinia. I view Sardinia as a great national force. Is that a good or an evil? It is a fact — and this fact, moreover, is monarchic. Are we to render it hostile to the cause of emancipation because it is so, or are we to turn it to good account, taking it as it is? The question is not a question for me, at all events. I declare that for my part I am ready to accept of monarchy, if monarchy is to give us an Italy independent and one."

The door had been gently pushed ajar while he was speaking, and the moment he stopped, a female voice — (ah! pity him, not that of his wife or daughter: both lay in their freshly opened graves) — a female voice said warningly, —

"Mr. Daniel, it is striking eleven; you know you have to go to Rue Pigalle."

"Thank you," said Manin to his careful *bonne*, "I am off;" and snatching a book from a table, and putting it under his arm, he led the way down the stairs to the street-door. There he stopped and said, with emotion, "Good-bye, my young friends; may all success attend

you in the pass you have chosen. Honour certainly will,
for it is the path of duty. My blessing goes with you.
To the rising generation which you represent, to the
simple in mind, and stout of heart, Providence reserves
the great work of Italian emancipation. Peace, peace
at all costs among the oppressed, that their united war-
cry may be like the trumpet before Jericho, at sound
of which the ramparts of the oppressors shall crumble
into dust. You will see that day, young men."

"And so will you," exclaimed Paolo and Salvator,
with enthusiasm.

"Not so, not so," replied Manin; "the spirit is strong,
but the flesh is weak. *Dies mei numerati sunt*, I may
say with the Psalmist, nor do I regret that it be so.
Once again, farewell." And with a friendly squeeze of
the hand of both, he hurried away. Paolo's heart sunk
within him as he watched the tottering steps of the noble
man, and he thought to himself, why this mysterious
dispensation which dooms the flower of a whole nation
to live and to die brokenhearted?

"Bravo!" cried Salvator; "a man worth his weight
in gold; every word of his hits the bull's-eye; though,
allow me to observe, that what he has said, much more
pointedly, I confess, is just what I had the honour of
telling you last night. By the bye, though, I should
like to know why he goes about with an Italian gram-
mar under his arm."

"Manin gives lessons to live, and therefore carries
with him the tools of his trade. Yes, oh! mockery of
fortune, the ex-dictator of Venice is reduced to sell
participles!"

Salvator mused a little, then said, —

"And why not? Poverty at all times has been the seal of true greatness. Deck Homer with a mantle of purple, seat Dante in a carriage and four, and see what a sorry figure they will cut."

CHAPTER XXIII.

Leave-taking.

PAOLO was for starting that same evening.

"But your passport?" objected Salvator.

Paolo was for starting without passport. Salvator shrugged his shoulders. A man does not travel from Rome to Palermo, and then to Paris, as he had done, without growing keenly alive to the importance of the item in question. He said accordingly, —

"More easily said than done, my dear friend — I mean as far as the arriving at our destination is concerned. Let us reserve extreme remedies for extreme evils, and first try what the Sardinian consulate will do for us."

Taking this good advice, Paolo with his wise little friend went thither. Strong in his good conscience, Paolo stated his case briefly and simply; he knew, he said, after making his request, that he had no specific claim upon the Sardinian government, yet he was not without hope that the anomaly of his situation, coupled with the object he had in view, that of enlisting for the Crimea, might entitle him to some consideration.

"Certainly," said the gentleman, to whom his application was made. "If I understand you right, your object is to reach Turin."

"Paolo bowed assent.

"Very well, excuse me for a moment," continued the official, leaving the room. He returned in a few minutes accompanied by another gentleman, who said to Paolo, —

"Can you give me the date at which you asked for a passport at the Nonciatura and were refused?"

Paolo named the beginning of the month of September.

"Nearly seven months ago — time enough indeed to come to resipiscence," said the second gentleman, smiling. "Such being the case, I think your best course will be now to renew your application there; if still unsuccessful, come to me again with two respectable fellow-countrymen of ours, who can testify to the refusal, and to your own identity, and I will give you a passport for Turin. It will be but a temporary one — to serve only for the journey. Will that do?"

"Perfectly," said Paolo; "I am much obliged to you."

Salvator here producing his passport, asked, —

"Will you accept of me as one of the witnesses you require for my friend?"

Glancing over the passport tendered to him, the Sardinian gentleman replied in the affirmative.

Renewing their thanks, the two young Romans took their leave, and following the advice they had received, went immediately to the Nonciatura. But the hearts that they found there were as hardened towards Paolo as Pharaoh's to the Jewish lawgiver. Salvator, however, took the opportunity of having his own passport *viséd* for Rome.

"Now then," said he, as they walked away from

the unaccommodating Nonciatura, "now for this second
witness.   Do you know any Italians in Paris?"

"Not one," said Paolo.

"Then we must apply to Du Genre," quoth Salvator, "he is the man to help us, he knows everybody."
But this suggestion was so evidently unpalatable to
Paolo, that Salvator, stopping short, turned upon his
companion with an inquisitive "What's your objection?"

Paolo could not bring himself to any specific explanation; so Salvator, with pitiless good sense, continued, —

"My good Paolo, when necessity drives, squeamishness must be got over.   Du Genre is the most service-
able fellow on earth, and I can't understand any one
hesitating to ask a favour of one so cordial.   We have
no time to lose, and recollect that he who will the end,
must will the means.   Come, let us go to Du Genre
without more ceremony."

The Frenchman being out, Paolo left a card, on
which he wrote his wish to see him.

The confession, withheld by Paolo from Salvator,
was, that of late a coolness had sprung up between him
and the realist.   Du Genre, being a man who put method in his dissipation, that is, one who made it a point
to keep within the limits of his purse, seeing that Paolo,
on the contrary, was living beyond his means, had
taken upon himself to remonstrate with him repeatedly,
and Paolo, too excited to listen to reason, had seen fit
to take offence at what he considered an encroachment
on his personal independence.   Hence a comparative
estrangement between the *quondam* inseparables.

Du Genre called on Paolo in the evening, and
warm was the greeting he gave to Salvator, whose pre-

sence took him quite by surprise. He evinced none, however, on hearing of Paolo's sudden resolve. "He was prepared for anything and everything," he said, "in that quarter; it wouldn't make him start if he met Paolo on the Boulevards with a tower of Notre Dame under each arm. Always in extremes, eh, Paolo? However, as it must be so, let me tell you that, extreme for extreme, I give my vote for a six months' campaign in the Crimea on short rations, in preference to that infernal gallop — excuse me for calling it so — which you have been keeping up for the last two months."

"You have characterized my life perfectly," said Paolo, good-humouredly; "be charitable enough to help my escape from it," and he proceeded to explain the service he needed. Du Genre took up the matter with all his old cordiality; of course, he would find a witness, twenty witnesses, any number of witnesses, from each and all of the Italian States, including the republic of San Marino, but he must have a little time.

Time was the only thing which Paolo could ill afford, but circumstances laid their bridle on his neck, and forced the curb between his lips. Champ the bit as he would, and scatter forth the foam of his impatience, three whole days he had to wait. Luckily he was not without some imperative occupation.

There was, first, his establishment to break up, and plenty of accounts to settle, but for these more money than time was required. As to the carriage and horses he had been fool enough to buy, Du Genre took charge of them, and would sell them, when a good opportunity occurred. Secondly, there was a duty not to be omitted — the few friends he had so long neglected, to see and take leave of.

Mr. Perrin, Mr. Pertuis, and Mr. Boniface gave the young Roman as hearty a reception, as if his last call had been paid the day before. Perhaps Mr. Boniface, with the good faith of an absent man, fancied such to be the case. Busy people in large cities, be their business speculative or active, are generally apt to overlook the flight of time; even the few exceptions to this rule affect to do so, in order to avoid unnecessary explanations.

On hearing that he was going to Turin — Paolo carefully abstained from breathing a word of the Crimea — both Mr. Perrin and Mr. Pertuis, taking it for granted that he meant to remain there, expressed their approbation of this choice. Sardinia, said Mr. Perrin, was fast becoming the centre of the Italian movement, and it was to be wished that all the scattered energy in the Peninsula should converge to that focus. Mr. Pertuis considered the last bold move of Piedmont in the affair of the Crimea, as a *chef d'œuvre* of statesmanship, and one which might have incalculable consequences. Paolo's heart swelled with joy as he listened to the golden opinions entertained by these talented men, of a country which he was in a manner to adopt as his own, and of a policy in support of which he was going to stake his life.

His visit to the Quai Montebello was reserved as a *bonne bouche* for the last. Prudence was the only one among Paolo's acquaintances, who seemed to have perceived the length of his absence.

"Oh, Mr. Paul!" she exclaimed, "what a stranger you have grown!"

Tears started into Paolo's eyes at this gentle rebuke.

"Would to God I had been less so!" he said,

feelingly; "it would have been better for me and others."

The busy Prosper had had no leisure for recollections; he was as simply overjoyed to see Mr. Paul as the children, who came and established themselves between their former playmate's knees, and needed no urging to empty his pockets of the toys and bonbons, with which they were crammed.

Benoît, telegraphed to from the back window, shuffled in presently, and, what with his astonishment and emotion, could find nothing better to do than to snatch at the famous meerschaum pipe which he wore dagger fashion in his belt, and to cry, as he flourished it, "Here it is." Day was closing in, and Benoît was under the influence of — vapour, as he Jesuitically termed it — a toxicological condition, which added to his pantomimic, what it took from his oratorical, powers.

The party being thus *au complet*, as Prosper professionally observed, kindly inquiries were exchanged, and such bits of information given and elicited *hinc inde*, as Prosper's frequent exits, and the ebb and flow of passengers in and out, allowed. The room in which they were sitting had undergone some repairs; the walls had been freshly papered, and a new and neat stove had taken the place of the old and rickety one. These improvements were pointed out by Prosper with no little pride.

"It is all the doing of the new administration," explained the elated little man — "the Compagnie Générale des Omnibus — all capitalists cased in millions — bought up all the lines at an immense outlay; there is nothing like centralization, you see. Between you and me, an affair of gold, and perfectly respectable."

"Are you better paid?" asked Paolo; "that is the most interesting question for me."

"No; my salary is not raised yet, Mr. Paul; but we have got a uniform — all our men have — handsome, is it not?" and Prosper drew himself up to his full height, and stood complacently to be looked at. It was only then that Paolo noticed the great fact of Prosper's blue overcoat, with its embroidered collar and cap to match. "Capital cloth; just feel it; smooth as velvet; and the embroidery of real silver; and we have a waterproof cloak for rainy days — here it is."

Paolo approved of the waterproof garment, but demurred as to the uniform. Prosper *mordicus* defended his new acquisition. From the Marshal of France down to the shop porters, he said, every one now-a-days had his uniform.

"It's the men's crinoline," said Prudence, laughing.

"Hang the crinoline!" cried Prosper, with sudden vehemence; "three-quarters of the complaints made to us are caused by that downright abomination. Now, a uniform, thank God, is in nobody's way, and most *comme il faut* it is, isn't it, *mon parrain?*"

At this appeal, *mon parrain*, who, during the debate, had been obstinately puffing at his empty meerschaum with the gravity of a Cherokee chief, got up, made a military salute, and said emphatically, "The uniform is the man, *quoi?*" — too profound a dictum not to settle the question.

After this, Paolo was called no to admire the children's copy-books, and to listen to La Fontaine's "Ant and the Grasshopper," recited by the eldest boy.

When the little ones, praised, caressed, and loaded with gifts, had gone off to bed, Paolo rose and said, —

"And now, my dear friends, I must also be off; I came to say good-byé to you before leaving Paris. I am on the move for Turin."

This announcement had the most exhilarating effect on the old trooper. He made a feint at Paolo's breast, ejaculating, —

"*Farceur, va* — none of that; ha! ha! ha! Turin! a good joke."

"Turin!" repeated Prosper, with a lengthened face; "far away, isn't it? I hope you don't mean to settle there for good and all."

"As to that I can say nothing, my good Prosper; you know that man's decisions are often set aside by circumstances."

"Because," continued Prosper, "be it said without meaning to disparage other countries, I have always heard that there is no place for comfort like Paris; only to speak of public conveyances, find me another city where, for instance, you can go as far as from Batignolles to the Jardin des Plantes, a little journey, for six sous."

Paolo assured him that there were plenty of public conveyances in Turin, and that the fare from one end of the town to the other was only four sous.

"That's very well — very well indeed; but, monsieur, I don't believe Turin covers the ground that Paris does. However, I am glad to hear what you say. Omnibuses speak well for the civilization of a place; but there are omnibuses and omnibuses, you know; and you may take my word for it, there's only one 'Compagnie Générale' in the world."

"Will you humour a childish fancy of mine?" whispered Paolo to Prudence. "Just let me have a peep at my old room, will you?"

"Most willingly," said she, lighting a candle, and leading the way.

Benoît saluted their exit with a fresh burst of laughter, and a "well done, old boy!". In what circumstance originated his delusion, that Paolo was joking as to his intention of leaving Paris, was, and must remain one of the unfathomable mysteries of tipsiness. Paolo surveyed the back parlour for a moment; it was empty, cold, and dismal enough, God knows, but even such as it was, full for him of sweet memories, of the sweetest of all those hallowed by disinterested affection. He took Prudence by the hand, and said, —

"I have sought for this moment of privacy to tell you —" there was a knot in his throat which stopped his words; "I want to ask your pardon — yes, your pardon — I ought to ask it on my knees — here, in this place. Don't look as if you did not understand for what. You know, and I know, that I have been ungrateful to you and yours; that I have kept away from you, my benefactress, my kind nurse — paid you back by shameful neglect for the boon of life, that, after God, I owe you. If you can say so truly, say that you forgive me."

"If it must be so," said Prudence, smiling through her tears, "I will say that I forgive you; though I have never felt angry; and that I bless you, dear Mr. Paul, with all my heart. And now, let me explain one thing. If I receive the news of your departure just now with seeming coolness, don't believe that it was from indifference, or resentment, indeed, it was neither. The truth is I was prepared for it. The moment you came in, I was sure you had come to say good-bye. I was sorry for myself, but glad for you; it is for your good, I know. You look pale and thin, not like what you were when you were writing for Mr. Boniface. You don't look happy." (Paolo here raised his eyes to the ceiling, in a way highly confirmatory of Prudence's hint.) "Will you let me give you a good recipe for happiness? I am but a poor uneducated woman, but women have good guesses about some things. Find out some nice young lady to love, and who will love you, and marry her, though she were a born princess."

"Suppose," said Paolo, won by this maternal affection to sudden confidence, "suppose the lady were already found, and that I feel myself to be unworthy of her."

"Fiddlesticks!" cried Prudence, with a laugh; "it's well enough to be modest, but too much of anything is bad. I am glad, at all events, that you are on the right track; it will come all right at last."

"Is there nothing in the world I can do for you?" asked Paolo, almost imploringly.

"Not in the way you mean," was Prudence's quick answer; "we are very comfortable indeed; but if not too inconvenient perhaps you will let us hear of you now and then."

Paolo promised, took her in his arms, kissed her, and left the room.

"Adieu, Prosper, adieu, *mon vieux*, God bless you all." And with another shake of the two men's hands, he was gone.

Good tidings were awaiting him in the Chaussée d'Antin. Du Genre had called, and left word with

Salvator that he had found the required witness, who
would be at the Sardinian Consulate the next day at
noon. No fear but that Paolo was punctual to the hour
of rendezvous. Everything went as smooth as oil, and
by three o'clock Paolo was the legitimate possessor of
a regular passport, duly *viséd* by the French police into
the bargain. He and Salvator accordingly fixed to take
their departure by that evening's express train for
Lyons.

Clothes, books, boots were tossed into trunks and
portmanteaus, which were no sooner filled than sent off
to the terminus, Du Genre making merry the while at
Paolo's expense. Paolo was in such dread of missing
the train, that they reached the débarcadère exactly two
hours too soon — considering which, and that none of
the three had dined, they with common consent sought
the refreshment room, and ordered dinner.

Du Genre ate little, but, contrary to his custom,
drank freely, talked rather more than usual, and was
more outrageously paradoxical than ever.

"An Italy independent and free!" quoth the realist,
tossing of a glass of Champagne in response to a toast
of Salvator's to that effect. "You speak of it at your
ease, my dear friends, without giving a thought to the
consequences. 'To digest or not to digest,' that is the
European question involved in the Italian one; and
what if I prove to you that the *status quo* of Italy is
the *sine quâ non* of a good digestion for nine-tenths of
Europe! Make the least attempt at change, and jaun-
dice will be the order of the day. You ask for evidence,
ye hard of understanding! Just handle, gently as a
zephyr plays with a rose, the Roman question — and
to be free, touch it you must — and two hundred mil-

lions of Catholics soon find their gastric juices impaired. Just give a wink to the *Italian* Tyrol — and wink in that direction you must, or no independence for you — and dyspepsia seizes on more than forty millions of your fellow-creatures, whose gospel it is — not the Gospel of Christ, though — that the saurkrautian element was *ab æterno* destined to lord it over the macaronian element. To come down from the wholesale to the retail. Suppress that providential Italian issue, and no class, no individual but will sorely suffer from the revulsion. Publicists, statisticians, journalists will be deprived of their richest mine of speculation, philanthropists of their favourite *dada*, parliamentary orators of their cue for indignation speeches, poets of their camposanto, over which to sing everlasting requiems, fair readers of *Le mie Prigióni* of a safety-valve for working off their surplus of sensibility; and, to sum up all, the mass of nonentities whom God has blessed with a country, will sadly miss a point of comparison, which tends greatly to their self-glorification. So that, you must see, every one will be the worse for the change, and none the better — no, not even the Italians. I anticipated the objection. You will be the first to suffer, and *probo*. What is it that gives breadth and elevation to the Italian character, and wins favour for it? It is the immateriality of their pursuit, and the spirit of sacrifice they carry into it. Amidst the hard race after material interests and enjoyments which characterizes the present age, and lowers all individuals to the same level, no one can help respecting and sympathizing with people original enough to stake everything, life included, on something that is not tangible, not visible — for an idea. Commonplace as we may have become ourselves, we are still tickled by originality in others. Well, now for this state of things you are indebted to Austria. Remove the cause, and you remove the effect; make an Italy independent, free and happy, and farewell spiritual ballast, farewell poetry, and originality; you fall to the ground flat and uninteresting as an exhausted balloon; in fact, you are like the rest of the world, worthy of revolving — *dignus intrare* — in the commonplace orbit, which is to-speculate in railways or the funds, get rich, in short, and *prendre du ventre.*"

Men are too often ashamed of appearing as good as they are. All the farrago of nonsense just delivered by Du Genre had no other object than to cover the depths of an emotion much to his credit, and which, do what he would to check it, still would assert itself in his looks and words at parting.

"Farewell, dear Salvator, farewell, dear Telemachus, and *sans rancune*, I trust. If I gave you cause of complaint, and probably I did, my judgment was the guilty party, and not my heart; believe me, old fellow, I have got a heart in spite of appearances, and the day this weary Italian question is fairly put, directly and not by *ricochet* — well, never mind the rest. Perhaps after all you are right; but right or wrong, remember I value your friendship, and am always at your service. Write sometimes, and now, *Partant pour la Syrie*, and *à revoir.*"

CHAPTER XXIV.

Salvator wins the Day.

Down to Lyons and Chambery with the speed of an arrow, and up the Mont Cenis, grand, solemn, snow-clad Mont Cenis. Paolo had never before seen the Alps, he had tried often and often to realize them from description; but what powers of imagination can approach such stupendous reality? Paolo felt the presence of God in His works, and adored.

The day was cold and clear, and the old fir-trees, covered all over with frost, sparkled in the sun like gigantic Venetian chandeliers. To lose none of the sublime harmonies of the spectacle, Paolo made the whole ascent on foot, revelling in that glorious sensation of having, as it were, no body, and being wafted along on wings. Salvator's stumpy legs did good service in their way, for, with the exception of two short lifts, he kept by his tall companion's side.

And thus the summit was reached; and lo! deep down below, running at first within narrow defiles, but quickly expanding as it stretched onwards, lay the valley of Susa — and Susa itself, that brown speck in the distance. "Behold her, Salvator," cried Paolo.

"Italy for ever!" shouted the little man, and for the first time since heaven knows how long, he sung forth a quotation, even more appropriate than usual to the occasion. *Ah! del cielo e della terra, Bella Italia sei l'onor.*

This passage of the Mont Cenis, Paolo affirms to this day, did more to tune his soul once more up to

an harmonious diapason, than all the books of all the
moralists put together.   Lucky that it was so, for
delays and disappointments were in wait for him at
Turin. From every quarter the two young Romans received the unpalatable intelligence, that no volunteers
were admitted into the Piedmontese expeditionary corps,
but such as had served already, and could prove their
services.   There was, it is true, in course of formation
a foreign legion for the service of England, in which
recruits were received without any similar condition,
and probably Salvator had confounded this with the
Piedmontese corps.   The ardent little fellow, however,
in no wise daunted, went to some of the deputies, whom
he had come across in his first visit to the Sardinian
capital, and upon this slender thread of acquaintance-
ship, he did manage to make his way, and obtain a
letter of introduction for a high official in the war office;
but nothing came of it but a confirmation of the fact,
that he and his friend were ineligible for service in the
Crimea.   "Even you yourself will, I am sure, acknowledge the necessity for strictness on this point," wound
up the man in office, with a consoling show of sympathy for the disappointment he was inflicting.   "We
are about to confront a formidable military power, and
that, under the eyes of the two best armies in Europe;
the honour of our country is doubly at stake, and we
should be inexcusable, did we trust that to other than
tried men."

No bad reasoning, thought to himself the unsuccessful suitor, as he went down the stairs, not the less provoking to me and Paolo, though.   I suppose it's no
use trying so see the minister himself, of course they
have settled one and all to sing the same song.   But

if I could get to the top of the tree — to the king —
he might help one. Full of this new idea, he turned
mechanically to the right, and was roused from his meditation by perceiving the royal palace right before
him. The iron gates being always wide open, Salvator walked into the spacious court, and looked long
at the king's dwelling. There must be some solace in
gazing at the windows of those who can influence our
destinies. Lovers, for instance, are never tired of a
mute contemplation of those of their beloved ones.

An officer of the National Guard, seemingly on
duty, was pacing up and down before the palace. He
had an open, communicative countenance. Salvator
directed his own steps so as to approach the officer
without appearance of design.

"A fine building," exclaimed the landscape painter.

"No doubt," replied the officer. "Excuse me, but
you seem to be a stranger to Turin."

"Yes, indeed, I am a Roman," answered Salvator.
"Are travellers allowed to see the interior of the
palace?"

"Not when his Majesty is there, as is the case at
this moment. After all, one must not grudge kings a
little privacy."

"I am not the man to grudge Victor Emmanuel
anything," retorted Salvator, briskly. After a little
pause, he added: "Pray, is his majesty difficult of
access?"

The Piedmontese smiled with a certain pride as he
said, —

"The palace you are looking at, sir, is not Schön-
brunn. Our king is not afraid to see anyone; if you
want to have an audience, all you have to do is to

forward a request in writing, stating the object you have in view, and get your ambassador's signature —"

"To tell the truth," interrupted Salvator, "I don't think myself entitled to ask to see his majesty on what is only an affair of consequence to myself; still I should like to have a peep of *Il Rè Galantuomo*, and liberty to say a dozen words to him."

"Then, why not accost him in the street?" suggested the officer. "He will not take it amiss."

"If I only knew when and where," cried Salvator, eagerly.

"That's easily discovered," said the obliging citizen-soldier. "You see that archway to the left of this court; go through it — you'll find a church on your right, skirt its walls till you come to a lane that runs behind it. On that side of the lane which adjoins the palace, several back-doors open. Through one or other of those private doors the king makes his exit almost daily between two and three o'clock in the afternoon. Mount guard there, and it's ten to one but that you will have your wish. But beware of looking alarmed or stammering when you address his majesty; nothing he dislikes more than timidity or slowness."

Salvator was so elated at the chance thus pointed out to him, that, had he followed his first impulse, he would have thrown himself, in a transport of gratitude, on the neck of his obliging informant; but, on second thoughts, he was wise enough to content himself with expressing his thanks in a Roman-accent, that sounded like soft music in answer to the sharp, snipped words of his north countryman. Through the archway, round the church, and he was in the lane blessed with the palace back-doors, in less time than it takes to record his movements.

Ha! ha! friend Salvator, thinks he to himself, here is a famous chance for you, if you know how to use it; lucky that you are in a fit condition to appear before any potentate. (The reader has perhaps forgotten that, since his elevation to the post of scene-painter, director of choruses, and prompter in ordinary to her ladyship Delfuego y Arcos, Salvator had adopted a rigorous dress suit of black, with white cravat, and frilled shirt.) Yes, a famous chance; provided the king comes, though. As to nervousness and stammering, and all that sort of thing, we'll try to scare his majesty as little as possible in that way.

In spite of this assurance, however, Salvator felt somewhat disturbed, as testified by the dialogue he was carrying on with himself aloud; a fact no sooner perceived than checked by a resolute, "None of that, sir," and humming a tune, he fell to examining the locality, with an eye to the back-doors all the while.

It had wanted a quarter to two when he took his position in the lane. Two o'clock struck. All the clocks in Turin seemed to have a rendezvous over his head — a quarter-past two, half-past two, and no arrival, save that of a shower of rain, short but heavy, which wet him to the skin. A quarter to three — three. Poor Salvator began to shake in his shoes. Either the king had gone out earlier than usual, or was not going out at all. Scarcely, however, had he come to this dispiriting conclusion, when one of the long-watched back-doors opened, and two figures issued from it. Both gentlemen were in plain clothes, but in the foremost Salvator immediately recognized the king, and to recognize and see the king bear down on him with a firm rapid step was one and the same thing.

Salvator drew back, and had to be quick as lightning in taking off his hat — and raising his hand in military fashion to his forehead, he stood stiff as a poker, ready to take advantage of the slightest notice. Attracted by the soldierly salute, his majesty stopped, and with a half smile at the queer figure with such eager eyes fixed on himself, asked,

"Have you anything to say?"

"Please your majesty," was the prompt answer, "we are two Romans, who have come all the way from Paris to enlist for the Crimea."

"For the Crimea? Are you big enough?" asked the king, glancing sharply at the little painter.

"Just the right size for a Bersagliere, please your majesty. My friend is as strong and as tall as a tower; we have both smelt gunpowder already, please your majesty."

"Where?" inquired the king.

"At the siege of Rome in 1849."

"What puts it into your head to go to the Crimea?"

"The wish to qualify ourselves for your next campaign in Lombardy, sire."

His majesty turned with a pleased smile to the gentleman accompanying him, then addressing Salvator:

"And suppose you are killed in the Crimea?"

"If so, *dulce et decorum est pro patria mori*, sire."

"Bravo," cried the king, "good Latin, and good sense. What is your name? where are you to be found?"

"Angelo Gigli, sire, at your service, and just now at the Locanda of the Dogana Vecchia."

"Addio," said the king, and raising a finger to his hat, he passed on. Salvator had maintained his military attitude throughout the short dialogue, nor indeed did he relinquish it till the king was fairly out of sight.

"But," objected Paolo, when the particulars of this meeting with the king were related to him, "you were wrong in mentioning two volunteers, you know that I go alone."

"See if you do," quoth Salvator.

"Surely you don't mean to go with me," urged Paolo.

"See if I don't," quoth Salvator.

"And Clelia?" pleaded Paolo.

"Clelia will have to wait till Sebastopol is taken, that's all," said poor Salvator, with very assumed glee.

"And suppose any — misfortune happens to you?"

"Just what his majesty graciously thought possible also, forgetting that misfortunes and cannon-balls prefer the great; besides," continued Salvator, with great gravity, "to satisfy you, I promise I'll duck down when I hear a whiz. My good Paolo, why grudge a little chap a few laurels to add to his height? But what's the use of talking? let us sing instead —

> "Se uniti negli affanni,
> Noi fummo sempre insieme," &c.

Early next morning a young officer came to the Locanda of the Dogana Vecchia to inquire for Signor Angelo Gigli. He was aide-de-camp to F —, a general, who distinguished himself in the campaigns of 1848 and 1849, and was now named to a high command in the Crimean expedition.

The king had taken such a fancy to the spirited young fellow, who spoke with so much assurance of a campaign in Lombardy, that he had requested General F —, the gentleman in attendance, to see what could be done for the would-be volunteer and his friend, and General F — had in his turn deputed his aide-de-camp to fulfil that duty.

"His majesty having expressed a wish favourable to you," continued the aide-de-camp, "of course my instructions are, that short of some insuperable disqualification, your services should be accepted. Signor Gigli is rather short, I must say, but active and supple, and will do for a sharpshooter. As to Signor —"

"Mancini," suggested Paolo.

"Signor Mancini will make a capital grenadier. Gentlemen, you are of right good stuff; but drill, hard constant drill, is necessary to make your good qualities of service. Having thus reassured you, permit me for a moment to play the part, as it is called, of the devil's advocate, and advise you to pause and consider well, before you take an irrevocable step. A soldier's life in the field is not the poetic thing enthusiastic youths are apt to imagine it; on the contrary, it is a terrible matter-of-fact business, with drawbacks innumerable. I don't allude to the mere common hardships of cold, rain, or broiling sun, of hunger and thirst — of days of exhausting fatigue, followed by sleepless nights — nor yet of sickness and the chances of wounds or death. But I speak of the hope deferred, that makes the heart sick, of the perpetual annihilation of all independent action, all independent judgment, of all individuality —

a positive torture to gifted minds. I speak of the maddening *ennui* of weeks and months of inaction, and which makes a soldier's life a life of unparalleled trial. Does such a picture tempt you?"

Paolo and Salvator declared that their resolution was not to be shaken.

"So much the better for the service," cried the officer, rising and shaking both by the hand. "The aide-de-camp has done his duty, now allow the volunteer of 1848 to congratulate you an your decision. Not that the picture I drew was exaggerated, far from it; but that I see that you have the true patriotic feeling, up to any sacrifice. *Ad augusta per angusta.* I was made a soldier by circumstances myself. I was preparing for the bar in 1848. I abandoned my profession, because I believed my country needed my arm. I enlisted — and would do so again, though I have gone through all that I have described to you. I even think my sufferings have ended by endearing a soldier's life to me. May it be so with you!"

Having now the certitude of being sent to the Crimea, Paolo on the morrow went to a public notary, and made his will. It was of the simplest; he left everything he possessed in the world to his dear and faithful friend, Angelo Gigli, and in the event of his death, then to Clelia Mauri, both of Rome. A few days after, Paolo entered the first regiment of the second infantry brigade, under the command of General Trotti, and Salvator the second battalion of Lamarmora's rifles. A whole month elapsed between the day of their enlistment, and that of their embarkation — a month of drill, and nothing but drill, and during which the friends consequently could see but little of one another.

Their voyage was made in different transports, and once at their destination, their chances of meeting were of the smallest, the corps to which they respectively belonged occupying the two opposite extremities of the Sardinian camp. But, as luck would have it, towards the end of June, the second brigade was transferred to the centre, and the difficulty of getting a peep of each other diminished in direct ratio with the diminished distance between their divisions.

Our concern being neither with the Crimean war, nor with the part played in it by the Piedmontese Contingent — both by this time matters of history, the streamlet of our narrative keeps clear of such mighty waters to remain constant to the humble track of Paolo's and Salvator's fortunes. These were neither stirring nor brilliant, and may be disposed of in very few words. We have, however, before doing so, a duty to discharge towards the reader, whom we suppose impatient to learn whether Paolo's new life has produced a change for the better in his morbidly gloomy mental perspective.

Paolo, let us hasten to state, was already cured before he landed in the Crimea — cured, we mean, of the obsession which had haunted him in Paris. Though ready to die for his country, he was reconciled to life — nay, more than that, deeply penitent for having despised that boon, and of having contemplated, even for a moment, the throwing of it aside as a burden. Physical and moral agencies, change of scene, bodily exertion, the stir of patriotic passions around him, the new elevating aim offered to his activity, the sense of his own usefulness, had one and all helped to bring about this result. Yet it must not be supposed that he had learned to view, with more indulgence than formerly, his late follies — no such thing — his abhorrence of them continued unabated, not so his utter hopelessness of ever being able to redeem those errors. They seemed so far away, too, those ill-omened days of Paris — while, by an opposite play of mental optics, other times, other images and scenes, of a far more distant date, seemed things of yesterday; for instance, that charming first interview with Lavinia in his studio, in Via Frattina — he heard again and again the soft rustling like summer air among the trees, which heralded her approach — again and again he was sensible of those ambrosial odours which ever floated around her; every graceful kind word or action of that happy lunch at the Palazzo Morlacchi, was again vividly before him, he saw her again, as he had seen and believed her then, the good genius of her uncle's household; and constant, more than all, was the living remembrance of their leave-taking at Rome; of the touching earnestness of her repentance, and the unconditional surrender of her own will to his, which had scaled the renewal of their former engagement.

On these crumbs of the past Paolo's soul fed, and throve; but not on them alone. It had besides a substantial honeycomb to feast upon — her last letter. He guarded it as he would have done "the instrumental parts of his religion." He had folded it carefully in soft paper, and carried it in his bosom, close to his heart, that, should he die, it might be buried with him. Knowing it thoroughly by heart, he still read it over and over again, and on many a dark, lonely night, had recited to himself its contents, finding in it a talisman against heavy thoughts. Does any one call this childlike infatuation? Childlike perhaps, but not the less attended with positive and beneficial results; for out of the few data in that letter, Paolo was reconstructing inch by inch his spiritual world — a Lavinia hallowed by adversity, his own love purified by humility — and withal all the lofty aspirations which refine and exalt human nature. Was this nothing?

And now to leave these poetical heights for the flat level of matter-of-fact every day life. Dull, dreary and trying enough was that of our two cidevant painters in their quarters on the Tchernaya.

The Piedmontese Contingent were paying to the deadly climate of the Crimea a heavy tribute. Sickness and death in their most repulsive shapes put out of question for a time all active operations on their part, and many a gallant fellow had much to do to bear up against the disheartening effects of the awful visitation, and the relative idleness and want of excitement consequent upon it. We say "relative idleness," for, of course, there was more than enough of mounting guard, of patrolling, and picketing, and raising of *épaulements* for the able-bodied; but these occupations, though affording a temporary relief, had too little of excitement in them, to counteract the gloom which hung over the sick camp.

Our two volunteers stood the ordeal bravely, and without flinching; no small praise, if it be true that—

> "It is the detail of blank interval,
> The patient sufferance where no action is,
> That proves our nature. Many are who act,
> But, oh, how few endure!"

Paolo and his little friend did more than endure, they helped and encouraged. Now it was that Salvator's

comic powers, and large stock of quotations from his
peculiar and favourite literature, proved of real practical use in cheering many a desponding heart. Nor
was he chary of his talents, though his blanched
cheeks of late were in pathetic contrast to his fun and
drollery.

For, even Salvator's inexhaustible flow of spirits
was no buckler against the grasp of disease. One Sunday, the last of the month of July, he was absent at
the church parade. To Paolo's anxious inquiries after
his friend, the reply was that "the little Roman" had
been taken ill and carried to the hospital marquee.

For obvious reasons, access to the temporary hospital of the Sardinians, was interdicted to all but those
having official business there, and Paolo could get no
admission ticket. However, through the kind offices of
General F—'s aide-de-camp — the same who had
come to the Locanda of the Dogana Vecchia in Turin,
and who had shown constant kindness to his *protégés*
during the campaign, Mancini received news of Salvator, which relieved his worst fears. His complaint,
according to the physicians, was not one attended by
dangerous symptoms; an intermittent fever, such as he
had had once before at Rome, likely to be long and
tedious, but not putting life in jeopardy. This *prima
facie* view of Salvator's case was confirmed later, when
at the end of the first week in August, the expectation
of an attack by the allies on the tower of Malakoff,
caused all the hospitals in camp to be cleared out, and
Paolo further learned to his great satisfaction, that his
sick friend had been transferred to Balaklava, from
whence, as soon as it could be done with safety, he
would be conveyed to the hospital of Scutari.

To prevent all false alarms or possible misconceptions, which Salvator's prolonged silence might entail on Clelia, Paolo thought it best to apprise her at once of the real state of affairs, by a letter which also contained a cheque for a considerable amount of scudi. By the same post, he wrote, as he had promised, to Prudence, informing her of his being, for the present, a soldier, and enlarging on the gallantry and the sociability of her own countrymen in the Crimea.

The next salient point in Paolo's Crimean life, was a reconnaissance made by the Sardinians on the 13th of August, and the most lively anticipations of which were unfortunately frustrated. The expeditionary corps swept over the plateau on the other side of the Tchernaya, and to the banks of the Tchontion, without finding a trace of the enemy.

The 16th of August dawned at last, a day which was to be one of hard but glorious work for the allies, and in which the Piedmontese were to have their share of hardship and glory.

At the break of day, the line of the Tchernaya was attacked in gallant style by the Russians, who, after a momentary success, and not without a most obstinate struggle, were finally thrown back with great loss. This battle of the Tchernaya, according to competent judges, sealed the fate of Sebastopol. Paolo had the good luck to be one of the division Trotti, which was engaged in the action; nay, to belong to the very battalion which was sent to harass the retreat of the enemy. Mancini did not at one stroke run his lance through half-a-dozen Russians — by-the-bye, he had no lance — nor did he achieve any other supernatural feat in the knight-errantry line; but his

behaviour throughout was steady and resolute enough
to be noticed by the men and officers of his company.
The greater their pity when they saw him stagger, reel,
and fall to the ground. It was the last discharge but
one of the retreating artillery which had done the
deed.

CHAPTER XXV.

Beneficial Catastrophe.

It is now high time to return to Paris, and see
what has been going on at Dr. Ternel's sanitary
establishment. Miss Clara's pen has been busily at
work during this interval, and her letters to Owlscombe
and Scutari, if textually given, would fill a goodsized
volume, which would raise the number of our volumes
to four. Now, it being against rule for a fashionable
novel, such as this professes to be, to go beyond the
sacred figure of three, we shall take the liberty of
squeezing out of Miss Clara's correspondence all the
facts of any importance, and offering the summary to
the reader.

Dr. Ternel having done all in his power by word
of mouth, to arouse in his English patient an understanding of the reality preparing for him, at length
thought the moment had come for taking a step further
in the same direction. Accordingly, one fine morning,
a letter directed to himself was put into Mr. Thornton's
hand — a letter dated from Owlscombe, bearing the
Wareham post-mark, written in Miss Clara's well-known
hand, and signed with her name in full. She wrote
that she had heard of his being in Paris in the Rue

St. Dominique, and that, being now in possession of his address, she had instantly determined on going to see her old friend. Would he not be glad to see her?

The doctor anxiously watched the effect of this letter: rather to his surprise, it was one far from satisfactory. Thornton looked thoughtful, was much absorbed after its perusal; talked a good deal to himself, but never spoke to the doctor. Mr. Ternel had to break the ice himself.

"Well," he began, cheerfully, "you have received good news, I know. Miss Clara is already on her way hither."

"How came you to know that?" asked Mortimer, after pondering awhile.

"I have a letter from her also. See, here it is," and the doctor produced it.

Thornton looked at it, then said sternly, —

"It is all a hoax; since when have the dead taken to writing?"

"But Miss Clara is not dead — that is a mere morbid fancy of yours. Miss Clara is full of life and energy and affection for her dear old friend."

Thornton shook his head despondingly.

"Who ought to know better than I, who am her murderer?"

"I hold in my hand a plain undeniable proof that you are mistaken," urged the doctor, tapping her letter. "You are quite right in saying that dead persons cannot write — now Miss Clara does write, you know her writing."

"Once upon a time I did," said the unfortunate Englishman; "but who can tell? hands are so easily counterfeited. Have you ever advertised for a missing friend?"

"Never," replied the doctor.

"Well then, do so; and you'll see what comes of it. There are plenty of people who trade in heartless hoaxes. When the steamship *President* was lost, there was no end of such. I have had experience, for I was taken in myself," and he went on to relate his trip to Havre, and his cruel disappointment.

No reasoning, no appeals from the doctor could undo this new twist of his patient's mind. It would be unsafe to venture on a more tangible proof of his error. Better wait for a favourable change of mood — such was the doctor's decision.

"We must not risk too hastily our last, our only chance," he said to Miss Clara. "Though the best-matured plan may fail, yet let us at least do all that humanly can be done, to have the odds on our side."

The first failure had not caused the indefatigable doctor to relax in his activity, he only varied the means to his end. What the sight of Miss Clara's handwriting had failed to do, perhaps her voice, that most powerful of instruments to strike home to the heart, might accomplish, especially if connected with old associations. In furtherance of this plan, Dr. Ternel had a piano put in a small room at the back of the establishment, adjoining his own study, and the only window of which looked into the park. In this species of light closet Miss Clara spent many anxious hours, recollecting and practising those tunes and songs, which she thought would most powerfully recall old times to Mortimer.

The doctor, on his side, undertook to persuade his patient to go out, and enjoy the sight of the first coming into leaf of the trees. Thornton's servant having already received instructions to take his master to the particular spot, which it was desirable he should visit. It was long before Mortimer could be prevailed upon to comply with the doctor's wish. Inclined at all times to be sedentary and solitary, he had grown still more so of late. One day, however, when it was least expected, out he went, and following on the steps of the servant, came under the closet window. A short prelude of chords, followed by Weber's *Dernière Pensée*, rooted him to the spot. He looked up to the window from whence the sound proceeded, and listened intently. The doctor from behind the blind studied the play of Thornton's physiognomy with intense interest. He desired Miss Clara to sing, and she began at once.

The effect of her voice was instantaneous upon the eager listener. He started violently, clasped his hands together, and his eyes filled with tears.

"Now or never," whispered Dr. Ternel in great excitement; "sing on, sing on, I'll bring him here at once. Courage!"

It took him but a minute to run down the stairs, and round the house to Thornton; but in that minute there had been time enough for a change. When the doctor came up to him, Thornton's brow was lowering, and his eye fixed on the ground.

"Miss Clara is there," said Doctor Ternel, pointing to the window above their heads.

Thornton looked up with a glance full of suspicion.

"She is singing for you," went on the physician; "you will go to her, will you not?"

Thornton slunk back in silence.

"Why don't you wish to see Miss Clara, your dear old friend?"

Thornton vehemently shook his head; without speaking a word recoiled still farther, and ended by hurrying away altogether.

Tears started into the good doctor's eyes at having to return alone to the anxious young lady, with news of this second discomfiture. Had Thornton's mood, at first hearing her voice, but lasted a few minutes longer, there was no saying what might have been the result. Cruel, cruel, indeed, to founder in sight of port. But what was delayed was not lost. The doctor had too thorough an experience of the habits of diseased minds, not to feel assured that Thornton would revisit the spot, where he had received so strong an impression. And then the missed opportunity might be found again. With such and other cheering predictions, the sympathizing doctor tried to allay the shock of Miss Clara's disappointment.

This opportunity, however, did not present itself for the next fortnight. Thornton went two or three times into the grounds during that period, but studiously avoided the place to which his servant would have enticed him. Dr. Ternel perceived also that he was more agitated, and his thoughts more disordered than before the last experiment.

One afternoon Miss Clara was sitting at the piano — it was a lovely, mild April day — and as her eyes rested on the bright tender green of the trees opposite, her fingers wandered half-unconsciously over the keys. All of a sudden she felt she was no longer alone. A figure was standing on her right, too tall to be Dr. Ternel; surely then it must be Thornton. Startled beyond all conception as she was, she had been too well warned and instructed by the doctor as to what was chiefly to be avoided in a like emergency, to show her agitation. She accordingly continued to strike the keys, striving the while to regain full self-control; at last, she gently turned towards him, and said, —

"Is that you, Mortimer; how do you do?" and without rising, she held out her hand to him.

He did not take it, but examined her face calmly enough, though with a shade of timidity.

"Shall I sing *Queen Mab* to you?" resumed Clara. "It used to be a great favourite of yours at Owlscombe; you recollect it, don't you?"

He did not answer the question, but, as if pondering, still gazed at her. At last he exclaimed, —

"Where can the other be, I wonder?"

"The other who?" said she, rising cautiously. "There is only one Clara, you know — your Clara. Won't you shake hands with her?"

She bent forwards a little as she spoke.

He looked pleased, and smiled, hesitated if he should take the proffered hand or not, then, with a childlike gesture, touched it rapidly, but immediately drew back his own, muttering to himself, with downcast eyes, —

"How can it be?"

Clara approached him softly, took both his hands in hers, and plunging her eyes into his, said, —

"Clara, your Clara."

Thus they stood, perhaps, ten seconds, hand in hand, face to face. To his had returned full consciousness, but a change speedily came over it. As waters touched by a sunbeam, when a cloud intervenes, lose their

transparency, and in a twinkling become livid, so did
Thornton's countenance lose all its limpidity, and grew
at once grey and haggard.

"Don't touch my hand," he cried, "it is cursed;
it is the hand of a murderer," and he struggled to
disengage himself from her grasp. She strove to maintain her hold, trying at the same time to soothe and
pacify him with gentle loving words. To no avail.
Just as, in the pitiable contest, they had unwittingly
got near to the open window, a man dashed noisily
into the room.

This proved more than sufficient to heighten
Thornton's excitement into positive madness. "The
avenger, the avenger!" he shouted, and, shaking off
Miss Clara violently, in another moment he had flung
himself out of the window. A double scream rent the
air; she looked out, saw a motionless form lying on
the ground; saw a red stream flow from under it, and
fell back senseless.

The person, whose sudden entrance had brought
about this frightful catastrophe, was Thornton's servant,
who, on missing his master, had first searched the
grounds, and not finding him there, had next gone to
report his disappearance to Dr. Ternel. Unluckily, the
doctor was not in his study, and the man becoming
sensible that some sort of scuffle was taking place in
the next room, had hurried in; with what result, we
know.

He immediately raised an alarm, that speedily
brought half the household to the spot, Dr. Ternel
among the rest. Consigning Miss Clara, now in violent
hysterics, to the care of one of his assistants, the doctor,
ashy pale but collected, hastened to see what could be

done for the more serious case. Thornton was carried with all speed to his own room, and upon examination it was found, that, beside many relatively unimportant injuries, his right thigh was broken. The fracture was instantly and successfully reduced, and stimulants administered; every resource of art, however, failed to restore the sufferer to consciousness. The day wore on, night came, and another day dawned, and still Thornton lay insensible, and but for his fainting, fluttering pulse, might have been supposed dead.

Great was the doctor's dread of a concussion of the brain, beyond the power of mortal skill to cure; but this dread he kept locked within his breast, while, under his own superintendence, every known remedy was unflinchingly persevered in; not a moment's rest did he take, only leaving Thornton's sick bed to bring words of encouragement to Miss Clara, lying in a feverish state in the room of one of the needlewomen of the establishment. Dr. Ternel, by turns physician and comforter, wrestled valiantly with both bodily and mental sufferings.

About noon of the day following that of the dire event, Clara, quite worn out, had fallen into a sleep, when the doctor entered her room. He looked greatly excited, and was evidently struggling for self-command. It often happens that the men most hardened to painful emotions lose all their power of self-control under the pressure of joy.

"He is dead!" screamed Clara, starting up in her bed, her eyes wide with terror.

"He is alive," shouted the doctor, with elation; "he is conscious — he is —— I am a great fool; prepare yourself for ——"

"Tell me, good doctor — oh! tell me," cried poor Clara.

"Cured! cured!" was all that the doctor managed to say, accompanied by something mightily like a caper. Clara threw up her arms in speechless gratitude, and fell back on her pillow in a paroxysm of tears.

There is no better sedative for overwrought feeling than a good fit of crying; and presently the young lady was calm enough to hear what the doctor had to relate. He told her, that after a twenty hours' application of the strongest stimulants, Thornton had at last revived, and the first thing he had done, was to motion to Dr. Ternel to lean down close to him, and then, in a scarcely audible whisper, had asked, "Where is Clara?"

"I told him," continued Dr. Ternel, "you were in the *lingerie*, and he desired me to come at once, and tell you that, thanks to you, he was cured, and that, if he lived, it would be to bless to the last day of his life, her, who had restored him to reason."

Three days later, Clara was allowed to show herself to her friend; literally but show herself, for it was only under an express condition that she would neither speak nor be spoken to, that Thornton and she were allowed to meet. A useless proviso, after all, for neither could have said a word, so choked were both by tears.

Tears served indeed for all explanation between them — nothing more, not a word, even after all embargo to conversation had been taken off. And when, installed in the sick room, with a female attendant as chaperone, Clara proved herself the most intelligent, tender, and devoted of nurses, never did Thornton make any allusion to the past, but it was speedily drowned in their mutual tears.

Thornton, as may easily be believed, was, under the circumstances, the most docile and grateful of patients; he spoke little, though he felt so much; but he murmured over and over again to himself, even in his sleep, "angel, angel," and often asked of some invisible friend what he had done to deserve this bliss of blisses. As to the kind doctor, he looked ten years younger than he had done the previous month, and his white cravat and shirt-frill, at one period rather neglected, shone with all their pristine lustre.

Thus a month went by, and then another, and the sun was warm, and the grounds all decked in green, and the parterres a mass of colour; and Thornton began to hobble about upon his crutches, or rather upon his crutch, for that on the side Miss Clara walked, was superseded by her arm. The sun presently grew almost too hot, and shady walks were preferred, and the wooden crutch disappeared; the other, the soft, slender arm, was always, oh! always there. And save a shade of lameness, which would vanish in time, Mortimer Thornton was, to all intents and purposes, his former self again — that is, his body; for, as to his mind, that had undergone a change indeed, and not for the worse.

With summer's glad time, little projects budded forth, and Mortimer began to feel the expediency of shifting his quarters, and of leaving room in the establishment, to him thrice blessed, for some other more in need of assistance than, thank God, he now was. It was then Miss Clara wrote to Nelly and

George that they were wanted, and George and Nelly set off without delay, and arrived in Paris in the first week of July.

CHAPTER XXVI.

All's well that ends well.

THE scene of this last stage of our journey is the court of the Barrack Hospital at Scutari, in the latter days of September. The court swarms with soldiers in all the varieties of the uniforms of the allied forces in the Crimea — English, French, and Piedmontese — but the British regimentals far predominate. A lamentable sight, including, as it does, every shape of human wreck, which the most lugubriously disposed fancy could evoke, from the poor fellow yonder, who hobbles along minus a frozen foot, to that misshapen bundle of living flesh, with no arms and no legs, that lies upon a bench. Many crawl about with all their limbs, whose wasted frames and cadaverous hues tell even a more pitiful tale than that of their mutilated brethren. Returning health and vigour shine in the looks of a few, but even returning health and vigour are sad here, from the melancholy contrast they offer to decay, past recovery.

Several of the convalescents are walking about, alone, in couples, or standing in little knots; many are seated, conversing or reading; here and there one dictates a letter to a more learned comrade. Occasionally, a female figure dressed in gray, wearing a band across her shoulder, with "Scutari Hospital" embroidered on it, flits through the crowd on some charitable errand;

and the crowd opens before the flitting figure, and all caps are lifted, and grateful glances meet hers, as if she were some gracious queen.

We must single a group out of the motley throng. A handsome young man, very pale, with jet-black hair closely cut, is on his knees before a bench, drawing, on a large sheet of paper. Though there is no wind stirring, his foraging cap lies on one corner of the paper, and a stone on the other, to fix it down. The gray capote of the Piedmontese infantry is thrown loosely over his shoulders, as if it were a cloak, the sleeves dangling empty behind. While drawing, he converses with a fine young woman, grave and dignified looking, in spite of her humble attire, and of her occupation, which just then was that of mending a stocking. Her southern origin is written in unmistakeable characters in her raven hair and eyes and soft olive complexion. A third person takes part now and then in the conversation, and rarely without producing an exhilarating effect. This third person is a little fellow in the short gray cloak of the Sardinian Bersaglieri, and the longest and most ludicrous of striped cotton caps, the tassel of which bobs perpetually back and forward, in obedience to the quick and never-ceasing jerks and twists of its owner's head. The business of this little Bersagliere seems to be to march round and round the bench, brandishing a long stick, and singing whenever not speaking —

"Su, da bravi, figliuoli, coraggio,
Che fra i sassi s' arriva alla gloria."

"Yes," said Clelia, "it is as I told you. He came on board our steamer at Leghorn, he was bent on reaching Balaklava."

"This beats all his past tricks," said Paolo, laughing. "Count Fortiguerra turned Polish nobleman — an exile of course, and singing to the guitar."

"And a very good affair he made of it, I assure you," continued Clelia; "copper, and even silver, rained into his begging plate. He has an excellent barytone voice, I must say, and he manages it well."

"A rival for you, Salvator," cried Paolo; "I'll bet you anything he makes his way to Scutari one of these days."

"If he does," said Salvator, "I'll take care to make him go back faster than he came."

"Mere professional rivalry," quoth Paolo. "The *primo tenor assoluto* is jealous of the barytone."

"Pray, Salvator, may we ask what this infallible charm is for getting rid of him?" said Clelia.

"The unmasking him, of course."

"Even if you wished to do so — which I much doubt if you once saw him," said Clelia, quietly; "poor fellow he is old, and sadly out at elbows — well, if you had all the will in the world, I doubt, Salvator, your power to get the better of Count Fortiguerra, or whatever he may now call himself. He is a consummate actor, and personates any character he assumes to the very life. To see him in his square Polish cap, and surtout all bebraided with loops and frogs, a white tuft on his chin, and large white moustaches, to hear him talking of the campaign of 1830, — impossible not to believe him to be one of the noble relics of the heroes of Ostrolenka. Not a soul on board the steamer — and some Poles were there — ever doubted for a moment his assumed nationality and story; and whoever had ventured to impeach the old rogue, would have fared ill, I assure you."

"Impudence, I perceive, is the safest capital in this world," observed Mancini. "Did you find out whether he recollected you?"

"'That he did," answered Clelia; "one day I spoke to him in Italian, and there was a full admission in the roguish wink that accompanied his reply, '*Parlare Italiano molto giovinetto, vecchio scordato tutto quanto.*'"

"You saw nothing of his Achates, the chevalier?"

Before Clelia could reply to Paolo's question, Salvator, in a startled tone, exclaimed, —

"By the Capitol, a younger brother of Mentor, I declare."

Paolo turned round, and saw a tall man in plain clothes striding across the court, on his way out.

"By heaven, it is himself," cried Paolo, jumping up, and darting after the retreating figure.

At the sound of his name, Thornton looked back, put up his eye-glass, and with the exclamation, "God be praised!" hurried towards Paolo. "Now then, I am indeed happy," added Thornton, pressing the young man's right hand within both his own.

Paolo fixed a long, eager, inquiring look on his benefactor. Changed, radically changed, the expression of his face, the tones of his voice — Thornton, indeed, but surely not the Thornton of Rome.

"Thank God, I see you so well — better than I ever hoped to see you!" said Paolo, with emotion.

"Happiness, Paolo, happiness has been the great magician. Yes, indeed, many things are altered since we parted, and I have been more lucky than I deserved. You see in me a man restored to health of mind and body, to a sound appreciation of men and things — a man made happy, in short, by love — the love of an angel, she whom I had most wronged. But let us not talk of me just now; tell me how it is you are here — what became of you in Paris — tell me."

"Come and sit down a moment," said Paolo, pointing to the bench where he had left Clelia and Salvator; "there are some more of your friends from Rome here."

"How glad my wife will be!" said Thornton.

"Your wife!"

"Did I not tell you I had an angel to take care of me? Lavinia is here too, Paolo."

"Lavinia?" gasped forth Mancini.

"Ay, indeed; she makes one of our family for the present. Oh, Paolo! merciful heavens! what is this?" cried Thornton suddenly, stopping short, his every feature working with emotion.

Thornton, in mentioning Lavinia, had affectionately put forth his hand to take hold of Paolo's left arm, when he suddenly discovered that there was none there.

"One of the many chances of war," said Paolo, with a quiet smile; "I am thankful it is the left and not the right."

"Oh, my noble boy!" exclaimed Mortimer, clasping Paolo to his bosom, and, all English as he was, and used to control his feelings, he burst fairly into a fit of crying.

Clelia and Salvator now approached, and greetings were exchanged. Too moved to say much, Thornton made up by warmth of manner for deficiency of speech. They all sat on a bench, and before everything else,

Paolo had to give a very minute account of all that
related to his wound, and consequent amputation. This
was followed by a short summary of what had befallen
him since his separation from Thornton; nor did he
spare himself when he got on the chapter of his Paris
dissipation. Mortimer, in his turn, related his own
strange story. The reader already knows most of its
gloomy, but only a little of its bright side. To complete this last, a few lines will suffice.

Thornton and Clara's marriage had taken place at
the British embassy in the month of August, and bride
and bridegroom were on the eve of starting for Cypress
Hall, accompanied, of course, by Mr. and Mrs. Aveling,
when they received very alarming tidings from Scutari.
Lavinia had been struck down by cholera. Thornton
forthwith proposed that they should go to Scutari. "We
shall thus realize your former plan," said he to Clara,
"and enter actively into that partnership in good works,
which we have agreed that our united life should be.
If we arrive too late — which God forbid! — to be of
use to our dear young friend, we may be in time, at
all events, to do some little good to others."

Mrs. Thornton wanted no persuasion, she had had
the very same thought. Dr. Ternel, consulted upon
this project, approved of it warmly. A poet like Mr.
Aveling could not but have his fancy tickled by the
prospect of a journey to the East. Mrs. Aveling had
no will but her husband's will; in short, the quatuor
embarked at Marseilles instead of at Boulogne, and
had the great consolation, on arriving at Scutari, to
find Lavinia out of danger, and fast recovering.

Within a few miles of the general hospital, where
Lavinia lay, was an untenanted country-house, the pro-

perty of an English merchant, who preferred remaining for the present in Constantinople. This villa, tolerably well furnished, the proprietor had willingly let to Thornton; and as soon as it could be safely done, the exhausted convalescent had been conveyed thither.

The general hospital, just mentioned above, it is scarcely necessary to explain, was not the same as that into whose court we have just introduced the reader, the common appellation of which was barrack hospital, and distant about half a mile from the general hospital. In this last it was that Lavinia had been on duty when taken ill; and to it, save an occasional visit to the other on special business, Thornton and his party had confined their charitable exertions. This was how it had happened, that neither Paolo, nor Salvator, nor Clelia, inmates long before Paolo of the barrack hospital, had ever met Thornton.

"Are you able for a short hour's ride?" asked Mortimer of Paolo, when their mutual explanations were over; "but I forgot you are no rider."

"I can ride pretty well now," answered Paolo reddening; "I have paid dear enough for my instruction."

"But are you sure it will not over-fatigue you?" insisted Thornton.

"Quite sure — I consider myself all but well."

"The road, if road it can be called, is so abominably bad, that it admits of no carriage; but we may make a leisurely ride of it. I know that my wife will not be satisfied unless you go to see her and her friend directly. What do you say, shall I come for you to-morrow morning at ten? Will that suit you? I will accompany you back in the evening."

"I see, I am doomed always to be a trouble to you," said Paolo.

"Trouble!" repeated Mortimer, "that is a word which won't do between you and me. I am going to re-assert all my rights as Mentor, my dear Telemachus, I give you fair warning," and with this kindly threat Mortimer took his departure.

Paolo had not a wink of sleep that night, and we might bet a good sum, safe to win, that his were not the only pair of eyes of our acquaintance, which, within the circuit of less than a hundred miles, obstinately refused to close in slumber.

With military precision, Thornton arrived at the barrack hospital at ten next morning; Paolo in a moment was in the saddle, and off they went. The road was execrable, Paolo did not find it out — the prospect was bewitching, he was blind to it — Thornton spoke — he was deaf to his words. Sight, hearing, sensations, were all engrossed by one image, Lavinia; one thought, he was about to see her again. His friend understood this state, and respected it, maintaining silence for a time; but when within half an hour of their destination, he forced Paolo's attention from Lavinia to Lavinia's history.

Paolo listened eagerly enough now, to Mortimer's account of her altered circumstances, how it had come out, shortly after Mrs. Jones's death that Lavinia was not Mr. Jones's niece nor in any way related to him, . but the child of a poor weaver, which out of interested motives had been substituted for the real Lavinia Jones;

how, on discovering this, Lavinia had left Mr. Jones's house to seek by her own exertions to support herself, and how it was in the course of such endeavours, that she had been brought in contact with the present Mrs. Thornton; how at last the consequence of this meeting had been that the two young women had volunteered to go to the East, whither, however, Lavinia alone had gone, her companion remaining behind in Paris for Thornton's sake.

Thornton made no mention of the circumstances, which had obliged Lavinia to quit Mr. Jones's house, in order not to give his friend gratuitous pain. He also withheld another fact, viz. that Lavinia's parents had never been married. This was another secret, and of so delicate a nature, that Thornton did not feel justified in divulging it without the express permission of the person it concerned.

"It was all for the dear girl's good," wound up Thornton; "she is come out of her trials a new and a charming creature. Thrice blessed. the man who may call her his own."

Paolo did not speak on this hint, and the rest of the ride passed in unbroken silence.

Two ladies were sitting in the porch of the villa, when the riders dismounted, neither of them Lavinia. These two ladies, so like each other that they could not be supposed other than two sisters, and a tall, rather absorbed-looking gentleman, with the most shaggy and disordered of natural wigs, came forward to shake hands with Paolo, and, taking possession of him, half led, half carried him into a sitting-room, forced him, in spite of

21*

his protestations that he was not in the least tired, to stretch himself out at full length on a sofa, covered him with shawls, and overpowered him with consommés, wines, kind looks, and kindest inquiries.

Paolo was still panting under this avalanche of cordiality, when Thornton appeared, leading in Lavinia.

"Here is our other interesting invalid," he said; "I think there is no need of any introduction."

The meeting between the two was such, as from their respective situations, and the circumstances under which they met, might have been anticipated; full of repressed emotion, and painful embarrassment. Mrs. Thornton was not slow in coming to the rescue; no sooner had they shaken hands without a word, than she passed her arm round Lavinia's waist, and led her to a seat, while Mrs. Aveling recommenced pressing on Paolo, who, on Lavinia's entrance, had jumped up from the couch, the expediency of lying down again, and allowing himself to be covered up. But this time he stoutly and successfully resisted her persuasions.

Paolo was the hero of the moment, the centre of the general interest and curiosity. He had to tell over again the story of his wound, and of the loss of his arm, of his illness in Paris, to describe the Prosper family, and all their kindness, and to explain what had led him to think of volunteering for the Crimea — a dangerous topic this last, and one on which the presence of the ladies forced him to some concealments. After this came Mr. Aveling with his never-ending inquiries about Rome, often interrupted by Thornton's, about some point of Paolo's recent life, as to which the good gentleman's curiosity was not easily satisfied.

She who ought to have had most to ask was the least forward to put questions. Lavinia spoke little, and the little she did say had no reference to the past; on the contrary, she took care to avoid any allusion to it. She expressed her pleasure in knowing that Clelia was so near, and said how glad she should be to see her again. Though by this time Paolo's and Lavinia's manner to one another had become natural and friendly enough, there was still a shade of reserve and constraint in it. Her eyes never rested on his, nor his on hers, with that full direct long glance, which penetrates beneath the surface — their glances glided over each other's, as if both were on their guard.

The change, which little more than a twelvemonth had effected in their appearance, a change rendered still more striking by Paolo's military dress, and Lavinia's garb of a sister of charity, might to some extent have accounted, had there been no other reason, for the difficulty they experienced in resuming anything of their former familiarity.

Lavinia was still beautiful, perhaps more beautiful than ever, but her beauty had assumed a different character to that he formerly admired. Sorrow, reflection, and the habit of gentle and lofty thoughts, had softened, and, as it were, spiritualized her countenance, had impressed on it a calm serenity and dignity, which made her quite a new being.

Paolo was not less altered on his side: the features of the youth had ripened and settled into those of the man, and repentance and humility had breathed a new spirit into them. The experience he had had of life and of himself, had sobered and subdued his manner. Add to this, his paleness and touching infirmity, and a complete transformation was the consequence.

But there was another reason than that of their outward change, for their looking ill at ease, and on their guard; and this was that they were actually on their guard. Paolo and Lavinia had so far profited by the lessons they had received, as to be strongly impressed with the conviction of being each unworthy of the other, and accordingly in duty bound to renounce each other. It was this preconception, which had made their first meeting so full of reticence, and so deep-rooted was it, that their first impulse, had they followed it, would have been to fall at each other's feet. How could she, the silly thing of yesterday, the outcast of to-day, ever lift up her eyes to him, the austere youth, the hero, the martyr? How could he, the fallen idealist, the impure sinner, the intentional *felo-de-se*, ever aspire to her as she now was, purified by trial, sanctified by self-sacrifice? Hence their studious attention, their vigilance, not to say or do anything which might be construed to imply the assertion of presumptuous claims, forfeited and abandoned for ever. And from this study, this vigilance, arose that constraint, hastily interpreted on both parts as the sign of altered feelings.

The full moon shone on the two friends' ride back to the hospital — a light so calm, so sweet, so melancholy, that Paolo could willingly have wept. It made him think of the night of the ball at Torlonia's and of Thornton's bitter confidences about the very woman who now formed his crown of bliss.

Mingled were the impressions, which the Roman brought back from his visit — regret and discouragement on one hand, unbounded admiration and sympathy on the other. Paolo was not a man to breathe the same atmosphere with such a better order of beings as the two sisters, without carrying away with him some of its elevating spirit.

"Well may you call yourself the luckiest fellow in creation," he burst forth enthusiastically; "Mrs. Thornton is an angel, and Mrs. Aveling is another."

"And Lavinia, pray what title is she to receive?" inquired Mortimer, half jocosely, yet not without some anxiety.

"She is worthy of her friends, and that is saying everything," was Paolo's reply.

"Then you agree with me that thrice blessed will be the man who gains that prize?"

"Surely; but he must be bold who aspires so high."

"I don't quite seize your meaning," observed Mortimer.

"My meaning, however, is clearly stated," said Paolo. "Where is the man worthy of her?"

"Yet I once knew a young rogue, who had the audacity to think himself worthy of her," laughed the Englishman.

"So did I," proceeded Paolo, "but she was not then what she is now; and the silly rogue you allude to, though presumptuous, was nevertheless pure and possessed of all his limbs, whereas he is now humble, stained, and a cripple."

"H—m! but is not humility after all a potent recommendation to the choicest of the fair sex?" asked Thornton. "And those you style cripples, when crippled from certain causes, are they not apt to look only the more

interesting in their eyes? to say nothing of the occasion
for devotedness which such cases afford. And as for
past sins, women are for ever ready to bestow forgiveness, and to render good for evil. Am I not myself a
case in point?"

"Yes," said Paolo, "but there are sins and sins."

"I'll lay you a hundred to one," returned Thornton,
"that your sins are easily forgiven. Will you commission
me to make your confession to Lavinia?"

"Do," answered Paolo; "till that is done, I shall
feel as if I were playing the hypocrite with her; but,
above all, extenuate nothing."

"I promise you I will not; but now, suppose she
passes a sponge over the past — wipes it all out."

"Tempter!" cried Paolo; "why try to lull my conscience with fallacious hopes?"

Thornton had a ready answer on his lips, but he
gulped it down. He remembered in time, that Paolo
did not yet know all Lavinia's story, and he judged it
better not to push the subject further, until he had spoken
to Lavinia.

A curiously analogous conversation was passing at
the same moment between Mrs. Thornton and Lavinia,
with similar but yet more definite results. "Never,
whatever her feelings might be," said Lavinia, "no,
not for worlds, would she fasten her disgrace on an
honourable man."

Thornton's horses, what with visitors and mes-
sengers, had a sorry time of it for the next ten days.
Merry Salvator obtained a great success with the English family; quiet Clelia, perhaps, even a greater, especially with Lavinia. The Roman girl not seldom car-

ried away morsels of comfort, which she bestowed in certain desponding quarters. She even once went so far as to be guilty of a great indiscretion, by revealing that an old pencil sketch, dated Rome, September, and signed P. M., a sketch of Mrs. Jones and Lavinia, and which somehow or other had accompanied the latter to the Crimea, occupied a prominent place on the walls of the young lady's bedroom. Nor was it long before Thornton reported that the revelations of Paolo's short-comings in Paris, had been received in a most Christian spirit. Under the many gentle incitements to courage he received, the young man's sense of his un-worthiness of the great prize began to lose something of its intensity, and hope to revive in his breast. Nevertheless, there was but a trifling amendment in the situation; the same painful restraint marred the pleasure of the unavowed lovers' intercourse.

In this awkward position of affairs, Mr. and Mrs. Thornton laid their wise heads together to find some means of producing a crisis.

"These two children adore each other," quoth Mortimer, "and are pining away, and making themselves miserable from the absurd notion, that neither is deserving of the other. How are we to get such nonsense out of their heads?"

"No one," said Clara, "can put it out of Lavinia's head but Signor Paolo; and as for Signor Paolo, I believe you are the only one to manage him. You must begin by him."

"I am ready to do anything," replied the husband; "but before further urging him to come to the point, I think it indispensable that he should be informed of the circumstance, on which Lavinia lays such a preposterous weight, and which I have kept from him till now."

"Why should we not outrun discretion for once," said Mrs. Thornton, "and take upon ourselves the responsibility, without distressing Lavinia by asking her consent? Let him know everything; and if the bar sinister in her escutcheon makes no difference in his feelings, why, then tell him that it is that, and that alone, which causes Lavinia's reserve towards him, and that I, Clara Thornton, know she loves him devotedly."

In pursuance of this plan, as Thornton was riding with Paolo the next day towards the villa, the Englishman said,

"Suppose there were some blot on Lavinia's birth, would that modify your views with regard to her?"

"How can you ask such an absurd question?" said Paolo. "No more than if you were to tell me, she was the heiress of the mightiest monarch in Europe. How can one be made responsible for an accident independent of one's will, and consequently excluding either merit or demerit? Whether Lavinia is the daughter of a Prince, or the child of a poor artisan, can that alter the essence of her being, make her less or more good, change her one iota from the lovely, blessed creature she is?"

"Certainly not," said Thornton. "Well, then, as you have doubtless already guessed from my question, there is a stigma attached to the dear girl's birth. Her parents were never married; and now you have the key to the reserve she maintains toward you. In her innocence she fancies that some disgrace attaches to her, and makes her unworthy of you; but, believe me, her happiness depends as much on you as yours on her. It is for you to overcome her scruples, Paolo."

"And so help me God, I will try," exclaimed Paolo with fervour. "If I succeed, and she accepts me, then I am blessed indeed; if not, I go by the steamer that leaves to-morrow."

Lavinia and Mrs. Thornton were sitting at work in a pleasant room over the porch; thither Thornton led Paolo whispering, —

"Now or never, I'll pave the way for you;" and going towards the ladies, he added aloud, "I advise you, ladies, to lay violent hands upon this traitor, who meditates a flight."

"Oh! Signor Paolo," remonstrated Clara in painful and unfeigned surprise, "surely you are not really going away?" Lavinia did not speak, but all colour left her cheek.

"I may possibly have to go. I am not sure yet," faltered Paolo, almost choked by emotion. "My going or staying will depend on — Miss Lavinia."

"On me?" cried Lavinia in sudden alarm.

"Yes, on you," pursued Paolo, now speaking with great resolution. "I have a petition to make, on the issue of which much more is at stake than my going or staying — I mean the whole happiness or unhappiness of my life. Lavinia, mine is a most ambitious request, and yet made in all the humility of my heart." Saying this, he knelt down on both knees, and took her two hands in his. "Lavinia, will you undertake to make me worthy of you, by bestowing on me the blessing of your companionship through life?"

Overcome by contending emotions, with eyes averted from his pleading ones, Lavinia cried in a broken voice, —

"Pray, Signor Paolo, spare me — it is impossible — you don't know —".

"I know this," resumed Paolo passionately, "that there stands between you and me a prejudice of yours, which I am here on my knees to remove. Lavinia, I entreat yeu, let me have the benefit of my long-cherished opinions, whatever others may think. I don't make them for this present emergency. Long, long ago, you heard me say, that merit or demerit were strictly personal, and that the transmission of a badge of honour or of dishonour to such as had done nothing to deserve the one or the other, was the acme of absurdity in my eyes; wrong or right, what I thought then I think now. Oh! Lavinia, Lavinia, don't sacrifice a loving heart to a mere misconception on your part. Trust me, my whole life shall be spent in proving to you, the high sense I have of the great boon I am asking from you."

Lavinia, for all answer, burst into a great fit of tears. And now Thornton and his wife, the greatly moved witnesses of this scene, joined their arguments to Paolo's entreaties.

The struggle was long and obstinate, but love had the best of it at last, and Paolo from that day became an inmate of the villa.

Towards the end of December our whole party of friends left Scutari for Turin, whither Clelia and Salvator had long preceded them. It was in the capital

of Piedmont, that the double marriage of Paolo and
Lavinia, and of Salvator and Clelia, took place on the
same day, and at the same church. Thus came to be
fulfilled Salvator's fantastic anticipation about his own
and his friend's wedding day, and thus our performance
is at an end, to the satisfaction, we hope, at least of
the lovers of gay finales. A tale which winds up with
three marriages ought to be as good as three vaude-
villes.

MORE LAST WORDS.

Paolo has had a house built after his own design on the Lago Maggiore, between Intra and Pallanza. It is as unpretending as its owner, but spacious and in a lovely situation. The garden in front stretches to the edge of the lake, and there is a hillock behind planted with Italian pines. A suite of rooms on the second story are exclusively destined for the Thorntons and Avelings, and at the top of the house, adjoining Paolo's atelier, are two rooms fitted up for Clelia and Salvator.

Paolo has taken to painting again, and can do so without inconvenience, thanks to a most skilfully contrived artificial arm. Great as his excellence is, his beau ideal still, as of yore, keeps flying before him, just beyond his reach: but he takes his disappointment more philosophically now, that he has, according to his own account, secured the beau ideal of a wife. Two little charming impediments in the shape of a boy and a girl, arriving in reasonable succession, came in the way for some time of the yearly visits, the Mancinis, according to agreements, were to pay to Cypress Hall and Owlscombe; and therefore the inmates of Owlscombe and Cypress Hall had to obey the proverb descended to us from Mahomet. But nothing has happened lately

to prevent our hero and heroine's journey to Dorsetshire.

The Thorntons and Avelings inhabit by turns, but
always together, Owlscombe and Cypress Hall, that is
when not in the Mancini Villa on the Lago Maggiore.
Living quietly and chiefly for themselves, and not for
their neighbours, they are rather unpopular with the
gentry around, but very popular with the cottagers,
especially with the needy and sick. Mr. Aveling has
just published with great success his new poem, *The
Gladiator*, conceived and begun in 1856, at Rome,
whither he and his wife went, and made some considerable stay, after the marriage of the Mancinis and
the Giglis.

Salvator and Clelia are settled at Turin. Salvator
is one of the scene painters at the Carignano Theatre,
and Clelia has passed her examination as a school-
mistress and teacher for one of the government schools.
Husband and wife earn enough to be able to economize,
and the vivacious little man has visions already of a
villa of his own near that of Paolo. Whenever he or
Clelia have a few spare moments, they run down to
Lago Maggiore, where they are always welcome.

Prosper and Prudence are no longer to be found
on the Quai Montebello, they have been promoted to
an omnibus bureau near the Madeleine, where they
labour on in unaltered contentment. Whenever the
Mancinis pass through Paris on their way to England
or back, they never fail to visit these their Parisian
friends, and great are the rejoicings on these occasions.

Benoît has made over his douche and vapour department to a younger man, who pays him a pension
of two francs and a half a day, and the abdicated

monarch of the bath has migrated to his godson's new
neighbourhood. He makes himself useful in many ways,
attends the youngsters to and from school, and takes
them on holidays for long walks.

Pelissier, alias Du Genre, has been as good as his
word. The moment the Italian question was *posée pour
tout de bon*, to use his own expression, he volunteered
as a common soldier, and went through the whole campaign with great bravery, and lucky fellow, returned
to Paris without a scratch; his only regret being, as he
wrote to Paolo, that he was stopped just when he was
beginning to take to a soldier's life.

Mr. Jones has married a young and handsome lady,
and is full of contentment at the birth of a long coveted
son and heir. His wealth and influence are still on
the increase, and literally he has nothing to wish for
but a change in his name. We see no other remedy
for that but a peerage. Who knows? Stranger things
have happened.

Lady Augusta, now Countess Terrol, is still Lavinia's most intimate friend, and their correspondence
goes on as regularly as in the days of the diary from
Rome. Her mother, Lady Willingford, also retains a
maternal interest in her former *protégée*.

As to the Marchioness Delfuego y Arcos, the latest
news of her ladyship is, that she rents a villa on the
Lake of Como, and swims and races and shoots and
sings there, with a select circle of bipeds and quadrupeds
about her, as of yore in the Villa Torralba.

THE END.

www.ingramcontent.com/pod-product-compliance
Lightning Source LLC
Chambersburg PA
CBHW031133120726
47905CB00006B/1675